Mountain

An Odyssey of Adventure, Survival, and Romance

To Bob
Merry Christmas

Dick Falzoi

Beyond the Far Mountain

An Odyssey of Adventure, Survival, and Romance

A Novel

Dick Falzoi

SUNSTONE
PRESS

SANTA FE

Sunstone books may be purchased for educational, business, or sales promotional use.
For information please write: Special Markets Department, Sunstone Press,
P.O. Box 2321, Santa Fe, New Mexico 87504-2321.
Cover art by Dick Falzoi
Book and Cover design › Vicki Ahl
Body typeface › WTC Bodoni
Printed on acid-free paper
∞
eBook 978-1-61139-278-4

Library of Congress Cataloging-in-Publication Data

Falzoi, Dick, 1941-
  Beyond the Far mountain : an odyssey of adventure, survival, and romance :
a novel / by Dick Falzoi.
    pages cm
  ISBN 978-0-86534-991-9 (softcover : alk. paper)
  1. Fugitives from justice--Fiction. 2. Appalachian Mountains--Fiction. I. Title.
  PS3606.A497B49 2014
  813'.6--dc23
                            2014013929

WWW.SUNSTONEPRESS.COM
SUNSTONE PRESS / POST OFFICE BOX 2321 / SANTA FE, NM 87504-2321 /USA
(505) 988-4418 / ORDERS ONLY (800) 243-5644 / FAX (505) 988-1025

For Ginny—don't know where I'd be without her, and to my dad—I wish he were still around to read this.

Acknowledgements

There are a number of people I would like to thank for helping bring my story to fruition.

Ginny, who shares my life, has plowed through the manuscript a number of times, offering (sometimes demanding) changes and keeping me from straying too far afield. My daughters: Jill who provided in depth editing, and Kama, who gave valuable initial input. Pat Swartz, leader of our writing group, for adding her expert editing and encouragement. My brother John for suffering my reading aloud the entire manuscript on a trip from New York to Georgia and back.

Finally, thanks to Jim and Carl at Sunstone Press for publishing my book.

Prologue

One day, late in the Nineteenth Century, a large male dog wanders into the mountains of southern West Virginia seeking small game. This dog once had a home but his human had died and left him to fend for himself. Generally, a dog doesn't survive well in the wild, but this dog retains an affinity for his feral ancestor, the wolf, one of nature's most cunning and adaptable creatures. The dog is huge and mostly white, with dark markings on his face and along his back and haunches. A bushy white tail curls up over his back like a plume.

His stance is heroic, like a statue.

This day, a female grey wolf hunts the same territory. She is large for a female, over one hundred pounds. She has become separated from her pack—her incessant howling fails to locate her running mate. It is winter and she would soon be in heat. The dog hears her plaintive call and feels drawn to investigate. Ignoring his hunger pains, he tracks her, and soon the two animals are facing each other, yet at a safe distance. He approaches her tentatively, displaying no menace.

The wolf shows interest; neither animal shows fear. Soon the two are nuzzling noses and a bonding takes place—not yet physical, but one of affection. They find a cave and sleep close together, curled around each other, touching and making soft whining sounds. Soon the dog senses the wolf's readiness to mate, and though the copulation is brief, their commitment to each other is to be for life.

The wolf bears her pups in the spring, a litter of four, while protected in the cave. One pup is totally white with reddish eyes, not the yellowish-gold eyes usual for a wolf. The dog tends to the mother wolf, providing her and the pups with food and protection. One day, while the pups are still small, the dog goes off in search of game and doesn't return. The mother wolf ventures out of the cave, not far from the pups. She howls for her mate, but to no avail.

▲ ▲ ▲

"Zeke, ya hear thet? Some damn wolf out thar got sep'rated from its pack. The damn thing's in trouble 'n ah think we got us a shot at it."

There are two of them, these mountain men; the one not called Zeke is huge. He is the leader, Zeke is the follower and he likes it that way. Neither is particularly intelligent, but Zeke figures it's better to tie up with a formidable man than to try to ferret out a living by himself. Life in the mountains is exacting for any man and Zeke knew his limitations.

"Ah'll bet thet's a she-wolf, Zeke," said the big man. "'N ah think mebbe she's got her some pups from the sound of her howl'n. What say we go have us a look-see. Ah smell bounty."

The wolf, in her attempt to summon her mate, neglected her usual precautions and becomes easy prey for the big man, who shoots her.

"Zeke, you git ta skinnin' thet creature. Ah'm gonna go 'n find her pups."

"Aw, Bear, how come ah always gotta do the skinnin'?"

"'Cause ya ain't got nary a brain ta do nothin' else useful. Ya figgerin' you could run this har op-er-a-shun?"

Zeke glares at the big man, but soon relents.

Bear easily locates the whimpering wolf pups.

"Whal, lookee here, Zeke," Bear shouts back to his cohort. Then, to himself, "Damn wolf did have pups, jes' like ah figger'd. 'N a white one, at thet. Judgin' from them red eyes, ah'd say we got us a muth'rlovin' albino har. Gotta be worth some money. Damn thing looks almost like a dog, don' he? Yeh, a wolf-dog."

Zeke gladly puts aside his skinning assignment and joins Bear.

"So what'll we do with 'em, Bear?"

"Hell, we kill 'em! We don' need no more blamed wolves in these har mountains. 'Cept fer thet thar white one. Look at 'im...jes' standin' thar, starin' right at me. He ain't afeared of me a'tall."

Bear looks into the pup's red eyes and feels a shiver pass through his body, as if his very soul is opened up. He gulps—hesitates. He suffers a

8

twinge of guilt, an emotion he had long ago abandoned. With the bravado yanked from his voice, he manages to say, "Jes' grab thet pup 'n let's git the hell away from this har place."

PART I
The Mines

▲ ▲ ▲

1

Jonas McNabb stepped out of the farmhouse and savored the early evening air. It was mid-September, yet the day's warmth lingered, resisting the oncoming night chills. The air had a palpable stillness about it. Jonas had accomplished little this day as he and Benji practically had to fight over the chores that needed doing, so scant was the fare for the two of them.

Not even dark and already Jonas's father was down for the night—a price he paid for his long days at the mines. Benji was wrapping up the chores, and Jonas felt this was a good time to go off by himself and sort through some things.

His favorite spot to do so was under a chestnut tree by the small creek that ran through the fatigued McNabb farmland. He sat under that tree now. Picturesque, late summer clouds lingered just above the tree line, reflecting the brilliant oranges and violets from the setting sun, the kind of clouds that stimulate the imagination to pick out shapes of willowy animals. But Jonas didn't allow himself any such frivolities just now. He had serious matters to ponder.

Jonas remembered coming to this spot with his pa, *in another life*, when his ma was still alive. They would sit under this very tree, maybe with a basket lunch of corndodgers his ma had put up. His pa would light up his old briar pipe and reminisce about his youth—his growing up in Pittsburgh, and what life was like in the big city and, best of all, his account of how he had met Jonas's ma. When telling of this, his pa's face would light up, his eyes would take on a sparkle, and his words would flow through smiling lips. But that was then. Now, his pa would seldom talk about Jonas's ma, and when he did, it was with sorrow and sometimes tears, even now, three years after she had died.

Jonas reached into his pocket, pulled out a tie-pouch of tobacco and spread a pinch of it onto a thin paper. He rolled the paper around the tobacco, licked the edge, and sealed the tobacco in. Settling back against the chestnut tree, he lit the cigarette and inhaled deeply, welcoming the calming effect.

He looked up toward the thick forestlands that rimmed the farm. Jonas and his pa, and later Benji too, had hiked far up into those woods, almost to the foothills that led into the Appalachian Mountains. Jonas learned to shoot and hunt on these excursions. He also learned to love the woods and hills and just about anything having to do with outdoor life. Now, Jonas made these hikes by himself, although occasionally Benji would tag along. But, never his pa. His pa...what had happened?

Jonas allowed his thoughts to drift back to earlier days—to better days, when his pa's stories had so intrigued him as a young boy:

Caleb McNabb was descended from Scotch-Irish immigrants who had journeyed across the Atlantic several generations ago. These hearty folks had settled around Pittsburgh, where they continued their Old Country trades as merchants. As a young man, Caleb was learning the shop-keeping trade, but the government had other plans for him—the Union government. There was a war brewing then, and at seventeen, Caleb's arsenal switched from apron and ledger to uniform and rifle. In mid-September, 1861, he joined the Union Army's push into West Virginia.

The West Virginia Campaign was a peripheral one, not really germane to the war effort. Battles were scattered, casualties light, and results indecisive. Jonas's father survived the battles of Rich Mountain and Kessler's Crosslanes, but received a head wound in close fighting at Carnifax Ferry. The Union Army claimed the victory there as the Confederate commander vacated the war arena under the cover of darkness, leaving behind a battlefield of approximately two-hundred-fifty dead and wounded soldiers. Caleb was one of these casualties.

Young Caleb McNabb landed in a makeshift field hospital in Jericho, West Virginia, some ten miles from the battle site. For the first week, he faded in and out of consciousness. When he finally became aware of his surroundings, he looked up into the eyes of an angel. Her soft blue eyes gazed down into his own and her sweet voice issued encouragements. One of her hands supported his head from behind and the other offered him warm liquid from a tin cup.

"Wha...where am I?" Caleb muttered.

"Wahl soldier, welcome to the land of the livin'."

Caleb struggled to get his elbows beneath him and lift himself up.

"Easy, soldier, let's not rush things. Just lie back down there. How're you feelin'?"

"In truth, like I got run over by a team of mules 'n hung out to dry."

The angel laughed. "Caleb McNabb...it says here," she said, checking a list. "Caleb, I'm Lonica Quinn, 'n I bin nursin' you fer about a week."

"Nursin'? Yer a nurse, not an angel? I thought shore I was in heaven."

"Nope, soldier. This shore ain't my idea of heaven. But I take kindly to you thinkin' I'm an angel. Maybe my efforts ain't gone wasted."

Caleb smiled broadly, now aware that his angel was a handsome young woman.

"Wahl, shoot. If I'd known I could git this kind of attenshun, I'd a got shot up a lot sooner."

Lonica Quinn had been paying particular attention to Caleb ever since he had arrived unconscious at the hospital. She was one of many women volunteers who attended the war wounded in such hospitals. The Quinn farm was nearby and she alone was left to run it, as she had lost her mother to small pox and both a father and a brother to the war.

Lonica hated the fighting; it made no sense to her. The killing, the maiming. She had family members on both sides, North and South. The thought of kin killing kin was unfathomable to her. Even so, she felt great compassion for the casualties of the war. *The least I can do is to lessen their pain.*

"Hey," called a voice from across the room. "What's a feller gotta do 'round here to git some a-ten-shun? Y'know, nursey dear, some's the rest of us could use a li'l lookin' after, too."

"I was jist about to git to you, Willy. Hang on."

Lonica justified the extra time she'd been spending with Caleb because since he had arrived she'd been putting in more volunteer hours. She wasn't really neglecting the other soldiers, just using the extra time to be with Caleb. Why, she wondered? Lonica had known other men, but none that impressed her nearly as did this young soldier. Maybe something about him reminded her of her father or brother, whose recent deaths had left a void in her life.

Even when Caleb was incoherent, Lonica had sensed in him a certain gentleness and sweetness. He was certainly a handsome boy. She would gently brush aside an unruly lock of sandy hair that would stubbornly splay over his eyes and wipe beads of sweat from his forehead with a damp cloth. Making sure no one was looking, she would run her finger over his generous mouth.

And now that he was fully awake, Lonica had also become aware of his sense of humor, a quirky sense of humor, judging from his recent comments. *Angel, indeed.*

"Caleb, excuse me for a minute. It seems my services are required elsewhere," said Lonica, as she gently eased Caleb back onto his pillow. "I'll be back."

The large room was filled to overflowing with wounded soldiers, mostly those injured in the same battle that inflicted Caleb. Lonica didn't mind attending to the other soldier's needs or even abiding their ill-manners. Her thinking was that these men had a right to be rude or angry or bitter or anything they wanted to be in lieu of all they had suffered. *So sad. Young boys missing arms or legs or both. What kind of future were they lookin' at? It was tough enough to make a livin' around here, but to be crippled at so young an age.*

Caleb laid awake awaiting Lonica's return. *Lonica, what a pretty name.* He had vaguely sensed her presence for the past week, penetrating his delirium and semi-consciousness—her smell, the softness of her touch, her gentle voice—like a dream. Now this dream had become real, in the form of a young woman. An angel.

▲ ▲ ▲

Jonas was touched by his pa's description of his ma and pa's first encounter. He never tired of hearing it told and wondered if some day he too might meet someone who would stir his heart in a like manner, maybe in a far-off land, maybe somewhere beyond the mountains.

As Jonas slouched beneath the chestnut tree, a grey squirrel scurried across his legs, perhaps believing him a fallen log, bringing Jonas out of his reverie.

"Go bother someone else, li'l fellow. I'm doin' some serious thinkin' here." Jonas's thoughts returned to his father's story.

Caleb shared the hospital room, which was actually Jericho's town hall, with thirty-seven other war casualties. Dr. Grover Adams was the temporary hospital's only doctor and the sole doctor in Jericho for the past fifteen years. Of late, he'd spent most of his time patching up wounded Union soldiers so they could return to the war front. "A damn shame," he would say. "I patch 'em up so they can be sent back to get blown apart again. A damn shame."

The majority of the wounds Dr. Adams treated were arm and leg injuries, many requiring an amputation. Thankfully, anesthetics were available at this time and helped numb the physical pain, but no anesthetic could curb the emotional duress that lingered afterwards. The loudest screaming was heard after an amputation, when the unfortunate soldier learned he had lost an arm or a leg.

Head wounds were a different matter. Failure to understand how to prevent infection discouraged most doctors from attempting surgery for serious head wounds which were likely to prove fatal anyway. The doctors and nurses understood that their time was better spent treating wounds that might offer a favorable outcome. Fortunately, Caleb's head wound resulted from a glancing blow—the bullet didn't lodge. There was a lot of blood, but Dr. Adams felt the wound was treatable and that Caleb would recover with the proper care. So Lonica was allowed to spend as much time with Caleb as she wished, much to Caleb's delight.

But he did wonder just what it was about him that this lovely young woman would pay him so much attention. Not that he objected. Quite the opposite. For during his three weeks in the Jericho field hospital, Caleb had fallen completely in love with Lonica Quinn and now considered himself an exceedingly lucky man on two accounts: one, he was still alive, and two, Lonica had promised herself to him—yes, *promised herself to him*. On a third issue though, Caleb was not so fortunate, as he had convalesced sufficiently that the military wanted him back in action.

"Hell," he thought. "I s'pose if' I only had one arm and half-a leg, they'd still want me back to fightin' the rebs."

Caleb McNabb was discharged from the hospital after a month and rejoined the West Virginia Campaign at Greenbrier River. Before he left he promised his young nurse that he would return to her as soon as the army was done with him.

The battle of Greenbrier River was inconclusive for both the Union and the Confederacy, but for Caleb the head wound would again be a problem—or rather a blessing, as he began to see double and was deemed unfit for duty. Later, Caleb would joke that the army let him go because they were already having trouble enough with "them orn'ry rebs, without me multiplyin' their numbers by seein' twice as many of 'em."

The Union Army discharged Caleb in late November of 1861, less than three months after his enlistment. Caleb returned to Jericho and married Lonica Quinn.

Lonica had inherited a farm from her father, since she was the only surviving child in a family cut down by war and sickness. The farm, though barely viable (like most farms in the area) had become run down as Lonica had spent so much of her time at the hospital, tending to the wounded and neglecting the farm's upkeep. Caleb had no objections when his new wife offered that he help her run the place. He vowed to do everything within his power to put it back on its feet, so was his devotion to Lonica. He knew nothing of farming, but would walk through hot coals if Lonica had so requested. And so the Quinn Farm became the McNabb Farm.

Stinging fingers brought Jonas back to the present. He flicked away the cigarette and crushed it under his boot, bringing the afflicted fingers to his lips.

"Best pay a bit more attention here," he thought to himself. He looked around.

Only a sliver of the sinking sun hung over the low mountains. Shadows had ceased and everything seemed flat—distances had become indeterminate. Even the far off mountains appeared close. "Someday," thought Jonas, "I aim to see the other side of them mountains." Jonas squirmed to a more comfortable position under the chestnut tree and returned to his thoughts of the past. *Gotta know where I been b'fore I kin know where I'm goin'.*

▲ ▲ ▲

The McNabb Farm was one of many in the region, a section of lower West Virginia known mostly for the beauty of its majestic mountains, its deep river valleys, and its vast forested lands. Yet, to farm the area was a brutal occupation. Early settlers struggled diligently to raise any kind of a decent crop, only to be frustrated by the hard crusted, scaly topsoil that dominated this rugged land and yielded little fertility.

It was a mountainous region—a part of the great Appalachian Range—as well as a forestland, interspersed with rivers and streams that cut winding paths through the hills and mountains, creating a topography that resisted domestication.

But the land was bountiful with coal, and it was coal mining, rather than farming, that gained dominance in the region. Over the years, the Appalachian farmers had withstood Indian attacks, droughts, floods, and even a Civil War. They had suffered much for the sake of their farms and were but scarcely compensated for their efforts.

The coal companies were but their latest antagonists.

Coal barons came swooping down like vultures to prey on their farms, employing shady and legalistic tactics to gain mining rights to the coal-rich farmlands. The farmers were no match for the opportunist land grabbers and ironically, in able to survive, many of them had no alternative but to seek employment with the very coal companies that had taken their lands.

▲ ▲ ▲

At first, the McNabb's farm had withstood the coal miners' incursion, but now it struggled for solvency. Their farm relied mainly on crops of potatoes and corn, and peripherally, a few pigs and chickens. Most of what they grew was for their own consumption, selling what remained to local markets. Farming this region was never lucrative, but what the McNabbs produced did manage to sustain them for a time. When the local market fell for potatoes and corn—as buyers turned to more lucrative markets, Caleb decided to try his hand at ginseng farming. This endeavor showed some promise in that the ginseng root had become popular as a medicinal tonic that was believed to have restorative powers. The drawback was that ginseng

needed to be grown wild, making it difficult to control the pests and predators. Mice, voles, and slugs devoured the roots. Rabbits ate the leaves. Still,
Caleb, although out of his element, struggled on, partly because of Lonica's
constant urging and support—but more significantly—as the family of two
was about to grow in number.

Jonas arrived first, and then, five years later, Benjamin. The proud
father would proclaim, "By gawd, I may not be able to produce much of a
crop, but I sure did produce two fine boys."

These recollections flowed through Jonas's mind as random impres-
sions, like dream images, jumping from one time-frame to another: his pa's
head wound, his ma nursing Caleb back to health, their falling in love, the
beginnings of their life on the farm, Jonas's own early childhood—memories of a struggling, yet happy household. But even the happy memories
were tainted by visions of his ma's saddened eyes as she lay dying. It was
as if he were reading a story for the second time, already knowing the outcome—feelings of joy and sorrow fighting for prominence within the same
recollection.

Particularly vivid were his mother's intimate words to him as she lay
on her deathbed. She had grasped Jonas's hand with a strength that seemed
beyond her present capacity and spoke words meant for him alone.

"Jonas, hear me now, for you need to know some things. Yer pa is a
good man, honest, decent, well-intended 'n devoted to this family. He'd do
anythin' fer us, anythin' he'd be capable of."

Lonica spoke hesitantly, each utterance a struggle that tore at Jonas's
heart.

"But Jonas, as loveable 'n easy goin' as yer pa is, there's many things
he ain't. Don't think bad about what I'm goin' to tell you, 'n even more,
ne'er think bad of yer pa."

She stared hard at her son. Her grip grew even tighter as she covered
his hand with both of hers. Tears formed in the corners of her eyes. She
looked tired and drawn after a long bout with her illness. Her words were
halting and she often gasped for breath. She asked Jonas for a glass of water,
the only relief that Dr. Adams had known to prescribe. She took a small sip
and again took Jonas's hands. Her eyes were stern.

"Jonas, I fear when I'm gone thet yer pa won't be able to take proper keer of you boys 'n the farm. He was ne'er cut out to be a farmer. He only did it fer me, 'n he worked hard at it, I'll give 'im thet. I almost feel guilty thet maybe I kept him from his real callin', whatev'r thet might be. He was real good with people, you know. Everyone he met liked 'im. He had a way of talkin' thet would keep folks int'risted. 'N he always left 'em smilin', or ev'n laughin' outright."

As she related this, Lonica even managed a chuckle, which turned into a coughing fit. Jonas felt his heart sink as he wiped the spittle from the corners of his mother's mouth. Even weaker now, she continued, "You remember how he was. 'N now you kin see the changes in him since I've grown ill."

Jonas had seen how his pa had changed. He ignored the farm and was given to bouts of silence, seeming helpless and lost, as his wife's health grew worse day by day.

"He's losin' hisself, Jonas, little by little. He ain't handlin' my sickness well a'tall. I ain't sure how well he'll hold up when I'm gone. He ain't nearly as strong willed as me, 'n you too, Jonas...never was. He's like a willow tree, sort of swayin' 'n bendin' in the breeze. And you, Jonas, yer like the oak tree, straight 'n strong. Don't disrespect him fer what he is. He ne'er pretended to be anythin' diff'rent. It was fer me thet he became a farmer... he did it for my sake, bless his soul."

Jonas treasured each of his mother's words, but wished she would not persist, so obvious was her struggle. But that was her way. She was the strength and fiber of the family. She would not abandon herself to rest until she'd had her say; until with the last ounce of her courage she had tried to make things right.

"What I'm tellin' you, Jonas, is thet soon you'll be the head of this family. You got inner strength like me, 'n yer good 'n decent too, like yer pa. Whate'er happens, you got to promise me thet you'll take care of yer pa and Benji. I know you kin. Yer as good a boy as any mother could hope fer. I ain't sayin' you got to stay fore'er obligated to this farm. I know you'll be figgerin' out yer own way, 'n it'll be right fer you, God willin'. But fer now, till maybe things get better fer yer pa, you got to be responsible fer this family."

His ma released his hand and reached around the back of her neck.

She unclasped the cameo necklace Jonas had always known her to wear and dropped it into his hand.

"Jonas, I want you to have this. Keep it with you to remember me by, 'n someday you kin give it to some young woman you'll come to love. Now I'm tired, Jonas." She raised her arms and beckoned him to her. Theirs was an endearing embrace and Jonas feared it might be their last.

2

Jonas stared up into the leaves of the chestnut tree, catching glimpses of the darkening sky. He'd always found solace here, under the chestnut tree, alone with his thoughts of imagined adventure beyond the confines of the farm. Now, with all the responsibilities thrust upon him, such thoughts seemed illusory.

Recalling his ma's words disturbed Jonas. He had welcomed the challenge at the time—a mere boy of fifteen, entrusted, even commissioned to be the man of the family. It felt almost heroic, but then, *what about the life he'd pictured for himself? A life beyond the mountains.*

His ma died of dysentery. She and his pa had but sixteen years as man and wife. She had been the glue that held the family together and no matter how hard the times, she always found ways to put food on the table and make the best of the poor crop yields. Then she was gone.

Caleb took Lonica's death very hard. He became depressed, his spirit broken, his strength gone. He performed his chores without zest or purpose. He was an aimless man meandering from one task to another, until the sun set and he could be off to bed.

Lonica had sensed this would happen, had told Jonas as such. Still, Jonas found his pa's decline difficult to accept. It saddened him, but never did he show disrespect or impatience with his pa. Rather, he would offer words of encouragement, hoping somehow to help Caleb regain his former self. One thing became clear to Jonas. He was now the head of the household and, like it or not, was obliged to honor his dying mother's wishes, *to care for the family 'n the farm.*

Jonas had now reached his eighteenth year and his brother Benjamin, his thirteenth. The boys now ran the farm. Caleb did little these days, still fighting a deep depression. Yet, perhaps out of obligation to his sons, or a feeling of guilt to his late wife, Caleb took the only alternative that seemed to be open to him—he went to work for the Becker Mining Company, which by now had become firmly established in the small mountain town of Jericho, West Virginia.

▲ ▲ ▲

Jonas rolled another cigarette and welcomed the settling calm. He sighed a billowy smoke ring, which floated up into the branches of the chestnut tree, dispersing among the leaves and spiny chestnut burs. His sigh reflected his own feelings of despair—that he had not kept his promise to his ma—the farm was failing and now his pa had abandoned the farm to work in the mines.

Jonas hated to see his pa go off to the mines each morning, hated to see what the rigorous demands of a miner's day did to him. Caleb would return home after a twelve hour day with his feet dragging and a haggard look in his eyes; a mere shadow of the joking and easy going father Jonas had once known.

Jonas held to one hope, that if he, and Benji, and his pa could make the farm productive once more, his pa could quit the mines. If they could put their full effort into the farm, maybe they could recapture some of the spirit they used to have as a family, when his mother was alive. For now, this remained Jonas's hope for the future. But even this prospect seemed unsettling, as other urges tugged at him. His ego was not such that he felt himself destined for great things, but neither did he feel he'd ever be satisfied with life in Jericho. Sometimes he wished he just could pack up and take off for those far off mountains, just to see where they might lead him.

Jonas continued to sit under the chestnut tree, staring into the darkening sky. Already a few stars were visible, faint pinholes in a sheet of grey. He was in that state of mind where dreams could smother reality. How inviting it would be to give in to these dreams—dreams of adventure, far off places, the life he'd imagined. But Jonas knew this was not to be his time. For now, his responsibility was to the family. But what could he do to make things better?

Jonas made a choice.

He was convinced that if the farm had any chance to survive, it would take an investiture of money, and sadly, the only way to make money around Jericho was to work for the mining company. To Jonas, the mines were hell itself, the antithesis of all he held dear—the open countryside with the fragrant aromas of the wildflowers, the smells and sounds emanating from the thick woodlands, the first warm days of spring as the sun chased away the winter blues. Working long days underground in the mines would rob him of all these joys.

But if I gotta shake hands with the devil, then that's what I gotta do.

A virtual orchestra of night sounds greeted Jonas as the last vestiges of the day faded—the chant of the whippoorwill, the chirping of the ubiquitous cricket, the trilling of the tiny tree frog, the singing chorus of the katydids. The night air was cool, causing Jonas to hug his elbows as a slight breeze brought him a chill.

"Guess it's about time to be gittin' on back. I sure didn't come prepared against the cold," he said to himself.

He stood and shook the cramps from his legs and rubbed the small of his back to relieve the ache that accrued from sitting on the hard ground.

The night now fully engulfed him. Clouds covered the stars and all was black. He felt no fear of the night, but rather welcomed the feeling that the dark made the world around him seem a smaller place, perhaps a more manageable place, bereft of the intrusions the light of day presented.

"I guess if I ever really want to take a good look at myself, it should be on a dark night like this. Seems then there ain't no escape from what's goin' on inside me," he thought.

On his trek back to the cabin, he heard the plaintive cry of the great horned owl.

Whoooo—whoooo.

"Whooo, you say? I'm Jonas McNabb, and it looks like I'm gonna be a miner."

▲ ▲ ▲

The McNabb farmhouse was by no means elaborate, with a main living area, replete with fireplace, potbelly stove, table, several chairs, and a separate room off to the side that once had been Caleb and Lonica's bedroom. Now only Caleb slept there. Jonas and Benji slept in the loft, which barely accommodated two bunks. Their sleeping area was but a crawl space under the roof's rafters, with a lone window allowing for daylight and fresh air. What little space remained in the loft contained Lonica's clothing and personal items, which Caleb was reluctant to be rid of.

The faint glow of an oil lamp welcomed Jonas back to the cabin. His father had been asleep for hours, as his workday at the mines extended from sunrise to sunset. After such a long grueling day of exacting work, Caleb found sleep an early evening friend. Jonas doused the lamp and climbed the ladder to the loft.

"Hey, Jonas."

"What say, Benji?" His brother was barely visible in the darkened loft. Jonas stripped down to his long johns and slipped under the blanket.

"Where've you bin? Yer comin' in kinda late."

"Had some figgerin' to do. Time sort of slipped on by, I guess."

"What kind of figgerin'?"

"Jes' some figgerin', 'n I ain't done yet. Don't fret about it. I'll let you know presently." Jonas turned to the window, signaling an end to the conversation.

Gazing outside, Jonas welcomed his view of the clear night sky, now sprinkled with tiny dots of light as the clouds had cleared—a visual panorama hinting at the mysteries of the universe. If only his own mind were so clear. A slight breeze stirred through the open window and Jonas filled his lungs with the refreshing air. It settled him much as the cigarette had settled him earlier. "Hell," he thought, "I don' suppose there's anythin' more difficult in life for a man than to make the right decisions. 'N there ain't no one around here to help me—Ma's gone 'n Pa ain't in no shape to advise me." He reviewed his decision to seek work at the mines.

Jonas knew his brother could handle what little work was needed for maintaining the farm. In fact, Benji would relish the opportunity. Growing up time. The ginseng was the only crop that required much care, mostly keeping the pests at bay. A scattering of pigs and chickens had to be fed and a vegetable garden that would need some attention. The livestock consisted of two cows for milking and a horse for plowing and pulling a wagon, when it was in working order. Benji could easily handle these tasks.

Jonas knew his brother had been through a difficult time, being so young when their ma died—deprived of a woman's touch and understanding, robbed of her gentility and sensitivity and her penchant for making a house a home. Jonas had done all he could to maintain his mother's spirit and vitality, but knew he could never replace her.

"Damn," he thought. "How can I be both mother and father and brother to Benji, while Pa...what? Fades away? Hell, he ain't but forty or so." Jonas fingered the treasured cameo necklace he wore around his neck. His eyes watered as he recalled his mother's final days and what losing her had cost the family.

The effects of the daily drudgery of Caleb's mining job showed in his attitude, his walk, and his speech. His face and hands were maps of fine line cracks delineated by the black coal dust. His was a daily aging, his lungs filling with the killer coal dust, the scourge of all miners.

But the mines were Jonas's only hope for employment outside the farm. So the mines it would be, for now, anticipating that with both he and his pa working for the mining company, they could put aside enough money to put the farm back in working order. Maybe add some livestock, some horses, some breeding stock, more pastureland. Add some genuine sweat and the McNabbs might yet make a go of it.

Jonas loathed to see what the mining company had done to despoil this land, bringing in their machinery and railways, throwing up shacks for the miners, spitting in the face of all nature had intended. And now he was considering working for the Becker Mining Company, the perpetuator of this travesty.

"Hell," thought Jonas, "what a mess! Who am I to think I can fix anything? Well, for Pa's sake, and Benji's sake, and for Ma, I'll be tryin' my damnedest." Jonas gazed at the stars and once more thought of his ma.

3

Frederick Becker was one of many who responded to a special set of circumstances in the post- Civil War, newly formed state of West Virginia. Thanks to the railroads.

Forging their way through the virgin forests of this pristine mountainous region, the Chesapeake and Ohio, and the Norfolk and Western Railroads created the Coal Heritage Trail: a one-hundred-mile stretch of boom towns that stretched all the way south to the Virginia border.

This trail attracted thousands of disillusioned soldiers, who, when returning from the war to their homelands, found only lost farms, ravished lands, and depleted families. With nothing to lose, many of these desperate men traveled the newly forged steel rails into the Appalachian foothills of West Virginia south.

The allure was coal. The railroads had opened up this region for the rapacious exploitation of its natural reservoirs of bituminous coal—that great Eastern United States commodity that was nature's gift to the developing country. The land was generous enough to provide copious supplies of this energy source, but at a drastic price, at least for the unfortunate miners employed by the coal companies.

The miners tunneled into the solid rock, exposing coal deposits often located at waist level or lower—demanding that they work on their knees or backs to free the black gold from it primordial repository. During twelve-hour shifts in dark, narrow corridors, breathing coal-dust-stale air, the workers labored under the threat of the collapse of inadequate supporting walls, or worse, a methane gas explosion.

Coal barons established coal companies, which in turn established coal camps, home for most of the miners. The camps might include schools, churches, stores, livery stables—the basics for any normal settlement. But coal camps were far from normal settlements. The land that these camps occupied remained under the ownership of the mining companies. Worker's families could expect no more than a tiny shanty for living quarters, rented from the coal companies. Generally, should a miner get out of line or attempt to quit or even think about unionizing, he and his family could be quickly evicted. Further, company stores charged extravagant rates, which the poorly paid miners could ill afford.

One of the foremost of these mining conglomerates was the Becker Mining Company.

Jericho was little more than a cluster of buildings before Becker's coal company invaded the territory. As a typical town for the period and the locale, Jericho had catered mostly to farmers. Folks would come to town to buy supplies, drink, dine, attend church, or even kick up their heels at infrequent dances. Young folks hung around to meet other young folks; old folks hung around the storefront or the hotel lobby to swap stories and chew and spit. Back then, Jericho was a slow moving, laid back, country town filled with country folks with their folksy ways.

When the Becker Mining Company established itself in the area, Jericho became a coal town, which meant that when folks came to town to buy supplies, or to drink or dine, portions of their pay made its way into the mining company's coffers.

When Jericho shifted from farm town to coal town, Saturday nights became much livelier as untoward establishments sprang up, replete with decorated ladies down from Charleston, anxious to trade favors for the miners' paychecks.

The Becker Estate lay just outside of Jericho and included a large country estate house (dubbed the "Manor"), bunkhouses for the help, a stable of horses, and acres upon acres of land, with one section bordering the McNabb Farm. Bustling about the Estate were servants, handymen, cooks, stable boys, and even a gardener—whatever was felt necessary to maintain such large holdings. Frederick Becker and his daughter, Laura, lived in the Manor.

Noticeably absent from the Estate was Laura's mother, Priscilla.

4

Laura Becker loved her horses. Two of her dad's stock she counted as her own. Lucifer, a sleek black stallion, was perhaps the more handsome of the two horses, but Laura preferred her dapple grey Appaloosa filly. She gave her an Indian name, Sacagawea, after the courageous Lewis and Clark Indian maiden scout, a tribute to the mare's courage and moxie.

Laura grew up on horses and excelled in her horsemanship. Her jaunts carried her across meadows, through woodlands, across streams, up rocky hillsides—places that would be dangerous for a less capable and daring rider. The vast Becker Estate allowed her ample opportunity to ride for hours without twice covering the same ground. Laura's father, Frederick Becker, had no objections to her long daily rides, but then her horsemanship was never the issue. The issue was where Laura chose to ride.

Jericho was a rough town, catering to disgruntled miners, attracting men of every unsavory bent and persuasion, not a place a father would want his daughter frequenting on her own. Yet, she had become a common sight riding astride Saca into the coal camps, the mines, and even into Jericho. This is what met with her father's disapproval.

Laura was a beautiful, young and spirited girl of seventeen and Becker feared for her safety around the miner types. Sure, she was the boss' daughter and it was unlikely that these men—many in his employ—would dare bother her, but you never knew around men like that, especially the young ones.

Amongst the miners and their families, Laura stood out like a rose among weeds. The young women of these impoverished families had a certain ashen look about them—sunken eyes, thin lips, lackluster hair—not their fault, but merely the consequences of the hard lives they endured.

Laura faced no such disadvantages. Her father's great wealth assured she be well cared for. Her face glowed with health, her cheeks were rosy, and her bright blue eyes sparkled with youth and vitality. Her father reserved the right to be protective of her. Any man would desire her, be he rich or poor.

Laura's insistence on riding into the miners' camps was not the antics of a peevish child, nor was her behavior designed to test her father's authority. She simply wished to help alleviate some of the miserable conditions endured by the miners' families—to give them encouragement, as well as donations of food and clothing.

Many a child in both Jericho and the miners' camps wore Laura's childhood clothes. Also, she supplied needy families with castoffs from her father's household help—anything she could confiscate. Even her father's wardrobe was not sacrosanct, some of which, to her father's chagrin, he spied suspiciously on the backs of some of his miners.

And Laura would bring food to needy families, either appropriated from the Manor's pantries or donated by some of the better off families. She listened to the poor families' concerns and promised to try to influence her father to improve their conditions. In this, she had been unsuccessful.

Becker's attempts to restrict his daughter, his only child, to the limits of the Estate were doomed to failure. He brought up his objections one night at the dinner table.

"Honey, there's plenty of Becker land for your rides. Why do you insist in defying me by riding into town?"

"Dad, you can't keep me cooped up here on our land," she insisted. "There's things I jis' feel strongly about, 'n visitin' with town's folks 'n the families of the farmers and miners is one of them. Besides, you've got eyes everywhere, you know I kaint come to no harm. 'N maybe if you paid more attention to the needs of folks around here, they wouldn't be so bad off."

"Now, Laura, be fair. I run my operation much the same as the other mining companies, even better than most."

"Better than most?" responded Laura. "Dad, is that what we're settlin' for...better than most?"

Becker always felt uneasy with his daughter's challenges. The iron hand he held over his men was a limp reed with Laura.

"Laura, you jes' don't understand how a man's got to run this business. Don't be judgin' me. You go pamperin' these ornery miners 'n the work jes' won't get done. You can't possibly know what I got to go through each day to keep them in line."

"Don't treat me like a child. I'm not a child, I'm a woman, 'n I'll ask you to respect that. I love you, father, you know that, but I kaint settle for 'better than most'. It jis' ain't right. I'm sorry, but right now I ain't too respectin' of you."

Laura left the dinner table in a huff.

"Damn," muttered her father.

Becker seldom won such confrontations with Laura and he certainly lost this one. But for his own peace of mind, he put the word out—in no unsure terms—that there would be no dalliances with his daughter or there'd be hell to pay. Besides, most everyone knew Becker favored his supervisor, Dirk Fisher, for Laura, and Fisher was not someone to mess with.

5

Ten years ago, when Laura was seven, Priscilla Becker abandoned her daughter and husband, deciding she could no longer abide rural living and, more particularly, the lack of a decent social life in the backcountry settlement of Jericho. She endured life there for five years, but longed for the lifestyle she'd previously known in Charleston as a well-to-do society debutante. Priscilla left Jericho and took up residence in Richmond, Virginia, while still supported by her husband, Frederick. In Richmond, Priscilla maintained that she could...*mix with civilized and cultured people.* Her mother's departure left a large gap in Laura's life that her father attempted to fill by hiring a live-in nanny and tutor, Miss Guinevere Bucher.

Guinevere was the daughter of Henri Bucher, a close friend of Frederick Becker's in Charleston and Becker's primary bookkeeper in his many business ventures there. Guinevere's mother, Elizabeth, maintained a dress shop that specialized in French styling, as both Henri and Elizabeth were first generation descendants of French immigrants. When Frederick left Charleston for Jericho, he had asked Henri to join him in a coal-mining venture. But Henri lacked Frederick's ambition and was quite satisfied with his life in Charleston, where he remained the chief bookkeeper in Frederick's old company, now under new ownership. Periodically Frederick would visit his old friend in Charleston.

Guinevere grew up bilingual and received a public school education. She then matriculated to a teaching academy and earned her teaching certification. After graduation, she divided her time between teaching in the Charleston public school system and working as a seamstress in her mother's dress shop.

Then, tragedy struck.

It was to be a family vacation—a trip to Huntington to visit family and take scenic buggy rides through the city and the surrounding countryside. The Buchers never made it to Huntington. Their train was derailed and claimed the lives of both of Guinevere's parents and left her with a severely mangled left foot.

Frederick Becker attended the funeral of his dear friends in Charleston and paid respects to Guinevere who was still hospitalized and unable to attend her parents' funeral. A year later, when Priscilla Becker abandoned her family for Richmond, Frederick returned to Charleston and sought out Guinevere Bucher.

He found a forlorn girl of twenty-one, desperately attempting to endure the rigors of her teaching position in lieu of her handicap. She was living over the dress shop she had inherited from her mother, and struggling to maintain it. To Frederick, it was obvious that even this was too demanding for the girl. He attempted to persuade Guinevere to accompany him to Jericho and become Laura's live-in companion and teacher.

"But why would I be more capable of that," she asked, "than I am of running a dress shop? Oh, I just don't know, Mr. Becker. I'd just be a burden."

"Guinevere, you're the daughter of one of the best men I've ever known. I know he raised you right, and you'd be perfect to help raise Laura, and Lord knows, I'll be needin' the help."

"But I'm crippled."

"You won't be asked to do any more than you feel capable of. Laura needs a woman's touch, somethin' I can't give her. And it'll be good for you too, to get away from here, away from past memories, to where you can get a fresh start. Guinevere, I want to do this for you, 'n for Laura. You'd be doing us a great favor."

"Mr. Becker, do you really think I could handle the responsibility, with my lame foot and all?"

"If I didn't, I wouldn't be askin'."

"Well, I *have* had offers to buy the dress shop, and the doctor says eventually my foot will get much better."

"Then it's settled. I'll help you sell the shop and get your affairs in order. Then, young lady, you'll be off to meet my Laura."

Becker didn't fancy his daughter attending school in Jericho, mixing with the miners' kids and other *underlings*, as he called them. Laura would be educated as a woman of wealth and position and Guinevere would be the person to make this possible.

▲ ▲ ▲

The raising and tutoring of young Laura Becker became Guinevere's only responsibility. She was not expected to cook or clean. She would share family meals with the Beckers and accompany them to community functions, but mostly, Guinevere was to be a constant companion for Laura.

She became more of a friend to Laura than a nanny, although Guinevere had almost fifteen years on Laura. Finding the name Guinevere too much of a mouthful, Laura shortened the name to *Gini*. She loved to hear Gini's stories about her life in the city. She also delighted in Gini's French accent, and even found a few French expressions creeping into her own vocabulary. Gini tried desperately to improve Laura's back-country manner of speaking, but to little avail.

"Gini, I'll learn all yer book learnin', 'n all you can teach me about manners 'n such, but down here in West Virginia, this is the way we talk. If I was to talk diff'rent than everyone else, I'd just feel out of place, 'n I'd be makin' myself to be somethin' I ain't."

Guinevere found Laura's reasoning refreshing and vowed never to insist on anything that would dampen her spirit.

Though a willing student and a quick learner, Laura's first love was horses. The stables were more of a home to her than the somber Manor House. Laura assisted the stable hands in the care, feeding, grooming, exercising, and nursing of all the horses of her father's ample stock, not just the two that belonged to her.

And how she loved to ride. She had already forsaken the traditional sidesaddle riding style demanded of proper young ladies, and now sought to do something about the long cumbersome dresses that cramped her freedom in the saddle.

Interrupting a tutoring session, Laura, dressed in her usual daytime attire of a full dress down to her ankles, expressed to Gini this particular concern of hers.

"Gini, I kaint ride Saca in this damned ole thing of a dress, sidesaddle or any other way, garments fly''n every which way. I need me some britches."

"Laura, we're in the middle of a lesson here. Just try to concentrate on your Latin."

"Gini, you know I think the world of yer teachin', but right now I got somethin' else in mind. 'N yer exactly the person to handle it. It has to do with this durn ole thing of a dress. Here's what I'd like you to do. Fashion me some riding britches like the boys wear, and maybe a blouse I kin jes' tuck in. I kaint ride in no full dress buttoned up to my chin."

As usual, Gini soon relented, and Laura was able to convince her companion to utilize her considerable seamstress skills to fashion her some trousers which were more suitable for the way she liked to ride.

"I'll make them for you, ma chérie, but you'll have to convince your father to allow you to wear them."

"Oh, he'll come around. 'N I got somethin' else in mind too. I'd like a shorter dress, like mid-calf length, with a split up the front, so I kin kick a leg up over the saddle and set Saca proper. That'll be for when I got to dress up better."

"Tu es impossible!" But actually, Gini admired her ward for her determination and spunk.

Gini applied her tailoring skills and soon provided Laura with the requested garments. So Laura now rode the way she liked, as the boys did— with complete abandon, unhampered by the long crinoline dresses and bulky undergarments generally worn by young ladies. Her father conceded to this due to Laura's unyielding insistence. However, the compromise was that she wear britches only when riding on the Becker property, not around the mines and never into town. There, she would wear her truncated version of the riding dress. She had anticipated this compromise.

"Hell, if yer mom was here, she'd never permit this," said Frederick, registering a parting objection.

And Laura rode without a hat. The sensible thing would be to pin up her hair and tuck it under a riding cap, or at least braid her hair into plaits. But Laura preferred the feel of the wind whipping through her hair, with Saca at full gallop—dust flying, trees and shrubs rushing by, the sound of Saca's hooves pounding the earth as they crossed grasslands, splashing across streams with a water-spray-fan tailing behind, scrambling up embankments, both horse and rider of one heartbeat and one soul.

This is what Laura truly loved—and this is what brought Jonas McNabb back again and again to watch her from the far meadow bordering the McNabb Farm and the Becker lands.

6

For the past week, Jonas had been watching Laura Becker ride the speckled gray mare across the meadow that bordered the McNabb Farm. He'd first spotted her while he was out hunting, hoping to scare up a rabbit or two in the thick shrubbery that lined the hillside bordering the McNabb Farm and a vast meadow of the Becker Estate.

Jonas was about to abandon his hunt, when he caught sight of the young woman in men's clothing riding wildly across the meadow, her long blond hair tossed freely in the wind. Jonas was frozen at the sight of her, as if a vise had gripped his chest.

Laura noticed the tall, lanky young man with the wide-brimmed, well-worn hat watching her from the down slope of the slight hillside, partially hidden by a thicket of thistles. She allowed her gaze to linger on him for a moment as she rode by.

Jonas recognized the young girl as Laura Becker, daughter of Frederick Becker, owner of the Becker Mining Company. Everyone knew her by sight as she often rode into Jericho and the surrounding areas. Jonas had never personally met Laura, as he, along with most young men in the area had to be content to hang back and admire her from afar.

At the same time the next day, Jonas returned to the same spot, hoping to catch sight of Laura again. He wasn't sure why—what possible good could come of it? He thought she'd glanced his way for a brief moment the previous day. Maybe she would be curious about him—he'd settle for curious.

Laura did return that next day, and every day for the next week, same time, same meadow. And Jonas would be there watching, as if drawn by a magnetic force.

He made little effort to conceal himself, and actually became bolder each day to assure that he'd be noticed. And how he loved to watch her ride—her golden hair whisking madly in the wind, her trim figure gliding in tandem with the horse's smooth gallop. She was a woodland sprite riding in frivolous revelry. Jonas remembered his ma reading to him from a book of fairy tales when he was a small child. One of his favorites was a fanciful tale with fairies and woodland sprites, elves and other magical figures. His ma read the story with warmth and delight, installing in the youthful Jonas a fascination for anything to do with the woods, meadows, and forests—and especially the creatures dwelling therein. Watching Laura brought back these warm memories.

She rode without a whip, urging her mare on with gentle touches of her heel or the prodding of her knees. She would whisper in the horse's ear and bury her head in its mane. The horse responded to Laura's gentleness as a lover would to a caress.

Jonas knew there was no way, not in his wildest dreams, that Laura would ever be more than a fantasy to him, and a fleeting fantasy at that. Still, he allowed the fantasy to linger, filling his thoughts each night as he drifted off to sleep. Sometimes he would imagine that she looked his way and that a smile crossed her face.

Lately, it seemed to Jonas that Laura's rides brought her closer to where he stood. And at times, it even seemed she slowed her pace as she passed him, but never did he smile at her or raise a hand in salutation. He would not display such arrogance or disrespect.

▲ ▲ ▲

This day it was raining hard. Still, he stood by the meadow hoping Laura would come by. Water dripped off the wide brim of his hat, obscuring his view as he strained to catch a glimpse of her, willing her to come.

How foolish. Of course, she wouldn't ride on a day such as this. The meadow had become slick with mud. Rivulets of water streamed off the thicketed slope and splashed his boots. Well, he'd give it a bit longer. He was already thoroughly soaked, so what difference would a little more time make. Just a bit longer.

And she did come, despite the rain and the mud and the driving wind. She rode a black stallion, not her usual mount. Jonas couldn't help but imagine that she came because of him, despite the downpour. The rain plastered her long hair against her face and neck. Her sopped clothing clung to her like a second skin. Laura rode toward him, closer than ever before, her pace slowed by the sodden earth. Jonas stood mesmerized. His stomach gnarled as the horse and rider drew even closer. He took a step toward her, growing bolder as the wind and rain seemed to create a bond between them, tearing down any barriers of time and space and circumstance.

Suddenly, she and the horse were down.

7

Frederick Becker sat behind the large desk in his home office. A meeting was in progress. In attendance were his three foremost employees: supervisors Jake Kellogg and Larry Jansen, and Becker's chief supervisor, Dirk Fisher, his second-in-command and most trusted manager. Becker favored the lad, possibly because he thought Dirk would make a good match for his daughter, Laura.

Becker was an imposing figure with a thunderous voice and a commanding presence. At fifty-eight, he still maintained all the strength and drive of his youth. The Becker Mining Company was his company and he ruled it with an iron hand and little in the way of compromise. But he was inclined to put too much trust in his supervisors, especially Dirk Fisher, and often relegated authority to them that should have remained in his own hands. He would come to regret this.

Becker spent his first thirty-three years in Charleston, West Virginia, where he established a lucrative freighting operation and amassed a sizable fortune. During the Civil War, his business was deemed critical to the North's war effort and Becker was exempted from military service. Following the Civil War, West Virginia experienced a railroad boom. The newly built railways soon connected West Virginia to eastern cities, facilitating the state's exportation of its natural resources—lumber, coal, natural gas, and oil. Frederick Becker seized upon the opportunity and entered the railroad business. He bought up large parcels of land and then sold the land to the railroads. Encouraged by his earlier successes in the freighting industry, he then established a second operation, the Becker Shipping Company, which specialized in locating and shipping coal and lumber to the recently completed railways.

Now a very rich man, he married Priscilla Thatcher, a young socialite from an upper-crust Charleston family. Becker was more a business man than a lady's man and considered himself fortunate to win Priscilla's hand. He was perhaps far down the line of the many men that had courted her, and sensed that she had chosen him more for his prospects than out of love. At her insistence, they moved into a modest gothic style mansion on the outskirts of Charleston, engaging housekeepers and a cook, which allowed Priscilla to perpetuate her high-society lifestyle.

Ten years later, and against Priscilla's wishes, Frederick sold the company at a tremendous profit. The Beckers, now including a two-year old daughter, Laura, then headed south to the small farm town of Jericho, West Virginia. There, Becker established his mining company and within ten years, his operation was among the largest in the state. This he accomplished by employing men much like himself—hardened men used to the rigors of the mining operation and able to control the miners. These chosen men he named the *Corps*.

In general, the miners were a disgruntled group with little incentive and, as such, difficult to motivate. The Corps provided the incentive and the motivation. They instilled in the miners not only the fear of losing their jobs, but also the fear of actual bodily harm should they step out of line. The Corps consisted of ten well-chosen men and included three supervisors. These three now met with Frederick Becker in his office.

Becker wore his usual workday attire; a dark gray, single breasted wool sack suit over a maroon vest, a white cotton shirt, and a thin black bowtie. Tucked into the vest pocket was a gold watch and chain. A bowler hat rested on a massive oak table, partially obscuring piles of paperwork. An ever-present cigar protruded from the side of his mouth, spewing a steady stream of smoke.

On hot days, Frederick might be without the coat and tie, but he was never without the vest. His manner of dress befitted his position and distinguished him from his supervisors, whose outfits consisted of linen pullover shirts with full sleeves and generous collars and long tails tucked into straight-legged trousers with a flap that buttoned to the waistband. Vests might be worn, particularly by Dirk, and hats were of the floppy variety with wide brims for sun and rain protection.

The Corpsmen were easily distinguished from the mineworkers in that they all wore red sashes around their waists, and were dubbed "Reds" by the miners.

Most of the Corps had billies tucked into their red sashes for intimidation, or actual use on unruly miners, such as northern boys and southern boys still fighting the war that ended two decades ago. Some miners even wore remnants of their military uniforms. And although they would wear any conglomeration of clothing that befitted the rugged dirty work in the mines, they would maintain at least one set of decent clothes for special occasions, such as church, dances, and other community functions.

"Dirk, this lad...what's his name...uh, Jonas, send him on in here," said Becker. "Damn, I wanna meet that boy."

"Sure, Frederick." Dirk was the only employee who dared call Becker by his first name. Becker allowed the familiarity, feeling that one day Dirk would be family. "I'll fetch him right up."

Dirk Fisher ushered Jonas into the spacious office. Becker rose, approached Jonas, grabbed his hand and pumped it hard.

"So yer the young lad I'm ever more indebted to. McNabb...then you'd be Caleb's boy?" said Becker.

"Yes, sir. That's me, Jonas."

"Well, damn, boy. That was a heads-up thing you did. I'm glad to tell you, my daughter's safe and restin' well. Ole Doc Adams says she'll be like new in a month or so. Sure gave us a scare though. Now sit yerself down here 'n tell me what happened. And incidentally, how did you happen to be there, anyway?" asked Becker.

Jonas sat, showing discomfort, nervously clutching the wide brim of his hat. He felt intimidated by the men surrounding him. *Yeh, what was I doing by that meadow?*

"Well, sir," started Jonas, hesitantly.

"Now lad, don't be nervous. Just give me the account," said Becker, glancing at his pocket watch and blowing a puff of smoke Jonas's way. The rest of the men shifted impatiently, conveying an attitude not lost on Jonas. He felt hemmed in, like a treed raccoon.

"Well, I was there, sir, by that meadow because that's where the McNabb land borders yours. Due to all the rain, I was checkin' to see if there might be some harm come to the crops." Becker wouldn't know that no crops were possible on that particular spot of land. "I seen Lau...your daughter ridin' in the meadow. It was hard to see in all that rain, 'n I thought it was odd, anyone bein' out ridin' durin' such a storm 'n all. She got closer, 'n suddenly, I saw her go down. I guess she got tripped up in some gully, so I ran to where I seen her last." Jonas winced as he continued, remembering the sight of Laura lying there, trapped beneath the black horse, not moving.

"Keep going, lad," said Becker, again displaying impatience.

"She was down all right, 'n trapped 'neath the big black. I think the horse was injured bad, 'n yer daughter sure wasn't movin'. I was able to get her out from under the horse, 'n I lifted her, real careful. I was afraid somethin' might be broke, or worse." Jonas gulped, then continued. "I didn't know what else to do but try to get her home. My place was closer, but we didn't have no way of transportin' her from there to here. Our wagon ain't serviceable just now. So I carried her to yer place. It took a while, but I got her here 'n then some lady took over from there. I told her about the horse, but I don't figure there was much hope for that black. Mr. Becker, I hope yer daughter's all right, that I din't cause her no further harm. That's about it, sir."

"Well, hell, you did just fine, boy. 'N you sure didn't cause her further harm. I'm entirely grateful to you. If she'd got left out there, no telling how it might have gone. Could be she even owes you her life. Now, somethin' like that can't go unrewarded. So, is there anything I can do for you, uh...Jonas, right?"

"Yes, sir. It's Jonas. Jonas McNabb." Jonas hesitated. "There is somethin' you could do for me, sir." He looked nervously around at the three supervisors. "I'd fancy a job at the mines."

Frederick Becker studied the young man. Another puff of smoke drifted Jonas's way. A good lookin' boy. Tall. A strapping lad. Becker had never heard of the boy's dad causing any trouble. Jonas sat uneasy, kneading the brim of his hat.

"So you think you'd like to work in the mines, do you, boy?"

"Sure...uh, yes, sir."

"Tell you what," said Becker, after further musing. "I'll put you in the mines, but just for a short time, so you can get familiar with how things are run around here. 'N if I'm guessing right, 'n I always am, I can use a lad like you as a go-b'tween. Someone who understands them damn miners, who's one of them 'n can talk their language. So, what do you say, boy, think you can handle all that?"

"Yes, sir. I'd be grateful for the opportunity."

"Then it's settled. 'N laddie, I'm the grateful one, for what you did fer my daughter. Don't be givin' me no cause not to be. Dirk, get Jonas here started. Take him down to the mines. Show him around, give him an idea about our operation here. He can start work in the morning. Jonas, you'll be reporting to me weekly, not here, but down at the mining office 'n I'll be wantin' to hear good things about you. Don't you be disappointin' me. Understood?"

"Yes, sir. Uh...Mr. Becker," Jonas started. "I was wonderin' if it might be possible..."

"What? If what might be possible? Come on, laddie, spit it out," barked Frederick, again looking at his timepiece.

"If I might look in on yer daughter?" stammered Jonas, "Jes' to see that she's all right."

With this, Dirk Fisher gave a start. "See here, who the hell do you think you are?" he said threateningly. "You impudent li'l..."

"Dirk. It's all right. I'll take care of this," said Becker. He studied the boy again, working the cigar around in the corner of his mouth. "Of course, I reckon I can see yer concern. Larry, go find Gini 'n fetch her over here. Have her tell Laura that she'll be bringing the McNabb boy to see her. 'N, Jonas, don't you be lingering there, just check on her 'n get out. Got it?"

"Yes, sir, 'n thank you, sir."

"Yeh, yeh. Just wait outside, Gini'll be right along. Come on men. Let's get back to business matters."

Jonas waited outside Becker's office. His pulse raced. Not because of the job offer, but because he was about to be in Laura's presence. In her room. Allowed to actually talk to her. How had he ever dared to suggest such a thing to her father? It could have gone so wrong, but when would he ever get another chance like this? While carrying Laura home from the accident, he had been so concerned for her welfare that nothing about the episode had been in the least bit enjoyable. But now that she was out of danger...a lump formed in his throat.

Gini arrived, walking with a slight limp. Despite this, Jonas thought her to be quite an attractive woman, dressed smartly in a long skirt and a frilly blouse, not at all what Jonas would have expected from someone of her position, whatever that might be. Gini escorted Jonas up a staircase and down a hallway, stopping before a partially open door. Gini peeked in.

"Laura, *ma chére*, you have a visitor," she said with a lilt in her voice.

"Oh, is it that young man who rescued me? Do send him in, Gini."

Gini and Jonas entered. The bedroom was large, highlighted by a floor to ceiling, three-panel Palladian window with rose-colored, billowy satin drapes drawn open to allow light to fill the room. A partially raised window admitted a breeze that caused the drapes to dance. Laura lay in bed, a coverlet pulled up to her waist. A heavily bandaged leg stuck out from under the covers. Jonas tried to hide his concern, but his face betrayed him.

"What? You've never seen a girl all wrapped up like a Christmas present before?" teased Laura.

Despite her condition, Jonas saw she was as pretty close up as he had imagined. The last time he had seen Laura, she had been unconscious and covered with mud. Now, the sight of her caused his face to flush as his hands wringed the brim of his hat, threatening to mangle it.

"So, this is the young man," Laura proffered coquettishly, enjoying his uneasiness. "The young man that saved me. I wish to shake yer hand if I might."

"Oh, I'm not sure that would be an all right thing to do, ma'am," he said, without conviction.

"Nonsense. Gini, you kin leave us now. I have some questions for this young man, of a personal nature."

"Why, of course, Miss Laura," Gini said, winking. "I'll be just outside the door, in case you should need me." Gini left, leaving the door ajar.

"Jonas...right?"

"Yes, ma'am. Jonas McNabb."

"Well, Jonas McNabb. Come here." Laura extended her hand. Jonas approached, cautiously taking her hand. She would not allow him to withdraw it. Now her soft blue eyes locked onto his. "Tell me, Mr. Jonas McNabb, why were you watchin' me out there in that pasture?"

The question took Jonas by surprise. "I...I don't know. I'm sorry. You were so...," he stammered.

"I was so...what?"

"Well...you were jes' so unusual, the way you rode, the way you looked. You were wonderful. I guess that's what I wanted to say."

Laura flushed. She lowered her eyes, then brought them up again. She had been toying with Jonas, but now warm feelings swept over her. Her eyes became glassy, like fine blue porcelain. She still held Jonas's hand and now there was a tingling to their touch.

For the moment, Jonas forgot who he was, and who she was. There was no other reality than the reality that now surged within him, warm and exotic, a feeling quite unlike anything he'd ever known before. Nothing existed outside of this room, nothing mattered but the feel of her touch and the message in her eyes. He could not believe other than she was feeling the same.

"Laura, *chére*." It was Gini. "Time for monsieur to leave."

"I...I'd better go, Miss Laura. I jes' wanted to make sure you were all right," said Jonas. He dropped her hand and backed away, visibly flustered. He turned to leave.

"It's jis' Laura, Jonas. Not Miss Laura. "N I think yer wonderful too."

Jonas left. Laura beckoned Gini to come back in. "Oh, Gini, isn't he somethin'? *Et tres beau*. What a perfectly wonderful, handsome young man! 'N savin' my life...like in a storybook. Gini, do you think there's any possibility that he 'n I might...oh, I don't know. It's kind of crazy, ain't it?"

"Laura, *ma chére*, it's more than crazy. Your father would tan your hide and nail that young man to a tree if he knew what you were thinking. But, knowing you, I'd sure be reluctant to say what's crazy and what isn't."

"Now ain't that the truth...," said Laura.

8

$5{:}30$ A.M. Still dark, with just a glow of promised daylight on the horizon. Jonas and his pa trekked the mile or so to the mines in silence. Jonas wondered what his pa might be thinking. Last night, Jonas had broken the news that he'd taken a job at the mines. His pa had just stared at him. Then his eyes had turned downcast and a pained look had crept over his face. He had turned and walked away, entered his room and closed the door. No words had been spoken—whatever occupied Caleb's mind was his alone to know.

They arrived at the mines at first light. Caleb joined the other workers at their prescribed tasks. And Jonas began his first full day at the mines, with many reservations, hoping his mining career would be a short one.

The plan was for Jonas to learn all aspects of the mining business from the bottom up, and become a viable laison to Becker. He was told to report to Lucas, a large black man, who would give him his first day's assignment. Lucas was the miners' main man, a role he attained and maintained because of his great size and his ability to outperform any two men. Even the Reds gave Lucas a wide berth. He wore Union Army blues, with his cap arrogantly tilted to the side.

Lucas couldn't wait to get his hands on Jonas. Word had trickled down that Jonas was the boss's lackey, planted in the mines to weed out troublemakers.

Jonas was aware of the miners' suspicions. Why wouldn't they be leery—nothing ever turned out in their favor. But Jonas was determined to apply himself to the job and win the miners' trust by his hard work and dedication to their needs.

Lucas gave Jonas the lowest of tasks, assigning him to chip coal with a pickax in the darkest and dirtiest of the tunnels. Jonas was forced to crawl on his hands and knees in the tightest of spaces, testing both his strength and resolve. Lucas kept Jonas separated from the other miners and kept on his back constantly, taunting him, physically prodding him to work harder, calling him "spy boy" and "sissy farmer." Jonas took all this humiliation the big man dished out, but inwardly cursed the fates that would put him in such a position.

The day wore on, seemingly, without end for Jonas. Finally, near dusk, a whistle sounded the end of the workday. Jonas walked from the mine, weary and disillusioned, only to find Lucas waiting for him.

"You, boy," said the big man, thrusting a hand against Jonas's chest. Jonas found himself encircled by a group of miners. "We don't abide no spies around here." Another shove from Lucas forced Jonas back against a coal car, the impact causing coal dust to spill over the car's edge, covering Jonas's head and shoulders.

"Well, looky here," said Lucas. Looks like we're kin."

" No, we ain't, we ain't no kinds of kin. Family treats each other with respect. They ain't bent on humiliatin' each other."

"Yeh, yer right about that, ain't no way I'd want you fer a brother."

Lucas pushed Jonas hard once again.

Jonas tripped backwards and lay sprawled on his back, the impact kicking up more puffs of coal dust.

"Enuff's enuff," said Jonas. He rose slowly, keeping a steady eye on his adversary. "You got it all wrong. I ain't no spy. I ain't no diff'rent than the rest of you. 'N I don't appr'ciate yer pushin' me around."

A voice came from one of the miners. *Show 'em Lucas. Show 'em what we think of spies around here.* Others joined in, urging Lucas to make an example of Jonas, the interloper.

Lucas swung hard at Jonas, but Jonas was ready this time. He ducked the blow and rammed his knee into Lucas's groin. Lucas was expecting that his huge size would overwhelm Jonas; the retaliation took him by surprise. He doubled up and was ill-prepared to fend off Jonas's ensuing onslaught of heavy blows.

The big man went down.

Jonas was angry, but still he understood why he was under attack, that the miners had every right to be suspicious of him.

Jonas extended a hand to help Lucas up.

But Lucas, taking advantage of Jonas's offering, barreled into him like a crazed bull and the contest was on. The ensuing tussle took on epic proportions, swaying this way and that with neither combatant gaining the advantage. The miners cheered, even took bets, wagering heavily on Lucas, but gradually favoring Jonas, as he displayed great courage and stamina in combating the bigger man.

Both men grew weary, lying side by side, drained by the prolonged physical engagement. They stared at each other. Lucas burst out in a fit of laughter.

"My gawd, you shore got some crust, boy."

The pugilists struggled to their feet and faced one another, neither seemed anxious to further engage the other.

"McNabb, tell me ya ain't jes' Becker's flunky."

"I ain't no man's flunky, Lucas. I ain't got no choice but to be here, jes' like the rest of you."

"I guess I misjudged you, boy."

Lucas offered his hand. "What say we start over?"

"Fine by me." They shook hands.

Jonas looked around. He located his father and thought he detected a slight smile on his face.

Not smiling was Dirk Fisher. Dirk knew of the imminent confrontation between Lucas and Jonas and made sure he was there to witness McNabb's humiliation. He harbored a growing dislike for Jonas McNabb and had hoped the big black man, Lucas, would stomp McNabb and send him back to the farm or whatever yahoo land he sprang from.

He derived no such satisfaction, as it seemed the confrontation had only strengthened Jonas's status with the miners and with Lucas in particular.

"Yeh, McNabb," thought Dirk, "you survived this one, but let's jes' see what the boss man'll have to say 'bout you pickin' a fight yer first day out."

Jonas needed about a half hour before he felt up to making the trip home. He received reassuring pats on his back from many of the departing miners, but nothing from his dad, who was long gone. When Jonas arrived back home, his dad was already down for the night.

▲ ▲ ▲

Little was said as Jonas and Caleb walked to the mines early the next morning, and nothing was mentioned of the events of the previous day.

Dirk Fisher was waiting at the mines for Jonas, grinning slyly.

"Yer comin' with me, boy. Becker wants to see you." His grin broadened.

Jonas followed Dirk to the field office. The office was significantly smaller than Becker's Estate office. Windows on three sides allowed Becker to observe the daily operations of the mines. Becker stood in front of a centrally located desk leafing through some papers, his back to Dirk and Jonas. Cigar smoke swirled around his head and permeated the office.

"Here he is, Boss," said Dirk.

Becker turned and sat on the edge of the desk, facing Jonas. He laid the papers aside.

"Well, McNabb," he said. "What you got to say for yerself? First day on the job I was so kind to give you, 'n you end up in a fist-fight."

"I tole you it was a mistake to put him on, Frederick," said Dirk. "He's nothin' but a trouble maker."

"Quiet, Dirk, I want to hear from McNabb here. So, speak up, boy."
Becker blew a puff of smoke Jonas's way. Jonas whisked it away with a sweep
of his hand.

"Well, sir, I don't see how I could've avoided it. He jes' come at me, 'n
I'd had 'bout all I could take."

Becker stared at Jonas, a stern look, and Jonas expected the worse.
Becker turned back to his desk and twisted his cigar out in a large ashtray.
When he turned back to Jonas, he was wearing a smile...and chuckling.

"Jonas, lad, it was a stroke of genius, you standin' up to Lucas like
that. Ain't many a man would do that. I had Lucas in here 'n got the whole
story. He tells it straight, ole Lucas does. 'N he says yer gonna work out just
fine. I told you I was never wrong, 'n by damn, yer gonna be my inside man,
just like I figured. Now, go see Lucas. He'll put you to some more reasonable
work from now on, seein' as you showed yer grit."

Jonas left with Dirk close behind.

"You got lucky, McNabb...this time. But I guarantee you ain't always
gonna be so lucky."

His inside man? thought Jonas. He wasn't sure how he felt about that,
thinking he'd hate to go against Frederick Becker, *Laura's dad*, but knowing
his heart was with the miners.

▲ ▲ ▲

Jonas won the confidence and trust of the miners, largely due to the
way he stood up to Lucas, their undisputed leader. If he accepted Jonas, so
would they. Not to say that Jonas and Lucas became best of buddies; no one
could make such a claim, as the big man preferred to maintain a separation
from his fellow workers, as would a general with his underlings. But Lucas
did now support Jonas as the miners' go-between.

Jonas labored hard and long, side by side with the workers, never
shirking his work, never taking advantage of his new status, doing whatever
dirty job needed doing without complaint. He assured the miners he would
not betray their trust and would do all he could in their behalf.

He was now able to observe firsthand the grueling day that the minors
endured. His pa seldom talked about his work in the mines and Jonas had
only seen the effect such work had on him, but now Jonas became aware of
just how outrageous were the difficulties the miners faced each day.

The work was hard; it was dirty and it was dangerous. The miners often worked in extreme wet conditions, sometimes standing or even lying in six inches to a foot of water. Coal was loosened from the tunnel walls with picks and shovels and then loaded into small shuttle cars to be pushed to a central loading point where mules would pull the cars out of the mines by rail.

Black Lung, a breathing ailment, was common among the miners from inhaling the ubiquitous coal dust. Gas explosions, fires, and cave-ins were constant threats. Stories of such tragedies were prevalent, although mostly whispered. Recently, in Illinois, seventy-four miners drowned when water from melting snow suddenly poured into the mine. For the miner, injury or death awaited at every turn.

Jonas paid heed to the miners' complaints, such as: the coal company didn't supply the workers with adequate rails and cars, making the removal of the coal difficult. And the mines were unsafe due to the lack of lumber for supporting the mineshafts. Jonas felt Becker could improve on these conditions if he were so inclined, but would Becker listen to his suggestions, or, more likely, would Jonas be labeled a troublemaker and be subjected to the punitive measures of the Corps?

The miners' most common complaint concerned their pay as the company had total control over their financial well-being. The meager wages barely covered their food and housing, let alone any extravagances. With the threat of eviction hanging over their heads and no prospects for other employment, the miners were forced to endure any hardships the mining company might wish to impose on them.

For the time being, Jonas kept his mouth shut. But he kept a close account of all he observed, hoping eventually to be able to present the miners' concerns to Becker in such a way that Becker might be moved to implement some changes.

Returning home after a long, hard workday, Jonas was beat; his muscles ached, the stench of coal dust lingered in his nostrils. He could only imagine how much worse it was for his father.

▲ ▲ ▲

In time, Frederick Becker felt Jonas was progressing favorably enough to bring him out of the mines and expose him to other aspects of the mining business.

Jonas now worked outside the mines, becoming responsible for the transportation of the coal to the railways. Still, Jonas listened to the miner's concerns and began to present them to Becker, slowly at first, small bits at a time, so as not to overwhelm his boss. And conversely, he was able to put Becker's demands to the miners in a somewhat palatable form. But, so far Jonas had been unable to influence Becker in any appreciable way.

By now, Jonas's obligations carried him all over the mining community, into Jericho, and often into the miners' homes—but never into the Becker home.

On many occasions, Jonas was able to observe first-hand the cruelty and unfairness of the Reds in action. Workers who complained too much or stepped out of line or spoke of unions might well receive bruises that didn't show. The Corps pushed the miners to the limit as greater production was their only concern.

Generally, Jonas did not attempt to interfere with the Corps, knowing he had no authority to change the way things were handled. He would bide his time, observe, make notes—though it was difficult for him not to act more aggressively to the improprieties he observed.

On one occasion he had intervened. An older worker had exited one of the mines, coughing and spitting up phlegm. Jonas was nearby and attended to him. He caught the attention of one of the supervisors, Dirk Fisher.

"This man is in bad shape and needs to be sent home," said Jonas.

"That right, McNabb?" said Fisher. "Since when'd you start callin' the shots 'round here?"

"Look, I'm only sayin'...."

"Well, Mr. McNabb, champeeeen of the people," taunted Fisher. "I've been wonderin' how long it'd be till you started stickin' yer nose in where it didn't belong. If the boss didn't somehow favor you, I'd-a had you outta here long ago. But yer on thin ice, boy. Jes' give me an excuse 'n not even Becker'll be able to save yer ass. I'll be watchin' you close, McNabb. Now git the hell outta here." Jonas had no choice but to watch the afflicted miner return to work. His heart sunk that he was unable to help.

Jonas knew if he were to help the miners, he would have to find ways around the Corps and the supervisors, particularly Fisher. He could only hope that Becker was unaware of how miserably these men treated the miners, and, if informed, might intercede on their behalf. But he felt the chance of that happening was slim, at best. Jonas seldom saw Becker down at the mines and suspected that the Corpsmen were taking advantage of his absence.

▲ ▲ ▲

Weeks later, Laura had healed sufficiently to be able to resume her riding excursions. Oddly, her jaunts quite often placed her in the same vicinity as Jonas McNabb. The two had extended salutations, smiles, an occasional word or two, sometimes even sharing a scoop of water against the summer heat. These occasions did not go unnoticed by Dirk Fisher.

Dirk thought he had the prize, Laura Becker, all but wrapped up. It was understood that one day he and Laura would wed. Yet, there had been no engagement announced and no intimacy had transpired. Still, until now, Dirk had perceived no rivals for Laura's hand. It was inconceivable that the upstart, lowlife farmer boy, Jonas McNabb, could possibly hope to gain the affections of Frederick Becker's only daughter.

Well, not if he had anything to say about it!

▲ ▲ ▲

One of the few amenities granted the mining community was the monthly Jericho Town Center dance. It was rare that the miners, management, and town's folks all came together in one place, but the dance was an exception. It was a gala affair and one of the few times Frederick Becker showed some consideration for the miners. The locals decorated the hall and the Becker Mining Company footed the bill for refreshments and music.

For the most part, at these affairs, miners stuck with miners and management stuck with management. But, that's not to say that dance floor couples might not be a mixture of young miners' daughters and over eager management lads. Still, it was one of the few times the coal camp folks were able to put aside the rigors of their daily routine and actually enjoy themselves.

Jonas was popular at these dances and the young ladies sought his attention. He wasn't without a bit of notoriety when it came to the ladies— good looking, humorous, and known for his prowess on the dance floor. Yet none of these girls had quite caught his fancy.

The night of the dance approached and not too soon for an impatient

Benji. He had just turned fourteen and was looking forward to meeting some young gal himself. Most young lads received their dancing education from their mothers or sisters, as had Jonas. Seeing Benji had neither available, Jonas had taken on the task of teaching his younger brother a few dance steps, so he wouldn't be completely inept come Saturday night.

"We can't have you shufflin' around like a wounded ox, now can we?" taunted Jonas.

Jonas enticed his pa to beat out various rhythms on a pan with a wooden spoon, while he pushed and pulled Benjamin to and fro, simulating the different styles of dance he might encounter.

"Okay, brother. I think you got the basics down now, at least enuff so you won't make a complete ass of yerself. Ha."

Saturday evening approached and the McNabb boys made ready for the Jericho affair. "Yep, Benji-boy, it's time to make a man out of you," kidded Jonas. "I know there's some li'l ole lassie out there jes' a hankerin' to git their grubby li'l ole claws into you."

Benjamin greatly admired his older brother and took his kidding without resentment. "You really think the gals will like me, Jonas?" he asked.

"Hell, yeh, li'l brother. You'll have to beat 'em off with a stick."

"No, really Jonas, I don't know nuthin' about how girls think. What if they don't take to me?"

"Hmmm," thought Jonas, "back to the mother role. Or should that be the father role. I guess the big brother role will have to do." Jonas studied his younger sibling. *A good-lookin' enough kid, maybe a bit gangly. 'N that shock of sandy hair covering his forehead, so much like his pa's.*

"I'll tell you what, Benji. There ain't no big secret. Jes' be yourself. If they like you, they like you. If not, that's their problem. 'N smile at 'em a lot, tell 'em they sure look pretty tonight. That should get you started. I suspect when they get to know you, you'll be in fine shape."

"Aw, Jonas. I don't know if that will be enough. You know lots of girls. What're they like, really?"

"What're they like. Well, I'll tell you one thing. They ain't like you or me. 'N that's the beauty of it. You can't really figger 'em out, so don't try. Jes' enjoy 'em best you can. 'N remember, most of 'em are prob'ly no more used to boys than you are to them. You best start off with one that's kinda shy, so she won't be overpowerin' you. Then you kin learn all about each other at the same time." Then, kidding again, "It's gonna take you a powerful lot of experience before you kin be a real lady's man like yer big brother. Okay. Enough on that. You'll do jes' fine, Benji. We'll be takin' the mare into town so we'll have to ride double. 'N I recommend you spruce yerself up there a bit. A little grease wouldn't hurt, maybe keep that mop of yers in place."

"Yeh, right. Yer hair looks like the back end of a mule," said Benji.

With that, Jonas got Benji in a head lock and rubbed his scalp roughly with his knuckles.

"You, fella, could use to learn a few manners, 'n a bit of respect for yer elders. Now come on, we gotta git movin'."

The boys spruced up, donning whatever clothes they could find that looked decent—or at least clean. They bid their dad goodnight and began the three-mile trek to town, doubling up on the mare.

9

The Town Center was gaily decorated and the fiddle band was in full swing. Couples clomped heavily round and round, sometimes facing each other and sometimes side by side, in jigs and country swings and modes of dance learned from generations of mountain country folk.

The band consisted of three musicians, basically, and any others that might want to join in. The fiddler led the music and was also the caller for the square dances. His fiddling provided a lively, twangy lead for the Irish jigs and Virginia reels. The banjo added pickin' and rhythmic accompaniment. The third member of the band, the guitar player, doubled on rhythm and melody, pounding out alternate bass notes to keep the dancers in step.

The locals often joined in with home-made style instruments such as jugs, spoons and bones.

The Town Center was little more than a barn with wide-boarded, wooden flooring. Sawdust was spread on the floor to allow the dancers to easily slide and shuffle and stomp without their feet sticking to the floorboards. The dance floor yielded and creaked as the heavy-stepping square dancers and cloggers and flatfoot dancers shook the building. Refreshments were biscuits and punch. A little extra was added to the punch as the evening wore on, which gave the festivities a little added kick. The music grew louder, the dancing livelier and the men folk bolder.

This wasn't Benji's first time at these monthly dances. But now, at fourteen, it was the first time he'd really taken an interest in the young ladies. And he had hopes of corralling some young gal to his liking. Already, his brother, Jonas, had attracted several girls, vying for his attention and dancing skills. Jonas asked the youngest of them to help his brother with his dance steps. Her name was Heather. She gamely escorted Benji onto the dance floor for a slow dance, for starters.

As Benji struggled with his steps, desperate to maintain a smooth glide, he noticed that Jonas and the several girls with Jonas were watching him, obviously stifling their laughter. Benji grew red. His dance steps became even more erratic and to his total and utter embarrassment, he stepped on Heather's foot, causing her to stumble backwards. Only Benji's quick reflexes prevented her from falling. Now Jonas was openly laughing, as were the girls with him and several other observers, especially those Benji had bumped when preventing Heather from falling. Mortified, Benji followed Heather off the dance floor and back to Jonas's group.

"Wahl, Benji. Now I don't remember teachin' you that step," taunted Jonas. "What was that...the Irish trip'n fall?" The girls giggled, even Heather. "C'mon Benji," Jonas continued, as he put his arm around his brother's shoulders. "Not so serious...I'm jes' funnin' you. You'll be dancin' up a storm in no time. Right girls?"

"Yeh, we're terr'ble for laughin' at you, Benji," said Jill, the older sister of Benji's first partner. She took Benji's hand. "Come with me, Benji, I'll learn you some proper steps." She dragged a reluctant Benji back onto the dance floor.

Dirk Fisher sought every dance with Laura, as if he were aware that she had intentions elsewhere. And, of course, she did. For Laura was always aware of where Jonas was—who he was dancing with or trying to fend off, or if perchance he might be glancing her way. She was wearing a Gini special—a dress simple, but fetching—floor length, light blue in color, with crocheted white lace around the sleeves and collar, the midriff drawn tight around her slim waist. She insisted that the dress be simple so she wouldn't appear pretentious. But despite her precautions, Laura Becker stood out as a young girl of astonishing beauty and grace.

"Dirk, kaint we just sit a few out," she implored. "I'd like to talk to some of the girls, maybe get my breath back."

"Sure, honey. I got a few people to see myself," he replied.

Laura joined Gini, not far from where Jonas was engaged in a dance. She was barely aware of the ensuing conversation, her attention being on Jonas. The young lady he was dancing with was fetching and danced well. She felt a twinge of jealousy, and wondered that she should feel so. The dance ended and Jonas made his way back to his brother, who was in conversation with his new friend, Jill. Jonas turned and looked Laura's way. She was looking at him...and then she was moving toward him. She approached, seeming to float across the dance floor, her feet barely visible beneath her long dress, her long, silky, golden hair bouncing as she strode up to Jonas.

"Could you fit a poor li'l ole gal into yer dance schedule mister?" she said.

"Now, I could hardly refuse the boss's daughter, could I?" *Damn, what a stupid thing to say*, he thought.

"Well, if that's all you think of me, you kin damn well refuse me. I'll jis' find myself a fella that's more apprec'ative."

Laura turned to leave. Jonas grabbed her hand. She turned back to him.

"Laura, I'm sorry. I think you know what I think of you."

"Well then, Jonas McNabb, escort me out to the dance floor, 'n no more sass, please."

Jonas sought to reply but the words stuck in his throat. *Ladies' man indeed*, he thought as he followed her onto the dance floor.

The dance was a slow one and Jonas hoped it would be a long one.

He knew he shouldn't be with her, not with *Laura Becker*, but just now he didn't care. They said little as their eyes locked. The music continued and their bodies drew closer. Much *too* close as far as Dirk Fisher was concerned.

He watched the two of them, rage building within him. He'd never before been challenged for Laura. This was an affront. Laura was his, and his alone. He was top man in the mining company, next to Becker. Damn it, she came with the territory, everyone knew that—including old man Becker himself. How dare this clod-buster son of a broken old miner even dare look at Laura, let alone touch her. Nor did Dirk like the way McNabb was being promoted in the Company. Dirk saw him as a threat to his authority. He'd have to deal with McNabb.

It felt so right to Laura to be in Jonas's arms. Feelings arose within her, feelings that were quite new to her. She was both confused and delighted at the same time. She felt his strength, yet his gentleness. Perhaps for the first time since childhood she felt vulnerable to another person. And she didn't mind at all. They talked little, at least not verbally. Their eyes said it all. Laura wished the music would never end.

When the music did stop, Jonas dropped his arms. He felt awkward standing there with Laura in the middle of the dance floor, knowing they were attracting attention and that he was out of order. To continue this behavior would only bring harm to both of them.

"Laura...I....," he stammered. "I can't do this to you. I only wish things could be diff'rent."

With that, Jonas walked away from Laura and rejoined his brother. Laura stared after him. She didn't understand. As far as she was concerned, people were people, on equal footing until they showed otherwise. Of course, she was aware that as Frederick Becker's daughter, she was considered to be out of reach for most of the young men hereabouts. Until now, that hadn't really bothered her. But now there was Jonas. If he felt about her as she did about him, no one, not even her father, could keep them apart.

She became aware that folks were staring at her. She hadn't moved from the spot where Jonas had left her. Gini came to her and guided her off the dance floor. Laura stood beside Gini—silent, confused. Eventually she looked around. She saw Jonas with a small group of young folks, but not paying much attention to any of them. He would glance at her briefly then lower his eyes.

Gini spoke to Laura. "Honey, Jonas knows there's no chance for the two of you. That's why he left you on the dance floor."

"Gini, that boy's the one I want, 'n I know he wants me. 'N there's all the chance in the world..."

Laura saw Dirk talking to several of his friends. He looked miffed. She knew Dirk favored her, but, somehow, she didn't trust him. He had never given her reason to dislike him, always polite and considerate. But she didn't really have feelings for him, not like what she now felt for Jonas. Dirk seemed to be giving instructions to the men, pointing this way and that. Then they all went outside. She assumed for a smoke or a drink, not an unusual occurrence at these dances. Soon one of the men re-entered. Laura knew it to be Jake—probably Dirk's closest friend. Jake walked directly over to Jonas and began talking to him, far from friendly. Jake became vehement, poking a finger to Jonas's chest. Jonas looked confused and ostensibly irked by Jake's aggressive manner. Then Jonas began to move to the door leading outside with Jake close behind. Jonas passed close to Laura and cast her a glance, but no words. She could read nothing in his eyes. He and Jake went outside.

Benji had caught the animated conversation between his brother and Jake. Jake had said something about Mr. Becker wanting to see Jonas outside and that it was important. When they went outside, Benji followed. He saw that Jake and Jonas now faced each other within a circle formed by a cluster of men. Becker was nowhere to be seen. Benji listened in. Jake had a way of calling Jonas "boy" and dragging Laura's name into the conversation such that Jonas became angry. Now the two were toe to toe and the verbal exchanges more heated.

Benji overheard Jake threaten Jonas, telling him to stay away from Laura. Laura's name and Dirk Fisher's name were bandied about a few more times and the level of agitation heightened. Jake stabbed a finger into Jonas's chest. Jonas swatted the finger away. Jake took a swing at Jonas, which Jonas ducked and parried with a stiff right hand, knocking Jake to the ground. Jake shook off the impact of the blow and regained his feet, now wielding a knife.

"Now yer really gonna git it," Jake snarled. The action was swift and somewhat obscure after that. Benji looked on in disbelief. He tried to think of how he could help Jonas, as he sensed an unfavorable outcome to the confrontation. He began to edge around the two combatants, who were now on the ground and out of his line of sight. Benji felt sure that Jonas would prevail but doubted that the other men, who were clearly urging Jake on, would allow Jonas to walk away unscathed. Benji meant to have the mare ready for Jonas in case there was a need for a quick departure.

Laura heard the commotion. Men-folk were streaming outside. She moved toward the door. Gini tried to stop her, but Laura was not to be deterred. When she arrived outside, she saw a group of men gathered around two men who were struggling against each other on the ground. Their struggle ceased and one of the men slowly gained his feet. Laura gasped. It was Jonas. And his arm was bloodied. He looked confused. The man on the ground remained still. Laura could not tell who it was, but she saw blood on him too. The men surrounding the combatants looked stunned. Jonas started to back away from the scene. He looked at Laura. His eyes pleaded with her. Then, his brother, Benji was beside him leading a horse. Some of the men began pointing to Jonas.

Stop him, he's kilt Jake...don't let 'im git away. Stop the murd'rin snake...the shouts rang out.

But Jonas had already mounted the mare and drawn Benji up behind him and they disappeared into the night. Laura stood in shock. *How could this be happening?* Some of the men shouted for Doc Adams and some for the sheriff. Others were seeking their mounts. Gini came out and joined Laura. "Laura, what's happened...all the shouting. *Oh, mon Dieu,* what is it?" she asked.

"Oh, Gini! It's Jonas. Something awful has happened. He's all bloody. I think he's kilt someone. Oh, Gini, I just kaint believe it." She buried her face into Gini's shoulder, sobbing. Dirk Fisher had eased up behind Laura. He leaned close to her ear. "Well, Laura sweetheart, what do you think of yer lover boy now?"

Dirk continued past Laura and joined his men who stood over Jake.

"Men, let's wait till the sheriff gits here before we go tearing off after that maverick." Dirk didn't really want Jonas caught. He didn't want him telling his side of the story. He just wanted Jonas out of the picture and out of Laura's life.

Jonas got the head start he needed and covered the three miles home as fast as he dared, riding double in a headlong plunge through the night. His arm hurt like hell, but his strength seemed to be holding up. He didn't want to think about what happened back there. Time for that later. Now only flight seemed plausible. He knew he was in trouble, that soon riders would be on his trail and they wouldn't be looking for explanations. His stop home would have to be brief. Jonas would need the mare and some provisions—enough to get him far from Jericho. *But to where?* He didn't have time to think about that—just time to grab what he needed and flee the area.

But before he fled, there was something he must do.

10

Gini escorted Laura home. Few words were exchanged. Once home, Gini consoled Laura once more with a hug and Laura sought the solitude of her bedroom.

Gini quietly stepped outside, settling down on the top porch step. The night was crisp, hinting that autumn was approaching. Scattered clouds mostly obscured the stars and the partial moon. She felt terrible for Laura. She could feel her pain and wished there were something she could do.

She and Laura were very close, companions since Laura's mother had abandoned the family. Gini admired Laura's free spirit, her fervor for life, and her deep concern for others, no matter their station in life. She hated to see her dear friend hurting like this.

"Psssst...over here, Gini." Gini was startled by a nearby whisper.

"Who's there?" she asked, nervously.

"It's me, Jonas. Please, don't be afraid. I only got a minute. But I have to see Laura, I have to talk to her. Please. I've got to explain what happened." He moved closer so Gini might recognize him in the dim moonlight. A slight glow emanated from inside the house, allowing Gini to distinguish that it was indeed Jonas that emerged from the darkness, leading a horse. His arm was in a sling. She had no fear of Jonas. She didn't believe that the accusations leveled on Jonas could be true.

"Please, Gini. Please, trust me. I must see Laura. I couldn't never cause her no harm."

Gini hesitated, studying him. "Jonas, wait around the side, it's darker there. There's just Laura and me here now, but no telling when Mr. Becker will return. I expect he's looking for you right now. Everyone is. If you hear anyone coming, lead your horse around the back. The woods are close by there. They'll give you cover so you can get away safely. Now, get around the side, I'll fetch Laura."

Soon Jonas saw Laura rushing toward him. She hesitated before reaching him. He saw tears in her eyes and confusion on her face. How had he any right to bring her into his plight?

"Laura, I know I shouldn't be here. I got no right to expect you to..." he started, hesitated. "Laura, I jes' want you to know what happened. I couldn't stand it if you thought bad of me."

"Jonas, are you hurt? I saw blood, 'n yer arm's all bandaged."

"No, it's nothing." *He lied.* "Pa bandaged it up pretty good. I'll be all right."

Her tears flowed again. She wrapped her arms around Jonas's waist, burying her head into his chest. She looked up at him.

"Jonas, you idiot. You got every right to be here. I know yer innocent. I know yer decent, you'd never hurt nobody on purpose. I couldn't feel like I do about you if I believed what those men were saying."

"Then that's all the more reason you should know what happened 'n what I gotta do. Laura, as far as I kin make out, 'n this ain't all too clear, even now. Jake told me yer pa was outside 'n wanted to see me, 'n that I was in some kind of troubl'. 'N he said some things about me 'n you I didn't care for. I think Jake was lick'erd up a bit. I followed him outside to find out what yer pa wanted. Some of the men Dirk hangs out with were out there. I didn't see yer pa anywhere, 'n I was startin' to get suspicious. Then Jake...he starts in on me. He told me I needed to be put in my place, that I ain't got no right to be seen with the likes of a lady like you. He said I was messing with Dirk Fisher's girl, 'n if Mr. Becker found out, he'd have me out of the county, or worse. Then Jake took a swing at me, but I ducked him 'n got in a pretty good shot myself. Jake went down 'n when he got back up he had a knife in his hand. Laura, I ain't never faced a knife before, 'n I expect I was scared. After that, it was pretty much a blur till we were both on the ground 'n Jake wasn't movin' no more. I guess you know what happened after that. Laura, everyone was sayin' it was me that pulled the knife. But I swear, it happened jes' like I said." Jonas tilted Laura's head up to his.

"What's gotta happen now, Laura, is that I got to clear out of here... prob'bly up into the mountains, maybe Virginia or Kentucky way. I know they'll be lookin' for me, so the rough country seems best."

"Oh, Jonas," said Laura, sniffling. She wiped her eyes and brushed at her runny nose. She stood up firmly. "Now, you listen. You do what you have to do. But know that I'm back here, 'n I'll be waitin' for you. You come back to me when you know how to set things straight, 'cause I know you can. There ain't no one here that means to me what you do. 'N if you want me, nobody's going to stop you from havin' me." She hesitated, said softly, "You got anything else to say to me, Jonas McNabb?"

"Laura, I never dreamed you'd feel that way. I never dared hope..."

"Nope. That ain't what I want to hear you sayin'."

Jonas looked into Laura's face, her beautiful face, eyes softened by tears. He touched her hair. His lips brushed hers. "Only that I love you, Laura." Now their lips met for real and, for a moment, obliterated all thoughts of the tragic events that brought Jonas here.

"'N I love you, too."

They'd known each other such a short time, but they knew what they felt and that it might be a long time before they would have another chance to express it.

"Jonas, you've got to go." It was Gini. "They're coming back. Hurry!"

"I'll find a way. I promise, Laura. Trust me," said Jonas. "In the meantime, I'll be wantin' you to be wearing this." Jonas handed Laura the necklace cameo his mother had given him. "Ma wanted this to go to somebody real special. I reckon that would be you."

"Jonas, it's beautiful," said Laura. She studied the cameo, then fastened it around her neck. Again, tears filled her eyes. Another fleeting kiss and Jonas led his horse around the back and vanished into the woods, just before Frederick Becker rode up with Dirk Fisher and several others. Laura tucked the necklace into her bodice, hiding it from view. She would wear it next to her heart awaiting Jonas's return.

When Frederick Becker burst through the front door, his daughter and Gini were calmly waiting in the living room. Becker had dismissed his men.

"Dad," said Laura, "you've been gone sich a long time. What's happened?" She tried not to appear too anxious.

"What? Oh, it was the damnedest thing. That McNabb boy, the one I got workin' for me...seems he got into a fight 'n knifed Jake Kellogg. Then he ran off. Some of the men followed him to his farm, but he'd already taken off. Hell, never expected him to be a troublemaker. Guess you jes' never know. Can't figger it. I gave him every opportunity, on account of what he did for you. I thought he was comin' along jes' fine. Sure proves you gotta be mighty careful who you deal favors to around here. Damn farmers ain't no better'n the miners."

"Is Jake all right? Is he...dead?" Laura asked.

"Not sure, Laura. Doc Adams says he'll most likely pull through. Ain't like a gunshot where you got to dig the bullet out. Hurt pretty bad though. What in hell got into that boy, pullin' a knife like that? I wouldn't have minded if he jes' settled it with fists, but damn...a knife. Anyway, we're sure rid of him now, no matter what. As far as I'm concerned, it's the sheriff's problem now. I don't figure on ever seein' the boy around here again."

"What about...his dad? You're goin' to keep him on ain't you? None of this was his fault."

"Caleb? Naw. He's fine. No reason to punish him for what his boy did." Frederick looked sternly at his daughter. "Damn, girl, what's yer concern here? Now that I think about it, there's talk about you 'n that McNabb boy cozyin' up to each other at the dance. Now, I'm not wantin' to believe that kind of talk, but I'm jes' tellin' you, remember who you are. You hear me?"

"Of course, Dad."

"Good. I'm going to bed. Hell of a night."

PART II
The Mountains

▲▲▲

11

Contrary to what Jonas had told Laura, his wound was serious and the pain excruciating. The knife had penetrated deeply into his upper arm; he only hoped nothing serious had been struck. In his hasty stopover at home, his dad had minimally treated the wound, time being of the essence, and put his arm into a sling. Now, as he made his way into the foothills, in the dark of night, miles from Jericho, Jonas's arm throbbed, acerbated by the constant jarring of the galloping mare. He hoped the wound wouldn't become infected, but he dared not stop and tend to it now—not until he'd put some distance between himself and any possible pursuit.

He assumed Sheriff Pete Turner would assemble some men and set out after him. Ole Pete would try to make it look good, like he was earning his pay. But night tracking would be difficult even for the best of trackers, which the sheriff wasn't. When his pursuers did get around to tailing him, most likely in the morning, they'd try to pick up his trail from the McNabb cabin, never figuring on him doubling back to the Becker Estate to see Laura.

Jonas figured he'd make his way south into the mountains and then maybe head west into Kentucky. Or wherever. His thinking wasn't too clear at this point.

Oh, lord, what have I gotten myself into?

He planned to travel all night and into the next day before he'd hole up somewhere to rest and tend to his wound. That was about all the real planning he'd done so far.

Jonas urged the mare on at a quick pace, but no longer a gallop. This was much easier on his arm and the horse. He carried a blanket in his saddlebag and the heaviest jacket he could come up with, anticipating the cold autumn nights in the mountains. He had packed in a hurry—dried meat, cans of dried fruit, pork and beans, soda biscuits, extra bandages, matches, eating utensils and cookware, and a canteen of water. And of course, his hunting rifle and ammo. Anything else he might need he figured to scrounge for as best he could. He had about ten dollars in his pocket, all the family could spare.

His familiarity with the countryside was limited in the direction he was headed, thirty miles being the farthest he'd ever been up into these hills. But he was confident in his survival skills. His hunting and camping excursions often kept him out for days at a time, and he was an excellent shot, often providing venison for neighboring families as well as his own. Still, he had never been all the way to the mountains and sensed that's where he would meet his greatest challenges.

Jonas felt the chill, but he rode on. Soon it would be much colder as he got up into the mountains. His arm continued to ache. It was full night now and progress was slow and dangerous, even in what was still familiar countryside. His mare wasn't accustomed to prolonged romps, as she was a farm animal, used for plowing and hauling. Now, Jonas was demanding a lot of her, and under the circumstances, even an adept riding horse would be tested to find sure footing and the proper path. The moon was about half and provided but slight illumination and even that was often lost as billowy clouds drifted across the moon face, creating silvery edges like ornamental lace. Ordinarily, such a vision might have thrilled Jonas, but now passed unheeded as his full concentration was on keeping the mare from a disastrous misstep. His pace had slowed considerably, as the woods thickened and overhanging branches could knock him from the saddle if he wasn't careful. Even so, his face was scratched from unseen twigs that reached out in the dark like claws from a beast in a child's nightmare.

"Pretty crazy, ain't it, ole girl?" He patted the mare gently on the neck. "I guess I'm askin' a powerful lot of you to git me outta here safe and all. But if you do, I promise you'll never have to pull another plow for as long as you live. I'm countin' on you, girl...and the Man up above. Please, God, don't let her break a leg or nothin'."

The night lingered on and by now Jonas had been four or five hours in the saddle. He was not used to lengthy riding such as this and his thighs rebelled against the effort, adding to the ongoing pain in his arm. He patted the mare and again thanked her for her perseverance. "I know you ain't used to this kind of thing either, ole girl. We're both pretty much out of our element."

The first semblances of dawn haloed the horizon, a welcome sight and an end to Jonas's frenzied nighttime flight. He issued a sigh of relief. Daylight and warmth might help to chase away the apprehensions that had been building as he rode. He sensed his life would completely change now and it was daunting for him. He was leaving behind all he had ever known and loved. He had no idea what lay ahead, but he wasn't one to shy away from danger or back down from a challenge. He was tired and hurting, but determined to survive and return to Laura and somehow clear his name.

Jonas stopped by a small stream and let his horse drink and graze while he rested and ate several soda biscuits. Half an hour later, now in full daylight, he once again rode on, entering a red spruce forest, following a deer trail. The woods became more dense with tall spruces casting long morning shadows across the trail like railroad ties. The increasing warmth of the sun felt comforting after his chilling night ride. A chipmunk scurried across the trail, barely avoiding the mare's hooves, then ducked into a safe-haven cubby hole amongst the gnarled roots of an ancient beech tree. Wild turkeys rose in a flock, the raucous flapping sound of their wings startling Jonas's horse. He had all he could do to keep his seat. He pointed a finger-gun at the birds as they tailed off over the treetops. "Pow," he said. "I hope you guys'll be around when I really need you."

The deer trail was narrow and the land rugged. Jonas guided the mare around fallen branches and sharp rocks, stooping to avoid low hanging tree limbs. At times he was forced to dismount in order to locate the trail, as it all but disappeared amidst the thick foliage.

Jonas could see the mountains up ahead, not too far distant. At their highest points the trees thinned out—not nearly as thick as the woodlands he now traversed. He trudged on, seeking the best route up and into the mountains as the deer trail had now played out.

The sun was now well past its zenith and Jonas figured about three more hours of daylight before he'd camp for the night. He was fatigued and confused as his mind never really strayed from the seriousness and devastation of the altercation in Jericho, or the pall that hung over him from having actually killed a man. He feared the consequences of the incident, which he knew would alter any future he had once envisioned for himself. Yet, the beauty of the approaching mountains was intoxicating. If anything could lessen the impact of that fateful night, surely it would be the majesty of the landscape which lie ahead.

"Whoa, boy, let's jes' sit here for a bit."

Jonas leaned on the saddle horn and spent a moment admiring the grandeur of the mountain vista. Balsam fir and beautiful spreading American chestnuts and mountain ash dominated the mountainside. The foliage was widely varied, creating a multiple-colored and multi-textured mosaic that covered most of the upward climb he now faced. Farther up the mountain, he could detect rocky crests and high bluffs as the canopy of trees thinned out. The steep escarpments were breathtaking in beauty but might be difficult to negotiate. Hopefully, he could find game trails that avoided the more treacherous aspects of his journey upward.

Jonas again urged the mare forward. What trails he discovered soon petered out. He searched for others and eventually stumbled upon what looked to be a well-worn path leading up the mountain.

"Well, I'm sure grateful for whatever or whoever beat out this path for us, be it deer, man or bear...well, maybe not bear. Think we got enough to handle without runnin' into one of them critters." He got down off the mare and began leading her up the trail. "Reckon you earned some walkin' time, ole gal, 'n I don't mind a bit of walkin' myself. My legs ain't used to all this time in the saddle. Let's see where this path leads us." After a considerable and often perilous ascent, the trail crested and then descended into a hidden valley, perhaps a mile across, with a burbling stream running its length. Fatigue was really setting in now, his strength further sapped by the knife wound.

About nightfall, he reached the stream and set up camp, allowing himself a modest fire against the dark. He would need the fire's warmth both for his body and for his sagging spirit as the marvels of the mountainside dissipated into dark feelings of loneliness and loss.

Jonas unsaddled the mare, tied her to a tree, and let her graze. He ate beans from a can heated over the small fire, figuring the walls of tall pines would hide the fire from view on at least three sides, leaving only the side facing the creek exposed. He'd chance it. Several soda biscuits dipped in water completed his meal. He cleaned his wound in the small creek and rewound it with fresh bandages, discarding the old bloody sling on the campfire. The cut was nasty, but didn't seem to be infected. *Thank God for that.* Finally, he arranged some pine boughs on the ground, fluffed them up, lay down and drew a blanket over his body, using his saddle for a pillow. He allowed himself a smoke as he assessed his situation. He thought of Laura and how she felt in his arms—their lips meeting, her professed love. These thoughts he treasured; these thoughts would be the fuel to carry him through whatever hardships lay ahead.

He thought about his pa. Would Becker dismiss him because of his son's misadventure?

The events of the previous evening kept running through Jonas's mind. Could he have handled it differently and avoided such a disastrous outcome? Eventually he slept.

▲ ▲ ▲

Next morning was frigid. A light frost covered the ground. The fire had died out and the one blanket he'd wrapped around him failed to fend off the cold. He rose shivering and retrieved the heavy coat from his saddlebag.

"Brrrr," he said. "If it's this cold already, what's it gonna be like when winter sets in?" He guessed he'd better be out of the mountains by then. He ate a few biscuits and washed them down with water and soon he and the mare were again under way.

Jonas no longer feared discovery. He even considered seeking someone who might live in the area. Maybe he could purchase supplies—food and warmer clothing. Few folks lived up here in the mountains, but maybe he'd come across some mountain man's cabin or even a small settlement.

The mountains were vast, endless miles of rugged landscape. Another thought slipped into his mind. *It would be so easy to become lost.*

"Hell, I'm not even sure I know where I am now. Must have covered better'n fifty miles, mostly south I hope. 'Bout time to start head'n west I figure." He gazed up at the morning sun, knowing it lay easterly. He mounted the mare, stroked her neck and whispered in her ear, "Well, ole girl, let's see what lies ahead," and prodded his horse on, the sun at his back.

The horse's breath sent out puffs of vapor into the chilly air, as did his own.

Jonas followed the valley westward, thinking he might by chance stumble upon someone if he followed the creek.

They traveled this way for hours, allowing the creek to dictate their route. At times, he would talk to himself, at times to his horse. "You know, girl, weren't but a short while ago I was wond'rin what it might be like to jes' make off into these mountains 'n see what might lay beyond for me. These ain't exactly the cir-cum-stances I imagined. Ha, that's puttin' it mildly." *Strange the way things work out. I might actually be enjoyin' all this, if it hadn't been for...but then, that was before I met Laura. Now I can't imagine any plans that don't include her. Hell, ain't that a laugh...include her in what, a jail cell?*

He listened to the sounds around him—the creek gurgling around rocks and splashing over shallow falls—chiding blue jays warning of his intrusion. For a while, Jonas was taking in all the sights and sounds, but as the soothing monotony of the mare's repetitive gait wore on, he drifted into a semi-trance, recalling earlier times.

His life had been free and easy then. His ma evoked nothing but warm memories. He thought of how his pa had struggled with the farm, his ma urging him on, encouraging him, patiently explaining farm work, then explaining again. His pa just wasn't cut out to be a farmer. But it was a happy household. They made do. Back then.

Then the farm had became Jonas's responsibility, as was raising his younger brother. Jonas wondered what Benji was doing right now. Was he alone on the farm while his pa was off to the mines? Was his pa even working in the mines? He hoped they wouldn't be suffering because of what he had done.

And Laura—the memory of her riding in the meadow next to his farm. Her hair billowing out, her face flushed—the joy and exhilaration in her eyes. Would it really be possible that they could ever be together? How could he even hope for that, especially now? Pure lunacy.

"Hell, I ain't even got a plan that makes much sense," he thought out-loud. "I killed a man 'n the law's after me. I'm an outlaw. I ain't got no idea how to prove it wasn't my doin'...that it wasn't me that pulled that knife."

The miles droned on, a horse oblivious to Jonas's plight, a rider sagging into a stupor of memories and regrets, all to the intoxicating murmur of a mountain stream.

12

"Hey mister, ya think ya could help me?" A plaintive voice brought Jonas to a stop.

"Wha..." Jonas snapped out of his reverie, looking down on a young girl.

"I seen ya comin' from outta the window," she said. "I need ya to help me out. My uncle's sick. I don' know what's ailin' 'im. Kin ya take a look, mister?"

It was difficult to tell how old she was, due to her unkempt appearance. Her hair straggled down around her shoulders, swatches of dirt or ashes dappled her nose and cheeks. She wore a simple frock, torn at the elbows and she was barefooted. Jonas thought it a poor outfit against the autumn chill up here in the mountains.

"Please, mister," she continued.

Jonas had happened upon a clearing, with a cabin and a small barn. A mule grazed in a fenced area near the barn. He got down off the mare, wincing from the lingering pain in his wounded arm. He tied the mare to a tree and followed the girl inside the cabin. The cabin was one large room with a table, a couple of chairs, and two bunks. A man occupied one of the bunks, a blanket pulled up under his chin. A fire blazed in an open stone fireplace.

"I don' know what's the matter with 'im. He fell sick a coupla days ago. Maybe you kin fix 'im up."

The man groaned. He was wet with perspiration. He gazed up at Jonas, blurry eyed, and coughed up a gob of phlegm, which dribbled down his chin. He struggled for speech, but was incoherent.

"I think he's gittin' worse. It jis' came o'er 'im sudd'n like. I don' know what ta do."

Neither did Jonas. His experience with sick people was limited to his mother and he had been helpless with her. He felt helpless now.

"Look, miss. I ain't no good with sick folks. He pro'bly needs a doctor."

"Wahl, d'you see a doc anywhar near. They's jis' you 'n me. So, d'you think he'll die?"

"I'm sorry, Miss, I jes' don' know what you expect me to do."

"Maybe you could jis' stay with him a while...'till he...you know..."

"I reckon I could do that, the least I could do." Jonas felt compelled to do something. But he had no idea what. The girl seemed helpless and the man was clearly in trouble, maybe dying. Jonas cursed himself that he couldn't be of more use. Or, possibly, it was a curse, that on top of everything else—now this.

"I guess we jes' try to keep 'im warm, 'n see what happens," said Jonas. He remembered how it was when his ma was dying, how she had just laid in bed for days, becoming worse and worse. "I'll stay with you. Maybe he'll come around."

By nightfall the man had died.

"I think he's gone," said the girl, flatly, as if a man dying were an everyday occurrence. "Maybe we better jis' bury 'im, 'n then we kin git the hell outta here. I kaint stay har by myself."

The girl's reaction puzzled Jonas. No remorse. No emotion. *Lord, her kin is dead here. She ought to feel somethin'.* In contrast, he remembered how his heart had been torn apart by the loss of his ma.

Jonas checked the man. He was dead all right. Jonas covered him with a blanket.

"I guess we better wait 'till mornin'," said Jonas. "Then we'll bury 'im, 'n figure out what to do from there."

"Suits me. My name's Callie. What's yers, mister?"

"I'm Jonas."

"Wahl, Jonas. Whatcha doin' up har in the mountains, anyhow? Ya don' look like no mountain man ta me. Aire ya huntin' er what? 'N what happened to yer arm, ya got it all bandaged up there."

Jonas thought for a second. He realized he should have been ready with an explanation for being in the mountains, in case he ever needed one—like right now.

"Yeh, up here huntin'. Lookin' for deer to take back home for the winter. 'N I fell off my mare a ways back. That's how I hurt my arm." Jonas knew his story sounded lame, but that's what came out.

"Okay, Jonas, if'n you say so." Callie sat on her bunk. "Now me, I bin here fer o'er two years, e'er since my paw died 'n his brother har took me in. I din't have no one else. Two years I bin stuck up har in this wilderness hardly ne'er seein' nobody. I bin cookin, 'n slavin' for thet old coot, 'n now I figger I'm freed up. I s'pose ya think I sound hateful, him bein' daid 'n all. Wahl, I'll tell ya, fella, I had all I could do ta keep 'im offa me. 'N I sure don't feel nuthin' fer him now, 'cept grat-i-tude I kin finally be gittin' outta har."

Gettin' outta here? This girl was now to be my responsibility?

Jonas brought in his bedroll and placed it by the fire, as far away from the dead man as possible.

"I su'pose I outta feed ya somethin'," said Callie. "You hungry, Jonas?"

Until then, Jonas hadn't realized how hungry he really was. "I reckon I could stand some of that stew I smell there."

"Yeh, we might as well eat it up. We kaint take it with us, 'n I shore ain't leavin' it fer no critters."

Callie ladled out a cup of the stew, added a biscuit, and handed it to Jonas. He made quick work of it.

The girl talked incessantly, as if it had been a long time since she'd had a chance to test her voice. Jonas was tired and wanted nothing more than to lie down by the fire and sleep. As soon as it was dark, he excused himself and climbed under his blanket. Sleep came quickly.

Sometime during the night, he woke to find the girl snuggled up against him beneath his cover. He rolled away from her and spent the rest of the night sitting by the dwindling fire, only half-dozing.

Early next morning the girl was up, packing her meager possessions in a cloth bundle. "C'mon mister, what's holdin' ya up? He's daid 'n gone. We got ta be movin' on. Yer responsibl' fer me now."

"Girl, take it easy. Gimme time to think. We gotta do this proper; give him a decent burial."

"I know that. Ya think I'm deft? Git it done, 'n let's be gittin' outta har."

Jonas started digging. He had no idea who the dead man was, if indeed he was the girl's uncle. All the while, she stood impatiently by. The ground was hard and digging was difficult, even more so with his injured arm. Finally, the man was laid to rest, buried, and covered up with dirt. "Any words you'd like to say over him?" asked Jonas.

"Hahl, no. What fer? He's jes' goin' get et by the worms 'n sich. Ain't ne'er seen nobody so sentimen'l as you aire. Let's jis' be gittin' on outta these hills b'fore it really gits cold. I've had my fill of these damn mount'in winters."

The girl had the mule all packed up, with room left for her to ride. She wore the same tattered dress, but now covered it with an oversized hairy coat, her uncle's most likely, and heavy boots. She mounted and they rode off, following the creek westward.

"I guess ya don' find me attrac-tive, Jonas", said the girl. "What, ya got a girlfriend somewhar hid away?"

Actually, Jonas did find her an attractive girl, despite her unkempt appearance and unsightly clothing. She was about his age, slender, and not without a certain grace. But most notable was her crop of fiery red hair.

"Girl, I'm more'n willin' to help you out. I ain't exac'ly in the best of predicaments myself. 'N I don't pretend to understand what's goin' thru yer mind. But I'm obliged to help you out. So, here's what I'm offer'n. I'll do my best to get you out of these mountains, 'cause that's where I'm headed myself, but then yer on yer own."

"Yer loss, mister, but it's a damn shame. Yer a fine lookin' boy, 'n I bin tole I'm a right purty gal."

Jonas wasn't at all sure he did still have a girl back home—*I'll be waitin' for you. You come back to me when you know how to set things straight.* Laura's promise lingered in his thoughts, though now it seemed so vague and far away.

They traveled on. Jonas couldn't count on Callie for directions so he continued with his original plan, following the creek westward.

Nightfall came and they made camp. Jonas built a fire and they ate and talked for a while before bedding down for the night. Jonas slept alone.

Sometime during the night, Jonas woke. He thought he'd heard something—a twig snapping? He sat up, alert to any sound. It was difficult to hear much over the noise of the rushing water of the nearby creek. Then the mare whinnied. Jonas slowly gained his feet, looking to where the mare was tied up. He could see little in the darkness as the fire had died down considerably. He thought he'd better do a better job banking the fire if he expected to keep the critters away.

"Jes' hold it right thar, mister." Two shadowy figures emerged from the darkness and now trained rifles on Jonas. Their features became clearer as they neared the fading campfire. Two men, one large, the other smaller. He heard a dog growl.

"Shet the hell up, you devil, or ah'll whack ya a good one," threatened one of the men. "Tie thet critter up to a tree'r somthin', Zeke. Hell, we shoulda left 'im back at ole Jeb's shack."

"Yeh, I tole ya so, Bear," said Zeke, lashing the dog's rope-leash to a tree. "Damn thing's more wolf than dog. When thet old coot gits back 'n finds his dog is gone he's gonna be comin' after us, shore as hell."

Sleep cleared from Jonas's eyes. He saw that the dog was muzzled by a loop of rope, with another short rope tied around its neck to serve as a leash. A third rope led from the rope around the dog's neck to a hind leg, effectively hobbling the dog. Obviously, the two men had a tough time controlling the animal. The dog was pure white and it was huge. And it had red eyes.

Bear, turned his attention to Jonas and the girl. Callie was now sitting up.

"Hell," said Bear, "this har ain't much more'n a boy 'n a lil ole gal. Now, ain't this a purty picture. Whataya think, Zeke, maybe somethin' awry goin' on har?" He laughed. "Yep, I think we done busted in on somethin' purely sinful har, 'n she ain't much more'n a squirt. What's the matter with yer arm, boy?"

Jonas looked down at his arm. The wound had reopened and leaked blood through the fresh bandage. "I said, what the hell's wrong with yer arm, boy?" Bear prodded Jonas's arm with the barrel of his rifle. Jonas winced. "Zeke, we got us a wounded sinner boy. Think we oughta shoot 'im 'n put him outta his misery?"

"Hell, yeh. We can feed 'im ta thet damn dog."

"Naw, thet dog's prob'ly used ta prime venison, not some stringy boy meat."

Jonas studied the two men. Mountain men most likely. He had heard stories about such men, grizzled men who called the mountains their home and who didn't generally abide intruders. He sensed he was in grave danger. Robbery—worse? He felt his best chance was to keep his mouth shut and not provoke them.

Then the girl spoke up. "Hell, y'all. Ya came jis' in the nick of time. This har fella was cartin' me off, 'n he's been tryin' ta have his way with me. I'm thinkin' ya've done rescued me."

"Wahl, Zeke, ya hear thet? I reckon this har lady's in need uv a bit uv a-sis-tance." And then Jonas's head exploded and all went black.

▲ ▲ ▲

Jonas woke slowly, his head throbbing. Pain shot up his side, maybe both sides, he couldn't tell for sure, but if he moved even slightly, the pain was nearly unbearable. "What the hell?" he said to himself. "I suspect they clobbered me with something, but what else did they do? I 'spose them scoundrels must've kicked me a few times, jes' for good measure. From the way it feels, someone must kick like a damn mule. Sure hope no ribs got broke."

As best he could determine, the girl was gone, as were the two men. His vision was clouded and his head pulsed with pain.

He felt something cold and wet on his face. A huge bulk of white hair lorded over him, emitting a low growl. A dog? A wolf? Hard to tell. The animal from last night? How long had he been unconscious?

The low growl was unsettling, but not threatening. The animal was no longer muzzled—its wet nose had revived Jonas. Jonas chose not to meet the animal's eyes, feeling the dog might take it as a challenge. He spoke softly.

"It's okay, boy. Good dog, if that's what you are, a dog." Jonas's gentle words seemed to placate the dog. The growling ceased and the animal backed off slightly, but stood his ground.

Jonas guessed the dog belonged to someone—*the old coot?*—and was not a wild scavenger or a killer. The mountain men must have treated the animal badly and brought out the worst in him. Now Jonas dared to look into the dog's eyes, his red eyes. He continued to talk softly and reassuringly to him, somehow trusting the dog. He sensed no menace in the dog's eyes.

"It's okay, boy. We jes' ain't goin' to hurt each other, are we?" *Like I'd be capable of it, the shape I'm in.* The dog seemed to know Jonas could be trusted. He inched forward, close enough for Jonas to weakly reach out to him. He licked Jonas's hand. "Well, I guess that means you like me okay. Leastwise, you ain't gonna eat me." Jonas felt his strength ebbing. He was drifting off, losing consciousness again, as his head continued to throb and his body rebelled against him.

Over the next few days, Jonas drifted in and out of consciousness, and always the dog was there. On the third day, he regained enough of his senses that he could look around and take stock of his situation. It didn't look good, but at least he was still alive. The mare was gone, along with most of his provisions. His cooking utensils remained by the campfire, which was now stone dead. He had his blanket, and fortunately his knife, which he had wisely placed under his blanket. He retained his canteen, thank God. Painfully, he unscrewed the top and drank. Every part of his body ached, but at least the cool water helped clear his head. After his initial survey of what his attackers had left him, Jonas thought of the mare. His attachment to the horse had grown during his desperate flight into the mountains—now he felt a heart-twanging loss—not only had the mare facilitated his escape, but she had been the remaining link to his family—to all he had left behind.

Jonas studied the dog. A short length of rope still hung from the dog's neck and Jonas figured the dog had chewed his way to freedom. He wasn't sure how he'd slipped the rope-muzzle.

"You must've jes' kept workin' at it, eh boy? 'N I guess them fellers left you behind 'cause you were jes' too much troubl' for 'em. Looks like they traded you for the girl." The dog allowed Jonas to remove the rope from around his neck.

Why the dog had stayed with Jonas was a mystery to him. Jonas had heard tales—fairytales?—about wolves caring for human children. But he was no child. Whatever the reason, he sensed that the dog's presence was essential to his survival. He had no doubt the mountain men had left him for dead. And the girl was at least partially responsible for his present situation—*trying to have his way with me.*

"Well, boy. I guess if I ever git out of this mess, we're a team. I'd give you a name, but I guess you belong to some ole feller back yonder somewhere, so I'll jes' call you Dog. Yeh, Dog, this is sure a fine mess. I wonder how long it's bin?" Jonas lapsed back into unconsciousness.

When he awoke, Dog lay in front of him. And at his feet was a half-eaten rabbit. Jonas laughed. "And what the hell am I s'posed to do with that? Don't s'pose you could cook it for me, eh, Dog?" He laughed again, which spiked the pain in his head and side. "Phew," he gasped, "guess laughin' ain't such a good idea."

His head settled into a nagging ache. He guessed he must be feeling a bit better because he was able to think more clearly now.

He tried to rise but the effort sent his head into an eruption of pain and dizziness. He found he could crawl, not painlessly, but enough to gain mobility. The side pain was almost bearable, so he figured no ribs were broken.

"Well, Dog, I got bruised ribs, a head half knocked off, 'n a bloody hole in my arm. Don't suppose you could fix any of that?" With great effort, and greater pain, Jonas gathered sticks enough to rekindle the fire. Fortunately, he'd kept his matches in his pant's pocket and not with the stolen gear.

Using his knife, he was able to skin the rabbit Dog had left for him. He didn't think his stomach would accept raw meat. In fact, he knew it wouldn't, something he'd learned the hard way. *An older kid had told a four-year-old Jonas that if he wanted to grow up big and strong, he should eat raw meat. This kid even had a sampling of raw rabbit meat with him, which he offered to Jonas. Jonas looked at the raw meat, which still dripped with blood. "Are you sure? I never heard of eatin' raw meat." "Course I'm sure. How d'ya think I got so big? If you don't want it, I'll jes' give it to someone else who might be more grateful."*

So Jonas had been properly enticed to actually stuff some of the rabbit into his mouth and swallow it. It wasn't long before he painfully coughed up the parcel of meat and spit it out. Even now, the thought of it about gagged

78

him. Whatever pain he must endure, he would cook this rabbit.

Dog continued to bring meat to Jonas, which Jonas continued to cook—rabbits, squirrels, even pheasant—"how had the dog managed to take down a pheasant?" thought Jonas. They shared the cooked meat for which Dog seemed to show a preference. "Yeh, purty soon I'll have you eatin' off a table with a knife and fork."

Jonas found he could crawl to the nearby creek for water and eventually was able to stand and move about without excessive pain. He didn't know how long he'd been recuperating by the stream in the middle of nowhere, but he did notice the nights were getting colder. Soon, they would become unbearable as he retained but light clothing, his heavy coat being lost with the mare.

Of late, Dog had been sharing his body warmth with Jonas as he slept. Jonas was in awe of the huge white dog. What a magnificent animal—be it dog or wolf—the only reason he was still alive. Jonas pledged his loyalty to this great beast. "I owe you, Dog...way b'yond what I can ev'r repay." The dog looked into Jonas's eyes as if understanding every word. Jonas was transfixed by the stare of the red eyes.

"Jes' who or what are you, my special friend?"

Jonas knew he had to be on the move soon, as he was ill-prepared to meet the frigid conditions that lie ahead. "Well, ole boy. What'd'ya think? Time to git on with it? Fate's done handed us a heavy load, for sure. But, I ain't quitting. Can't jes' lie here and wait for a snowy grave, now can I? Not after all you done for me."

The dominance Dog had maintained at first, he now instinctively relinquished to Jonas. A dog, a new master—a team for survival.

13

At first, Jonas could travel in but short stints, supporting himself with a wooden crutch he'd fashioned from a vee-notched tree
branch, resting often. He and the dog continued to follow the stream. As his
strength gradually returned, he was able to discard the crutch. Dog continued to provide the meat, always grateful to have it cooked. To his own diet,
Jonas added some blackberries, chestnuts, tubers, and other late-season
pickings. The nights continued to grow colder and the deciduous trees began releasing their foliage of reds, yellows, and oranges, making silent travel
impossible as dried leaves crunched beneath their feet. But stealth was no
longer a consideration. His concern was for the oncoming frigid conditions
he would encounter if he didn't soon find a way out of the mountains.

Dog stood guard at night while Jonas slept. There were many dangers
imminent in these mountains—mountain lions, wolves, bear, *man*—but
Jonas felt safe with his huge white friend as a sentry. Dog would be intimidating to any intruder, man or beast, night or day.

Jonas cursed losing his rifle. He needed it for protection, but more
importantly, for hunting. If he could bring down a deer, he could skin it and
use the hide for warmth, maybe even fashion himself a coat of some sort.

"You're lucky, Dog. You got a nice natural, heavy coat, ain't you boy?"

Chance had it that the twosome encountered a dead deer. In truth,
Dog found the deer and drew it to Jonas's attention. Jonas knew the deer
had died recently as its body still retained heat. He guessed the unfortunate
animal had lost its footing on the cliffs above and tumbled down into the
ravine, impaling itself on a sharp branch of a dead tree. Jonas wasn't sure
if he should trust the meat of the deer, but he sure could use the hide.
"Unlucky for you fella, but shore lucky for me. Dog, you got an uncanny
knack for seein' to my needs, don' you, boy? Don' suppose you could rustle
me up a horse, could you?"

Jonas had no trouble removing the deer's hide, even though he was not yet up to full strength. He'd skinned many a deer, but it was the meat he was after back then, now it was the hide. With determined patience, he was able to scrape the inside of the hide fairly clean. He washed it in the nearby creek and hung it on a tree branch to dry overnight. Next morning, he slung the stiff hide around his shoulders and traveled on. He had no way of curing the hide, so periodically he would soften it by beating it with a rock. The hide served as a second blanket by night and a cloak by day. To secure the cloak around him, he fashioned ties from thin strips cut from the deer hide.

On this, their third day out, Jonas and Dog traveled westward toward the Allegheny Plateau. Jonas had heard stories about the severity of the winters in this region—how the Plateau would become a rugged mountain hellhole, buffeted by high winds that swirled the snow and ice into a frenzy that could cut a man's body to pieces—as well as his soul. Jonas knew he needed to be through this rough country before such conditions set in. His very survival depended upon it.

By now, Dog was establishing the pace, forging ahead as if he had a particular destination in mind. Jonas, still healing, was forced to hurry just to keep up with his white guide, ignoring the twinges of pain. The creek they had been following had dwindled as they approached its source in the mountains.

As night approached, Jonas lost sight of Dog. This was not unusual as Dog often surged ahead on his own. Jonas would catch a glimpse of him, sometimes on the higher trails or even farther up on craggy outreaches. But Dog would always return—sometimes with game, sometimes with his fur covered in burdocks, entreating Jonas's help in removing them. Jonas had grown accustomed to Dog's ways.

But, this night was different.

Jonas heard the urgent barking and growling somewhere up ahead. And the ruckus did not emanate from Dog alone.

Jonas stepped up his pace, heading toward the commotion. A rifle shot rang out, causing Jonas to proceed more cautiously. Up ahead he saw a campfire, revealing an unbelievable scene. Two dead—a wolf and a mule—a second wolf in mortal combat with Dog and a third wolf being held at bay by an old man wielding a knife in one hand and a burning stick in the other.

The growling, the snarling, the snapping—the vicious, raucous sounds of combat filled the night air. The third wolf went in low on the old man, clasping its powerful jaws on his upper leg. The man went down, still thrusting at the beast with a large hunting knife. Jonas rushed in, reasoning aside, but driven to help. The old man had dropped the knife, which Jonas retrieved. He then leaped onto the wolf's back and drove the blade deep into its neck. He drove the knife in again and again until the wolf released his hold on the old man's thigh and slumped to the ground, dead. Jonas rolled off the wolf's body, physically spent. He heard Dog whimper. He turned to see the dog by the downed man's side, nuzzling his face. The wolf that Dog was battling was nowhere to be seen. Jonas reasoned that it had run off. The left side of Dog's body was bloody and a forepaw limp.

The old man whispered, "Savage..." then lost consciousness.

Dog lay at his side, panting, still whimpering.

"What is it, boy? You know this old feller," said Jonas, "or are you jes' natur'ly drawn to folks in trouble?"

Jonas tended as best he could to the old man's leg, washing it down with water from his canteen and wrapping it with the last of his bandages. Then he splinted Dog's leg, while the animal licked at his other wounds. Dog resumed his protective position at the old man's side. Jonas covered them both with his blanket and sat near the warmth of the fire, maintaining vigil in case the dead mule might attract more wolves or even other predators.

Jonas looked about him, taking in the carnage. How could so much turmoil beset him in so short a time—the knife fight in Jericho, his escape into the mountains, the girl, Callie, and the mountain men leaving him for dead, the incredible great white dog...*and now this*! But a short time ago he had been in Laura's arms, envisioning a future life with her. Now it seemed a nightmare had set in. He looked to the heavens, pondering just what he had done to deserve such a fate.

The night passed without further incident.

The morning light revealed a grisly scene. Two dead wolves, a dead mule, a wounded dog, and an old man badly hurt. Jonas knew the death stench would soon be unbearable and he hoped to be out of here by then. The old man stirred and Dog got up and stood guard over him.

"Savage, is thet you...?" the old man asked weakly. He reached out and the dog licked his hand. He grasped the dog by the ruff of his neck and drew him close. "I thought I lost you, ole boy." He pointed to Jonas. "'N who's yer new friend? Wahl, stranger...reckon ya saved me. Sure as hell figur'd I was a goner. Don't know what brought ya by...but I'm shore obliged to ya." The old man spoke haltingly, grimacing often.

Jonas sat by the old man and gave him a drink. "Name's Jonas. I reckon it was the dog brought me by, 'n none too soon. That's a mighty nasty bite you took there on yer leg. And the dog's ripped up some too."

The old man extended a hand. "Jebediah, thet'd be me. But call me Jeb, least' yer...hankerin' ta spit out a whole mouthful ever'time ya address me...haw. 'N this har's Savage. He 'n me...we go way back. Ya did a right nice job on thet leg...his 'n mine. What a pair we aire now. Wahl, reckon I better git up...'n we best be gittin' outta here, b'fore thars more troublin'. Hep me up...would ya mister? Jonas is it? I figger I kin travel, with...some help. My cabin's not mor'n a day'r so from har. 'N fetch my hat fer me would ya... wharev'r it got to. My rifle should be around har somewhar, too. Guess thet cus-sed wolf knocked it outta my hands."

"I got yer rifle. Found it last night 'n stood guard with it. Not sure you can travel, Jeb, but we'll give it a shot."

Jonas retrieved Jeb's hat. He judged the old man to be a mountain man, based on his buckskin clothing and wide brimmed hat. His hair was silver white—long and matted, encasing a leathery face with an unruly mustache and an equally unkempt beard. Leather strips fringed the shoulders, arms, and sleeves of his heavy leather coat. No telling how old he was, his age was probably exaggerated by the rigors of mountain life. His boots were of thick leather, suitable for the regimens of the mountain terrain and cold weather. Yet, there was an amiable twinkle in his eyes that gave Jonas a comfortable feeling.

Jonas got Jebediah to his feet.

"Easy there, boy," said Jeb, grimacing. "I ain't no sack of flour."

"Sorry. You sure yer up to this, old timer?"

"Hell, boy. I bin banged up worse'n this. Jes' gimme yer arm."

"Okay. I guess we might be able to manage if we take our time," said Jonas. "I ain't in that great shape myself."

Jonas had stripped the mule of the few supplies it was carrying, wrapped them in his blanket, and slung the whole affair over his shoulder, the one not supporting Jebediah. Jeb carried the rifle in his free hand. The dog walked gingerly, but steadily ahead of them, maintaining guard.

"Hell, we look like we're...returnin' from thet damn bloody war. All we need's a drummer boy a-leading the way," Jebediah commented and laughed weakly.

14

The trip to Jebediah's cabin was slow and tedious, the wounded needing frequent stops for rest. The old man grew progressively weaker, making Jonas's burden more difficult. Savage took the lead, despite his injuries.

Jonas learned that Jebediah had been searching for Savage for about a week and was just returning home when he encountered the wolves.

"I left Savage b'hind whilst I went out huntin' fer deer. Had ta stock-pile some meat fer the winter comin' up. I don' ord-in-ar'ly leave my dog behind, but I had some skins needed protectin'n...thet 'n Savage seemed ta be ailin' a bit. When I got back, Savage was gone 'n the thievin' scoundr'ls had ransacked my cabin, lookin' fer somethin' I suspec'. Not thet there was much ta take, not thet they could find leastwise. Thet's when I set out ta find Savage. I gave it up after a few days 'n started back, thinkin' mebbe he found his way back ta the cabin. 'Bout dark last night, I made camp, figgerin' on makin' the last leg home the next mornin'. My mule must've attracted the wolves. Hell, them beasts were on me b'fore I had a chance ta react proper. Gittin' old, I suspec'. So how 'bout you, boy, how'd you happen by?"

Jonas told how he'd happened upon Savage—related the whole story, giving the dog all the credit he deserved. He omitted how he happened to be in the mountains in the first place.

"Two men, eh? Yep, mount'n men most likely. Thar's some good 'uns around, then thar's some like thet damn pair of scallywags you encounter'd. Gives us respect'ble old turds a bad name. Strange 'bout the gal, though. I don' recall comin' upon no young gal 'n her uncle. I thought I knowed most the folks up har in the mountains. 'N ya say she was quite fetchin', eh? Don' know if'n I'd wanna be in her shoes...not tailin' along with them varmin's. Mebbe, if she's as sassy as ya say, she mighta struck up some sorta bargain with 'em."

Jonas was uneasy with Jebediah's incessant chatter. But it was nearly impossible to keep the old man quiet, despite Jonas's admonitions that Jeb save his strength for the trek back to his cabin.

"So, the way I figger it," continued Jeb, still talking haltingly, "them two hombres left Savage 'cause he was jes' too much trouble, 'n most likely they left you for dead. They musta took the girl, or accordin' to you, rescued her from the des-pic-abl' desperado thet you aire. Haw. Now, what they intended ta do with her is the question. Shore, the obvious, if she was a purty li'l thing like ya say. Not thet it would matter much ta the likes of them two...s'long as both her legs reached ta the ground. Haw."

Jeb paused to catch his breath. Jonas was aware of the pain the old man must be enduring as he prattled on. "Most likely," continued Jeb, "they'll try'n git some money for her down in Sprucetown. They could sell her off fer some critter's wife, 'r maybe whore 'er out ta some saloon owner. They's always cryin' fer fresh young things."

For the last hour, only moonlight guided them. Jonas's head continued to throb and his arm ached. By the time they reached Jeb's cabin they were all nearly depleted—Savage, still feeling the effects of his wounds, Jonas, with waning strength, and Jebediah, his condition exacerbated by all his palaver. Once inside the cabin, Jeb located and lit a lantern and purveyed the damage. The interior of the cabin looked like a whirlwind had hit it. The table and chairs were overturned; pots, dishes and crockery had been swept from the shelves. The bedding was shredded and strewn on the floor.

"Yep, them rascals shore was lookin' fer somethin'," said Jeb, "somethin' they didn't find." Jeb collected what he could of the desecrated mattress and bedding, threw it onto the only cot, and collapsed upon it. Savage nestled beside the cot and maintained vigil over his master. The cabin was cold, and before Jonas surrendered to a much needed sleep, he set kindling in the fireplace, lit a fire, and added firewood enough to fend off the chill of the night, then settled in before the warmth of the fire, pulling the deerskin wrap around him. Soon all three weary travelers surrendered to sleep.

▲ ▲ ▲

Jonas awoke to Savage licking his face. "Ahh, you still love me, don' you boy?" He inspected the dog's wounds and was satisfied that the dog would be fine. Jeb was another story. The bite on his thigh was deep and ragged and Jonas was afraid infection might set in.

"Jeb, wake up, Jeb. We gotta see to that wound b'fore it infects."

"Huh?" It took the old man a few moments to get his wits about him.

"Sorry, old-timer. Gotta git you up. We gotta look after that wound of yers. We don't want it festerin'"

"Okay, yeh. Better do thet. There's some good stuff up there'n the cubbert, 'lessen them two varmin's took it. See if thar ain't a tube of oint-ment. Thet should do the trick, always has. Should be some bandagin' in thar too." Jeb delivered the information with a good deal of effort.

Jonas found the ointment and bandages. He cleaned the wound, treated, and bandaged it. He also took the opportunity to clean and rewrap his own arm.

It was clear the old man would be incapacitated for some time. Jonas intended to stay with Jebediah until he was back on his feet and able to care for himself, which wouldn't be anytime soon.

"I guess it'll be up to me to straighten up this mess them two moun-tain men left," thought Jonas. "Wonder what they were lookin' for, *that they didn't find?*"

Jonas set to straightening up the cabin. Despite the mess, he was impressed by the old man's quarters. The furnishings were modest and most likely were homemade: a table with two chairs—one being a rocking chair—one bunk, and a wood-burning cook-stove. Open cupboards lined one wall just above a sink and water pump. A lantern hung over the sink, a second lantern lay smashed on the floor. The windows were glass and still intact, facing opposite ends of the room. A solid oak door fit snuggly in the entranceway, with a heavy bar to slide in place for locking. An open trap door in the floor likely led to a root cellar. Jonas closed it. A large stone fireplace took up half the back wall.

Jonas picked up a small woodcarving, one of about a dozen scattered around the floor. He studied it—a duck portrayed in full flight. He noted the attention to detail as he slowly turned it in his hands. The small sculpture seemed to have a life of its own, as if an actual duck had been shrunk and magically transformed into wood.

He gathered up the other sculptures strewn about the cabin—raccoons, beavers, delicate birds, deer, bobcats, and a magnificent mountain lion. Each animal was depicted in dramatic poses—birds with spread wings as if soaring, a hawk captured in the act of snatching a rabbit, talons extended and threatening. Most spectacular was the mountain lion perched on the back of a deer, his jaws clamping deep into the victim's neck. Jonas had seen woodcarvings before, but nothing that approached the beauty and realism and intensity of these. A few were broken and Jonas cursed the mountain men for their lack of respect for such brilliantly crafted pieces. He gently placed the carvings on the shelves that lined several of the walls. "I guess this is where you had 'em displayed, ole-timer. I sure got to ask you 'bout these."

Jonas walked outside. He figured it to be mid-October by now. The air was crisp in the mountains, but daytime was still quite pleasant, the nights not nearly so. The deciduous trees had mostly surrendered their foliage, but plentiful evergreens would shield the cabin from the fierce, bitter, cold winds that hammered these mountains in wintertime. A rippling stream emptied into a small pond but a few hundred feet from Jeb's doorstep. Could be fish in there, Jonas thought. Out back of the cabin was an out shed, which Jonas guessed was for curing and storing furs, and storing firewood.

Jonas wondered if he might winter here. Made sense—take care of Jeb while he himself hid out. He hadn't formulated any other plans that made much sense. Of course, he'd have to run it by Jebediah.

The old man slept right on through the rest of the day and all night too, for which Jonas was grateful. They could all use the rest. Once Jebediah woke, Jonas unveiled his plan.

"Jeb, you ain't in no shape to set yer place up for the winter, 'n I could sure use somewhere to hole up. So what say we come to an agreement? You put me up 'n I'll see to yer bandagin' 'n upkeep. You got wood needs cuttin' 'n you sure ain't up to that. 'N I kin bring in game. Ain't no one e'er doubted my shootin' ability. I figure you can do most of the cookin', which I ain't much good at anyways. 'N Savage, he still needs some healing too. So, I'm suggestin' I take care of the both of you through the winter, seein's how the dog pretty much saved me 'n we're all kinda thrown in here together."

"Ya won't git no arg-u-mint from me, young feller. I jes' might enjoy a bit of comp'ny this winter."

So it was settled. The old man would get a helping hand to get him through the winter, both he and the dog would get time to heal, and Jonas would get time and distance from his troubles back in Jericho.

15

Laura treasured her last moments with Jonas—the embrace, the kiss, the declaration of love, the promise of his return. She felt she must share her feelings with someone, someone she could trust to keep her secret from her father, or anyone else.

She knocked on Gini's door. "Gini, it's me. Is it okay if I come in?"

"Of course, ma chère."

Laura entered to find her mentor and friend putting the finishing touches on a dress. "How beautiful. What's it for?"

"It's for you, dear, a little something to help you get your mind off certain other matters."

Laura moved through the room to the garment draped over a dress-makers form. She ran her fingers down its soft material. Though simple in design, the dress was pink and bright in color, with folds, drapes, and pleats, and just a touch of lace. She gave Gini a quick hug. "It's a wonderful dress, 'n thank you Gini. But I'm afraid it'd take even more'n a beautiful dress to take my mind off...oh Gini, I've got to talk to you. I'm jis' bustin' up inside."

Gini placed a hand on Laura's shoulder. "Dear, you'll get over it, I know it hurts now but..."

"No, no. It don't hurt. It feels wonderful," said Laura, now directly facing Gini. "Can't you tell? I never felt like this before 'n I'm needin' to tell someone about it."

"But Laura, you and Jonas had so little time together."

Laura placed her hands on her hips. "Six times. We were together six times, Gini. The first time in my bedroom, three times at the well down by the mines, then at the dance, 'n finally jis' before he had to take off. I remember every little thing he said, everything he did. Oh Gini, I knew from the first he was special. Then at the dance, when he held me...'n then, most of all, that night he came to the house to tell me goodbye 'n he held me, 'n we kissed." Laura reached inside her bodice and brought out the cameo. "This cameo was his mother's. She gave it to Jonas on her deathbed 'n tole 'im to give it to someone special...he gave it to me, Gini. To me! Then he told me he loved me."

Tears filled Laura's eyes. She sunk onto Gini's bed. Gini sat beside her and placed her arm around her.

"Oh, Gini, I think about him all the time. When I get dressed in the morning, I wonder if he'd like me in a blue dress, or a white dress. If he'd like me better with my hair down or pulled back with a ribbon. Seems practic'ly ev'rything I do is tied up with him. Every day I ride Saca out to the meadow where I first saw him watchin' me. He'd been watchin' me for about a week before I had the accident. Did you know that? That's why he happened to be there 'n was able to help me. Now, each day I ride out there to the tree where he stood 'n I imagine he's standin' there." She buried her head against Gini's shoulder as the tears continued.

Gini rocked Laura in her arms. "You poor child."

Laura wiped her eyes and stood, looking resolutely at Gini. "I'm not a child anymore, Gini. I'm a woman 'n I have a woman's feelin's. I love Jonas, 'n he loves me, 'n what's more, I know he will come back to me. Kain't you see that?"

Gini rose and held Laura shoulders. "You are a woman, probably the best and most unusual woman I've ever known. And Jonas must be an exceptional person for you to be so taken with him. Laura, honey, forgive me for making light of your feelings. If you love him, then I love him too, and I have no doubt the two of you will work this out. But we mustn't let anyone else know about this, especially your father, not until the time is right. *Compris?*"

"Of course, I compree." She hugged Gini. "Thank you for yer understandin', Gini. I really needed to tell someone, someone who'd understand. Now let's try on that gorgeous dress."

▲ ▲ ▲

Fresh from her revelations to Gini, Laura spent this bright autumn afternoon atop Saca, retracing her ride from some months past when she lost her black stallion to the slippery elements.

She stopped at the spot where Jonas had stood that day, drenched by the heavy downpour. Had he taken several paces toward her? She was reining toward him, this time intending to stop and speak to the mysterious young man. Who was he and why was he so intent upon her? She only knew that her heart fluttered each succeeding day when she anticipated seeing him again.

It was an adventure, she told herself, just a curiosity. Something to stir her imaginative spirit. A laugh to be shared with Gini, later.

Laura was no stranger to the interest of boys. Many had sought her attentions, only to be discouraged by her father, who would allow none but the best for his Laura. Only Dirk Fisher seemed to measure up as a suitor. But Laura had no feelings for Dirk. Then, along comes this young stranger, whom she had yet to see up close, and her feelings ran wild with all kinds of imaginings. Who was he? What did he want? Why should she even care?

That day, that rainy day, Laura meant to have a closer look, *just out of curiosity, of course.* She'd sensed nothing threatening in his demeanor or posture but, somehow, this young man had stirred feelings within her that she had not before experienced in all her young years.

Then she had fallen and the anticipated meeting took an unexpected turn.

It was not until she lay in her recovery bed that the meeting did

90

take place. Laura had almost gasped when he entered her bedroom—a respectfully shy young man, tall, handsome, with unruly sandy locks curling about his brow. She had insisted he take her hand. She had toyed with him, refusing to let his hand go. She would know more of this boy, who had dared to seek her presence—a brash act considering who her father was. Laura, unlike her father, knew Jonas was not merely there to inquire about her injuries. Was that the moment—holding his hand, locked into his eyes, that Laura had first come to know that Jonas was to be special?...*you're jes' so... wonderful,* he had said.

From that moment on, Jonas had occupied her every thought. Laura had sought him out down at the mines when she had recovered enough to ride. She knew she wasn't being discreet; matters of the heart seldom yield to good judgment. At the dance, she'd had but one intention—to be with Jonas. And despite what anyone might think, she had meant to capture Jonas's heart, as he had hers. It was destiny; she could feel it.

Even as fate had dealt a severe blow, Laura remained secure in her belief in this destiny and it was fortified by their meeting just before Jonas had to leave. They had professed their love for each other, and no calamity would ever betray that. She felt so strongly in this that she rejected the possibility that anything might happen to prevent Jonas's return.

Laura touched the cameo necklace Jonas had given her, as she urged Saca back toward home.

Sharing her feelings with Gini was what Laura needed to quell an anxiety that had been building within her since Jonas's departure. Her feelings were in delicate balance—her ebullience over Jonas's professed love, and the apprehension she felt for his safety. Yet, she adopted an assurance of a favorable outcome. Destiny dare not have it any other way. Comforted and fortified by this conviction, Laura was determined to be the woman that would make Jonas proud.

To this end, Laura began again to make her friendly rounds into the camps, visiting the miner's families, determined to do whatever she could to alleviate their poor living conditions. She had so much, they had so little. She implored her father to improve the lot of the miners and hoped such persistence would eventually make a difference.

Laura paid surreptitious visits to the McNabb cottage, where she could feel close to Jonas. She told Caleb of Jonas's parting visitation. Caleb sensed the girl was taken with his son and he did not approve—such a relationship could only lead to trouble. Frederick Becker would never allow it.

But Caleb would not interfere, nor would he even voice his objections. The girl seemed genuine. There was no condescension in her attitude. Caleb almost wished Jonas might end up with this young woman, but doubted it could ever happen.

Benji was thrilled with Laura's visits. He pestered Laura to relate anything and everything Jonas had said to her, word for word. He idolized his big brother and envied him his adventure. To Benji, it was storybook stuff. He only wished he could be with Jonas rather than being left to the tedium of his everyday farm life. Jonas—his heroic brother, fleeing the law, living by his wits and facing glorious challenges, with the beautiful Laura awaiting his return—an epic tale in the making.

Laura was not nearly as confident in Jonas's well-being as was Benji, and she had troubles of her own...

To her dismay, Dirk Fisher had been stepping up his efforts to advance their relationship. Laura was convinced that Dirk had instigated the fight the night of the dance. It was mostly Dirk's men that comprised the group surrounding Jake and Jonas. They said it was Jonas that had pulled the knife, but Laura knew that wasn't true. She implicitly trusted Jonas's account of the incident.

Jake hadn't died of the stab wound and had soon recovered. Then, Dirk had fired him. Laura felt sure this was Dirk's attempt to disassociate himself from any complicity in the stabbing. Any respect Laura might have had for Dirk was now gone. She now faced the task of fending off his attentions.

▲ ▲ ▲

Laura, her dad, and Gini were finishing dinner and involved in a conversation most displeasing to Laura.

"Laura," her father began, "Dirk's a fine lad, 'n he's got a real future in my company. I know he's got intentions on you, but you don't seem to be takin' much of an interest. I think it's about time you started to get more serious about that boy."

"Dad, I think that's my decision. I'm not nearly ready to be settlin' down with nobody yet, 'n I don't think Dirk Fisher's all so grand as you think he is."

"Now look," her father persisted. "Gini's done a damn good job raisin' you since your mother left us. Now it's time you found yourself someone 'n thought about startin' a family."

"Well, I'll tell you, Dad. If that right man comes along, I'll certainly entertain thoughts along that line." Then teasingly, "But right now, you're the only man I need in my life."

"Now gal, don't get cute with me. I've even heard it said you might have some feelin's for that McNabb boy, the one that knifed Jake 'n ran off. Now please tell me that ain't so."

"I'll tell you one thing. I don't believe for a dag-gummed second that Jonas started that fight, 'n he certainly wasn't the one that pulled the knife. I don't believe that for an instant."

Frederick Becker gave his daughter a long, hard look. He threw his napkin down and shoved his chair back.

"Well, that about tears it," he said. "You are sweet on that McNabb boy. Well, I just won't have it. Damn it, girl. I've jes' been givin' you too much loose-rein. You scurryin' all around the countryside, stirrin' up the miners' families. 'N now this. By damn…" Frederick hesitated, controlling his anger. He turned to Gini. "Gini, I want you to contact Priscilla, in Richmond. Tell her that her daughter will be comin' to stay with her a while."

"No, please," Laura pleaded. "I don't belong in no city, 'n Mother wouldn't want me there anyhow."

"Don't matter what she wants. It's me that's paying her way, while she fritters away her days 'n nights with fancy teas 'n dances 'n such. Time she took some responsibility in this family. 'N it won't hurt you none to gain a little finery yerself. Maybe a little culturin' will knock some of the nonsense out of you."

Frederick rose from the table. "Now, Gini. You get that arranged, 'n the sooner the better. My God…Jonas McNabb!" Frederick stomped from the room.

"I'm sorry, Laura, I have no choice," said Gini.

Laura was in tears. "No, you don't. Father is God around here. Well, I'll go ta his Richmond. But it won't change me none. 'N Saca goes with me. Ya won't kitch me a sittin' around all day in them thar frilly dresses, sippin' tea 'n suckin' sassafras 'r whate'er them society folks do." Laura deliberately let her grammar slide a notch in protest.

Gini made arrangements for Laura's trip to Richmond. Her mother dared not deny Frederick's demand, but to lessen the burden of her responsibility for Laura, Priscilla arranged for her daughter to attend The Richmond Academy for Girls, a finishing school for young ladies. Laura would be allowed to take her horse, Sacagawea, who could be stabled near the Academy. Also, by design, Laura would spend a weekend at her mother's place in Richmond before beginning classes at the Academy the following Monday. Her mother feigned delight at the prospect of seeing Laura, but in reality, she didn't want to be bothered by the child raised in the hills of West Virginia.

▲ ▲ ▲

Laura arrived in Richmond by rail. Over the past ten years, she had accompanied her father on his rare visits to Richmond but twice. On these occasions, her mother had seemed a stranger, aloof and distant—indifferent to the longing in Laura's heart.

Her mother met her at the station. Laura yearned for any indication that her mother might be happy to see her, but the greeting was perfunctory, a peck on the cheek as one would greet a casual acquaintance. Laura noted that her mother was still fetching in a dignified manner, her deep blue eyes much the same as her own, her blonde hair bunched up beneath a feathered bonnet. Nothing in Laura's wardrobe could approach the finery of her mother's burgundy-colored satin dress, full and resplendent, shaming any attire Laura had encountered back home.

Laura's baggage was placed in a horse drawn carriage. But before Laura would accompany her mother, she insisted on seeing that her beloved horse be properly attended to.

"Laura, dear," said her mother, "I'm sure the station people will see to it that your horse is taken to the stables. You can see to her later. Right now, we must be getting home."

"Mother, please. I don't want to be difficult, but I kaint go with you till I know Saca's properly keered for."

"Oh dear, the language. Well, I'm sure the Academy will change your

94

hillbilly ways. All right, we'll see to the horse first. But after that, I'll expect you to be more cooperative, young lady."

"Yes, Mother, I promise."

Laura saw to it that Sacagawea was properly stabled and that good care would be given her. When satisfied, she and Priscilla proceeded on their way, crossing Richmond by carriage.

Richmond had recently undergone a major reconstruction. Large parts of the city had been devastated in the aftermath of the Civil War. Ironically, most of the destruction was at the hands of its own Confederate army. When the Confederate President, Jefferson Davis, abandoned Richmond, the retreating southern soldiers received orders to set fire to the bridges, the armory, and the supply warehouses. These fires spread out of control and destroyed major sections of the city. The Reconstruction extended to around 1880, but evidence of the damage still remained. Priscilla called Laura's attention to only the better aspects of Richmond, ignoring those areas still in ruins.

"Look, Laura," said her mother as their carriage crossed the Richmond downtown section, "an electrically-powered trolley car. Richmond is the first city to have such a system. This is a fine city once again, Laura. You're going to love it, I'm sure."

Laura was fascinated by what she was seeing. What a far cry from the small towns she knew in West Virginia. Block long buildings rose three to four stories high, railways snaked along the city streets sporting trolleys, some horse drawn and as her mother pointed out, some electrically powered. How strange it looked to see the trolleys moving along the thoroughfares with no horses to draw them.

And people were everywhere—lining the street corners waiting to cross, bustling here and there, carrying parcels from an endless array of stores of every kind. There were stores that sold nothing but hats, and others that specialized in shoes and boots, even shops selling nothing but cooking utensils. There were museums, opera houses, dance halls, music halls—even a gymnasium, whatever that was.

"Laura," said her mother, "I have a stop to make...to take care of some business. Driver, stop in front of that building, please." Priscilla indicated a two-story structure with a storefront at ground level and apartments above.

"Laura, you can look around on your own. I'll only be about an hour. Don't stray so far that you can't find your way back...one hour."

Priscilla knocked on the door of a side entrance that led to the apartments above. A stylishly dressed man greeted her with a hug and led her inside.

"Hmmmm..." thought Laura, "I wonder what kind of business that could be?"

Laura was surprised that her mother would leave her on her own, even for a short time, as she was unaccustomed to the ways of a big city. "Well," she thought, "I guess I should be used to it. Not the first time she's abandoned me."

"Okay." thought Laura, "Here I am in the big city, all on my own. Might as well make the best of it." She was curious about the trappings of such a large city and did wonder what city folks might be like.

She delighted in window shopping, seeing all the wares quaintly displayed for public viewing. Until now, her shopping had always been at country stores where there were but one or two selections of anything. The Richmond stores offered endless arrays of styles to choose from, whether it be hats, dresses, boots—even women's undergarments *on public display*. She entered such a store, being curious to know how a girl could possibly allow herself to be seen publicly purchasing such frilly articles, like lace underwear or long stockings and garters. The thought of this caused Laura to snicker, which caught the attention of a male clerk.

"Perhaps, madam would care to try on one of our specialty garments. We have a changing room and I would be happy to assist you in any way I might."

"Sir," said Laura, petulantly. "Aire you off'rin' to help me try on one of these here female personal articles? 'Cause if you aire, I jis' might have my brother come in here 'n you kin repeat yer prop-er-si-tion in front of him. I figger him to be about twice yer size." With that, Laura turned and walked from the shop, leaving a rather puzzled clerk at a loss for words.

Laura spent the rest of her allotted time at a small café across the street from the apartment her mother had entered, allowing her to keep an eye out for her. "Enough of city folks for now," she thought. The café offered a vast selection of food. She settled on a cocoa and a sweet roll.

It was here that she met Charly Cooper.

"Hi. Mind if I share yer table?" asked a young woman of about Laura's age. "My name's Charly."

"Oh, please do. Sit yerself down. Be glad to have yer comp'ny. I'm Laura. 'N yer Charly? You sure don' look like no boy."

"West Virginia," said Charly, as she sat.

"I guess it's purty hard to hide," said Laura, laughing.

"Well, I'm glad to meet anuther country gal down here. I come from upstate, the Shenandoah Valley, to be exact. And Charly was my father's choice. Guess he was wantin' a boy. Hell, I wouldn't mind one myself." Both girls laughed. "I don't mind the name, Charly, no more, I've gotten used to it. Actually, I think it makes me feel sort of special. How many gals can boast the name, Charly?"

Laura and Charly became immediate friends. Moreover, they discovered, to their delight, that they were both to attend the Richmond Academy for Girls. About that time, Laura's mother reappeared, looking up and down the street in search of her daughter.

"Welp, there's my mother. I better git goin'. I'm sure lookin' forward to seein' you at that school. Maybe it won't be so bad awful after all."

Priscilla's apartment covered two floors in an upscale section of Richmond—the cultural district, home of museums, music halls, and an opera house. Across the street, Laura noticed a small park with a huge statue with General Robert E. Lee astride a rearing horse with sword wielded as if signaling a charge.

Laura was ushered into a spacious living room and noted that several other rooms led off it. A grand spiral staircase led upstairs. Laura, of course, was used to finery as the Becker Estate lacked little in furnishings. But her mother's place seemed luxurious by comparison—decorated with a woman's touch, with paintings and statuary, opulent furniture, exotic carpeting and long flowing drapes, all color coordinated in pastels with rich burgundy and golden accents. Priscilla retained a butler, a housekeeper, and a cook. The housekeeper, Caroline, showed Laura upstairs to her room. Laura was to freshen up and come down for dinner.

Three guests arrived for dinner—the Stappleton's. Mr. George Stappleton, Mrs. Eleanor Stappleton, and Richard, their son. Richard appeared to be about Laura's age and Laura suspected complicity. Introductions were made and they all sat down to an exquisitely set table and a fine array of delicacies. All meant to impress the Stappleton's, thought Laura, *certainly not me.*

"Laura is here for the weekend," explained her mother. "After which she'll be attending the very fine Richmond Academy for Girls. I was thinking young Richard here could show Laura around our fair city, maybe introduce her to some people her own age. Perhaps they could take in a show, or maybe go dancing."

"Mother," objected Laura, "I'm sure Richard has his own plans. I wouldn't wanna interfere."

"Not at all," said Richard, quickly. "I'd be delighted." Laura was a beautiful girl and Richard found her country-way of speaking amusing. He knew his circle of friends would be intrigued by her. "I just happen to have all day Saturday free. Laura, consider me to be your humble and honored escort."

"Good. Then it's settled," said Priscilla. "Laura will be ready for you at noon."

Laura was rather quiet during the meal. She was not thrilled with the prospect of spending the next day with Richard and his friends. She had rather hoped to get to know her mother better. Well, maybe Sunday.

Saturday, around noon, Richard came by with a carriage.

"You two have fun," said her mother, as they departed. She never asked about Richard's plans for the day.

Soon after Richard and Laura left, an elegantly dressed man pulled up in front of Priscilla's apartment in a similar carriage and whisked Priscilla away. Had Laura still been there, she would have recognized the man as the one her mother had seen the day before.

It seems Richard Stappleton had no intentions of following the suggestions Laura's mother had offered. He had his own agenda. He took her to *The Paree*, a bistro of European flavor and a favorite hangout for the young rich of Richmond. The seating spilled out onto the sidewalk and boasted about a dozen small tables with umbrellas to block the sun. The wine list included some of France's best and stronger spirits were also available. The food was considered gourmet and of a European persuasion.

A small group of Richard's friends, all nattily dressed, and seemingly paired off, greeted Laura and her escort outside the Bistro. Richard introduced Laura around and she soon became the object of attention, as she and Richard joined his friends at an outside table.

"Wherever did you get that accent?" asked one of the girls. "It's positively quaint."

"Wahl, I'm from West Virginia. 'N I don' talk no diff'rent than no one else there."

"*Waaahhhllll...you sho' 'nuff* talk *diff'rent* than we do," mocked another girl. "Is thet what they call *hill-billy* talk?"

"Hey guys, ease up," said Richard, "you're making Laura uncomfortable. Where in hell are your manners? Come on, Laura, we'll go inside, away from certain rude *ladies*, and I use the term loosely."

Inside the bistro were more tables and a bar lined with stools. The clientele was mostly young and indistinguishable from those outside, and even at this early hour, they were well into the inebriants. Richard led Laura to a table which was candle lit, despite the overhead electric lighting. The atmosphere was cozy—Laura could imagine many a rendezvous occurring here. The menu boasted appetizers and every variety of sandwiches imaginable.

"Don't pay any attention to them," said Richard, indicating the group outside. "They're just jealous, that's all. Because you're the most handsome female in the place. What say we order some lunch?"

Laura was willing to give Richard a second chance, in spite of his rude friends. Besides, she was hungry. She settled on a seafood entree but refused the wine.

"Just a small glass, Laura. The wine is excellent."

"I'm not much for drinkin'. I think I'll pass."

"Okay, I'll bring you a lemonade." He ordered the drink at the bar, but had the bartender slip in a touch of gin. Laura noticed the off taste but attributed it to a "European" influence. During the course of the afternoon, Richard brought several more such drinks to Laura. By now, some of Richard's friends from outside had joined them.

"Allow us to apologize for the rudeness of the girls," one fellow said. "We'll try to keep them in line, I promise."

"So, Dickie boy," said the same fellow, "how long is li'l Miss West Virginny going to be with us?" He winked.

Laura stood.

"Jis' today," she responded quickly. The several spiked lemonades had loosened her tongue a bit. "'N I'd appreciate if you'd call me by my name. It's Laura. 'N I don' appreciate yer superior attitude, like somehow yer better'n me. Where I come from, folks'r polite. 'N men folk got more important things to do than sittin' 'round all day drinkin' 'n eatin' 'n insultin' good people. 'N women know how to keep a civil tongue 'bout them." Laura felt slightly light-headed and suddenly realized why her lemonade had such a peculiar taste. "*Dickie boy*, you kin take me back now. I've had jis' 'bout enuff of yer friends, and yer lemonade." Laura walked out of the bistro.

Richard caught up with her outside. "Laura, I'm so sorry. You're absolutely right; they are incredible boors. I'll have the carriage brought around."

"I have no idea what a boor is, but it sure sounds like the right word for them friends of yers."

The carriage arrived and Richard gave Laura a boost up. He took the reins and they clattered off.

"Look, Laura, I know this hasn't been a pleasant afternoon for you, but it's still early. Let me show you some of Richmond. Please, let me make it up to you. We could take a ride in one of those new electric trolleys."

Now this was appealing to Laura and about the only thing Richard could have offered her that could have tempted her to remain in his company.

"Yes," she said. "I think I'd like that."

Richard secured the carriage to a hitching post and he and Laura awaited the horseless trolley. The trolley approached, the bell clanging their stop. They got on and found seats, Laura by a window, Richard beside her. She was thrilled by the ride, the gin adding to her delight. She'd never been on a trolley, horseless or not. Richard pointed out Richmond's sights as they passed by. People got off and on at each stop, keeping the trolley to capacity.

"Laura, you know, the prettiest sight in Richmond right now is sitting right here beside me."

Laura turned toward Richard. "Look, Richard...I..."

"All I mean is, I'm having a wonderful time with you. I think I'm really attracted to you." He reached into his coat and pulled out a small flask, unscrewed its top and took a deep swig. "I don't suppose you'd care for some refreshment?" He offered the flask to Laura. She waved him off.

"No, of course you wouldn't." He returned the flask to his inner pocket. He smiled at her, then took her hand in his and brought her hand to his lips, brushing it gently. Laura withdrew it abruptly.

"Aw, come on Laura. You know why your mother put us together as well as I do. She's hoping to marry you off to a well-to-do family, same as my folks are. Well, we got to get started someplace." He grabbed her shoulders and pulled her to him, attempting a kiss. Laura pulled back and slapped him hard. She stood and squeezed past him, moving quickly to the front of the trolley car and demanded that the driver let her off.

"Laura, you can't just get off in the middle of Richmond," Richard called after her, following her up the aisle. "You don't even know where you are."

Laura glared at him in anger. "Yer worse than yer friends. Jis' keep away from me." People on the trolley were staring at the two of them. "Driver, please let me off this thing."

"Laura, you can't..."

"I can, 'n I aim to."

"Hey, let her be, fella," a voice from a passenger.

"Yeh. Leave her alone," from another.

A woman spoke up. "You tell 'em, girl. Good for y'all." A fellow country gal, obviously.

The trolley finally stopped and Laura jumped off. Richard followed close behind.

Laura turned, "Stop!" she demanded. "Stop right there. Don' you dare follow after me."

"But you don't know your way back. Be reasonable."

"Reasonable? Like you were? I'd rather take my chances with gittin' lost. If you don't keep away, I swear I'll scream."

"Okay. You win, Laura dear." He held up his hands in defeat and a broad smile crossed his face. "I bloody well pity the unlucky sap that ends up with you. Good luck finding your way back." He walked off, chuckling like a prankster who'd pulled a fast one.

"Uh oh," thought Laura. "Now what?"

She had no idea where she was or how to get back to her mother's apartment. *The cultural district*, she thought. *Somewhere in the cultural district*. Then she remembered the statue of General Lee. Surely, someone would know where that was located. Her mother's place was just across the street from that statue. Laura thanked herself for being so observant.

She sought help in a small shop with a window display of an array of saddles and various other leather items. The smell of leather made her think of home.

"Can I help you miss?" It was the shopkeeper.

"Oh, I do hope so. I guess I'm lost. I need to know where's the statue of General Lee, 'n how to git there."

"Lady, this is Richmond, Virginia. There's General Lee's all over the place."

"Well, he's ridin' a horse, 'n he looks like he's goin' into battle. He's got a big sword out 'n he's got it raised up like in a charge. 'N the statue is big, real big." Laura so indicated, raising her hands high over her head.

"Yep. I know that one." The shopkeeper took pity on Laura's plight, warming to the vulnerable and likeable young lady. She was obviously a country girl and lost as to city ways. "I can hail you a carriage. You got any money?"

"I got a little. But I kin git more when I git to my mother's place."

"Okay. Here's what we'll do. I'll get you a carriage. You could probably get there by trolley, but it'd be too hard to explain how. You tell the carriage driver to take you to Lee St., in the cultural district. Explain about the statue. He'll know where it is. You pay him what you can; I'll cover the rest. He'll know I'm good for it."

"But I couldn't ask you to..."

"Yes, you could, and you will. Now stay put while I get you a ride."

"I sure thank you, mister. It's good to know there's some decent folks around here. I was beginnin' to wonder. What's yer name?"

"Gary Prentice, ma'am, 'n glad to be of assistance."

"Wahl, Mr. Prentice, I'll sure be remem'brin' you."

Laura arrived back to her mother's apartment in the late afternoon. Her mother was not home. She went to her room, flopped down on the bed, and thought of folks back home. Mostly she thought of Jonas.

The next day, when Laura's mother questioned her on the previous day's activity, Laura pretended that all had gone fine.

"Well, are you seeing that nice young man today?" her mother asked.

"Mother, I'd jes' like to take Saca ridin' today. Please?"

Her mother acquiesced and Laura spent a pleasant day riding, reunited with a friend she trusted, Sacagawea.

Monday meant Laura was to start school at the Richmond Academy for Girls.

"This school will make a lady out of you, dear," Laura's mother emphasized. "Lord knows your father couldn't."

16

Jonas would soon know the full fury of an Allegheny Mountain winter. Jebediah's cabin was located deep within these mountains, not far from where they tapered off into the Allegheny Plateau. Wintering so close to the Plateau was a test for man and beast alike, as it featured some of the roughest mountainside and the most tempestuous winters in all of the Alleghenies. Jebediah had chosen this location for his home, in part because he welcomed the challenge the elements put to him—*makes a man come alive!*—but mostly because of its unsurpassed beauty—a beauty that persisted even in the ferocity of its winters. Here, Jeb found a serenity and fulfillment he wished to share with no one, which was not a problem, as very few others were tempted to endure such hardships. Of course, being laid up, he was grateful to have Jonas around to help him through this particular winter.

As prescribed in their new allegiance, Jonas performed the heavy work as Jebediah could barely hobble around the cabin. There was plenty for Jonas to do, most of which needed to be completed before the snows set in. He chopped enough wood to last until spring. He shot deer, rabbit, and turkey to keep them supplied well into the winter season, intending to hunt more game as weather permitted. With Jeb's help, he built a bunk for himself and fashioned serviceable clothing from deer hides which would protect him from the challenging, wintry onslaught that lay ahead. Jeb's root cellar was already well supplied with potatoes, beans, bacon, salt, flour, and both dried and canned fruit.

By December the snows came, heavy and often, and effectively snowed Jeb and Jonas in. Fierce winds howled constantly, piling snow half-way up the windows. Jeb had built the cabin well, chinking the logs sufficiently to hold off the bitter cold. He had located the cabin such that the front received the least bombardment from the elements, allowing Jonas to keep the doorway cleared for access to the shed for wood and other supplies. Drinking water was procured by melting snow in a wooden barrel placed by the fireplace, as the sink pump was frozen.

A wood-burning cook-stove allowed for hot meals, while the stone fireplace provided heat. Jonas was amazed that a small fire could keep the well-built one room cabin so comfortable.

Jeb had discarded the crutch and was now moving about quite freely. This day, as the high winds buffeted the cabin and timbers creaked and windows clattered, he filled two tin plates with beans from a heavy black pot on the cook stove and set them on the table. He sat opposite Jonas and they both dug in.

"Welcome to winter in the mountains, my friend," said Jeb through a mouthful of beans and corn bread. "Compared to this, yer Jericho must seem like some sorta resort," he taunted.

True, thought Jonas. Jericho lay in a valley, protected from the severe winter conditions by the surrounding hills, mountains, and forests. "You said a mouthful there, old timer."

Just before the heavy snows arrived, Jeb had instructed Jonas to rig a rope from the cabin door to the shed as there would be times when the blinding wind-swept snow could cause a person to lose his way. Now, with the wind at full fury, Jonas stepped outside to fetch firewood from the shed. He was met with fierce winds and blasting snow, pummeling his face with an intensity that forced his head down. It was only by a hand-over-hand progress, following Jeb's rope that he was able to struggle forward. *Why would Jeb choose this life?* The trip back to the cabin with an armful of firewood was even more fitful—tripping in knee-deep drifts, retrieving dropped firewood, and finally, stumbling through the cabin door, collapsing on the floor, sending firewood every which way.

"Mind shet'n thet door, yer lettin' in the cold," said Jeb. He didn't acknowledge Jonas's ensuing curses.

Savage's leg had healed up nicely and the dog was able to accompany Jonas on any outdoor ventures, weather permitting. Often, when Jonas had been unable to find any game, Savage would return with a rabbit, a pheasant, or a squirrel and drop it at Jonas's feet.

"Ole boy, yer sure some kinda help. What would we ever do without you?" Jonas couldn't know how prophetic those words were.

▲ ▲ ▲

One day, as frigid winds disallowed any outdoor ventures, Jonas asked Jebediah how he happened to come by Savage, his huge white dog that always seemed to be there when disaster was imminent.

Jeb sat by the fireplace in his rocker, puffing his briar pipe with Savage lying at his side. He reached down and patted the dog on the head. "Grab a seat, Jonas, 'n I'll sure tell ya 'bout this har beast." Savage whimpered.

"I got Savage as a pup from two mountain men down in Sprucetown. I was somewhat familiar with the gents 'n knowed they'd be diff'cult to deal with. Ne'er did like 'em much. Anyways, they wanted a lot fer the frisky white pup.

"The larger of the two said somethin' like, 'Hell, fella, this har pup's got a lotta wolf in 'im. I figger thet white hide of his jacks up the price consider'ble. So take it 'r leave it, old man, I got lots more folks int'risted.'

"When I picked up the pup 'n looked into his red eyes, I felt a bond. Ain't no one else was to git thet white pup but me. I was glad ta pay their price.

"Now this har pup seemed 'bout as much wolf as dog, so I named him Savage. Whal, we b'came in-sep'rable. Savage grew to maturity 'n weighed in at o'er a hundert-fifty pounds. Now thet's huge for a dog, or a wolf, whate'er he is. Let me tell ya somethin' 'bout a wolf. We're talkin' 'bout one of the smartest 'n cun-in-ist 'n most fearless creatures they is around. I'm thinkin' my Savage har retained most of them wolf at-tri-butes, but then too, he showed the gen-til-ity 'n faith-ful-ness of a dog.

"I'll tell ya, I felt secure with sich an animal as a companion. Predators were attracted to the meat 'n other foodstuff I kept in the shed 'n this har dog would warn me whenev'r a wolf 'r bear 'r wildcat 'r any other marauder was near, includin' man.

"Savage became known ever'whar har-abouts. Whene'er the two of us went down into Sprucetown, folks would gather around the dog 'n rave 'bout what a mag-nif-i-cent creature he was. I got offered huge sums of money fer thet dog, but I'd sooner part with an arm than give 'im up."

Jeb again reached down and patted Savage, who had now lapsed into sleep.

"Ya ain't bored by my story aire ya, ya un-grateful mutt? Haw."

"Well, I sure ain't," said Jonas. "Keep goin', Jeb."

Jeb leaned back in his rocker and exhaled a puff of smoke to join the smoke cloud gathered at the ceiling. He continued:

"Now, Savage's real gentle around people, especially childrins, so gen-er-ally folks ain't in-tim-i-dated by his presence. But I'll tell ya one thing true, if'n this har animal sensed a body was up ta no good...wahl, they'd best jes' steer clear. Like I say, it seemed he could be a dog when a dog was called fer, 'r a wolf when a wolf was needed."

"So, Jeb, how was it that them two mountain men were able to over-come Savage when they took 'im?" Jonas asked.

"Y'know. Now, thet's the strangest thing. Like I tole ya b'fore, I left ole Savage be'hind, 'cause he seemed ta be ailin' a bit. Now them two ras-cals thet took 'im musta bin the same one's what sold 'im ta me. I suspec' Savage musta recollect'd 'em, 'n allowed 'em ta git close. 'N considerin' he weren't up ta snuff, I reckon he wasn't as alert as usual. Ain't no other way them two owlhoots coulda got the jump on 'im. I sur-mise they got a rope on 'im, 'n muzzled 'im b'fore he figger'd out they meant ta do 'im harm, damn their orn'ry hides. I could tell by the tracks he weren't goin' along willin'ly. I suspec' they meant ta sell 'im somewhar. Ain't sure though whar they intended to take 'im thet folks wouldn't know who he belonged to. 'N wouldn't you jes'know, he'd be a-returnin' in the nick-a-time ta save me from them wolves. 'N it was durn for-tu-nit fer you he was thar ta help after them two scoundrels waylaid you. Someday, ah'm gonna catch up with them two snakes, 'n thar'll be hell ta pay."

▲ ▲ ▲

At times, spending extended periods of time cooped up in Jeb's cabin preyed on Jonas's mind. Never in his life had he been so restricted, unable to wander at will. As much as he liked Jeb, the old man's constant jabbering left Jonas longing for relief. Out of respect, he wasn't about to tell him to shut up. He approached the problem obliquely.

"Savage, ole boy, said Jonas, scratching behind the dog's ears as they both stretched out before the open fireplace. "I suppose Jeb must've about talked yer ears off when there weren't nobody else around to spend his winters with. Nothin' personal Jeb, but you do go on and on."

Jeb had begun a new woodcarving, which he now set aside. He struck a match and relit his old briar pipe, blackened and singed from years of use, its bowl now ragged as if gnawed on by a rodent. He glared at Jonas. "Hell, boy, I guess you'd rather listen to the wind a-howlin' 'n this ole place a-creakin'. Thet's some grat'r'tude for ya."

"You know, Jeb. There is somethin' I bin wantin' to hear you talk about," said Jonas, relenting somewhat. "That's how you come to be up here in the mountains in the first place."

"Ya sure yer ears kin take it...?"

"Sorry 'bout what I said before. I'd really like to hear yer story."

Properly placated, Jeb went on to tell how he'd chosen this particular way of life.

Originally, he related, he had lived in a small town in the southwest neck of Virginia. He was an only child. Maybe his mom was unable to have any more children, or maybe Jeb was just more than his parents had bargained for and they decided one child was more than enough.

Jeb's dad was the town sheriff. "Yep, I was one proud kid, my pa bein' sheriff 'n all, big ole gun on his hip. I wanted ta be jes' like 'im. It was mostly a peaceful-like town; thar weren't no gunfights like we'd heard 'bout out West. 'Till one day, when I was 'bout twelve, pap caught up with a coupla horse thiefs 'n he got shot daid." Jeb hesitated. "Thet was the last chance I got ta be a kid. Hell, I was only 'bout twelve at the time.

"Ma didn't have no occupation, 'n we had no way of supportin' ourselves with my pa gone. We heard thar were coal mines openin' up o'er in West Virginny—o'er yer way, Jonas, but further east, nearer the mountains. So we sold ever'thin' we could, packed up the rest, 'n headed up east. I told the mining people thar I was fifteen. Not thet they'd care one way or t'other. Them minin' companies were hiring boys as young as twelve, 'n gals too. Young kids who could squeeze into the tight spaces in them mine shafts, places too tiny fer reg'lar size folks."

Jeb related that he worked in the mines until he was eighteen—six long, grueling years. He said he hated it, hated being trapped inside dark caves ten to twelve hours a day, digging out coal deposits from the unyielding rock. "I knew somethin' was awry; thet a man jes' weren't s'posed ta live thet a-way, thet it were agin God's intenshuns fer us ta be hackin' away 'n puttin' ugly holes inta His backyard like thet. I say it was an affront ta nature, 'n the miserabl' lives we led was jes' nature's re-venge on the lot of us. Six years of thet 'n I was longin' for the fresh air 'n open spaces. I'd stare at them distant mountains 'n feel drawn to 'em. But I stuck it out ta support my ma. Then, wouldn't ya jes' know it, she jes' up 'n found herself a man 'n run off with the buzzard. I ne'er heard from her agin. Thet was my first mis'venture with a woman, ev'n though it was my ma."

Jeb rose from his rocker and stepped to the fireplace, tapping the dead ashes from his pipe into the low-burning logs. He reloaded the briar from his tobacco pouch, lit up, and stood, back to the fire. Jonas's cigarette fixings had run out and he savored the tobacco aroma as it filled the cabin. He took the opportunity to stoke the fire and add another log. Savage sought a cooler spot under the table.

Jeb continued his account. "Welp," he said, "I ups 'n got married myself. Hell of a thing. Met her at a dance—purty li'l thing she was, daughter of some shopkeep'r. I guess I figger'd my drab life might be more intrestin' with a young filly around. Wahl, she moved in, 'n we made a purty good go of it for a while. Then, she run back to her daddy. Kaint say I blamed her none; bein' a coal miner's wife ain't much of a life. Wahl hey, thet's poetry—a coal miner's wife ain't much of a life. I think mebbee I missed my callin'. Haw."

Jonas winced. "Maybe we could git on with yer story."

"Wahl, hell, boy, loosen up, you'll live longer. Anyway, I'll tell ya true, I'm a whole lot soured on wimmins. They jes' seem ta run off on a feller. Ya gots ta be kerful who you hook up with."

Jeb related that by this time he was fed up with the "das-t'rd-ly" life he'd fashioned for himself. He'd heard talk of there being gold up in the mountains. Over the years he'd managed to save some money, enough, he figured, to stake him in a gold prospecting venture.

He started asking around, learning all he could about prospecting. Then, one day he just up and quit the mines, loaded up a mule with all his belongings and what other supplies he might need, and headed for the mountains—in search of gold.

Once he got there, he knew right away he'd found his element. It was springtime and the mountains were buzzing with new life. He couldn't yet identify the new greenery that sprung from the earth, or the birds that filled the air with their sweet music, or from what source the wind carried the fresh aromas that filled his nostrils and chased away the lingering musty smell accumulated from his six years in the mines.

He didn't yet have a sense for the dangers that might lie ahead or the demanding rigors of life in the mountains, but he just knew this was the life he wanted and no matter what, he'd make it work for him.

"Yeh, boy. I sure did luv it. Didn't know the first thing 'bout survivin' up har though. But I knew right off, I was in the right place. A man kin feel good 'bout hisself if'n he's livin' right with his surroundin's." Jonas recalled the drudgery of his own time in the mines and sensed why he too had felt the tug of the hills and mountains, much the same as Jeb.

"Thet first summer 'n fall-time were easy 'nuff," continued Jeb. "I got me a shack built right off 'n ventured ev'ry which way from thar. They was always plenty ta eat, game all o'er the durn place. Thar was a town not more'n fifteen miles away, a day's trip fer when I needed supplies or anythin'. 'N I got goin' right away on the gold prospectin'. While waitin' fer thet ta git per-duc-tive, I took up trappin', 'n sellin' furs down in town. I had me a dog. Nuthin' like Savage here, but I figgered I needed a companion. The first winter was the roughest, as ya might well imagin'. A lesser man might ne'er have made it through..."

Savage moaned from the fireside, his eyes squinting at his master.

"Shet up, ya orn'ry cur. This har's my story 'n I'll tell it any damn way I please. Anyways, me 'n my mule had managed ta lug a small potbelly stove up to my shack. Took a bit of in-gin-u-ity, but we got it done. I reckon hadn't bin for thet stove I'd a bin a goner thet first winter. Hell, I'd a friz up solid, 'n wouldn't of thawed out till spring. Har. I laarned a powerful lot thet first winter. But I got through. Bin up har many a winter since. I still luv it. 'Cept fer the loneliness. Don't see many folks. Sometimes thet's good. Most times it's good, but lately I've bin havin' a hankrin' ta be around folks agin."

Jeb left the fireside and returned to his rocker. Jonas took a chair at the table. Though Jeb talked a lot, he had seldom mentioned his personal life. Jonas was deep in thought. Jeb's story might have been his, were it not for Laura. He turned to Jeb who had resumed his carving. He started to say something, maybe about his reason for being in the mountains, but lost the words.

Instead, Jonas asked about Jeb's woodcarvings.

"Jes' somethin' ta be idlin' away the hours," said Jeb.

Jonas stood and selected a wood sculpture from a shelf over the sink, studying it from various angles. It depicted an eagle in flight.

"You know, Jeb, when I look at this carvin', I feel somethin' stirrin' inside of me. Somethin' I can't explain. It makes any troubl's I might be feelin' seem small, like maybe things ain't all so bad as I imagin' them to be."

"Hell, boy, I don' know 'bout all thet, I jes' carve 'em. Jes' somethin' ta pass the time up har in the mountains, 'specially when the snows got me all bottl'd up. You wanna make somthin' else of 'em, wahl, thet's yer business."

"You ev'r show 'em around? I think folks oughta see 'em. You got a real gift here, Jeb."

"Naw, boy. Let's not make 'em out fer any more than they aire. I carve 'em fer myself. Don' matter none what other folks think of 'em. So quit fussin' 'bout 'em. Don' know why folks think they gotta figger ev'rthin' out. You enjoy somethin', or ya don't, or somewhar in b'tween. What's the need of di-sectin' ev'r li'l thing?"

Jeb stood and limped over to the black kettle of beans simmering on the cookstove. He gave them a stir. "Keeping food on the table, thet's what's important."

17

Jeb was feeling more fit now, and when the winds allowed, he and Jonas and Savage dared to venture outside. The snow was deep but not impassable, and well worth the effort as the scenery could take a man's breath away and the peaceful quiet could well put his mind to rest. Jonas welcomed the quiet calm of the serene wintry landscape, a release from the struggles of the past several months. At such times he felt an affinity for Jeb's world.

One windless day, with a bright sun creating a sparkling vista of magical proportions, Jeb, Jonas, and Savage stood outside the cabin taking in the still beauty of the wintry panorama that stretched before them.

"Kinda overwhelms ya, don' it," said Jeb. "I've lived in these mountains fer longer'n I'd care to admit, 'n they ne'er cease to amaze me. Winter's the purtiest, but it's the damn orneriest, too. Ya gotta be careful; it's unpredict'ble. Ya git too far from shelter 'n thet wind whips up, yer in a heap of troubl'."

"Say," continued Jeb. "Why'nt we take a look down thar at the pond. I got a fishin' pole, 'n sometimes thet pond is jes' plumb o'erloaded with bullhead. I'm thinkin' we could sure use a bit of *var-i-a-tee* in our diets. We gotta chop us a hole in that ice though, if'n it ain't too thick. Jonas, you git the ax 'n I'll fetch up a fishin' pole 'n some sourdough balls fer bait."

Jonas ventured out onto the ice, wielding the ax. Jebediah and Savage waited on shore.

"Thet seems 'bout as good a spot as any," shouted Jeb, stopping Jonas somewhere near the middle of the small pond.

Jonas hacked away at the ice and eventually produced a sizable hole. Unfortunately, his hacking also produced large escalating cracks in the ice. Water oozed up through these fissures and the ice became extremely slippery.

"Uh-oh," cried Jonas, as his feet slipped out from under him and he slid into the frigid water. He flailed and splashed around, trying to gain solid ice and safety, but the ice kept breaking under him. Jonas could swim well enough to keep afloat, but he knew he wouldn't last long in the freezing water.

"A little help here…if you wouldn't mind." Jonas was directing his plea to Jebediah, but as usual it was Savage that responded to his plight. The dog came bounding out onto the ice. Both Jonas and Jebediah called for Savage to halt, knowing there was little he could do to retrieve Jonas from the icy hole. Jonas watched wide-eyed as Savage came rushing at him. The dog tried to stop on the slippery surface, then tried to reverse his direction, but although his legs were pumping in one direction, his progress preferred another—straight into the ice hole. Now the two of them were clawing at the edge of the hole, trying to get out but only succeeding in further breaking up the ice.

"Wahl, now ain't the two of ya some sight," said Jeb. "Hell, they ain't goin' be a fish within a mile of har now, with all thet racket yer makin'… haw." Jeb inched his way close to the ice hole, carrying a thick stick. "Here, boy, latch yerself on ta this stick." Jeb extended the stick to Savage who clamped onto it with his jaws. Jeb lay sprawled out on the ice, belly down to distribute his weight evenly over its surface and lessen any chance of causing further breakup. "Give Savage a boost from behind, Jonas. I'll pull from this end." In that manner, they got Savage to safety. Jeb then extended the stick to Jonas and pulled him from the frigid water.

"We better get ya back in front of the fire, afore ya ketch yer death. It sure is a hell of a way ya got of fishin' there, boy. What was ya figgerin' on, jumpin' into thet hole 'n throwin' the fish out? Haw." Savage stood dripping beside Jeb and commenced to shake, spraying Jeb with a fusillade of ice cold water. "Hey thar, ya orn'ry cuss, I think ya did thet on purpose."

▲ ▲ ▲

Jonas wondered about Jebediah's lifestyle, truly an adventurous one, maybe not too different from the life Jonas had imagined for himself back when he was stuck on the farm. But that was before he'd met Laura. Now he couldn't imagine a life without her. Yet, the path Jeb had chosen did have a certain attraction. In many respects, Jonas envied Jeb his simple life—owing to no one, accountable to none but himself, away from the improprieties of fellow humans, subsisting by his wits and courage—one man's working alliance with nature, in total contrast to the affront to nature perpetrated by the coal mining industry. "Not a bad way to live," thought Jonas.

Jeb hunted and trapped for fur, taking muskrat, red fox, wolf, raccoon, otter, and beaver, but no more than he needed. He skinned and dried the furs by tacking them to a board. When dry, he cured the pelts with salt to preserve them until he could sell them in Sprucetown, the nearest town. The furs would be taken elsewhere for tanning.

Jeb's income came primarily from the selling of his furs. He didn't need a whole lot of money, being that he lived so simply. He'd built the cabin himself, as well as all the furnishings. Although he could have gotten his water from the nearby stream, he'd dug a well and laid pipe to the cabin so he could have an inside pump.

Jonas felt that Jeb's day was filled with tasks a man could feel good about, tasks a man was meant to do, tasks far different from the degrading work of the miner crawling around in dark, dirty tunnels in the bowels of the earth.

But mostly Jeb professed to be a prospector, a prospector for gold. He'd traipsed these hills for decades searching for that elusive yellow rock upon which dreams are made. He'd panned for gold in the many mountain streams. He'd hacked at large, promising quartz deposits with a pick ax on rocky mountainsides, in hopes of emancipating a rich vein. He'd explored caves and dried creek beds, dug in loose gravel, and picked through rocks and boulders by hand, always feeling he was but a step away from pay dirt. But Jeb never intimated to Jonas that he'd had any luck at all with this occupation.

▲ ▲ ▲

One day, with the winds tapering off a bit and the sun finding some success through the clouds, Jeb led Jonas to a secluded spot up on the hillside, within shouting distance of the cabin. Savage took the opportunity to romp off in search of game, stretching his now healed leg. Jeb and Jonas approached a shack, well hidden by thick surrounding brush and evergreens, with a prominent smokestack emerging from the roof and spewing a steady stream of wispy, white smoke. A person would have to be practically on top of it to notice it at all.

"This har's my pride 'n joy," Jeb declared. "I bin sneakin' off 'n preparing' this fer you." Neither Jonas nor Jeb had been inclined to keep track of the other's every movement. After all, it wasn't a marriage.

Inside the shack was a large wood stove with a fire burning briskly within it. Sacks of sugar and corn meal lined one wall, and a half-dozen cloth covered buckets sat against another wall. But most prominent was an odd-looking contraption sitting atop the wood stove and consisting of a large covered copper pot with a length of copper tubing extending from its top and coiling through a wooden tub filled with running water. Liquid dripping from the end of the coil was collecting in a mason jar. Jebediah ladled a bit of liquid from the jar and lit a match under it.

"Yep, s'long as this har juice don' ketch afire, it's ready fer some aging," he explained. Jeb wasn't sure why this would be true but he liked the added drama. He grabbed a jug from a shelf containing a row of similar jugs. Each gallon jug was labeled "Ole Jebs". "I figure this one's jes' 'bout ripe." He pulled the cork and took a swig. Grimacing slightly, he passed the jug to Jonas. "Kinda mild, but take a crack at 'er," he said. Jonas lifted the jug to his lips and swallowed. Fire leaped from his mouth as he spit out most of the brew.

"Yep, reckon this batch's almost ready ta take to town." A wide grin spread across Jeb's face. "But I thought I'd give ya a preview. Haw."

"Ya know," continued Jeb. "I came out here one day 'n you'll never guess what I en-count-er'd." Jeb sat on a bench and took another swig from the jug. "Yep, strangest damn thing I ev'r saw." A smile crossed his face and his eyes twinkled. "Seems an ole black bahr somehow bust in har. Wahl, he got into the brew; musta thought it was honey. Hell, them bahrs'll eat most anythin' ain't tied down. By the time I got har, thet bahr was a-hoppin' 'n prancin' around outside most like he was act-ur-ly dancin'. His old snoot was tilted up in the air 'n he was makin' some sort of keenin' sound like he was a-callin' a square dance. Wahl, he saw me standin' thar 'n sorta did a stagger-waltz o'er to me. He lifted a paw, real gentle-like. I sur-mized he was offerin' thet paw ta me, so's I took it, 'n we proceeded ta do us a bit of a jig, jes'a-twirlin' about till the moon came up. Now ain't thet somethin'?"

Jonas looked at Jeb, shaking his head. "Jeb, if you aint the ornery-ist, most con-fab-u-lat-in' ole fool I ev'r met...," and he burst out laughing.

Later, Jonas learned that Jeb, aside from his personal use, sold his "shine" to a few fellows he knew up here in the mountains. Jeb's moonshine was reputed to be about the best around these parts.

"Shore, now 'n agin' I'll pack up a mess of these jugs 'n haul 'em into town on my ole mule, Hank..." The old man hesitated, remembering the loss of his mule to the wolves. "Guess I'll be need'n me a'nuther mule."

18

Thus far, Jonas hadn't told Jebediah his story—how he had happened to be in these mountains. Jeb hadn't inquired, respecting Jonas's right to privacy. One day, restricted to the cabin because of a resurgence of raging winds and warmed by the fire, and a few drags on Jeb's jug of ripened juice, Jonas did tell his story. He told the complete story—starting with his ma dying and his pa falling into depression and how he'd had to take over the reins of the family. About the failing farm and the need to go to work in the coal mines, and how he was given the opportunity to gain a position in the mining company because he'd saved the owner's daughter. He told how all this was lost because he had likely killed someone in a knife fight. And Jonas told Jeb all about Laura— everything—watching her from the meadow, the accident, carrying her unconscious, rain soaked body back to her home, the love that had developed between them and how it now seemed nearly impossible that they could ever be together. All this gushed out of Jonas like a burst pipe.

"Hey, young feller, yer shore carryin' a load," said Jeb. "So what's yer plan fer har on out. I don' figger ya fer the mountaineerin' type."

Jonas hesitated. He really didn't have much of a plan. He'd thought about it a lot, of course, but thus far hadn't formulated much.

"I guess," he began, "my thinkin' is to go west, over into Kentucky— maybe find me a job 'n somehow scrape together a grubstake." Jonas was almost making this up as he went along. "Maybe then I kin buy me a small farm, like a starter farm. I guess I'd like to try to raise some horses. I know that sounds crazy, but...well, Laura loves horses, 'n she knows all about 'em, so maybe if I could git a horse place goin', she'd be willin' to...oh, hell, it's jes' too crazy to ev'n be thinkin' about."

"Tarnation, boy, t'ain't crazy a'tall. If'n a man wants somethin' bad enuff, he'll find him a way ta git it. 'N if she loves you like ya said she did, she'll come around if ya git thet farm goin'. But, how 'bout thet mess ya got back home? Ya figgered out some way around thet?"

"Nope. Reckon I ain't. That fight weren't of my makin' 'n it sure weren't my knife. Somehow, I got to git back there'n prove that. I jes' ain't yet figgered out how to do that, or 'bout the horse farm part either."

"Wahl, boy. You jes' keep figgerin' on it 'n I jes' might be able ta help ya some with what yer talkin' 'bout. I jes' might have a few surprises fer ya."

Jonas looked at the old man oddly, "'N jes' what kind of surprises you talkin' about old- timer?"

"Jes' you ne'er mind for now. When the time's right, we'll be talkin' about it. 'N 'nuther thing, ya li'l whippersnapper, I'll stop callin' you boy, if'n you'll stop callin' me old timer."

"Okay...Jeb, 'n you know, I'm thinkin' maybe you'n me ain't all that much diff'rent. Yer pro'bly right, I ain't the mountaineerin' type, but still, we got a lot in common. You knew workin' in the coal mines weren't no kind of life, 'n you took off for the mountains, same's I did. 'Cept you went by choice, 'n I was driven to it. But I always had a yearnin' to be up in these mountains, or beyond, jes' to see what might be there for me. 'N when I dwell on it, it seems to me some kind of fate brought us together. I had quite a time gittin' here, 'n I'll tell you true, there were a coupla times I actu'ly cursed God for the mess I was in. Now I'm thinkin' maybe God had a plan for me a lot bigger'n my own, whatever that was. I don't know what's yer feelin's 'bout God 'n all, but somehow I think He's put me in the right place 'bout now."

Savage rose from his resting spot near the hearth and looked intently at Jonas.

"'N this great dog of yers...how is it he's always there when we need him most? Seems almost unreal."

Savage's red eyes locked onto Jonas. They were kindly, but penetrating. Jonas stammered his next few words. "There's jes' somethin' about that dog."

Jeb knelt beside Savage and ruffled the thick hair on the back of his neck. "I'll tell you, Jonas. I ain't thet big on churches 'n such. Seems ta me them places jes' take what rightly b'longs in a man's heart 'n tries ta make all sorts of laws about it. Shore, I got my feelin's 'bout God, 'n I'll tell ya true, they's all wrapped up in these har mountains, 'n in this critter here."

▲ ▲ ▲

Winter was showing signs of quitting. The temperatures were up and the winds were down. Jonas decided to risk an outing, to spend a day out in this mountain winter wonderland before spring came and turned everthing green. Maybe do some hunting—might even camp out for a night if the weather were accommodating. He'd take Savage along to give the great dog a chance to romp a bit. They both needed a respite from several months of cabin fever.

Snowshoes were a necessity. With Jeb's help, Jonas had constructed his own shoes, fashioned from lengths of mountain ash, then steamed and bent over special snowshoe molds. After several weeks of drying time, he added strips of rawhide as netting.

Savage had natural snowshoes, the thick wide pads on the bottoms of his feet. But even then, he would at times sink deeply into the softer snow making progress difficult and slow.

But a slow pace was just fine with Jonas. He'd carry a rifle and a small backpack containing a bit of food, some camping implements, and a bed roll, just in case the elements allowed for an overnight. This was to be a venture out into the snow-covered beauty of the mountains and a chance to think about what lay ahead for him, all facilitated by the supreme stillness and serenity of the quiet wintry landscape.

So he and Savage abandoned the warmth of the cabin and began their trek into the silent and irresistible beauty of the late winter mountainscape. As Jonas filled his lungs with the cold fresh air, his body became alive and invigorated, his mind clear and refreshed.

The sun was bright in a rare cloudless sky causing him to squint despite the darkened wood char swatches he'd applied under his eyes. The branches of spruce and pines bent downward under the heavy snow covering, melding them with the ground snow as if they were part of it. In places, the ground was a crusted sheet of crystallized ice that sparkled like diamonds and crunched to Jonas's step. Giant icicles clung to the rocky escarpments, glistening in the sun like glass stilettos. Jonas felt himself in a fairyland and only wished he could share this rapture with Laura.

He kept the stream in sight, always aware that he could become lost if he didn't maintain a reliable landmark for his return journey. Enraptured by the beauty of his surroundings, his mind wandered. Jonas did love the mountains but knew that Jeb's life could never be his life, not isolated and alone like the old man. All of his future dreams and plans included Laura. But how would he ever realize those dreams? He was practically penniless; a wanted man...a killer. It was pure foolishness to hope for a life with Laura, pure folly to believe he'd ever have anything to offer her.

It was too painful to continue these thoughts, and Jonas abandoned them, chosing to get lost in the beauty of the snow-clad mountains and in the reprieve they offered him.

About mid-day, Jonas lost track of Savage. "Yeh, boy, have fun. I guess its bin a while since you've had a chance to stretch yer legs." Jonas passed under a low hanging branch. A cascade of snow fell on him from above. He looked up and gazed into the ferocious yellow eyes of a huge mountain lion. The tawny colored beast was crouched near the base of the overhanging branch, only several feet away. Its tail was twitching wildly, its ears upright. The lion emitted a threatening, agitated snarl. The ears bent back and the lion leaped for Jonas. All Jonas could do was raise his arms and hands to protect his face. The impact of the lion threw Jonas off his feet and over the edge of a deep gully. He tumbled helplessly to the bottom, some twenty feet below. A strange thought occurred to him: *What the hell's a mountain lion doin' up in a tree...damn it all, I thought they jumped around on rocks and boulders and such things.*

Deep snow arrested Jonas's descent. His arm hurt and it was bloody. He looked back up the incline. The lion was about to leap again. Jonas's rifle was no longer strapped over his shoulder. He searched frantically for it and saw it laying several feet away, half buried in the deep snow. He dove for it just as the lion leaped. He heard a horrifying screech. He cringed, awaiting the impact of the huge cat. None came. He heard Savage growling, he heard hissing. He gained his rifle and turned toward the sounds.

"My God," he exclaimed. Savage had intercepted the lion in mid-flight. They now faced each other in menacing postures. "The hell with this," said Jonas, and he shot the lion. "I know you could've taken him, boy, but one of us banged up is enough."

Jonas checked his arm. His shirtsleeve was tattered and blood dripped off his fingertips. "Damn, the same arm as before. I got another arm, you'd think *they'd* git that one now 'n then...hmmmm...who'm I talkin' about here, God, or ole Lucifer, himself? Sometimes I ain't sure who's pullin' the strings 'round here." Savage was nudging the dead cat, growling slightly. He went over to Jonas who was still sprawled in the snow.

Jonas rubbed the dog's neck. "Thanks again, boy. I think I'll live. Looks like you've saved me once more." He hugged the dog as best he could with the damaged arm. "Guess I should try'n git up 'n see if I got any strength left." Jonas managed to rise, but felt woozy. "Well, regardless, we gotta travel, boy. We gotta get back to the cabin. Ain't wantin' to be out here come dark, not in the shape I'm in."

Jonas looked up the embankment he'd just tumbled down. It was practically sheer. "No wonder my bones ache so. No way I'm goin' to make it back up there, not even on my best of days. 'N this sure ain't one of 'em. 'Cept that I'm still alive." He rubbed the dog's neck. "Well, boy, you saved me, now you s'pose you can git us the hell outta here?"

Jonas studied his predicament. He was in a ravine. The snow was deep and he'd lost his snowshoes. He couldn't see them anywhere around and figured he'd lost them right away, up near the top of the steep incline and that put them out of his reach, for sure. The ravine was thick with trees and brush, preventing Jonas from seeing very far in either direction along the bottom of the gully.

"Well, Savage, we can go that way, or we can go that way, but we can't go that way, or that way," indicating the four directions, two of which were steep rises and inaccessible. "Seems like we were comin' from that way, so's that's the way we'll be headin' back 'n hopin' we're right."

They started down the ravine, with Jonas looking for a way up and out. Savage was able to stay on top of the crusted snow, but the crust was not solid enough to support Jonas's weight and he sunk to knee depth with each step. This made travel difficult for him and he was weakening quickly. He discovered the snow was shallower and travel easier a ways up the side of the ravine, before it got too steep. He grabbed one sapling after another for support to keep him on the incline as he progressed. "Jes' about like square dancing," he said aloud. "Do-se-do 'n all that."

Gradually, the ravine became less deep and eventually petered out. Jonas recognized he was now in familiar territory. "Well, Savage, at least it looks like we chose the right direction." He had regained some strength, although his arm still throbbed with pain. He knew he still had about a mile to go to get back to the cabin.

Savage seemed to sense that Jonas was out of danger and no longer felt it necessary to stick to him. He also knew this territory well and took off, maybe looking for small game—or doing whatever it is dogs do when they run off. "See you later, boy, maybe you kin find a cougar to take down by yerself. Ha."

Finally, Jonas saw the cabin up ahead. He was weary and his arm was hurting. Still, he sensed something was wrong. There were tracks in the snow, too many tracks leading up to the cabin. And two sets of snowshoes protruded from the snow by the front door. Jeb had visitors. He hadn't had visitors all winter, so this was unusual and Jonas felt the need to be cautious. He edged in closer, keeping low. Voices emerged from the cabin, angry voices. Jonas sidled up to the window and peered in. Jeb sat in a chair and two men loomed over him, prodding him with their rifles. Jonas knew these men—a big one, and his shadow—*the same men who left me for dead.*

Jonas could overhear their conversation.

"Why'nt ya make it easy on yerself, old man," said the big man. "We know ya hit pay dirt somewhar. Word is ya bin depositin' a heap of cash o'er in the Sprucetown Bank. Ya struck it rich, didn't ya, ya ole weasel. Ya shore din't make no deposit'ble cash from yer fur sellin'. We jes' wanna know whar yer stake is at, old man."

"Ya know, it jes' ain't fair," Bear continued, "you havin' all thet money 'n us piss-poor. Seems like ya'd be moved ta share yer good fortune with yer ole mountain buddies. Hell, what's an old coot like you want with all thet gold anyhow. Now, all's we're askin' is thet ya jes' spread it around a little. Me 'n Zeke, we could put it ta prop'r use, like con-trib-u-tin' ta some charitabl' organ-i-za-shun. Now ya wouldn't want ta interfere with the Lord's work, would you?"

"The only Lord's work around har would be ta send both you varmin's to hell," replied Jeb.

"Haw, thet's a good one, Jeb. I like a sense of humor, but fun time's over fer you, old man, we ain't har on no humor ex-pi-di-shun. Zeke, you got thet poker fired up yet?"

"Hotter'n a bar room whore, Bear," said Zeke.

"Wahl, hand it ov'r har, let's see if ole Jeb would rather be stumblin' around blind, 'r be fessin' up 'bout his gold strike."

Jonas knew he had to act quickly, as Jeb would never give in to the likes of these two. Jonas had his rifle with him, but figured by the time he could break the window and fire off a shot, at least one of the intruders would get a shot at him. Especially as he had only one good arm to shoot with. Another plan came to mind, which he immediately implemented.

Jonas threw a sizable rock through the window, shattering the glass and causing the two mountain men to turn toward the commotion. He then burst through the front door and before the intruders could redirect their attention to him, he got off the first shot, felling the one called Zeke. The big one had his rifle trained on Jonas by this time and was about to squeeze off a round when Savage came crashing through the other window. Before the big man could fire, the dog's jaws closed on his wrist, sending his firearm flying across the room. Almost as quickly, Jebediah grabbed a knife from Zeke's belt and thrust it into Bear's midsection. The knife went in deep and upward toward the heart. The big man went down, gasped, and drew his last breath.

"Wahl, tarnation," said Jebediah. "You two done saved me agin. But looks like we're gonna need us some new winder glass." He inspected the dog. "'N you, ole boy, yer cut up purty bad." Jeb noticed Jonas's bloody arm. "Now what in tarna-shun happ'ned ta you? Don't look like no gunshot wound."

Jonas explained about the mountain lion. "So, now Savage has gone 'n saved the both of us the same day," said Jeb. "Ain't thet somethin...ain't thet *really somethin'* ? Wahl, let's git the two of ya patched up. 'N looks like we gotta clear us out some garbage, too," referring to the two dead mountain men. "These're the two scallywags thet attacked you too, Jonas, if'n I ain't mistook."

"You ain't wrong, Jeb. I ain't likely to forget them two."

"'N I'd wager they wish they'd ne'er sold me thet dog in the first place. Haw. Like they could e'er wish fer anythin' agin. How 'bout helpin' me git 'em outside? Then we'll patch up you 'n Savage har. We kin bury these two scavengers later. I don't figger anyone's gonna come callin' fer 'em."

After the two mountain men were duly deposited in unmarked graves, Jebediah confronted Jonas inside the cabin. Jeb gave Jonas a lengthy look from across the table, making Jonas nervous. A lit lantern sat between them, dispelling what darkness the fireplace couldn't handle. "I figure ya heard what was said earlier," started Jeb, "what them two critters was sayin', 'bout me runnin' up a purty good bank account 'n all. I ain't said nuthin' 'bout my gold profits 'n you ain't asked me nuthin' about 'em. Wahl, they were right 'bout thet. Back a ways, I got real lucky 'n come across a powerful rich vein. It worked out thet I was able ta build up a sizabl' fortune 'n git it deposited in that bank down thar in Sprucetown."

Jebediah looked straight at Jonas. "I like ya boy, 'n I trust ya, 'n I kaint say thet 'bout many folks. 'N I ain't overlookin' ya done saved my blamed life...hell, twice now. Now I ain't sayin' I owe ya, 'cause I don't want it ta be that way b'tween us. We done spent us a whole winter together without gittin' at each other's throats, 'n thet's sayin' a lot fer me."

The old man fiddled a bit, shifted in his chair. "Welp, I got a prop-er-si-shun fer ya." Jonas wondered where this was going, but kept his tongue.

"Lately, I bin thinkin' seriously of gittin' down out of these mountains. Bin up har a long time, 'n I guess I'm jes' gittin' a mite tucker'd out.

The prospectin' kept me int'risted fer a while, but I got more money than I know what ta do with now, 'n it seems a bit foolish like ta keep poundin' them hills 'n pannin' them cricks. I ain't got it in me no more. Besides, my main strike's jes' 'bout played out, 'n I bin lookin' fer somethin' ta do with my money. I figure you got the plan but ya ain't got no way ta im-pli-ment it. So, my good friend, I intend ta bankroll yer horse farm venture for ya. Whatcha got ta say to thet?"

At first, Jonas said nothing, he just stared at the old man, incredulously. Finally, "Jeb, I couldn't ask you to do nuthin' like that. It jes' don't make no sense."

"Of course ya could ask me, 'n it shore 'nuff makes plenty of sense. Now, mind ya, it ain't jes' no gift out of grat-er-tude, neither. I'm intendin' ta own a piece of thet thar farm too...like a partnership. 'Cept'n, you'll mostly be runnin' it, you 'n thet lady friend of yers. I'm figgerin' on doin' a lot of porch sittin' 'n rockin' 'n maybe a bit of cookin', dependin' on how the lady of the house wants ta sort things out."

Jonas sat there, stupefied, studying the old man. The offer was beyond his wildest dreams. And to include Laura. "Jeb, I thought you hated women."

"Now stop right there, young feller. How I feel 'bout wimmins, thet's about me—how you feel 'bout yer lady friend, wahl, thet's about you, 'n I ain't about ta interfere with thet. My offer stands as stated."

"Y'know, I think yer serious." Jonas continued to stare. He began to smile. "'N if you are, a man would have to be a damn fool not to take you up on it."

"Well then, let's shake on it, 'n git ta planning' this thing out."

Jebediah had some suggestions for Jonas concerning his horse farm. Jonas was more than open to any suggestions being that he really had no firm plan anyway.

"I'll tell ya, Kin-tuc-kee's not the way ta go," said Jeb. "I've spent a good deal of time up in Virginny, 'n I'll tell ya, thar ain't no purtier land on this har earth than up thar in the Shenandoer Valley. 'N the horses must jes' love it, 'cause thar's horse farms e'er which way. Now, I ain't got nuthin' agin Kin-tuc-kee, but I figger a feller oughta stick with what he knows best, 'n I know a heap of a lot more 'bout Virginny then I do 'bout Kin-tuc-kee. I figure we can follow these mountains right up thar into northern Virginny without no prospects of being detected, in case thar might still be someone a-lookin' fer you. We can git outfitted for the trip o'er there in Sprucetown, 'n ask around for someone who kin steer us to the right folks to contact 'bout buying us a farm up in the Shenandoer. I know a few folks already thet might be able ta help."

"Jeb, you got things figgered out like you bin thinkin' 'bout this for some time."

"Yer right there, young feller. I as-cer-tained it was 'bout time fer me ta give up this mountain life 'n find some way ta enjoy my remainin' years in a bit more com-fert. Seems ta me you've provided me thet op-per-toonity."

"Well, Jeb. Seein's I got no better plan, 'n yours sounds more'n reasonable, I think we got ourselves a deal. I'll jes' go along with what you suggest." Jonas felt something he hadn't felt for some time—hope.

19

Winter in Richmond. What little snow fell failed to take, but still, the days were chilly and the nights much colder. It was Monday and Laura Becker, country girl from Jericho, West Virginia was to be enrolled in the Richmond Academy for Girls, with the expectation that she might become a proper young lady. This, of course, was not Laura's expectation.

The school lay in the outskirts of Richmond and not far from the stables that boarded Sacagawea. During Laura's acclimation period—which, like the snow in Richmond, didn't take—Saca was to be her link to her home life.

What little adjustment to Academy life she managed was due to her new friend and kindred spirit, Charly Cooper. The two girls soon developed a close friendship, perhaps the closest Laura had ever had to a girl her own age. Laura had been unable to form real friendships with girls around Jericho as they tended to shy away from her due to the prominence of her family name.

Charly was a bright, springy sort of girl with a bit of deviltry about her, not unlike Laura in this regard. She too, was seventeen, and quite pretty, maybe just a bit plump but pleasantly so. Cascades of blonde curls framed a freckled face that beamed when she was excited, or when she was up to mischief. Laura took to Charly right away because she also was a country girl, an anomaly at this school. And they shared another bond, an unfortunate one. Charly had lost her mother several years ago and her father hadn't remarried. And Laura had been without a real mother for about ten years.

But it was their love of horses that ultimately bonded them. Charly's family had a large horse ranch in upstate Virginia, in the Shenandoah Valley, and she talked of it often and made no secret that she wished to be back there now, and not at this stuck-up Richmond Academy for *snobbish* Girls, as she put it. She had brought her favorite horse to Richmond, a Paint she called Chestnut. The horse was indeed chestnut colored with splotches of white decorating her face, hind feet, and sections of her chest and back. Chestnut was bright and friendly, just like Charly. Most of the upcoming weekends would find Laura and her new friend roving the near-by hills aboard their beloved mounts—their way of contending with the school they both abhorred.

Most of the young girls attending the Academy were from the Richmond area, the daughters of the city's elite families. They were here to learn to become perfect young ladies, with the intent that they might then attract just the right man and perpetuate the families' high ranking in Richmond society. Laura was truly the outsider among these girls. Charly, less conspicuously so. In particular, Laura was singled out for ridicule because of her back-woods way of speaking. Proper young ladies didn't say "ain't" or "y'all" or use—God forbid—"double negatives". But these affronts didn't bother Laura. It wasn't that Laura couldn't improve her manner of speaking, if she so desired. But she was quite satisfied with who she was and saw no need to change her ways just to impress anyone who seemed to think themself superior just because they used more proper English.

"Y'know, it's a funny thing," Laura once intimated to Charly, "back home, I guess I'm considered sorta upper-crust, but here I'm looked down on like I was inferior or somethin'. Sometimes I jes' ain't sure where I do belong."

The Academy assigned two girls to a room, and Laura and Charly had managed to swap around so that they shared the same room. Oddly, Laura, despite her perceived lower rank, became viewed as a curiosity by the other girls. Small groups of girls began to gather in Laura's room to hear her stories about back home. Laura didn't disappoint.

She delighted in relating tales—true and almost true—about bears, wild cats, wolves, and other long toothed, sharp clawed "critters" that stalked every man, woman, and child in and around Jericho. In time, these small groups of Academy girls became larger groups crowding into Laura's room, anxious to hear of her alleged rugged and adventuresome life, a life so foreign to them. But mostly, they wanted to hear about Jonas.

Laura became elevated in their eyes—already in love at such a young age. Not only in love, but in love with a ruffian, an escapee who was being hunted all over the state. Laura was not reluctant to enhance her stories. She showed the cameo Jonas had given her, and further delighted the girls by relating how Jonas had stolen back to her house, in the dead of night, right under the nose of her father, the sheriff, the posse, and everyone else, just to see her one last time, to ". . . impart his undying declaration of love for her, and crush her against his body, and kiss her into swooning oblivion."

"Uggghhhh!" declared one of the girls, "To kiss a lowly farmer and dirty miner. Must have been like kissing a stable hand."

"Well, maybe you should try it sometime. You might like it," shot back Laura. The girl blushed amid the jeers and laughter of the others girls.

One girl, rather young, dared ask Laura if she had actually *done* it with him?

"Well, what d'you think?" Although Laura's reply was rather flippant, she had often thought about being with Jonas in that way. Sometimes she actually wished they'd have had more time during his hasty departure to seal their relationship with a more substantial declaration of their love, something he would be unlikely to forget, no matter the distance or circumstances that separated them.

So, ironically, Laura became a celebrity among the Academy girls. Not all the girls were won over, but enough so that the Academy teachers became concerned about a most disturbing trend. It seemed many of the girls were so intrigued by Laura that it became fashionable to imitate her way of talking and other untoward mannerisms. *Ain'ts* and *y'alls* were creeping into their language. And *tom-boyishness* was infiltrating their proper lady-like training. It was considered chic to talk, look, and act like Laura Becker.

The concern of the Academy administration was such that Laura was summoned to the president's office and informed that she must put aside her roguish upbringing and strive to become a lady. Further, she was told that after the upcoming two-week Christmas holiday, which she would be spending with her mother, she would either show improvement or be asked to leave the school. Her disruptive influence would no longer be tolerated.

The prospect of spending the holiday break with her mother aroused a quandary of feelings in Laura. She felt a need to know her mother better, to establish some kind of relationship beyond the formal dalliances of her previous weekend. But, in truth, she actually preferred the Academy to the strained time she and her mother had spent together.

Charly Cooper would be spending the holidays at her Shenandoah Valley home. So Laura would be stranded, alone with her mother until school started again, and she was of the opinion that her mother would prefer that she were back in West Virginia and not her responsibility.

Laura was full of apprehensions. The short stay at her mother's apartment before school began had been difficult enough. Now she was to spend two weeks there. She could only hope that this time things would work out better. But that was not to be. The first evening at her mother's apartment was to be indicative of Laura's entire stay. A gentleman showed up and whisked her mother off for an evening at the opera. Laura might have been interested had she been invited to accompany them. She had never been to an opera.

Curiously, the same gentleman showed up on subsequent evenings to escort her mother to other functions. Laura was never included. Several nights, Laura did not even hear her mother return home. Nor did she see her until the afternoon of the next day. *Curious indeed...*

With Priscilla away so often, Laura became the responsibility of her mother's housekeeper, Caroline. Caroline was attentive, but much older than Laura, hardly apt company for a young woman. But Caroline was game. On an unusually warm day, with the sun shining brightly and the wintry chills taking a day off, Caroline introduced Laura to a new phenomenon that was intriguing Richmond society—bicycle riding. Now, the bicycle was essentially a man's vehicle. For the ladies there was the "high wheel" tricycle, which was especially designed to accommodate their long skirts and corsets, as well as their modesty. This riding machine had two rather large wheels in back and a smaller one in front. While men were risking life and limb on two wheelers, with the small wheel in back and an exceedingly large one in front, ladies could pedal quite safely with the stability afforded by the tri-wheel system.

Caroline had retrieved two of these tricycles from a shed in back of the apartment building. Priscilla had purchased them because they were the *latest thing*, but had yet to utilize the vehicles. However, Laura was always open to a challenge. "I s'pose you want me to crawl up on that thing," she declared to Caroline.

"That's the general idea."

"Wahl, then, let's git at it."

Caroline explained to Laura the rudiments of bike riding. The seat was such that it was not necessary to straddle it. Rather, it was more a bench, allowing a girl to seat it quite comfortably, without compromising her respectability. Laura climbed daintily up onto the seat, parodying the manner that might befit a young lady.

"Now then, shouldn't I be a-twirlin' a parasol?" Laura joked. Then, in contrast, "So, whar's the stirrups for this dang thing? C'mon, giddy-up, giddy-up."

"My dear, just pedal the damn thing." Caroline wasn't angry, she was actually amused by Laura's antics.

"Okay, okay. Hold yer horses. Or bikes, or trikes, or whatever." Laura started pedaling but failed to steer the vehicle properly and abruptly collided with Caroline's bike. "Oops. I guess you have to steer this thing, too."

After a few more mishaps, Laura got the hang of the tricycle and Caroline felt confident to accompany her for a more extended outing. Soon they were riding the streets of Richmond with great pomp and ceremony, an occasion that did not go unnoticed among the male gentry, who tipped their hats and even whistled as Caroline, and particularly Laura, guided their machines down the boulevard. Laura thought it to be great fun and vowed to get herself one of these "contraptions". Then on second thought, she dismissed the notion, thinking it would be indecent for her to be riding up and down the streets of Jericho on an extravagance such as this. But she had no such reservations here in Richmond. Caroline had chosen a route with little traffic, since the tricycle could prove quite dangerous in jockeying for position amid all the trolley cars and horse drawn buggies and pedestrians and such. Again, Laura's thoughts returned to that same old refrain, "I wonder what Jonas would think if he saw me now?"

Laura and Caroline stopped for lunch at Chesterton's, a very proper eatery just down the block from Priscilla's apartment. They both ordered a simple lunch—soup and sandwiches. Laura thought she would take this opportunity to ask about her mother.

"Caroline," she started. "You've bin with my mother for quite some spell. I was hopin' you could tell me somethin' about her. I was real young when she left, I guess I jis' don' quite understand." Laura's eyes showed hurt. This was a sore point with her and not easy for her to approach.

Caroline was somewhat guarded on the subject, Priscilla being her employer. She was aware that Laura and her mother had little in common, other than family ties, but she felt sympathy for Laura. How could a mother not adore such a delightful child?

"Laura, I've grown quite fond of you. Whatever I say to you now must stay strictly between us. Understood?" Laura nodded yes. "I know an employee should remain faithful to their employer, but I don't feel that what I'm about to tell you is in violation of that faith, because a mother-daughter relationship is such a dear thing. Generally, it's none of my business what your mother does, or doesn't do, me being just a housekeeper. But, in all fairness, she is your mother and should feel an obligation to you. Mind you, your mother doesn't confide in me, but I see things and I hear things. So, that being understood, there are some things I can tell you, but it's just between you and me."

Caroline continued her account as they dabbled at their food.

"Dear girl, I don't think your mother has anything against either you or your father, but she does speak poorly of the life she had back in West Virginia. I assume your father has told you about your family history, about your mother being unhappy living there."

"Dad's told me some things, but not too much. I guess I'd jis' like you to tell me more. I wonder about her a lot—what's she like, 'n all that."

"I know you do, Laura. It's only natural. I don't want to be judging your mother too much, but it's my opinion that she's been wrong. I hope you won't think poorly of me, but it angers me that any mother would abandon a child, especially one so precious as you. Laura, your mother just seems caught up in herself. She has her own little world and doesn't seem to want to be concerned by anything outside it. Sometimes, I think I shouldn't be working for her, feeling like I do. But in many ways, she's a good person. She treats me well and the work is pleasant enough. I just can't understand how she could just...up and leave you and your father."

"Caroline...does she ever say anything about...me?"

"Dear, I'm sorry. I just don't know what to tell you. I only know she gets sad sometimes. Then she doesn't want anyone around. Afterwards, I can tell she's been crying. Maybe she's thinking about her family, about you. But, it doesn't mean she'll ever come back to you. You mustn't count on that. I don't know what goes on in her mind."

"She has men friends, don't she? I guess she prefers them to dad 'n me." Tears began to form in Laura's eyes. She placed her hand on Caroline's arm. "I thank you for tellin' me all this. I know you didn't have to; you could've lied. No one will ever know that you've tole me these things."

"Dear, I'm so sorry. Maybe someday your mother will—"

"No, Caroline. It's all right," Laura interrupted, wiping away a tear with her sleeve. "I guess I already knew most of what you tole me. It's time I jis' accepted it. Dad 'n me ain't bin doin' so bad. Anyway, I love this here bike ridin'. We gotta do it agin sometime."

Unfortunately, this unusually mild day was the only one suitable to bike riding during Laura's stay with her mother.

But not so for horse riding. Laura endured the remainder of the week by riding Saca each day. Then, on Christmas Eve, her mother went out, leaving Laura alone again with Caroline. They shared eggnogs, which were not without a certain kick and designed to dispel any feelings Laura might have of being abandoned by her mother, *on Christmas Eve of all things.*

Caroline showed Laura how to play Conquian, a new card game gaining popularity in Richmond. They played for pennies. Soon Laura got the knack for the game and relished raking in Caroline's money. She thanked Caroline for the evening's entertainment and went to bed, wondering how Jonas would be spending his Christmas, yet saddened that her mother had not been present.

Christmas Day consisted of opening a present from her dad—a riding crop, and one from her mother—a book on etiquette. *Ha.* Well, at least she did get to spend Christmas Day with her mother, a time that was stiff and uneasy for both of them.

After the dreadful two-week break, Laura returned to the Richmond Academy. The warnings were reissued that unless she should show a marked improvement in her behavior and begin to seriously improve her speech and manners and adhere to the program taught by the Academy, she would be dismissed and sent back home. This of course, was Laura's wish and intention, which she precipitated by skipping classes and becoming even more coarse in speech and dress. Soon, deeming her to be incorrigible, the school officials summarily dismissed Laura from the Academy. Her only regret was parting with her friend Charly, whom she promised to soon visit in her beautiful Shenandoah Valley. It was not an idle promise.

▲ ▲ ▲

"Laura...Laura...Laura. What am I to do with you?" her father said. They stood in the large living room of the Becker Estate house. Laura's travel bags lay at her feet. She stood defiantly. "I got letters from that school," Frederick continued. "Let's see..." He took a pair of reading glasses from his vest pocket and slipped them on. His cigar smoke was coming from urgent puffs. From one letter, *"Incorrigible...skippin' classes."* From another letter, *"...terrible grammar.* And what's this?...*a bad influence on the other girls."* Laura couldn't hold back a smile. Frederick Becker stared firmly at his daughter. "My God! My God," and a smile formed on his face. He began to chuckle and soon was laughing uproariously. "Well, daughter. One thing for sure, you shore don't take after yer mother." And they were both laughing. They embraced. "Good to have you home honey. And..." he added. "Just one thing. Try to be a little more open to Dirk Fisher. Maybe give it a chance to work."

Laura nodded her acquiescence, wondering how long she'd have to maintain the charade as she awaited Jonas's return.

20

Springtime finally asserted its presence, pushing the cold Appalachian winter aside. Jeb brought his rocking chair outside and was rocking and enjoying the warmth of a sun-lit day. Savage sprawled at his feet while Jonas lounged nearby, propped against a shade oak.

"Hey Jeb," said Jonas, "looks like we got us a boarder."

Jonas pointed to a freshly built robin's nest nestled into a crevice just over the cabin's front door with twigs and stuffing scattered below.

Jeb gazed up. "Hell of a place ta build a nest, with us goin' 'n out. Don' suppose she'll git much privacy fer raisin' her chicks. Most likely she'll jes' abandon the project."

Jonas noticed the robin standing some twenty feet off, watching them intently. Savage rose slowly and fixed his eyes on the red-breasted intruder. The robin shook her head and seemed to nod. She then flew to her nest and settled in, disregarding Jeb and Jonas's presence. Savage settled down once again at Jeb's feet.

"Now don' thet beat all?" said Jebediah. He stared up at the bird, then back at Savage. "N'er seen no bird so bold as thet. Savage, now you wouldn't have anythin' ta do with thet, would ya?"

Over the next few weeks, Jeb and Jonas watched as the mother robin went about her motherly duties, laying her eggs, warming them with her body, and nurturing the emerging chicks, seemingly in contempt of their human presence.

"Wahl, I don' su'pose we'll be around ta see them young'uns fly off," stated Jeb. "I figger it's 'bout time fer us ta be gittin' down offa this mountain."

Jeb and Jonas were without a horse or mule, so on their trip to Sprucetown they would cart only what what they could carry on their backs and on a stout travois they would drag behind, Indian style. Jeb knew that the best time to start out of the mountains would be in the early spring when there would still be snow enough to facilitate dragging the travois, but not so much as to impede travel.

Jonas had no belongings to speak of and Jeb didn't mind leaving most of his meager possessions behind. He figured on starting anew wherever they ended up anyway. He did, however insist on several jugs of his mountain brew. "Someday, someone'll stumble on ta my *shine factory* har, 'n they'll have 'im a hell of a time." They would also take Jeb's entire collection of woodcarvings, which they'd carefully packed to avoid breakage.

From under a floorboard of the cabin, Jeb retrieved a small flour sack, filled with a lumpy material.

"This here's the last of my gold diggings. It's what them two scallywags was lookin' fer. I kept it on hand in case of some e-mer-gency." He opened the sack and spilled the contents onto the table. "This har's the stuffs thet'll be providin' fer our futures, Jonas. Kinda purty, ain't it?"

Jonas picked up a few of the nuggets. "I've never seen the likes of it b'fore, Jeb. Maybe purty ain't a strong 'nuff word for it."

The mountain cabin had been Jebediah's home for many years and leaving it was not without considerable regret. Jonas discerned a sadness in the old man's eyes.

"I imagin' you're leavin' behind a lot of good memories, Jeb."

"Yep, shore am. 'N so's Savage. The only home he's ever knowd since he was a pup. I 'spect it's the end of one way of life, 'n the beginnin' of a'nuther. It's hard ta let thet kind of thing go by without a man gits a little worked up."

"Are you sure 'bout this Jeb?"

"I'm sure. Real sure. Yer the closest thing I ev'r had to a pard, 'n if I'm gonna be changin' ev'rythin' around...wahl, hell, it's gonna be with someone I trust. Jes' give me 'n my dog a minute ta bid my farewells."

▲ ▲ ▲

Jonas McNabb and Jebediah Hart began their journey north to Spruce-town in the early spring. The snow had receded significantly, clinging mostly to the higher peaks. Still, patches of snow dotted the hillsides. Wildflowers had sprung up everywhere, lending bright color to the drab ground and lingering snow. Dripping water from snow melting off the pines and spruces engendered a gentle sonorous background as the three travelers began their trek—Savage from the only home he had ever known and Jeb from his home of many years. For Jonas, it was not so much what he was leaving behind, but what lay ahead.

▲ ▲ ▲

Sprucetown was a mountain town lying about fifteen miles northeast of Jeb's cabin. It was where Jeb did most of his business—selling his furs and his "Ole Jebs" brew, purchasing needed supplies, and depositing his money in the Sprucetown Banking and Trust Company. There wasn't much to Sprucetown. A livery of course—hotel, mercantile, bank, saloon, church, schoolhouse, and a municipal building with a court house and offices for town officials—lawyers and such. Residencies and various businesses filled in the rest of Sprucetown's borders.

Jebediah drew enough money out of the bank to cover expenses for the foreseeable future. When he needed more, particularly for the purchase of a horse farm, he'd use bank drafts, drawn against this bank.

Jeb and Jonas left the bulk of their gear in storage at the livery. They procured a room at the Sprucetown Hotel and took a meal downstairs in the restaurant. It was the first time Jonas had been out of the mountains since he'd fled Jericho about seven months ago—to him it seemed an eternity. He savored the food, fresh fruit and vegetables, and for the occasion, he and Jeb had fat Angus steaks. They fed Savage from the table. Nobody seemed to object.

"What say to a li'l cel'bratin' b'fore we retire," said Jebediah. "I'm thinkin' we earned it. They's a saloon down the street what's got our name on it, thet's what I'm thinkin'."

Jonas wasn't yet in the celebrating mood. His mind was on the journey that lay ahead and he was anxious to be underway. Celebrating could wait. But, he went along for Jeb's sake.

They entered the Red Lady Saloon through batwing doors and found but a few patrons inside, as it was early evening. No one occupied the room's few tables; three men stood at the bar nursing drinks. The bartender was idling, wiping down the spacious bar top.

"What'll it be?" said Sam, the bartender.

"Wahl," said Jeb. "We'll start with a coupla beers."

Jonas finished his drink and told Jeb he was plumb tired and thought he'd head back to the hotel.

"Plumb tired? What they makin' you young-uns outta these days? Hell, thet weren't no cel-e-bra-shun. Thet weren't more'n a *howdy-ya-do*."

"'N that's all the howdy-ya-dooin' I'm gonna be doin' for tonight, Jeb."

"Wahl, suit yerself. I ain't even got my whistle wet yet."

"Well, wet away, Jeb, but remember, we got us a long trip come morning."

"Long trip, my arse. Thet ain't no long trip. I've taken longer trips on my hands 'n knees. So, run along, pup. I'll see ya come mornin'."

Jonas left Savage outside the Red Lady Saloon. "Watch out for 'im boy, he's an orn'ry old coot."

Inside, Jeb motioned the barkeep over. "Hell, now thet the am-a-tures has left, give me some of yer good stuff. Yer best whiskey."

In a room overhead, Callie Brown wriggled into a skin-tight, low-cut, emerald-colored gown, which favorably set off her bright red hair. She pinned her hair back with sparkly green combs, accentuating its red cast. Callie felt it important to draw attention to her hair—her fame and popularity rested on it. She was pretty enough, and young and well-endowed. But it was the flaming red hair that brought the customers back time and time again and kept them talking about her.

Now, with a bit of rouge to the cheeks, a dab of greenish tint to the eyelids, and a green sequin added to her cleavage, the mirror told her she was ready for the evening. "I guess I'm a purty lucky li'l ole gal," she said, gazing at her reflection. She thought about her trip down off the mountain with the two brutish mountain men. "One favor each was all they demanded—not a bad price ta pay. Shore a whole lot better'n the price thet feller with me paid. Hell, serves 'im right for not takin' up with me."

Callie's bedroom featured a canopied bed with brightly colored satin sheets, and two windows sporting red, frilly curtains. From outside at night, there was no mistaken the purpose of the room, the reddish glow broadcasting its invitation.

The two mountain men had brought her here to Sprucetown and turned her over to Sam, the owner of the one saloon in town. He was thrilled to have her, well worth the price he paid to the mountain men. His business took an abrupt upturn after Callie's arrival. Later, he offered his *star attraction* a part ownership, a small part, to keep her on. From then on, the saloon became the Red Lady Saloon.

Jeb pounded a fist on the bar. "Keep 'em comin', barkeep," he ordered, "now thet the chil'uns have left."

"Comin right up, old timer," replied Sam.

Jeb was one of the few customers at the bar. A card game had commenced at one of the tables. Presently, a red-headed girl in a low-cut emerald gown sidled up next to Jeb and asked if he'd buy her a drink.

"Why shore, git the lady a brew, barkeep. 'N jes' what might yer name be, gal?"

"Wahl, my name's Callie. Ya might have seen thet this place is called The Red Lady. Wahl, I'm the Red Lady."

"Hell if you ain't," said Jeb, noticing her hair. "Ain't seen red like thet since I chopped the head off a turkey buzzard."

"Ha, thet's sure a good one, fella. But I don' reckon I think too kindly of the comparison. Now what say ya be a bit nicer to a lady," she said, cozying up to Jebediah,

By now, Jeb was starting to feel his liquor. He suspected that young "red hair" here was aware that he carried a sizable bankroll, either on him or back at the hotel—news gets around in a small town. Combine that with his overall suspicion of women, since his bride had run off on him years ago, and Jeb wasn't about to fall for Callie's obvious intentions. But he wasn't above having a bit of fun with her either. Just not the physical kind.

"I'd shore be nice to a lady, if'n there was one around. But durned if I kin see one."

Callie wasn't easily deterred, she smelled an easy mark. She traced her finger along Jeb's chest. "Now mister, be nice. You be nice ta me, 'n I'll shore be nice ta you."

"Wahl, li'l lady, let me tell ya somethin'. I once had me a young filly like you. Then she up 'n run off on me, back to her maw. Since then, I ain't had much use fer wimmins. I think I'd druther have me a rattler fer comp'ny."

"I don' think I keer much for yer at-ti-tude, ya old coot."

"'N I don't think too much of it either, ole man," added Sam, who was lingering nearby. "You bin up in the mountains too long. Now what say you apologize to the lady?"

Jeb slugged down another whiskey. "Wahl sure...lady, I'm sorrrrreeee ya got hair red like a gobler's waddl'."

"That's it," said Sam. "You're outta here." Sam, a big man, came out from behind the bar, grabbed Jebediah by the front of his shirt and marched him out through the front batwing doors. He deposited him ingloriously into the street. "Haw," laughed Jeb. "I s'pose I might've overdid it jes' a bit." He began his walk back to the hotel.

The evening's imbibing dulled Jeb's wits and he didn't notice that a man had followed him from the bar. As Jeb passed a dark alleyway, the man stepped out, training a gun on Jeb.

"I'm thinkin' that purse seems a bit too heavy for an old man to be carryin' about. What say you fork it ov..." Before the would-be robber could finish his demand, Savage came flying out of the dark, knocking the gun from his hand and pushing him to the ground. The dog stood over the man, growling through his teeth, an inch from his face.

"Oh, I see yuv met my pard, Savage," said Jeb. "'N ya seem ta be friends already. Now thet's odd, he don' us'ully take ta folks right off. I thought shore he was gonna tear yer face off. Wahl, Savage, ole boy, let yer new friend up. Seems he needs ta clean up his pant-a-loons a bit."

The man got up slowly and backed away, his eyes intent on the dog. "Hmmmmm, Savage, seems ya've lost yer new friend. I've tole ya not ta sit on 'em right off like thet. Seems ta skeer 'em. Wahl, 'nuff fun for one night." Jeb and Savage headed back to the hotel.

▲ ▲ ▲

The next day was a full one with a whole lot for Jeb and Jonas to accomplish. Their first stop was the livery. They'd need two horses and a mule for their trip through the mountains. "I ain't got much in horse stock right now," said the livery man, "I kin provide ya with the mule, 'n one suitable horse, but after thet, the only thing I got in a horse is some ole mare I got stuck with a while back. Ain't nobody wants her so I kin give 'er to ya cheap if ya got a hankerin'." Jonas walked up to the mare and threw his arm around her neck.

"It's you, ole girl", and suddenly Jonas felt a further ray of hope, as if he'd reconnected with his family. *You'll never have to pull a plow again.* Jonas paid the man twice what he'd asked.

From the mercantile, they were able to procure all the supplies they'd need for the northward trek up into the mountains. Anything else they might eventually need, they'd purchase when they reached their destination. Jonas allowed Jeb to make most of the purchases, being that Jeb was more experienced at outfitting such a journey as lay ahead. That settled, Jonas and Jeb asked around and got the name of someone who might help advise them on some of the particulars of the business end of their venture. But first Jonas had some other business to take care of. Jeb had told him about his adventure, or misadventure of the previous evening. Jonas was especially interested in the red headed saloon girl named Callie.

"Wahl," said Jeb, "if'n it's the same gal ya ran into up on the mountain, she sure seems to know how ta git the better of us."

"Yeh, 'n if it is Callie, I got a few things to settle with her."

"Now, Jonas, jes' what is it yer hopin' ta accomplish? Ya don't wanna be startin' nuthin' ya ain't got no idear how ta finish."

"I reckon I'm obliged to call her out for what she did. I wouldn't be much of a man if I didn't."

"I s'pose yer aire obliged at thet. Ya want I should come with you, kinda back ya up?"

"Not rightly so, Jeb. I'm thinkin' it's somethin' I got to do on my own. B'sides, we're not even sure it's the same girl."

"Wahl, me 'n Savage'll wait outside, then. You need us, jes' give a whistle."

Jonas entered the Red Lady and saw right away that the red haired girl sitting at one of the tables was indeed the same Callie he had encountered in the mountains. It was early in the day and the bar was sparsely populated. Callie sat by herself at a table. Two men stood nearby at the bar in conversation with Sam. Jonas approached Callie's table.

"I don't reckon you ever expected to see me agin, leastwise, not alive." said Jonas.

Callie had seen Jonas approach and glanced to the two men standing nearby, putting them on alert. She looked back to Jonas. "Mister, a gal's gotta do what a gal's gotta do. You was a goner anyhow, weren't much I could do fer you."

"You left me for dead, after you tole them two varmin's that I was set on mistreatin' you. I figger you was largely responsible for what happened to me."

"Wahl, hell fella, ya think I should be cryin' fer you, a big boy like yerself? Maybe you need yer maw along ta keer for you." This brought jeering laughter from the two men, who had been following the confrontation closely.

Jonas wasn't sure where to take things from here. Anger and embarrassment were building up inside him. Had he felt this same sort of anger last year in Jericho, when he and Jake had it out? One thing for sure, he'd have to finish what he started here. "This yer saloon, Callie?" he said.

"I got a part of it. What biz-niz is it of yers?"

"Well, if this here's yer table, I thought I might borrow it for a bit." Jonas grabbed Callie's table and tipped it over, sending Callie sprawling backwards as her chair toppled. "And this here chair, I need to borrow it too." He threw the chair through a side window. Callie regained her footing and motioned to the two men.

"Mule, Harry, you wanna take keer of this fool?" The two men approached Jonas, wearing snide smiles. One man was huge and ugly. The other looked soft.

"Wahl...Mule 'n Harry," said Jonas. "Right proud to make yer acquaint'nces. Now let's see...which one of you could be Mule, I wonder. Must be the one that looks like the ass-end of a mule. This one here I think," said Jonas as he smashed a chair over the big man's head. Mule went down. Harry moved in on Jonas, but somewhat reluctantly. Jonas put him down with a fist to his soft midsection. So far, Jonas figured he had been able to get the better of his two adversaries through quickness and surprise. He didn't think in the long-run he'd have much of a chance against Mule who had him by about eighty pounds. As the two men regained their feet, they became aware of a snarling noise coming from behind them. They turned around slowly.

"Howdy, gentl'men," said Jebediah, who had just entered the bar. "May I in-ter-duce ya to Savage, my friendly dog? Ya may of seen 'im around. I imagine if'n you were ta move er anythin', he jes' might go for yer innards. So, Jonas, ya got any more biz'niz har?"

Mule and Harry backed off, now with their backs tight against the bar, as far from Savage as retreat would allow.

"Well...let's see," said Jonas. "Up in the mountains, I lost my horse, most my supplies, 'n damn near my life. So far, I've destroyed a window, two chairs, 'n a table. What'dya think, Callie? We 'bout even?"

"Why'nt ya jes' leave, mister. I ain't never wantin' ta see the likes of either of ya agin."

"Sure, Callie, 'n I reckon if you ever do see us agin, you won't git off so easy."

On his way out, Jonas flipped over a few more tables, then stopped and righted one of the tables. "See'ins I got my mare back, I'll leave this table as is."

▲ ▲ ▲

Lloyd Bainsfield was a Sprucetown lawyer, businessman, real estate agent, and probably even the town barber. His office was part of the complex that housed the courtroom and other official offices. Jebediah obtained his name from the president of the bank, who was only too willing to assist his number one depositor. Jeb and Jonas walked into Bainsfield's office, fresh from their encounter at the Red Lady Saloon. The lawyer rose from behind a large mahogany desk—a large man, more in girth than stature. His frock coat and bowler hat hung on a hook next to a floor length window. The window backed up his desk, admitting a stream of sunlight that silhouetted his massive frame, adding to his already daunting figure. Documents dotted his walls to attest to his authenticity. He wore a patch over his left eye. Bainsfield extended a hand to his visitors as introductions were made and cordialities dispensed.

"Have a seat, fellas," said the lawyer. "Now, what can I do for you?"

Jonas laid out his plan—as far as it had been formulated—stating that he and Jebediah were looking to purchase land for a horse farm up in the Shenandoah Valley region.

Bainsfield looked the two over, wondering if he really wanted to get involved with two such ill-clad characters. Although Jeb and Jonas had made all the purchases they felt necessary for their trip north, they had neglected their attire and still appeared as hard-to-do mountain men. "Hmmm...and you have the means to purchase such a place?"

"I know we look a bit scruffy," said Jeb. "But don' be thinkin' we ain't well-heeled." Jeb produced a note from the Sprucetown bank president attesting to his holdings there and slammed it onto the lawyer's desk. "Think this jes' might convince ya 'bout our means."

Bainsfield eyed the note and whistled softly through his teeth.

"Hey, no offense intended. You've convinced me. I jes' wanted to make sure you weren't wastin' yer time. Now, I don't deal in real estate all that much, but what I can do is put you in touch with the right people up north in Waynesboro. You'll most likely be goin' through there on yer way to the Shenandoah. I know people up that way. Now look up a gent named Tom McIvor, that's the man you want. He deals in real estate and we go way back. You can trust him. N jes' drop my name, boys, 'n you'll git treated right. If you ain't, you tell 'em he'll have Lloyd Bainsfield to answer to."

Jeb had been staring at the eye patch over Bainsfield's left eye. "What's with the patch, mister? War wound 'r somethin'?" There were still many walking wounded from the not too distant war between the states, so Jeb's deduction seemed reasonable.

"Naw, wasn't the war. Doc says I got a weak right eye. I got to wear this patch on the left one to strengthen the durned right one. Supposedly, makes the weak eye work harder. Funny thing though, damned eye seems to wander on me."

Bainsfield jotted down some names on his stationery and passed it to Jeb.

"Oh...and one more thing, boys," said Bainsfield. His uncovered eye strayed inward. He gave that side of his face a slap and the offending eye straightened out. "I hesitate to say anythin', but I'd guess it's been a while since you've had the opportunity to take baths. Maybe when you git back to the hotel, you can work in a bath somehow, before you go meetin' with too many more folks."

"We'll sure look into that," said Jonas, thinking he'd better speak up before Jebediah took exception to Bainsfield's suggestion. "'N we're mighty obligin' to you for the information. If we got any more lawyer business to transact, we'll sure look you up."

"Hell," said Jeb as they were leaving Bainsfields's office, "why take me a bath now, I'll jes' need 'nuther one when we git up north."

Jeb and Jonas had everything set for their trip. They spent one more night in Sprucetown, which did include baths for each of them. The next morning they left the mountain town, under a sky of darkening clouds and into a wind, brisk even for March. Jeb would have preferred to ride the mule, but it was needed to carry supplies, so both he and Jonas were on horseback, Jonas on his recently reaquired mare. Jonas welcomed the familiarity of the mare beneath him, linking him to the life that had so abruptly been taken from him. Soon the travelers were back on a mountain trail, heading north.

"If all goes well," said Jeb, "we should reach our destination 'n 'bout three 'r four days, providin' we don't git blow'd away. I figure it to be some-whar in excess of a hundert miles. Settin' out in early spring like this, we'll be missin' the black flies. 'N ya don' want no part of them abominations. They'd eat the mule 'n then take 'em ole Savage for dessert."

▲ ▲ ▲

Although they were too early for the black fly season, which terror-ized these mountains beginning in mid-May and lasting the summer, Jeb and Jonas were just in time for an early spring rainstorm, which began the afternoon of their first day out. It came suddenly and hard. They were well-outfitted with parkas and hoods, but for Jonas the relentless downpour presented an inauspicious beginning, dimishing the high hopes he'd held at the journey's outset .

They rode in silence finding it next to impossible to converse over the din of the pelting rain. The wizened old man and the young Jonas became ghostly gray figures, leaning into the buffeting wind and driving rain.

Jebediah knew of a passable route northward through the forested mountains that would allow the sure-footed horses to keep to the trail, despite the slippery conditions. Soon the beleaguered travelers entered the Blue Ridge Range, which was not nearly as demanding as the mountain chain they had just left. But even Jeb's familiarity with the trail didn't guarantee success in the blinding storm. At times, their best hope was to prod their horses in the right direction, trusting them to seek the safest path.

The rain continued its attack, accelerating Jonas's doubts, his confidence in his plans for the future dwindling—*what did he know of horse ranching? Would Laura still care for him after his prolonged absence? Or would she have second thoughts, maybe find someone else? How would he ever sort out that mess back in Jericho and clear his name?* Jonas felt lost—far from home and unsure of the future.

▲ ▲ ▲

Toward evening, Savage began acting edgy, casting frequent glances behind him. Jebediah was aware of this and his own instincts told him something was awry. He reined in close to Jonas.

"Jonas, I think we maybe picked us up a tail. I s'spect them two galoots from the saloon is lookin' ta way-lay us. I reckon they think we're totin' some valu'bles, 'n I imagine they's pissed 'bout the way ya mistreated their damn hides."

"I don't know, Jeb, how kin you tell in this hell we're in? I kin hardly hear myself think."

"It ain't what ya hear. It's what ya sense. 'N Savage is spooked. Thet tells me somethhin' fer shore. After bein' up in the mountains fer so many years, I got me a sense fer danger. Now, this next part's gonna be kind of tricky, so pay attenshun. You'n Savage keep on a-goin', I'm gonna wait fer them critters off the trail a bit. When you git up thar 'bout a hundert yards 'r so, git off yer horse like yer restin' 'r somethin'. Now, if ya hear a shot, 'r anythin' unusual, duck fer cover. Got it?"

"Sure, Jeb..." replied Jonas, half humoring the old man. Jonas's mind was still miles away, lost in doubt and despondency.

Nevertheless, he continued on, while Jeb disappeared into the foliage. At the specified distance, Jonas dismounted and sat against a tree, Savage alert at his side.

Jeb found a spot that afforded him a reasonable view of both Jonas's position and the trail behind. He then waited.

Jebediah wasn't caught up in depressing thoughts such as burdened Jonas. Jeb lived for the here and now. If there's a problem, solve it. He made no allowances for self-pity or remorse about his past. Just get the job done and move on to the next challenge. That was Jeb's life. And even now, he was excited about the challenge of dealing with this latest suspected peril.

Presently, Jeb saw the two men from the Red Lady—Mule and Harry—emerging through the rain. They stopped abruptly when they caught sight of Jonas up ahead, resting against a tree. Slowly they dismounted. The shorter of the two, Harry, drew a carbine from the sheath on his horse. He placed the firearm in the crotch of a tree to steady his hand, but, before he could pull the trigger a shot rang out and he slumped to the ground. The larger man, with his pistol drawn, looked toward the source of the shot. He saw Jeb approaching with his rifle leveled at him.

"I don' think I'd try nuthin', big feller. Yer partner's a done con-clu-shun. Now ya kin join 'im, or ya kin drop yer weapon 'n maybe have yerself a long 'n enjoyable life. Yer choice." Mule let his gun slip to the ground. "Okay, now I figger yer partner was the brains of the outfit, assumin' they's half a brain be-twixt the two of ya. So why'nt ya jes' haul yer com-padre back ta town, 'n tell thet red-headed lady thet it's all over, lest ya'd all like ta join yer pard here."

By now, Jonas had joined Jeb. Mule accepted Jeb's offer and headed back down the trail with his late partner in tow.

"Jeb," said Jonas, "Allow me to ne'er doubt you agin."

▲ ▲ ▲

The first night, Jonas and Jeb slept on the trail—grabbing what little shelter was available beneath overhanging trees and brush, any respite from the relentless rain. Sleep was fitful. Next day, Jonas, both tired and sullen, rode on like a zombie, the perpetual downpour only heightening his growing depression.

The following night the beleaguered travelers lucked upon shelter in an old abandoned cabin. It was rundown and leaking profusely, but to Jonas it was a palace. Fortunately, there was a fireplace and enough dry wood scattered around for a small fire.

"Hell of a thing, all this blasted rainin'," said Jebediah. "Really gits a feller down, don' it?"

With the heat of the fire, and hot food, Jonas's spirits had improved. He grinned at Jeb's obvious attempt to brighten his mood. "You said a mouthful there, Jeb."

144

21

Next morning, the rain slackened. By midday, occasional bursts of sun broke through the cloud cover. Footing was still treacherous for the horses, but the trail had become easier to negotiate, as Jeb and Jonas had left behind the higher peaks. Even so, at times they were forced to walk the horses through rain-slickened narrow passages, banked by sheer ridges and escarpments, demanding that they seek alternate routes. Savage generally scampered ahead, with no difficulty. On their third day out they encountered a segment of the trail that had completely washed away.

"Wahl, hell, boy," said Jeb, "seems ta me we're meant ta sit here fer a spell'n take us a rest, b'fore we figger us a way 'round this mess."

"Tell you what, Jeb. Why don't you go ahead and rest up a bit. I think I'll jes' take a look around 'n see if there ain't some way to get around this washout. Keep ole Savage with you for company."

Jonas knew Jeb was a hearty old geezer, but not half what he once was. Jonas wanted to afford him a chance to sit a while and rest up, somewhere other than a horse's back. They'd been in the saddle a long time over the past few days, a long and treacherous time, and old Jeb just wasn't accustomed to long spells on horseback. He could sure use the break.

So Jonas rode off while Jebediah rested. The sun made a rare appearance and the old man took advantage. He found a dry log to rest against, closed his eyes, and dozed off, as the warmth of the sun's rays evoked pleasant dreams.

Jebediah awoke suddenly to Savage's loud barking and growling. There was urgency in the dog's tone. Not twenty feet away from where Jeb sat was the one entity that a body would least wish to encounter on the trail—a grizzly. This grizzly was huge. Jeb guessed it to be over a thousand pounds and towering to eight feet when rearing, as it was now. Jeb feared it to be a rogue bear, fierce and unpredictable. Generally, bears—even large grizzlies don't attack humans unless threatened. But a rogue would kill and eat a man and "spit out his bones 'n pick their teeth with the splinters," Jeb thought to himself, a strange thought, considering the circumstances.

Savage was doing his best to protect Jebediah and keep the great beast at bay—darting in and out and barking and nipping at the bear's feet and hindquarters, narrowly avoiding the rearing beast's deadly claws at each advance. Jeb's rifle was sheathed with his horse, but the horse was nowhere to be seen, undoubtedly having sensed the bear's approach and run off.

Savage continued his evasive attack. His instinct was to protect his master. He knew he was no match for the giant bear and ordinarily would not confront one. But he would die before he would allow the grizzly to harm Jeb—such was his devotion to his long time master.

Jeb watched in horror, knowing he was helpless without the rifle. All he had on him was his hunting knife, "about as useful as a blamed peashooter agin a cannon," thought Jeb. Savage could not avoid the bear's vicious swipes for long and eventually a powerful sweeping blow from the bear's great paw sent the dog flying through the air and over a steep incline, and out of sight.

An agonizing yelp was the last sound Jeb heard from his beloved companion.

Now the beast faced Jebediah and the paltry knife he wielded. Even in fear, Jebediah could not help but admire the great animal, distinguished by a large shoulder hump, all gristle and muscle.

The beast popped its jaws. Jeb knew that meant it was ready to charge. Jeb gained his feet and began to back away, knowing that if he ran, the bear would be on him in no time at all, as Jeb was no match for the speed a grizzly could generate. The bear was too close for him to consider climbing a tree, even if he'd been capable, but Jeb didn't panic. He'd been in similar situations, though not nearly as hopeless as this one.

The bear closed on him and Jeb continued to back away. He had no illusions as to his fate. A few months ago, he would have accepted such a fate, but now he truly wanted to begin the new life he and Jonas had envisioned. He talked to the bear, yelled at it, raised his arms over his head to appear

146

larger, maybe scare the bear off. "Ha, fat chance of thet," he thought. The bear charged. Jebediah fell to ground, face down, and laid perfectly still, covering his neck with his hands—probably futile defenses, but about the only chance he had.

Jeb didn't hear the shots. He didn't hear anything for a while. He felt light-headed, as if he was floating in a trance.

"Jeb...Jeb...are you all right?" he heard from afar. The voice grew nearer, louder. "Jeb. It's okay now. It's me, Jonas."

Jeb opened his eyes, slowly regaining his senses. "What...how did..." He looked around and saw the huge bear laying dead at his feet, scarcely two feet away.

"I shot 'em Jeb. Jes' b'fore he could git to you. I heard the commotion. Guess I got back here jes' in time."

Jeb looked around again. "Savage...is he...did ya see 'im?"

"I only heard him. I'll see if I kin find him." Jonas didn't want to say so, but he'd heard the dog's final heart wrenching yowl and could only fear the worst.

"Here, hep me up," said Jeb. "I saw 'im go over thet bank o'er thar. He might still be alive."

The other side of the embankment was a steep incline that fell off into a narrow ravine. A swift, swollen springtime stream roared through the ravine, some fifty feet below, rimmed with jagged boulders and jutting tree stumps. Both Jonas and Jebediah knew that if the bear's claws hadn't killed the dog, the fall surely would have. They could see no way down into the ravine, no way to attempt to retrieve their lost friend.

"That big ole dog saved me agin. If'n he hadn'a halted thet bahr, 'n put up all thet racket, you'd a never come runnin' back har in time, 'n I'd shore bin a goner."

Jebediah went back to the huge beast. He still held the knife in his hand. He kneeled at the bear's side and sliced the beast open from throat to groin. He inserted a stick into the bear's gut to wedge the pelt aside, exposing the innards. "Let the animals, 'n the black flies, 'n the crows have thar pickin's at this gawd-almighty a-tro-city. Gawd damn his black soul. He ain't one thimble's worth of my Savage."

Jonas had no trouble retrieving Jeb's horse, which he had passed on his way back. Soon he and Jeb were on their way again, but without the great white dog. Their mood was understandably somber. Both men dearly loved that dog. He'd saved their lives numerous times, but the loss was especially intense for Jebediah, who had no other love in his life.

Jonas considered his own behavior for the past few days—his despondency and hopelessness. Jeb had just endured a devastating setback—the loss of his incredible companion, Savage. Jonas approached Jeb.

"Jeb, there's no excuse for the way I've behaved of late. I've been like a whimpering, spoiled school boy. What's happened to you is way beyond anything I've had to endure. I jes' got caught up in myself. There ain't goin' to be no more self-pitying on my part. I'm here for you, Jeb. You've given me all the hope I could ever wish for. We're goin' to be all right, you and me."

"Wahl, Jonas. Time you came around. A man's jes' gotta do the best with what is." Jonas marveled at his partner's self-control, considering the magnitude of his loss.

PART III
The Shenandoah

▲ ▲ ▲

22

The sojourners continued northward through the Blue Ridge Range without further incident. Nearing their destination, Jeb led Jonas out of the mountains and westward down through the Rockfish Gap and into the town of Waynesboro, Virginia, which guarded the southern entrance into the Shenandoah Valley. The Valley lay between the Allegheny Mountains to the west and the Blue Ridge Mountains to the east.

Waynesboro was the largest settlement Jonas had ever seen. There seemed to be two or three of everything—stores, churches, office buildings—and people everywhere.

"Sort-a makes ya wonder, don' it," said Jeb, "whar these folks'er all-a goin' thet seems so gal-danged impo'tant. Anyways, we fer sure got impo'tant business har. We best be gittin' at it."

Jeb sold his mule and bought a buckboard, saying he was "jes' plumb tuckered out a-stradlin' a cayuse, 'n he shore preferred ridin' a buckboard fer comfert 'n enjoyment." They retained Jeb's horse to draw the buckboard with Jonas's mare trailing behind.

"B'fore we get started lookin' for someone on that list we got from Bainsfield, we'd better find us a room here in town, 'n get cleaned up a bit," suggested Jonas. "Make ourselves a little more presentabl' when we approach 'em 'bout our biz'niz. 'N maybe we could find us some better outfits, so's we can look a li'l more respectabl'."

"Ya got a point thar, Jonas. Time I scrapped these ole mountain duds, see'in's we got a whole diff'rent life ahead of us. But I don' see myself as no dandy. Let's see what they got 'n rancher-type at-tire."

▲ ▲ ▲

When Jeb and Jonas entered the Waynesboro Town Center, they little resembled the two scruffy travelers that had weathered the rain and mud of the arduous journey through the mountains. Jonas was clean-shaven, bathed, and decked out in new jeans and a cotton shirt, still with the broad brimmed floppy hat, but a new one. Jeb, too, had bathed and was similarly outfitted, but retained the beard and mustache, though trimmed to reasonable length.

"I say, Jeb. I didn't know you was a human bein'. I thought you was my pet bear."

"Yeh, wahl if I'd a knowd I was partnerin' up with sich a dandy, I'd a brought me along a picnic basket. Haw."

The Town Center was a complex of offices particularly designated for the town officials—the mayor, sheriff, lawyers and such. Jeb had a name—Tom McIvor, from the list provided by Lloyd Bainsfield back in Sprucetown.

While still musing over the myriad of offices, Jeb and Jonas were approached by a diminutive man in business attire.

"You boys looked confused, maybe I could help," he offered. Sparkling teeth showed through a wide grin. His mustache was trimmed to a thin sliver, like it was drawn on with a piece of charcoal.

"We're lookin' fer a man name of Tom McIvor," said Jeb.

"McIvor...hmmm, McIvor. Yeh, I know him. But you boys missed him by a few days. He's out of town for a while, but Tom and me do a lot of business together. In fact, I'm handling his affairs 'till he gets back. I'd be more than happy to help you out. Names' Lincoln. Robert E. Lincoln, attorney at law and real estate agent, all in one. Why don't you boys step into my office?" Lincoln placed a hand each on Jeb and Jonas's shoulders and ushered them into a small office.

He motioned his potential clients to take a seat, while he made a show of tidying his desktop. "Business is booming, but I've always got time to help out when needed. Now, what can I do for you gents?"

"You say yer fillin' in fer thet McIvor fellow," stated Jeb, "'n yer name's Lincoln?"

"That's' right. Robert E. Lincoln at your service."

"Wahl, Lincoln. Spose I was ta tell ya we're lookin' ta buy land fer a horse farm. Think ya could handl' thet?"

"You know...hold on, boys. Something came in recently," said Lincoln, shuffling through some papers. "Ah, here it is. I think this might interest you."

He extended a document to Jeb. "Right here is a mighty fine parcel of land and I can get it for you at a bargain price, the owner being anxious to sell due to a death in the family. The widow, Mrs. Peters, recently lost her husband and doesn't figure she can manage all that land by herself."

Jeb glanced through the one-page document. "Jonas," he said, "I'd like ya ta take a look at this har doc-u-mint. My eyes ain't thet good no more fer readin' up close." Jeb handed Jonas the deed. "Par-ti-u-lar-ly, this har par-a-graf."

Jonas read out loud. "A forty percent down payment is due upon the signin' of this deed. The details for remittance of the balance of the mortgage to be worked out at a later date."

"Do you see the name, Mrs. Peters, in thar anywhar?"

"Nope, jes' the name, Robert E. Lincoln."

"Yep, thet's jes' 'bout how I read it, too."

"A widder you say...er...Mr. Lincoln? 'N at a rock bottom price, ya say?" said Jeb.

"You got it. But I can't hold the property for long, I got other offers. But I like you boys and I'm willing to give you the first crack at it."

"Now, that's mighty con-sid-er-at' of ya, Lincoln." Jeb stood and placed his hands on Lincoln's desk, leaning into him. "I guess ya figger us fer a coupla green-horns, fresh outta the hills, 'n ripe for the pickin'. Wahl, I've seen yer kind b'fore, 'n yer lucky I don't wring yer connivin' neck. If'n my Savage was har, he'd-a sniffed ya out right off for the four-flusher you aire. Jonas, we'll be de-partin' this har scallywag's presence."

"Well, Bob," a voice from a man standing in the doorway. "Looks like you've been found out. Still tryin' to pawn off that worthless piece of scrub land you got stuck with, I see."

"McIvor, this ain't none of your damn business."

"Don't look like it'll be any of your business either, Bob."

"McIvor? Thet'd be Tom McIvor?" asked Jeb.

"Sure is. Were you boys looking for me?"

"Thet we was," said Jeb, "afore we got way-layed by this har Lincoln critter. A feller up in Sprucetown—Bainsfield, b'lieve it was, said you'd be the man ta look up har in Waynesboro."

"Bob, "said McIvor, "you wouldn't mind if I was to take these fellows off your hands, would you? Come on, boys, I'm sure Mr. Lincoln can rustle up other...eager clients."

Jonas was impressed at how Jeb had handled Lincoln. "Seems there's always someone out there tryin' to git the best of a man," he thought. "Lots more to that old man than I figger'd." With Jeb's savy, he now felt more confident in any future business dealings.

McIvor led Jeb and Jonas into his office. "Take a seat, boys, 'n call me Mac, everyone does." McIvor settled in behind a modest desk as Jeb and Jonas sat in two chairs facing him. McIvor was dressed more casually than Lincoln—a white shirt with the sleeves rolled up and a loosened tie. He wore spectacles that constantly slipped down his nose, requiring that he keep adjusting them. A gray waistcoat hung on a coat tree in a corner of his small office.

"So, Lloyd sent you to me, eh? Now I'm thinkin' that's high commendation. And just what is it I can do for you boys?"

Jebediah and Jonas took turns explaining to Mac just what they had in mind. Tom McIvor listened to their proposal behind a tent made with his fingers. After they finished, he put the tent away and leaned over his desktop. "That's a pretty ambitious undertaking you've got in mind, but I think I can help you out. But first, I've got to know just how much money you're figuring on putting up. Horse farms don't come cheap."

Jeb grinned. "Hell, boy. I kin draw me up a bank draft har in town thet'll pop yer eyes out." For authentication and punctuation, Jeb showed McIvor a promissory note from the bank in Sprucetown denoting his worth.

Mac smiled. "Well, now. I can't see where money will be a problem," his glasses slipping down his nose a fraction. "Boys, what say we get out of this stuffy office. We can best settle our business over a few brewskies 'n I know just the place." He slipped into his waistcoat and led the "boys" out of the office and up the street to Nick's Place, his favorite whistle stop.

▲ ▲ ▲

McIvor was a short man, with a protruding belly and a bulbous ruddy nose that bespoke of his propensity for drink. Most everything he said was upbeat, like there was a joke in there somewhere. Jeb took to him immediately, as they shared drinks at Nick's and sorted things out.

"Now, there is a man, name of John Cooper," Mac began. "He's got a lot of land just north of here, smack dab in the most beautiful country you ever laid eyes on, up in the Shenandoah Valley. I estimate he's got more land than he kin ever use. I'm pretty sure he'll part with a parcel of it. My suggestion is that we go 'n see ole John about just that very thing. He'll quote you a fair price. John's a good man 'n ain't no way he'd take advantage of you."

The next day, Jeb, Jonas, and McIvor set off by buckboard for the Cooper Ranch, about ten miles out of Waynesboro. They were fortunate to catch John Cooper at a convenient time.

"Howdy Mac, who's yer friends here?" John Cooper greeted the arrivals in front of a spacious ranch house.

"John, these're a couple of fellows came to see me in town. Said there're looking to start 'em a horse farm. I told them you might have some acreage you'd be willing to part with."

"Well, climb down offa that buckboard'n come on inside. Let's see what we can figger out."

The Cooper Ranch was sizable. Corrals teeming with horse stock engulfed the large farmhouse. The horses were beautiful and spirited and of a wide variety. As far as the eye could see, flatlands and rolling hills stretched off into the distance. Ranch hands scurried about, tending their various duties. Wonder swelled up in Jonas's chest—the beauty of it all, the openness—the enthusiasm of the ranch hands, the camaraderie, so unlike the dismal conditions of miners back home.

They entered the home of John Cooper, crossing a wrap-around covered porch populated with ample wicker chairs and tables. The living room was huge with light streaming from large windows that afforded a spectacular view of the vast Cooper property and the mountains beyond. Cooper invited the three men to join him at a large table surrounded by elegant high-backed chairs.

"Charly," signaled the host. "Come on in here, gal. We got some company." Charly Cooper appeared. "'N bring in some coffee if you would, we got some business to discuss, I expect."

Moments later Charly reappeared with a tray containing a coffee pot and five cups. She poured coffee for the four men and one for herself. She then sat down next to Jonas as if her inclusion was understood.

"This is my daughter, Charly. She's gittin' a break from her schoolin' down in Richmond. Charly, meet Jonas and Jeb. I think you remember Mac, here. Guys, anything you got to say to me, you can say in front of my daughter. So, let's proceed. What's on yer minds?"

At this point Jeb took over the conversation. Charly was glancing rather interestedly at Jonas.

"Mr. Cooper," Jeb began. "We're lookin' fer land. Mac here, he done rec'mended ya to us. Now Jonas, he come up from Jericho way. We met up in the mountains 'n part'ner'd up. 'N Mac says ya might be a good one ta contact concernin' startin' us up a horse ranch."

"Jericho?" said Charly. "You mean Jericho, West Virginia?" She gave Jonas a long look. "Yer from Jericho? You wouldn't happen to know Laura Becker, would you?"

Jonas straightened. "Laura...you know Laura?"

"Sure do, I met her at the Academy, the Richmond Academy for Girls. We were great friends...wait...Jonas? You can't be...no, that can't be possible. Are you the same Jonas that saved her when her horse fell, 'n had all that trouble at that dance, and...no way, you can't be Laura's Jonas, it's too incredible."

"I...I..."

"Well, hot damn!" Charly exclaimed. "Ev'ry gal at that Academy's half in love with you, and Laura sure is. You and Laura's story was the talk of the whole school."

Jonas was stunned, his eyes glazed over and his tongue was a knot. "You...you know my Laura, 'n she still cares for me after all that's happened...all this time?"

"Jonas...Laura's Jonas. I can't hardly believe it. That you'd show up here. Laura is the dearest, most wonderful friend I ever had 'n yes, she dearly cares for you. 'N it don't matter how much time's passed, or what yer thinkin' might've swayed her against you. She ain't no society gal, nor will she ever be one. Ha, it's soooo humorous. They kicked her out of the Academy because she was influencing the girls to be more like her, rather than 'purfect young ladies." At this point Charly became so overwhelmed with Jonas's presence that she wrapped her arms around him and gave him a warm hug. "Oh, she's going to be so happy to know yer safe."

"Well, I'll be damned," said John Cooper. "Don' that beat all."

23

Charly dismissed herself, making Jonas promise to see her before he left. Jonas found it difficult to concentrate as the discussions proceeded. At one point, Jeb prodded him with an elbow, "What say we git this biz'niz taken care of. Ya kin think 'bout yer girlie friend later," he said with a wink.

"Sorry," said Jonas, "I guess my mind was somewhere else."

"Well, Jonas," said Cooper. "From what I know about Laura, I can understand why yer mind's wanderin'. Now, getting' back to the business of sellin' you boys some land, jes' what makes you think you'd be any good at raising horses? I know Mac wouldn't bring you all the way out here if he didn't think you had possibilities, but there's a lot more to a horse farm than you might expect."

Jonas answered. "All I can say is I been 'round horses all my life. We had a small place, 'n a few horses at one time. Lately, though, times have bin a bit rough 'n the farm ain't been too productive. So we were down to one horse..."

"Damn, boy. I don't mean no plow horses. They ain't nuthin' to care for compared to the fine animals we got 'round here, no disrespect intended. But, it takes some know how to raise horses for ridin', 'n racin', 'n such. How 'bout you Jeb, you got any experience with horses?"

"Nope, I ain't. Jes' mules. Kaint see thar's much diff'rence though. They both got four legs, 'n will bite the hell out of ya if'n ya ain't keerful."

157

Cooper burst out laughing. "I like you fellers. At least yer honest. What say, Mac, think they might be able to make a go of it?"

"Like you say, I wouldn't have brought them all the way out here if I didn't think so."

Cooper gave Jebediah and Jonas a final scrutiny. "Well, I don't see why we shouldn't be able to come up with some sort of a deal. But it sure looks like you'll be needin' some help. I got a coupla good men I can loan you, to help you get started, sorta teach you the ropes. Now, Jonas, Laura's been up here to the ranch, 'n I know her to be a fine gal. 'N she sure knows her horses. If she's chose you for her man, you got to be all right. 'N this ole whippersnapper of a pard of yours, I got a feelin' it's gonna be real fun havin' him for a neighbor."

"What?" interrupted Jonas. "Laura was here at yer ranch?"

"Sure was," said Cooper. "You missed her by about a week. But my daughter'd be the one to tell you about all that. Right now, let's just get our business settled."

"But, she was here...?"

"Pard," said Jeb, laying a hand on Jonas's shoulder. "Like the man says, ya kin go o'er all thet with his daughter. Now, stay with us on this har ranch biz'niz. Go ahead, Cooper, what was ya sayin'?"

"Well, my thinkin' is," said Cooper, "I'll have Mac get the papers drawn up tomorrow in Waynes'bro 'n we'll get you boys set up. First, though, I suggest we take a ride out 'n take a look at the land I got in mind. We'll take my buckboard. It'll seat four a bit more comfortably."

"Make that three," said Mac. "I think I'll jus' sit 'n relax on your porch for a spell." With that, he produced a small flask from inside his coat jacket, unscrewed its top, and poured a generous amount of liquid into his coffee. "If I nod off, give me a shake when you get back. I got no doubt these fellers will be in the buying mood when they see what you've got to offer."

▲ ▲ ▲

The land John Cooper had in mind for Jeb and Jonas lay between the Cooper Ranch and Waynesboro, comprising about two-hundred acres, its southernmost boundary not more than a couple of miles from town. As they rode out, Jeb and Jonas were greeted by rolling hills surrounding a beautiful valley with a bright stream running through. The land was mostly open, but mountain ash, oak, chestnut, and various evergreens added just the right amount of tree cover to keep the landscape picturesque. Jonas thought he had never seen a lovelier sight. And Jeb proclaimed that he felt "a feller could be right happy here, yep, right happy".

Cooper went on to explain that the stream had its beginnings up in the mountains, being spring fed and would never run dry. "You'll have all the fresh water you could ever need 'n it wouldn't be no trouble to dam the stream up 'n make a pond. The horse stock could water there, 'n you could have it brimmin' with fish in no time. When you and Laura's young'uns come along," Cooper said with a wink, "they're gonna jes' love a pond for fishin' and swimmin'." Cooper explained that two-hundred acres would give them a pretty sizable spread and if they ever needed more, he'd be glad to accommodate them.

"I jes' wanted to give you gents a look-see," said Cooper. "From the looks on yer faces, I guess you approve, sure enough."

Jonas more than approved. He couldn't believe he was looking at a vast expanse of storybook land destined to be his own. He sensed the concept was more than he could handle just now, suspecting the full impact of this day would catch up to him later. *I'll never sleep tonight*, he thought. *Between this, 'n the news of Laura.*

Arriving back at the Cooper Ranch, Jeb and Jonas begged off a dinner invite, wanting to be back in Waynesboro before dark.

But before Jonas left, he sought out Charly, as promised. He hoped his eagerness wouldn't be obvious.

"Oh, Jonas. She's such a wonderful girl. You two will make a great couple," said Charly.

"Charly, Laura was here? When? How long ago? How did she look?"

"Hey, mister. One question at a time." She laughed. "You ain't anxious or nuthin' are you? Yep, she was here not a week ago, soon's the weather was fit for travelin'. She spent four wonderful days here. 'N how she loved the horses. She jes' couldn't git enough of them. I think she rode everything with four legs."

"So I jes' missed her. Damn. I sure could've used seein' her, jes' to be sure she still...thought about me. It's hard to believe she'd really want me, after I kilt thet fella."

"What? Jonas, you didn't kill nobody. Laura said that man that got stabbed recovered jis' fine."

"He didn't die? But all that blood, 'n he weren't movin' at all." Jonas was puzzled. "Then I ain't no murder'r. I can't believe it. This is great news. More great news. But it still don't git me off the hook. They'll still figger I done the stabbin'...thet it was my knife. No way I'm gonna be welcome back in Jericho."

"Well, Laura knows it wasn't your fault. She tole me so. And she thinks that Dirk fella that keeps houndin' her had somethin' to do with settin' up that confrontation. And then, Dirk ups and fires the one that got stabbed. Jake, I think he was called. She said how Jake jes' keeps to himself most the time now, disturbed 'bout something''n drinkin' a whole lot. Maybe Jake's the one you oughta see. Maybe he can help clear things up."

"Charly, you jes' might be right about that. We'll sure have to talk some more 'bout all this."

"Well, I'll be headin' back to Richmond in a coupla days. I'll be schoolin' on through the summer, 'n finishin' up in the fall. I could send Laura a letter, 'n tell her all about what happened here, 'n that you're all right."

"No...please. I don't want her to know about me yet. Not till I git things here all wrapped up 'n I've got somethin' to offer her. 'N even then, not till I can figger a way to set things right back home. I sure don' want Laura endin' up with someone everyone thinks is a no account. She's so well thought of, 'n I won't be respons'ble for spoilin' what people think of her. So please, don't say nuthin' to her about me."

"Okay, Jonas. I'll respect yer wishes. But I think yer bein' foolish. That gal loves you and she deserves to know you're okay. But I'll do as you ask." Charly smiled at Jonas. She couldn't have been more impressed with Laura's young man from West Virginia.

24

John Cooper met with Jonas, Jebediah, and the real estate agent, Tom McIvor, the next morning in Waynesboro. The papers were drawn up to legalize the sale of two-hundred acres of Cooper land to the new co-owners, Jonas McNabb and Jebediah Hart. The signing put a lump in Jonas's throat. This was the beginning of a plan that would ultimately bring him and Laura together, and hopefully reunite him with his father and brother. It had always been his intention that his father and Benji would join him in his horse farm venture, and more particularly, get them away from the mines.

"Well, Jeb, you sure got the money to get the job done," Cooper said, "'n Jonas, you got a heap'a work and figgerin' ahead of you. You can consult with me anytime you feel the need. But, basically, here's how yer money will be spent. You're gonna need a house, barn, and stables of course, 'n a well. Figure on a lotta fencin', 'n a bunkhouse for all the crew yer gonna need to bring in to construct all that. Later, the bunkhouse will be quarters for any hired hands you'll be needin' for the ranch. Mac can help you find a crew and set you up with a contractor. I think most of the supplies you'll be requirin' will be available in Waynesb'ro. Anythin' else you kin send for. Maybe by late summer you'll be ready to bring in yer horse stock, which I can sure help you with. 'N I can recommend a few good ranch hands."

"Really obliged to you, Mr. Cooper," said Jonas, shaking his hand. "This here dream's seemin' more real ev'ry minute."

"You boys'll be jes' fine. Welp, gotta be takin' off, but you know where I am if you need anything".

"Boys, what say we go see a contractor friend of mine 'n get this whole shebang under way," said McIvor.

By buckboard it would take Jeb and Jonas about a half hour to travel from Waynesboro to the "J&J Ranch"—a name they settled upon for their horse ranch. But even a half hour was more time than Jonas wished to be away from his new land. He convinced Jeb they should camp out on the property until the bunkhouse was completed. Then they would take up residence in the bunkhouse with the construction crew until the ranch house was ready for occupancy.

"Don' see why we gotta be sleepin' on the hard ground when we got us pur-fect-ly good soft beds back in town," said Jeb, contrary as usual.

▲ ▲ ▲

McIvor's contractor proved to be more than capable in procuring all the necessary materials, as well as the work crew. He was a giant of a man, known as "Big Ben" Gables, but might well have been called "No Nonsense" Gables. He was as demanding of his men as he was of himself—driven, stern and with zero tolerance for incompetence. Big Ben was once known as "Big Black Ben", but he would not have himself labeled as black, and many a man had paid the price by designating him as such. He was to be Big Ben, equal to any man, white or black—an assertion few wished to dispute.

Along with Ben and his crew came the cook, known only as "Gerty". No one asked her last name, as she discouraged all inquiries of a personal nature. She was as elusive as Big Ben was intimidating. Her accent was deeply Scottish and difficult to understand. Her auburn hair was always in a bun, her attire of the sloppy sort—loose pants tied at the waist with rope, a baggy shirt buttoned to the neck. It was evident that she enjoyed her own cooking as ample breasts sagged onto a belly that poured over her rope belt.

Her presence particularly annoyed Jeb, whose intention was to do the cooking himself. Her mess was set up out of the back of a covered cook-wagon, later to be transferred to the bunkhouse when it was completed. Gerty now labored over a large pot set on a hot cook-stove. Jeb approached her, never to be daunted by any personage.

"Now, see har," he said. "I aims ta do the cookin' around har. I own a half-part in this har ranch, 'n I'm tellin' ya ta pack up yer gear and pull out."

Gerty glared at the old man. She walked around the cook-stove and waved a large wooden spoon in his face. "Ye git. Gerty is cook. You'll not be spoiling my stew or anything else." She smacked Jeb on the shoulder with the spoon. "Git, I say."

"Better do as she says, old timer." Big Ben had strolled into the confrontation. "I know this woman. Likely as not she be pourin' that pot of stew over yer head if you don't do like she says."

"Dag-nab-it," said Jeb as he turned and walked away, muttering something about "wimmins".

▲ ▲ ▲

First, the well was dug, then a windmill was implemented to distribute water to pumps and to wherever else it would be needed—the bunkhouse, the stables, the barn, and the main house. The fresh stream was damed up to form a pond which would provide abundant water for the horse stock. Then construction began on the bunkhouse, complete with cooking facilities to house and feed the workmen. Wagonloads of lumber arrived to the ranch site, along with hardware, roofing material, window glass, door knobs and latches, bedding, tables, chairs, a pot bellied stove...the list went on and on.

As contractor for the J&J Ranch, Big Ben towered over his workers and utilized his great size to keep them in line. He could not abide slackers, and anyone not carrying their load was summarily sent packing. There were plenty of eager replacements in Waynesboro. Consequently, he wasn't particularly well liked by his men. But, to his credit, Big Ben got more out of his men than could rightly be expected and the work proceeded smoothly and on schedule.

Jeb, in particular, had a problem with Big Ben. Having been on his own for so many years, Jeb was not inclined to be ordered about, which Big Ben had a tendency to do, even though Jeb was Ben's employer. Jeb hadn't yet figured where he wanted to fit into all this construction business so he just sat around most of the time. Big Ben was not amenable to such frivolities and said so, to Jeb's face. The big man stood before Jeb, who'd taken up lounging in a rocker in front of the nearly completed bunkhouse. Ben had already stated his objection to Jeb's lack of contributions to the work effort. Jeb ceased his rocking and stood.

"I like ya Big Ben," stated Jeb. "I admire the way ya git things done, but ya gotta loosen up a bit. Now, I ain't in-ta orderin' ya around, ev'n though it's my right, but what say we go 'round the corner har. I'd like ta in-ter-duce ya to a few friends of mine."

Jeb led Big Ben to a buckboard around the side of the bunkhouse. From under a tarp, Jeb extracted a jug of his fine "mountain-shine" and offered it to Big Ben.

"Ain't ne'er seen a man more'n need of some of this har med'cin then you, Big Ben."

The workers saw little of Big Ben for the rest of the afternoon and for parts of the days that lay ahead. The work didn't suffer all that much and the workers noticed a more amicable affiliation between their boss and ole Jeb, and a more relaxed attitude overall.

▲ ▲ ▲

Jeb was impressed at how well the work was progressing. Workers "scurryin' 'bout," like bees on a honeycomb. He felt no guilt about his lack of participation in the actual labor—no need to impress anyone or to 'splain hisself, if he didn't feel like it. He figured he was entitled to just sit back and take it easy, especially now that Gerty had chased him from the cook tent. Anyone that don' like it, be hanged, was his stance.

No one objected. Not even Big Ben of late. Jeb was a colorful character and his outlandish tales kept the crew in stitches. Jeb wasn't expected to be digging holes or hauling around heavy timbers in the hot sun. He did volunteer to pound a few nails, but, "...only if'n I kin keep my feet planted on the ground. Don' take to no heights, fella could git himself hurt...haw."

And then there were Jeb's carvings, those he carted out from his mountain home, and those he continued to work on in his ample spare time. The carvings were an instant hit with the workers. It seemed each of the crew boasted one of Jeb's sculptures, proudly displayed on shelves over their bunks. Even Gerty accepted one of Jeb's works, a crowing rooster, and was so pleased with it that at times she allowed Jeb to sample her soups, but never to assist in their making. Jeb asked for no recompense for his carvings, being satisfied that "now he wouldn't have ta be luggin' 'em around ev'rywhar he went". Each new sculpture was heavily vied for, but nowhere among his work, new or old, was to be found a bear, which Jeb refused to retain or carve due to the loss of Savage.

Word of Jeb's art reached Wayneboro, and he was approached by shop owners and collectors offering substantial money for his carvings. Jeb refused all such offers saying that he appreciated that they liked his work but he sought no profit from them. "Fer one thing, I don' need the money, 'n fer anuther, I don' keer fer the fuss," he declared.

Regardless, a number of Jeb's sculptures eventually showed up in the Waynesboro Museum and in various shops.

One sweltering afternoon, with the sun radiating a rare early season heat, Jeb sat by the well with a scoop of cool refreshing well water and surveyed his surroundings. "Ne'er thought I'd be a part of anythin' like this," he thought. "Life kin sure git strange on ya." His one regret was that his beloved dog Savage wasn't here to enjoy it with him.

Jeb took another sip of well water and poured the remaining liquid over his head. Then his mind wandered as he stared off toward the hills and far mountains, remembering times past, when he and Savage...his eyes registered a lone distant moving speck coming out of the hills. His mind was still focused on past memories and was slow to identify the approaching object. Little by little, awareness kicked in. As the object drew nearer, Jeb began to make out certain features. He rose to his feet, shading his eyes from the sun, squinting for better focus. He began to walk forward, slowly at first, then faster.

Then he was running, tears forming in his eyes.

"Jonas...JONAS!" Jeb shouted. "Look, it's Savage!" Soon Jeb was clutching the dog in a hard embrace. "Oh dog...dog...I thought shore ya was a goner." By now, Jonas had joined in the celebration, hugging Savage, and Jebediah. The dog was thin and tired looking. A wicked scar ran down the left side of his face. One ear was gone and a badly healed scar marred the left side of his body. He walked with a limp. But to Jeb he couldn't have been more beautiful.

"Damn, boy. I sure wish ya could talk," said Jeb. "What ya musta gone through. Wahl, we'll gitcha patched up proper, 'n ya'll be yer old self agin'."

"'N welcome to yer new home, boy," added Jonas. "I think yer sure gonna like it here."

The deep heart-felt ache that Jebediah had endured since he'd thought he'd lost his beloved dog was now lifted.

▲ ▲ ▲

John Cooper sent over the two men he promised, Denis "Frenchie" Martin and Red Phillips, both of whom would prove invaluable with the organizing and overseeing of the construction of the J&J Ranch, without interfering with Big Ben, of course.

The construction of the J&J progressed smoothly, and Jonas and Red became good friends. Red was three years Jonas's senior and had been around horses since he was old enough to straddle one. He'd been in Cooper's employ since he was sixteen and knew just about everything there was to know about running a horse ranch and hoped to eventually become John Cooper's foreman.

Red was aptly named. He sported a crop of thick, wiry hair and a full mustache and beard, all bright reddish orange. And Jonas felt a particular affinity for Phillips, as Red professed a fondness for Charly, whom Jonas now knew to be a close friend to his Laura.

Red was patient with Jonas, exposing him to all the various aspects of horse farming and Jonas was a willing and apt student, anxious to learn every little thing Red threw his way. Initially, Jonas had become involved in this venture because of Laura, knowing of her love for horses. But as the spread developed, he became totally immersed in the project and knew it was something he also dearly wanted for himself. This land was now owned by him and Jebediah—their land, their farm—two hundred acres—beyond his wildest dreams.

The bunkhouse was now standing. Jeb and Jonas abandoned the "hard ground" and took up residence in the bunkhouse with the workers. Jonas had no qualms with this. He enjoyed hearing the worker's stories and sharing in the camaraderie. From them he learned much about life in the Shenandoah. And they accepted him. To them, he was just one of the boys, *who talked funny*. And they particularly loved Jeb, the old wizened mountain man with stories, both true and tall that shook the imagination, *and he talked even funnier*. And who couldn't admire Savage, the huge wolf-dog? Jeb's stories about the great dog attained legendary status, his battle scars but adding to his stature. Even Big Ben warmed to the big dog, whose penetrating red eyes made a man think in terms of worth and truth.

And, of course, there was "Jeb's brew." At Jeb's insistence, a small addition was added to the bunkhouse, which housed his "shine" equipment. Soon, jugs of corn liquor lined the walls. "'N someday boys," asserted Jeb, "I'll be expandin' my expertise, 'n providin' y'all with my newest concoction—genuinely home brewed 'n bottl'd Virginny berb'n, matured in genuine oak barrels, set afire 'n blowed out. Now thet's the secret, the firin' her up fer jes' the right length of time. 'Course it takes at least a coupla yaars of maturin', but they jes' ain't nothin' like it. Smooth as a girlie's cheek."

Not that the workers became a drunken lot. They had too much admiration for Jeb and Jonas, plus a fear of Big Ben to allow Jeb's brew to interfere with their duties. And although Big Ben had softened, he still saw to it that his crew submitted a proper day's work.

By late summer, the stables, corrals, and barn were well underway. The ranch house was now completed and Jonas and Jeb were able to move in. Jonas was in awe of the house. It was not a mansion by any means, but to Jonas it was huge, many times the size of his farmhouse back home. It was a two-story structure, the first floor consisting of a living room, a separate dining room, a large kitchen, a small office area, and a large room in the back, which would be Jeb's private domain. Upstairs were four bedrooms. Jonas felt that Laura would be pleased with this house and he longed for the day they would call it their home. Laura was never far from Jonas's thoughts as all his plans revolved around her.

The house boasted a large front porch with a roof to keep the sun and rain off. This was Jeb's pride and joy—a front porch, for, as he put it…"jes' a-sittin' and rockin' 'n lookin' at the hills 'n far off mountains, with Savage beside me, 'n mebbe a spot a berb'n, if'n it's ev'r ready."

Though structurally completed, the house was still bare bones in regard to furnishings. Red suggested that Charly help pick out a few things for the place once she got home from school. To Jonas that made sense. It would certainly be more attractive to Laura were there a woman's touch involved. Yep, all thoughts led back to Laura.

Now they could turn their attention to the stables—the very heart of the horse ranch. Red explained that the stables needed special attention. Keeping horses happy and healthy was what horse farming was all about. The plans for the stables needed many considerations; for instance: the size of each stall, what material was needed for flooring, how to ensure the correct drainage, and that the proper ventilation be assured. How the horses were to be utilized was another matter—whether they were meant for riding, racing, show, breeding—whatever. Red Phillips didn't burden Jonas with excessive details at this point, knowing that Jonas's real education would begin when the horses were actually brought in. There was just too much to be learned for Jonas to digest it all at once. Red and Jonas maintained a constant dialog concerning all these matters.

They stood in the now completed stable. "Red," said Jonas. "You're still a young man, how 'n hell d'you know so much 'bout everythin' to do with horses?"

"Guess it comes natural. It's all I ev'r bin interested in. 'N I had a good teacher in John Cooper. You got a natural inclination for it too, Jonas. Yer goin' to be able to handle things jes' fine."

Jeb wandered into the stables with Savage, just as Red was leaving. Jonas was sitting before a stall, a look of concern on his face. Jeb sat down beside him.

"Lad, everythin's goin' jes' splen-did, so what's troublin' ya?"

Savage looked up at Jonas as if also seeking an answer to Jeb's query. Jonas hesitated, thought a bit. "Yeh, Jeb, somethin' is botherin' me. It jes' don' seem right, you doin' all the financin' for our ranch. I ain't got no way to pay you back at all. I jes' kaint see where I'd be deservin' all this good fortune. I guess I jes' feel guilty 'bout it. That's 'bout the whole of it."

"Deservin' ya say? Who in hell is deservin' of anythin' in this har cock-a-min-y world, be it good fortune 'r bad. Ya think I deserved ta hit thet rich vein? I shore ain't never done nuthin' so good as ta deserve thet. 'N look at the other side of things. You think them dirt-poor miners of yers deserve the kinda life they got? Hell, they don't ev'n got a pot ta tinkle in. So don't tell me 'bout deservin', boy. 'N if we all got what we deserved, most of us'd be smold'rin' in a pit somewhar."

Jeb slowly shook his head and went on, "Tar-na-shun, boy. I thought we had all thet sorted out, 'n now ya come back at me 'bout deservin'. Now listen har. I'm an old man, 'n a tired one at thet. I already had most of my livin' 'n now I got no one 'cept you 'n ole Savage har. 'N look what ya done fer me...saved my worthless hide sev'ral times over, you'n Savage. Who done looked after me all last winter? Ya think I could've cut all thet firewood by m'self? More'n likely I'd-a froze. Who done all the huntin', 'n most of the cookin'...if ya kin call it that? It's me that's obligin' ta you, Jonas."

Jeb paused and scratched at his wiry chin growth.

168

"Ain't up to us ta determine who deserves what, or who don'. We jes' take things as they come along 'n try ta make the best of it. We got us a deal, boy, 'n I'm standin' by it. 'N it's the last I wanna hear on the subject. Understood?"

"Yeh, I guess. Jeb, yer really somethin'." He kissed the old man on the top of his head.

"Git the hell outta har, what're ya, strange 'r somethin'?"

Jonas decided to take a ride, feeling he needed to ponder things a bit. Maybe he could find a place to sit and think, like he used to do back home under the chestnut tree beside the small creek. But he wasn't to be alone as Savage was soon trotting along by his side.

"Okay, ole boy. It'll be good to have you along."

Jonas chose a spot that seemed likely, except that it was a large sprawling oak, rather than a chestnut tree. He dismounted and gained a comfortable position under the oak. Savage hunkered down beside him. Jonas rolled a smoke, lit up, and began to relax.

"There's a powerful lot's happened to me, Savage. I'm not really sure I kin figger it all out."

Jonas thought about how bad fortune had led to good fortune, and how the two fortunes, good and bad, seemed to take turns coming his way. He concluded that at this time the good far outweighed the bad; the only things missing were his family, and Laura, of course. Jonas knew his father and Benji would be more than happy to be a part of his new life, he only wished he were so confident about Laura.

"But I'll tell you, dog, there's got to be a reason for all this happenin'. 'N if I can't take advantage of it, there's gotta be somethin' lackin' in me." Jonas mused over the twists and turns his life had taken of late as Savage lay content by his side, his head in Jonas's lap, his red eyes beaming with understanding.

25

Laura, recently back from her difficult time in Richmond was now finding life around the Becker Estate equally trying. She still rode often and took good care of her father's riding stock. Her father allowed her much more latitude in her visits to town as she continued her good-will visits to the miners' families, and she still urged her father to improve the miner's living conditions, supplications that mostly fell on deaf ears.

The problem was Dirk Fisher.

With her father's blessing, he had become much more attentive to her. Laura tried to discourage him as best she could but Dirk was relentless, feeling that marriage to Laura could mean the Becker Empire would one day be his. Laura still believed that Dirk was behind the trouble that drove Jonas away. It was a quandary for Laura. If she rejected Dirk, her father might discern that she still hoped for Jonas's return, and she might again be sent away. So she had to seem somewhat interested in Dirk, while still fending off his advances.

This was not easy as Dirk's persistence grew. At the dances he would try to hold her much tighter than she wished to be held, even attempting a kiss at times. Laura feared he might at some point tire of her rejections and force himself on her. But then, Dirk would lose her father's trust should that happen—although her father had stated that, "Sometimes, gal, I wish that boy would jes' sweep you up 'n carry you off, git all this dilly-dallying over with."

▲ ▲ ▲

September. *Almost a year since Laura had last seen Jonas.* She thought about that as she awaited her good friend Charly Cooper at the Jericho train station. Charly was done with the Academy and told Laura in a letter that she was anxious to see if those "West Virginny hill'billies" were all like

Laura. How good it would be to see Charly again. Her stay in Jericho would be brief—just a few days—then she and Laura would journey to Charly's home, the ranch in the Shenandoah Valley. Laura still dreamed about her first visit there—all the wonderful horses, the beautiful countryside.

Charly's train pulled into the station and soon she and Laura were embracing and fighting back the tears.

"Sure is good to be done with the Richmond Academy for Snooty Girls," said Charly, with a laugh. "Not that it made much of a diff'rence in this ole country gal."

So Charly got her much anticipated trip to Jericho, West Virginia and got to see firsthand all the country folks of Laura's stories. "Gawd-a-mighty, they all talk jes' like you do, Laura."

Laura introduced Charly to Jonas's dad on one of her rare trips to the McNabb ranch. She dared not go often, fearing that her father might learn of it and suspect that she still had feelings for Jonas. Benji, as usual, dominated most of Laura's time.

Charly took the opportunity to take Caleb aside. She told him about her meeting Jonas at her ranch up in the Shenandoah Valley, but asked him not to mention anything about it to Laura, or to Benji, who she feared might blurt it out to Laura.

Caleb felt relief that his son was all right. He never really doubted Jonas would survive his ordeal, but...

"The Shenandoah? Howev'r did he end up there?" said Caleb. "Ain't heard nothin' from him for the past year."

"Soon, Jonas will be able to tell you everythin'", said Charly. "I want it to be his news. But I'll tell you this, you and Benji ain't gonna believe it all. Jonas is one of the finest young men I've ever met, 'n believe me, he'll be able to set everythin' right."

Charly dearly wanted to tell Caleb more. She wanted to see the delight in his face as he learned of the J&J Ranch and of his son's wedding plans with Laura. The news was busting to come out, but she refrained.

As much as Charly admired the Jericho countryside and the country folks, she was saddened by the living conditions of the miner's families, so different from her ranch-style life in the Shenandoah Valley. During her stay at the Becker Estate, she dared not say much to Laura's dad, her host, but wondered why he would allow such conditions to exist when he surely had the means to improve them.

26

After a long train ride from Jericho to Waynesboro, and an ensuing hour and a half buggy ride, Laura and Charly arrived at the Cooper Ranch, with Saca in tow. Charly insisted that Laura bring Sacagawea with them, anxious for her father to see the magnificent Appaloosa mare.

The next morning, as the last vestiges of summer hung in the air, lazy and timeless, heedless of the approaching season of change, Charly urged Laura to ride south and check out the new neighbors.

"Dad sold off some land to a coupla fellas, 'n I'll tell you, the old guy's a hoot. You'll love him. 'N there's a younger fella, kinda shy and polite, not much your type," Charly said, holding back a smile.

Laura sure didn't need much urging to go out riding, but did wonder about Charly sending her off alone to visit the neighbors. But, no matter, she loved the grassy pasturelands and the rolling hills of this beautiful Shenandoah Valley countryside,with the mountains looming in the distance. This day she chose to ride the beautiful and spirited Paint, Chestnut, Charly's horse. Saca was being fussed over by Charly's father and the ranch hands.

Laura began a leisurely ride to the neighboring ranch, in no particular hurry. The beauty of the countryside was captivating; no ride anywhere had thrilled her more. She envisioned what it would be like to live here, engulfed by the grasslands and hills and streams, the far off mountains, and particularly, living a life centered on horses. Jonas would love it here, she thought. How perfect that would be. Jonas was never far from her thoughts.

Eventually, eclipsing a hilltop, Laura spotted the J&J Ranch, with the modest two-story house, the barn, the stables, and the beginnings of the fencing for the corrals and surrounding pastureland. As she rode up to the house, she noticed a rather old man and a huge white dog on the porch.

"Well, howdy, old feller. Is that dog safe, or should I hightail it outta here?"

"Well, ma'am, this here dog is a perceptive kinda critter, 'n he ain't 'bout ta drive off no ones as purty as you. 'N I ain't as old as ya might think," he said, with a wink.

Laura laughed. "Well then, howdy, *mister*," said Laura dismounting. "I'm Laura Becker. I'm staying with Charly Cooper over yonder at the Cooper Ranch for a spell. She suggested I ride over here for a visit, 'n I'm glad to make yer acquaintance." She offered her hand, which Jeb took, with a huge grin.

"Laura Becker, ya say? Whar you hail from, Laura Becker?"

"I'm from down Jericho way, West Virginia," Laura said proudly. "My dad owns the Becker Mining Company," she said, not quite so proudly.

"Well, ain't that jes' the dog-gon-dist thang," said Jebediah, still grinning. "Now you jes' wait here whilst I summons my pard. Hey, young fella," Jeb shouted to the house. "Come on out har. Someone ya jes'might wanna meet."

Presently, a man backed out of the front door, holding a shirt he was about to slip over his bare top. He turned slowly. "So who is...?" Then he saw Laura and stopped in his tracks. Laura's hands went to her face in disbelief.

"Jonas...?" she stammered.

"Laura...is it you? How...?"

"Well, ya damn fools," interjected Jebediah. "Course it's you, 'n it's you, too. Now git yerselfs together thar, 'n spare an old man any more heart-jerkin'," he said, dabbing at his eyes with his hanky. "Dag-nabbit-all anyways, how's an old man 's'posed to stay com-posed amid this har fairytale goin's on." Jebediah went inside, leaving Jonas and Laura by themselves. Savage stayed to inspect the new arrival.

"Oh Jonas, it is you!" She ran to his arms. They embraced wordlessly, both in tears. Their lips met and held. Eventually, Laura looked down at Savage. "Oh, what a beautiful animal." She kneeled and cupped the dog's head in her hands. Their eyes met and she sensed that somehow their destinies would intertwine. Finally, she tore her gaze from the engaging red eyes and stood, facing Jonas. "'N you, young man. You got some explainin' to do."

Jonas was still bewildered. Laura's presence held him in awe. How was it possible that she was here, like a beatific apparition materializing before him. He reached out and drew a hand down her silky golden hair—then gently gripped her shoulders. She was just as he remembered her, even better with flushed cheeks from her ride and sapphire eyes grown teary in his presence.

"Jonas, if I'd known you'd be here, I would've fixed myself up a bit."

"You couldn't look purtier, Laura, no way on God's earth. So many long nights I've pictured you jes' like this. Yer what carried me through."

"Well, mister, you gonna continue to eat me up with yer eyes, or are you gonna tell me 'bout all those long nights and days you've been gone...'n what in hell yer doin' here."

"I am, Laura, but first I think you'll be needin' to sit down."

They sat close to each other on a wooden bench swing suspended from the porch ceiling. Savage lay at Laura's feet. Fluffy, white cumulous clouds drifted across a deep azure mid-September sky, casting ghostly shadows across the nearly completed corrals, then continuing their lazy path across the flat grazing lands, eventually melding with the distant velvet mountains. The shrill two-note whistle of a male chickadee floated from a nearby red maple, already aflame with the approaching autumn.

Jonas told his story as Laura listened in utter amazement. He left out nothing, willing to share every aspect of his life with her.

"Oh Jonas...bears, mountain lions, killers, blizzards...if I'd a known, I'd a bin worried sick."

"Don't forgit fallin' thru the ice, 'n ole Jeb bustin' a gut over it."

"Now, Jonas, I'm serious. I coulda lost you any number of times."

"Yeh, I guess I've jes' about lived a whole lifetime in the past year."

"'N I guess I'm gonna have to keep a close watch on you, so you don't git into no more troublin.'"

"Now, that'll be some feat. Me 'n troubl' seem to be in a head-buttin' contest."

Laura laughed. "Then I guess its jes' somethin' I'm goin' to have to git used to...somethin' more to love."

Laura was intrigued by Savage's role in Jonas's account—how the dog had saved Jonas and Jebediah on numerous occasions.

"And, Savage," Laura exclaimed as she bent to the dog. "I'm gonna give you a hundert kisses for savin' Jonas." Then to Jonas, "If I had lost you...I...I jes' don't want to think about it."

Jonas told Laura about him partnering up with Jebediah and that Jeb had insisted on financing the horse ranch.

"Jonas, I jes' can't absorb it all. It's so overwhelmin'. Why my year's bin like...like a bed of roses compared to what you've been through. Jis' thank God yer all right." She hugged him again.

"C'mon Jonas, git yerself a mount and let's ride. I wanna see yer place, all of it. 'N we got about a million other things to talk about."

They rode and they talked. Jonas explained that the horse ranch was mostly for her—that he felt he needed to offer her something attractive enough that she would want to leave her home and join him here. *It was still difficult for Jonas to believe that the beautiful Laura Becker would want to be a part of his life.* Laura just smiled. "Git it on, slowpoke. See if you kin ketch me." She took off at a gallop.

Jonas took off after her, but was no match for Laura. He loved to watch her ride—she seemed glued to the horse—a goddess astride a winged Pegasus. Not until she slowed could he catch up to her. She had found a small clearing within a pine grove. The ground was soft and covered with pine needles. She dismounted as he pulled up. Jonas jumped to the ground and came to her.

"I'll show you what I think of yer plan, Jonas McNabb." She pulled him down beside her and they lay side-by-side beneath the pines. She kissed him, long and hard. "Oh, Jonas, I was so worried. For a whole year...not knowing."

"Then you will come here to live, 'n this can be our place? I guess you know, ev'ry inch of it was built with you in mind."

"Don' ya think you ought to ask me somethin' else first, Jonas?"

"Well, of course we'll git hitched...er, married. I mean, you will marry me...won't you Laura? I love you so much. You're all I thought 'bout this past year."

"Damn right we'll git...hitched. 'N I can't imagin' any other place I'd ruther live. Oh, Jonas..."

They embraced and kissed again, then laid back and gazed up into the clouds.

"Laura, I got some other business to take care of b'fore we can think about gittin' married. I wouldn't dream of cartin' you off, without clearing up my name first. Yer father's got to know I ain't responsibl' for what happened back home."

"Do you know how you plan on doin' that?"

"Not yet, not really. I ain't quite got it worked out yet. Yer friend, Charly, tole me back last spring..."

"What?" Laura sat up. "Last spring? Charly knew you was here all along? She knew you was here 'n she never said nuthin'. Wait till I see her..."

"Now, Laura. It weren't her fault. I told her not to say nothin'. Not till I had this place up and runnin' so's I'd have somethin' to offer you. Now stop yer interruptin' till I git this out. Charly said you thought Dirk Fisher might've had somethin' to do with Jake comin' at me like that. My thinkin' is that Dirk sent Jake 'n the rest of 'em to scare me off, him figgerin' you was his girl. Then Jake took a swing at me 'n we got to fightin'. Jake came up with a knife 'n come at me. Somehow, in the fracas that followed, we ended up on the ground, 'n Jake was stabbed bad. I guess you was there to hear what happened after that. The men with Jake were hollerin' that I kilt him, 'n that it was my knife. I had to run, Laura. I guess I thought Jake was done for, 'n I couldn't see no other way out of it but to run. My thinkin' wasn't too clear at that point. Then I saw you standin' there. I saw the look on yer face. The look jes' tugged the heart out of me." Jonas had told all this to Laura before, the night he came to see her before taking off for the mountains, but he felt a need to re-establish his reasoning in Laura's mind.

"Oh, Jonas. I never thought you was to blame for that. 'N I sure figger'd Dirk had somethin' to do with it."

"Laura, tell me 'bout Jake. Charly says Dirk fired him 'n Jake kinda fell apart...drinkin' 'n all."

"Well, Jake recovered from the knifin' all right. I'm not sure why Dirk let 'em go, but afterwards, Jake took him a room in town 'n started drinkin' hard, 'n carousin', 'n who knows what else. I lost track of him."

"Any idea how Jake could afford a room? He didn't have no job. "N the boozin' 'n all costs money too."

"Well, I sure don' know," shrugged Laura.

"Tell you what I'm thinkin'," continued Jonas. "Maybe Dirk paid Jake to keep his mouth shut, because Dirk put 'im up to that fight. 'N what else I'm thinkin' is that Jake ain't in very good shape right now, 'n maybe he resents bein' fired like that. Maybe I kin convince him to tell the way things really happened that night."

"Yes. Yes. Oh, Jonas, I think you're right." She hugged him in her enthusiasm.

For a long time Laura and Jonas sat beneath the pines, talking about future plans and glowing in each other's company.

By the time they arrived back, they had worked out a semblance of a plan. Laura would continue her stay with Charly for the planned two weeks, seeing Jonas often. Then she would return to Jericho and discretely find out everything she could concerning Jake—his whereabouts, what kind of shape he was in—anything that might help. Maybe even see if Dirk would tip his hand about what happened with Jake. But, this possibility was quickly dismissed as being far too dangerous for Laura. She was to say nothing to Dirk that might arouse his suspicions about her and Jonas.

Jonas would stay at the J&J Ranch, seeing to its completion. Then, in spring, he and Jeb would travel to Jericho. Jonas would disguise himself in such a manner as to defy being recognized. In Jericho, he and Jeb would confront Jake as concerned strangers, and somehow, get Jake to tell the truth about the night of the stabbing. Jonas didn't figure he could work out the details until he was actually back in Jericho, to see how things lay.

▲ ▲ ▲

Laura divided her time between the Cooper Ranch and the JJ&L (the new name for the ranch as agreed upon Jeb, Jonas, and Laura). Each day, early, she would ride over to see Jonas and help out in any way she could, particularly to complete the furnishing of the farmhouse. She needed to add only a few things, her *personal touch*. Some items she would bring from Jericho when she returned, after she and Jonas were "hitched". Evenings and nights, Laura stayed with Charly at the Cooper Ranch.

No one at the JJ&L took exception to Jonas spending so much time

with Laura. Everyone there was thoroughly impressed with her and wondered why Jonas didn't spend all his time with her.

Jonas treasured each moment he and Laura were together. For the
past year, she had filled his thoughts. Now she was here with him and she
was everything he'd hoped for, and more. This day, Jonas and Laura were out
riding and again assumed their favorite spot beneath the pines. It was late
September and nearing a time when Laura would be returning to Jericho.
Oaks and cottonwoods still retained their greenery and the clouds were
beginning to boast their full and picturesque autumn formations.

It was about this time, a year ago that Laura was at the Richmond
Academy. She told Jonas all about the time she spent there. She described
the buildings, the electric trolley, the shops, and her ill-fated outing with
Richard Stappleton.

"Sounds like the rich, city boy could use a few country manners," said
Jonas. "But you sure put him in his place."

Jonas hesitated, " I guess I jes' git a li'l crazy thinkin' of other fella's
takin' an interest in you, 'n me bein' so far away, 'n unable to do much about
it. I guess I couldn't of blamed you if you'd found someone else."

"Well, silly boy, it wasn't all that hard, knowin' you were waitin' for
me. 'N Jonas, none of them city folks was worth a hoot next to us country
folks. Well, the shopkeeper was kindly, the one that got me headed back to
mother's place. 'N the school...it's laughable. They kicked me out 'cause
instead of makin' a lady of me, I was makin' hillbillies outta their 'proper'
young ladies. I don't know how I would've survived that school as long as
I did, hadn't bin for Charly, 'n Saca, of course. I'm sad about my mother,
though. Jonas, she had herself a boyfriend. I'm sure she did. Seems like
she was all the time tryin' to git rid of me. I guess so she could keep her
'rendezvous'. But, I'd never tell dad about it. He pro'bly knows anyway. It's
just so sad."

27

Laura and Jonas sat on the front porch of the JJ&L ranch house making last minute plans before Laura's departure. Red Phillips strolled over and took a seat on the top step. He removed his hat and ran a shirtsleeve over his brow, clearing the perspiration accrued from the late summer hot, muggy afternoon.

"Hot day, ain't it?" he said. "But I imagin' it gits a powerful lot worse down West Virginny way. Anyways, Laura, we got a surprise for you. We got this horse race tradition. Ordinar'ly we don' hold the race till next month, but we moved it up to tomorrow so's you could participate."

"What kinda race you talkin' about Red?" asked Laura, her curiosity piqued.

"Jes' hold yer horses darlin', I'm 'bout to git to that. The boss likes to see what he's got in quality horse stock, so each year we have us a com-pe-ti-shun. He likes to test some of his younger stock agin' some of the more experienced horses. It also gives the men, 'n ladies too, a chance to show their skills."

"And you want me to be in it?," said Laura.

"Shush 'till I git finished woman. Hell, Jonas, can't you train this lassy to shet up when a man's talkin'," said Red, with a wink. Laura stuck her tongue out at Red.

"Now then, this ain't no ordinary horse race, mind you. This here race will test a critter damn proper. Any old nag kin run out a mile, 'round a pole, 'n back agin. But in this race, we got jumps, 'n hills, 'n steep descents, ev'n a stream crossing. All kinds of diff'culty to test a horse 'n rider. The winnin' cayuse has to be fast, 'n sure footed, 'n strong, 'n smart, 'n needs a powerful amount of endurance. The rider has to know how to guide that horse through a hell of a testin'."

"Now, Laura," continued Red. "Me 'n the boys been eying that big ole Appaloosa of yers. Being a West Virginny horse 'n all, she prob'bly wouldn't stand much of a chance agin our classy Shenandoah stock. But jes' outta curiosity, we bin hopin' you might jes' wanna run yer nag agin us...in the race, that is."

"Hmmmm," said Laura. "I'm not too sure Saca would want to be caught in the company of them swaybacks of yers, but I think she jes' might be persuaded, jes' to show y'all up."

"Hell, yeh," exclaimed Red. "So, I guess that means yer in. This is gonna be some kinda race. The boys're gonna be de-lighted."

▲ ▲ ▲

The race was to take place on Cooper's land, with fifteen riders signed up. The course had been laid out years ago and each year it seemed to gain in difficulty. It was slated to start at two o'clock the next afternoon.

Early, the morning of the race, Red took Laura and Jonas out to acquaint them with the racecourse, figuring it only fair that they actually see what they were up against. Not wanting to tire the mounts they would be riding in the contest, they rode horses that would not be in the competition. The sun had been up for several hours and Laura relished the warming rays of the late summer day that gave promise for ideal conditions for racing. A few fluffy clouds drifted lazily overhead. Darker, approaching clouds were hidden by the far off mountains.

The racecourse was to be five miles in length. Red guided Laura and Jonas over the first mile, a flat expanse leading to the foothills. "Some of the men like an all-out sprint o'er this flat part, maybe git an early lead," explained Red. "But you gotta be smart. The course gits a lot tougher up ahead, you don't want to be wearing yer horse out right off."

"The second mile here gets pretty damn tricky," said Red, as he led Laura and Jonas up a thickly wooded, steep incline. "Not only do you have to be goin' up this steep grade, but you gotta be goin' in and out amongst all these trees. The trail is pretty clear. Ya jes' follow the yellow flags. Hard to pass anybody here though, but if yer behind, 'n yer horse maneuvers well, this is one place you might make up some ground."

Although Laura and Red negotiated the circuitous route with ease, Jonas—a less experienced horseman—had his difficulties and saw many possibilities for a rider to come to harm. He had reservations about Laura racing through this kind of terrain, against the throw-caution-to-the-wind seasoned ranch hands. He hadn't intended to enter the race but now was determined to find a mount just to keep an eye on Laura.

The racecourse broke out of the trees and leveled off, following a ridge as they reached the halfway point. From the ridge, Laura could see the Cooper Ranch farmhouse and stables. The rest of the Cooper land, as Red explained, stretched out in three directions as far as the eye could see. Red went on to point out the remainder of the racecourse from this vantage point.

"We jes' slide down this steep grade here," said Red, indicating what looked to Jonas like a vertical drop off the ridge. "Yep, not for the squeamish," continued Red, noting Jonas's discomfort. "But it ain't all that dangerous. Jes' let the horse do the work. But, if a rider ain't up to it, they kin ride around this here steep slope 'n take the gent'ler path down. But it'll cost 'em a minute or two, 'n most likely the race. From there, the course winds down through that meadow, along the crick for a spell, crossin' it several times, 'n out onto the flatlands below." Red traced the route with his finger as he described it. "And finally, for the last mile, it's an all out sprint back to the barn, 'n the finish line. Seem reasonable?"

"Aw geez, Red," started Jonas, studying the steep grade before him. "Ain't it kinda dangerous goin' down this...?"

Before Jonas could finish, Red pushed off the ridge and headed down the steep slope. This demanded the utmost co-operation between horse and rider, least they both be tumbling head over heels down the incline. Mostly what Jonas could see from on top the ridge was a dust storm kicked up by Red's mount, as the horse plummeted down the steep grade. At the bottom, Red waved his hat indicating for them to follow. Jonas watched in dread as Laura guided her mount down off the ridge. *If anythin' happened to her...*

Now both Red and Laura were motioning for Jonas to come down. Jonas never considered himself much of a rider. The only horses he'd known were farm animals, more meant for the plow than speed, and most of his riding was to get from one place to another, not for enjoyment. But what would Laura think if he didn't face up to the challenge, and of course he'd never hear the last of it from Red. Jonas urged his horse over the edge of the ridge and maybe he closed his eyes after that because the next thing he knew he was at the bottom and still intact and white as a sheet.

"Now that weren't so bad, was it?" said Red, as he broke into laughter.

They continued their survey of the racecourse, the yellow flags making the route fairly obvious. Jonas was leery of the several natural jumps over fallen trees that blocked the trail alongside the creek. And several of the creek crossings actually involved that the horse swim against a strong current.

"Red, you call this a crick?" objected Jonas. "More like a ragin' torrent."

"Wahl, we intend to set up the kiddie rides in the corral, if that's more to yer likin'. Haw."

Jonas laughed at the ribbing but still maintained his apprehensions, mostly concerning Laura.

All that remained of the racecourse was the mile long stretch of flat land leading back to the finish line, the same mile stretch that marked the beginning of the race.

▲ ▲ ▲

The time for the start of the race was quickly approaching. Activity had escalated—the riders were preparing their mounts and receiving last minute instructions, amidst the hubbub of the enthusiastic wagering. The heavy money was on Red Phillips and his big, white Arabian stallion. Red had won the race three years running and was the odds on favorite. But Laura's Appaloosa had been attracting a certain amount of attention, definitely the sentimental favorite, at five to one odds. Many of the JJ&L workers had the day off and were backing Laura and a few of the Cooper hands, too. Jeb declared that he "wouldn't be caught daid on one of them fire-snortin' orn'ry sons-a-bitchin' an'mals."

Red drew Jonas and Laura aside.

"I surmise you haven't raced all that much, if at all, 'n I want you to have a chance. Now, we got some good horses runnin'. Maybe half a dozen quarter horses, but you ain't gotta worry too much 'bout them. They git off fast, but they fade fast too. The boss is trying a coupla new breeds this year, to see how they fare. That Morgan o'er there, for instance." Red pointed to the big brown stallion with the black tail. "'N them two spirited guys o'er there, they're Standardbreds 'n they'll give you a run for yer money. But mostly it's the Arabians you need to be concerned with, like my Dusty, this big white beauty here." Red held the reins of a giant horse that to Jonas seemed to be snorting fire. "Yeh, they kin be kinda ornery," said Red, "for sure they got spunk, 'n they win races like this one, where they gotta have speed 'n endurance 'n be sure of foot.

"Jonas, you'll be sittin' that Paint o'er there. That's Charly's horse, 'n she told me special she wanted you up on Chestnut, where'd you'd be safe... haw. But, seriously, Chestnut's a good all around horse, so give 'er some rein 'n let 'er run. She's always fared well in these races, usually with Charly up on her. Charly ain't ridin' this year 'cause she wants to watch you and Laura. Thinks that will be more fun."

Laura had been watching a beautiful, sleek, long-legged horse. "What about that dark bay o'er there," she asked.

"Now that one is the boss's' prize critter," said Red. "It's our first Thoroughbred, 'n he's faster'n blue blazes. Boss don't want nothin' to happen to that horse, so Clancy's up on him, 'n they don't come no better'n him. We're runnin' the Thoroughbred to see what he's got in endurance, not jes' speed.

"Mind you don't wear yer ponies down right off at the start; you got to save 'em for the end run. That's where this race is gen'rally won. I don't reckon any of our horses kin beat the Thoroughbred over flat terrain, but we'll see how he fares when he gits up into the hills.

"Well, that's about it, ladies and gentlemen. I 'spose we best be saddlin' up 'n gittin' ready for this shin-ding. Oh, 'n I forgot to mention, the boss is putting up five hundert dollars in prize money for the winner."

At two in the afternoon, the horses and riders were lined up, side-by-side, awaiting John Cooper's signal for the start of the race. The sun still shone brightly, though a few more clouds were drifting in from the West. Darker, denser clouds hovered over the mountains, but no one seemed concerned.

John Cooper rode his mount in front of the line of anxious horses, shouting best wishes for a good race to the contestants. It was difficult to keep the spirited horses in anything that remotely resembled a straight line.

Some were pawing the dirt, more like rodeo bulls than racing horses. One of the Arabians reared and almost threw his rider.

"This ain't no race for the faint hearted," thought Jonas. He and Laura were side by side, astride Saca and Chestnut. He reached over and gave Laura's hand a squeeze.

"Don't worry Jonas," said Laura, smiling encouragingly, "you'll be fine...I'll be fine."

When Cooper reached the last horse in line, he stopped, turned, and faced the hopeful riders. He raised a pistol into the air and fired it, signaling the start of the race.

Fifteen horses sprinted across the flat mile stretch. As expected, the quarter horses took the early lead, but by the time the upgrade was reached, fourteen horses were looking at the rear hooves of the flying Thoroughbred.

Laura was keeping Saca at a reasonable pace, close to the leaders. She wasn't sure what to expect from a challenge such as this. Her plan was to save Saca for the last mile sprint to the finish, as Red had recommended. But it was difficult to hold her horse back, as Saca seemed to want the lead—not be stuck in the middle of the dust and confusion created by the other horses. Laura let Saca run a bit harder than she had originally intended and when she reached the upgrade, the only horses ahead of her were the Thoroughbred, two Arabians (including Red's big white mount) and another horse she couldn't identify. She had lost track of Jonas in all the dust kicked up by the hard driving animals.

The trail up to the top of the ridge involved some fancy maneuvering on the part of the riders. The course wound around trees and bushes and up steep grades, at times requiring jumps over fallen trees. Passing was difficult—the demands of the course funneling the riders into a single file for much of the climb. But Laura did take one of the leaders with a dangerous pass on a steep incline of loose gravel. She was close on the horse's tail when the horse lost its footing and slipped back into Laura's path. Saca adroitly sidestepped the danger and scooted up into fourth place. The first three contenders formed a tight group as they reached the hill's summit and started along the ridge on top. Laura was not far behind. "Only three horses to ketch," she whispered into Saca's ear.

Laura felt a sprinkling of light rain on her face. She looked skyward and noticed that dense black clouds now hid the sun that had brightened the start of the race. In the short time consumed by her scamper along the top of the ridge, the rain burst out of the clouds like a cannon blast. Laura knew she was approaching the steep descent off the ridge and feared it would be too dangerous to undertake. And she was concerned as to how Jonas would fare in in the suddenly untoward conditions of the racecourse.

Up ahead, Laura saw that Red's horse and the other Arabian had passed the Thoroughbred, which seemed to be tiring. Red was now in second place, close behind the leader. They reached the steep slope leading down off the ridge. The lead Arabian took off over the rim and out of Laura's line of sight. When Laura reached the rim, both Red and the Thoroughbred had halted. Laura brought Saca to a stop. Red was pointing down the slope. Laura looked over the edge. The lead horse and rider had fallen near the bottom of the steep incline. The horse righted itself and continued the last few feet to the bottom of the ridge, seemingly unhurt. The rider wasn't so lucky. His horse must have rolled on him and he had all he could do to limp the rest of the way to the bottom. He yelled to the riders back up on top. It was hard to hear him over the pounding rain, but eventually he made it clear that he wasn't badly hurt, but couldn't continue the race. He shouted to them that the slope was too dangerous and they should take the gentler path down. He would remain there at the bottom and warn the rest of the riders not to attempt the descent.

"Welp," said Red, "I guess we take Chuck at his word 'n take the safe way around this slope." No one objected.

The three riders took off, skirting the ridge and avoiding the steep incline that had eliminated Chuck from the competition—Red first, then the Thoroughbred, then Laura.

The rain continued its attack. Laura wished she'd worn a hat, as her hair was thoroughly soaked and plastered to her face, making visibility difficult.

The alternate slope down off the ridge was gradual, but the riders were reluctant to let the horses run full out in such slippery conditions. Even so, Laura was not aware that any of the riders behind her were gaining ground. She wondered how Jonas was doing.

At the bottom of the ridge, the course flattened out and for several hundred yards followed alongside the creek. The footing was more secure here and this is where Laura took the Thoroughbred and bore down on Red and his white Arabian. She figured she would stay tight on Red's tail because in this downpour, were she to take the lead, she might be unable to locate the course markers. And she was concerned for Saca's safety should she veer off the course.

Laura followed the big White along the tricky course, following the creek, crisscrossing it numerous times. In places, the creek was deep enough that Saca had to swim, with Laura hanging on for dear life in the swift current.

Laura lost sight of the Thoroughbred behind her. It seemed now there was just her and Red. Red crossed the creek one last time and burst out into the flat meadow that led to the finish line, about a mile distant.

Laura was hot on Red's heels. The ground was not as hard as Laura would have liked as the rain had softened it considerably. And visibility was poor. Laura knew the ranch house and corral were somewhere ahead and that she faced a flat course the rest of the way, but so far she could see nothing ahead but the driving rain and the tail of the white horse.

Laura decided to let Saca run all out, trusting the horse's instinct to contend with the elements. She pulled alongside of Red and gradually inched past him. For the first time in the race, she had the lead. "I should feel wonderful," she thought, "but something is wrong." She thought of another time in conditions similar to this. Her bad judgment then had cost the life of her black stallion, Lucifer. Now here she was endangering her beloved Sacagawea.

She splashed through a puddle. *Saca could have tripped in that puddle...*Laura began to slow down. Soon Red overtook her. She slowed even more and soon had Saca walking. Red came back.

"What is it Laura? Is yer horse hurt?"

"No Red, 'n she ain't gonna be. I lost a horse once in conditions like this, I ain't gonna lose Saca. I'll jes' wait here for Jonas 'n we'll both come in together." Laura halted Saca and dismounted.

"Well, I reckon I'll wait right along here with you then. Can't see winnin' no race against reasonin' like that. I reckon you had this race won anyhow." He dismounted. Clancy reined up with the Thoroughbred. "What gives, Red?"

"Nothing to worry about here. Go ahead and finish the race, Clancy, and send a wagon back for Chuck. He ain't walkin' so good."

Jonas had found the race surprisingly trouble-free. Charly's Paint was so easy to handle, all Jonas had to do was hold on. He figured he was somewhere in the middle of the pack by the time it started raining. Maybe even toward the front. But he lost ground in the rain. He didn't want to endanger Charly's horse, so he just slowed down. He didn't mind the other riders passing him under such circumstances. He was into the last leg now, the long stretch leading to the finish line.

Up ahead, through the heavy rain, Jonas saw two vague images. They appeared to be two horses, both without riders. As he got closer, he could distinguish Red's white mount. The other horse looked like...oh no, he thought. His stomach knotted. *Not again...*

He urged the Paint on as the dreaded memory gripped him. Then he saw Laura. She'd been hidden behind her horse. She was waving at him and appeared to be all right.

"Jonas," yelled Laura. "I was beginning to worry."

She was moving toward Jonas now, and as Jonas got near, he reined up and hopped off the Paint. He ran to Laura and embraced her.

"Jonas, whatever brought this on?"

"Laura, when I saw yer horse with no rider, I was afraid you'd got hurt agin. But yer all right...ain't you?"

Several more riders had arrived and Red waved them on.

"I'm fine," said Laura. "I jis' didn't wanna endanger Saca, so I decided I'd wait for you, 'n we could jis' ride on in together, nice 'n easy."

"'N I decided to wait with her," said Red. "Hell, she had the race won, 'n as far as I'm concerned, she did win it."

"Laura, honey," said Jonas, "you never cease to amaze me."

When Laura, Jonas, and Red finally reached the finish line, an anxious John Cooper awaited them. All the other riders, except Chuck, were in by now. They stood by their mounts, thoroughly soaked, but lingering in the downpour to learn why three riders were walking their horses to the finish line. Most of the onlookers had sought shelter in the barn and were watching the finish of the race from the open doorway.

"What in tarnation happened to the three of you?" asked Cooper. "The boys say you was stopped halfway across the homestretch. Anyone hurt?"

Red went on to explain about Laura's decision that the downpour had made racing unsafe for her horse.

"She sure had the race won, Boss, no doubt in my mind. 'N I jes' didn't wanna win with her givin' it up to protect her horse."

Cooper mulled that over. "Now ain't that the damn'dest thing. Now my thinkin is that Laura and Red and Jonas here did a noble thing and the rest of you should be ashamed...including myself. Ain't no race worth the loss of a good horse. Laura, you feelin' about horses the way you do, you're goin' do jes' fine in raising a bunch of 'em."

"Boys," continued Cooper, addressing the other riders, "what say we split that prize money right down the middle, between Clancy here on the Thoroughbred, 'n the rightful winner, Laura Becker, 'n her Appaloosa."

"What say we give the whole bundle to Laura," said Clancy. She gawd-all-mighty deserves it."

To that suggestion, a roar went up from the other riders, backing Clancy's suggestion.

"I appreciate yer offer," said Laura. "But why not jis' let the pot hold over till next year, 'n then on some sunny day, I'll trim all yer butts, fair 'n square."

Everyone cheered that and John Cooper made her suggestion official.

"'N by the way," said Cooper, "due to the strangeness of the circumstances, all bets are off." A groan went through the men.

Since Laura would be leaving for Jericho the next morning, Jonas and Jeb spent the night at the Cooper Ranch, intending to bid their goodbyes to her in the morning.

The past couple of weeks had been pure joy for Laura, knowing that soon she would be Jonas's wife, and would be living on their horse ranch in the beautiful Shenandoah Valley. During her brief stay at the Cooper Ranch she'd impressed everyone with her knowledge and love of horses—the ranch hands, John Cooper, Red, Frenchie—experienced horse people, all. Perhaps

Jeb was the most impressed with Laura, actually admitting, "Thet li'l ole West Virginny gal has all but changed my at-ter-tude towards wimmins."

And Laura made known her feelings for Savage. "You saved my man, 'n you saved my future, 'n maybe I luv you most of all." As she looked into the dog's eyes, however, she detected a sadness. "What is it boy? What do you know?"

A lingering apprehension gnawed at her, the foreboding she had sensed when first she had met Savage—the look in his red eyes.

28

Laura returned to West Virginia and now Jonas gave his full attention to the ranch. With the assurance that Laura would soon share the JJ&L, as his bride, he proceeded with a new energy and spirit, intending that the ranch be in perfect shape for her return.

The signs of fall were evident. The oaks and maples were donning colorful cloaks of yellows, reds and oranges. Honking geese headed south in irregular V's, silhouetted against the billowy autumnal clouds.

The ranch house itself was completed, the final touches being the furnishings, initially implemented by Charly and later augmented by Laura during her two-week stay. The two girls had taken a wagon to Waynesboro and returned with it loaded with items deftly selected to fill the JJ&L's empty rooms. Jeb, watching the wagon pull in, patted Savage on the head and commented, "Wahl, hell, boy, kaint see's there's goin' be much room left o'er in this house fer us. Guess maybe we'll be campin' out under the stars." Jeb's concern was unfounded, as Laura and Charly's buying spree had yielded to good judgment and the trappings for the ranch house were utilitarian and tasteful, none infringing on Jeb's domain.

Shortly after Laura's departure, Red Phillips joined Jeb and Jonas on the front porch of the JJ&L ranch-house.

"Wahl," said Red, "seems to me the time is 'bout ripe to add the most impo'tant ingredient to this here operation of yers. Yep, time to bring in the horses. What say we git e'ryone together 'n have us a pow-wow."

The e'ryone mentioned by Red turned out to be himself and Frenchie, John Cooper and his daughter Charly, and, of course, Jebediah and Jonas. These six now congregated around the dining room table at the JJ&L Ranch to discuss the issue of selecting horse stock for the nearly completed ranch. Jeb was satisfied to just stand aside. "I'll jes' keep yer cups filled with coffee. You do all the figgerin."

Laura had given Jonas a list of horsestock she felt needed to be brought into the JJ&L, a starting point. That was about all he and Jeb could contribute to the negotiations as they yielded to the expertise of the seasoned ranchers.

The consensus was that the breeding and selling of horses would give the JJ&L the best chance for immediate success. Practically every country family required a horse or two, for transportation and for pleasure. Another consideration was to board horses, for a fee.

"And," said John Cooper, "if you get lucky, a horse might come along suitable for racin'. Such a horse would require specialized training to best develop its speed and endurance. But," he emphasized, "that's getting' ahead of ourselves. For now, let's just concentrate on the basics. After that, you can experiment a bit."

For the time being Red would assume the role of horse trainer and manager of the JJ&L, a role that would one day be turned over to Jonas and Laura, particularly, Laura.

"I'll tell ya, Jonas," said Red, "I don't think you'll need to hire no horse trainer. That gal of yers knows 'bout all they is to know 'bout horses. With her as yer trainer, 'n you managin' the place, I figger you'll be in fine shape. Of course, me 'n Frenchie'll still give you a hand here 'n there, if needed."

Eventually, Red and Frenchie would return to their jobs at the Cooper Ranch, but they agreed to stay on with Jonas and Jeb at least until late spring. By then, Jonas hoped he'd have affairs settled in Jericho and have returned to the Shenandoah with Laura as the new Mrs. McNabb.

Jeb was more than willing to finance the stock purchases. "You jes' git me the best critters ya kin lay yer hands on, 'n as many of the dad-burned beasts thet we're gonna need, 'n more. This ain't gonna be no rinky-dink op-er-a-shun."

For a start, John Cooper was willing to sell Jeb and Jonas some of his own stock. They could acquire the rest of the horses they'd need at auctions, which were periodically held throughout the state and up into Pennsylvania. Eventually, they could venture into Kentucky and Tennessee as well, in search of more varied stock. The best Thoroughbreds were said to be coming out of Tennessee.

Charly took notes. Her notes looked like this:

WHAT THE HORSES WOULD BE USED FOR
Riding, Racing, Show, Breeding, Jumping, Rodeo,
Pulling carriages and wagons, Work animals
HOW MUCH STOCK
To Start—25 mares, 10 stallions, 10 yearlings
WHAT BREEDS – (For this part of the country)
Appaloosas (at Laura's insistence)
 -For beauty, speed, spirit, intelligence
Arabians (like my Red's Dusty)
 -High spirited, speed merchant
Missouri Fox Trotter
 -Most versatile, easy to ride, high endurance,
 Sure footed (an asset in the mountains)
 Suitable for plowing & hauling, drawing a buggy,
 family riding horse.
Thoroughbred
 -Racing and jumping
Quarter Horse
 -Rodeos, working cattle
American Saddle Breed
 -Excellent riding horse

▲ ▲ ▲

By the end of November, Jonas, Red, and Frenchie had selected thirty horses at various auctions. With the stock from John Cooper, the JJ&L stables now boasted forty-two horses—*forty-two horses!* thought Jonas. A year ago, the possibility of owning forty-two horses would have seemed a bad joke.

Jonas could not have been more pleased. The JJ&L now was a bona fide and ready-to-go horse ranch and he profusely thanked anyone and everyone that had contributed to it, but Jeb seemed somewhat indifferent. He revealed to Jonas that he was not all that fond of horses and much preferred mules.

"Well, don' that beat all," observed Jonas. "Here you are, about to become a horse rancher, 'n you don' even like horses."

"Wahl, never said I did, now did I. I'm jes' the fi-nan-ceer. You gits ta run the show as far as I'm concerned. 'N when you gits Laura har, I aims ta jes' sit back'n relax most the time."

"Haw, so you say. I 'spect you'll have yer nose a-pokin' into ever'thin' goes on around here."

"You jes' git me some of them li'l chil'uns ta bounce on my knee, if'n I last thet long."

▲ ▲ ▲

Jonas soon found out that with the arrival of the horses, the real learning began. Everything up to this point had been but a prelude to the main event, like setting the table before the food arrived. Now Red became his constant companion and mentor.

Jonas was familiar with some of the involvement, having worked a farm back home. But that was small scale compared to what he now faced. The stables required constant attention and fences always needed repair. The horses had to be exercised daily and kept in fresh oats and clean hay—pastures needed to be kept picture-perfect and the soil constantly tested to assure the horses were getting their proper nutrients. Jonas had never suspected that a horse must be bathed outside whenever possible, then covered, brought inside, toweled off, covered again, and walked until dry, to prevent chills. *Phew.* Jonas thought about the family mare and his promise to her—a queen's treatment. She now roamed the pasture lands with nary a duty expected of her.

Jonas's training continued: that only about a week's worth of grain and a day's worth of hay should be kept in the feed room and there needed to be a separate tack room—maintained dust free so that clean tack, i.e. bridles, saddles, etc., could be ready for the horses. And that was just for starters. Thankfully, Red was an excellent teacher, showing great patience with the often overwhelmed Jonas.

Fall gave way to winter in the Shenandoah. Any profits the fledgling ranch might yield would be minimal in this, the off-season. Come spring, the serious business of putting the ranch on a paying basis would begin. But, come spring, Jeb and Jonas planned to be elsewhere.

Jonas was pitching hay around in the stables when Red sauntered in.

"Guess you'n Jeb'll be headed back to Jericho b'fore too long," said Red.

"That's the plan. Think you can manage without us for a bit?"

"Hell, with you gone, me'n Frenchie'll finally be able to git some work done around here, seein' we won't have to be mother-hennin' you all the time."

Jonas pitched the next load of hay at Red's legs.

"Haw, Pard," said Red. "Do I look like one of them nags of yers?"

"You really want me to answer that? Anyway, Red, when I return to the JJ&L, it will be with a clean slate and with Laura as my bride."

"Won't that be great?" Red exclaimed. "You'n Laura livin' here at the JJ&L, 'n Charly 'n me set up at the Cooper Ranch. Shhhh...don't spread that around yet 'bout Charly 'n me. She'll be wantin' to break that news. But, I'll tell you, a man couldn't want for better neighbors."

"Sounds mighty fine to me, Red, 'n Charly's a great li'l gal. Don't think you could do no better. You bein' so ugly 'n all."

"Hmmm...yer sure gittin' the hang of things. At least you got the talk down."

In spite of the felicity, Jonas was apprehensive as to how he would accomplish his exoneration back in Jericho.

It was set that Red and Frenchie would run the JJ&L Ranch while Jonas and Jebediah returned to Jericho. "Jes' take as long as you need, pard," said Red. "We'll have this place runnin' like a freshly greased wagon wheel when you git back."

▲ ▲ ▲

One late, winter day, with a fresh coat of snow blanketing the ground, Red returned to the JJ&L from one of his frequent visits back to the Cooper Ranch to see Charly. He met Jonas down at the stables.

"Who's yer friend?" asked Jonas.

"This here beast is Snowball, Charly's dog. She insisted I bring her over to keep me comp'ny seein' you 'n Jeb'll be leavin' soon."

Snowball was aptly named, a white Malamute, almost as large as Savage. The she-dog began to emit a low growl as Jeb entered the stable with Savage trailing close behind.

"Easy, girl," said Red, gripping the Malamute by the scruff of her neck. "I guess she ain't used to no dog bigger'n she is."

Savage stood unperturbed beside Jeb. "Don' worry 'bout it, Red," said Jeb. "Savage'll have her friendly in no time a'tall."

PART IV
The Return

▲ ▲ ▲

29

At the first signs of spring, three travelers prepared to leave the JJ&L horse ranch and journey west into West Virginia, then on down to Jericho. There was a grizzled old man, there was a tall rangy man, and there was a huge one-eared dog that limped. Jonas no longer much resembled the lad who had fled his home a year and a half ago. He was slightly taller and definitely broader. The rigors of his mountain adventure and the demands of working the horse ranch had toughened him, filling out his lanky frame. His face was lean and hardened. He wore a heavy beard and full mustache. His clothing was shabby, and a weather beaten wide brimmed hat partially hid his long scraggly hair—all part of Jonas's disguise to defy detection. In effect, two weathered mountain men and a damaged dog were headed for West Virginia. They took the easiest and most direct route back to Jericho. No need to stick to the mountains as it was unlikely anyone would still be looking for Jonas.

Laura had received a letter from Charly that Jonas was on his way home, and she in turn had informed Jonas's family. She told them nothing of the impending marriage or of Jonas's perilous adventures.

▲ ▲ ▲

The three travelers reached Jericho at night, after three days travel and took a room at the Claremont Hotel. The first floor of the hotel featured a bar and restaurant; rooms for let were upstairs. The travelers settled in and made plans for the next day.

Neither Laura nor Jonas's family were to visit him at the hotel. Too risky. Jeb could travel freely around town and the surrounding countryside, as he was unknown in these parts.

So Jeb would do most of the investigative work. But first he arranged a meeting between Jonas and his family in a secluded spot not far from their farm. Although it would be a daylight rendezvous, there was little chance that Jonas would be seen, and even less chance that anyone would recognize him.

The two ill-clad mountain men—one legit and one an imposter—approached Benji and Caleb in the small clearing. A giant white dog limped behind.

"My Gawd...is that you, Jonas?" asked Caleb. "I'd hardly've known you 'n I'm yer pa. For sure, no one else would." Benji just stared at his brother in disbelief and awe.

"Yer a man...yer a full-growed man," said Benji.

"That I am, n look at you li'l brother. You ain't much short of a man yerself. Is that fuzz I see o'er yer lip?"

Benji's face erupted into a proud smile as they hugged.

"This here's my pard, Jebediah," continued Jonas. "We got us a biz'niz deal cooked up. I'll tell ya 'bout it later. I brought ya back yer mare, Pa, there's a lot of story behind that. 'N this here white beast of an animal is Savage. 'N I'll sure tell you about him later, too. Go ahead, git to know 'im, he won't hurt you, 'less'n you're up to no good." Benji kneeled down to the dog. "He looks more like a wolf," he said, as he offered a hand to Savage, who gave it a reassuring lick. "Guess he likes me well enuff."

Jeb hung back, preferring that Jonas enjoy his reunion with his family without him butting in.

Jonas turned to his father. "How're you doin', Pa?"

They hugged. "All right, I guess. As best can be expected," said Caleb. "The minin's kinda got me down, son. Maybe I'm too old for it. This 'n that's sore most all the time." Jonas sensed his father's depression had gotten worse, with Jonas's absence only adding to the problem.

"The farm ain't producin' much anymore, Jonas," said Benji, still occupied with Savage. "I been thinkin' 'bout takin' work at the mines myself."

"The hell you say," exclaimed Jonas. "Purty soon there ain't goin' be no miners in this family."

"Huh, what do you mean by that?" asked his brother.

"Jes' this. Sit down. Me 'n Jeb got a hell of a story to tell you. 'N yer gonna have a tough time believin' it all."

Jonas went on to tell his father and brother all that happened to him during the past year and a half. He told them about how he met Jebediah and Savage and about all the "life savin' that went on". He explained about Jeb's offer and their subsequent partnership.

"We got us a legitimate, genuine, ever-lovin' horse ranch up in the purtiest countryside you ev'r seen. As soon as I get this mess cleared up around here, 'bout the stabbin 'n all, we're all gonna live on that horse ranch. No more mining, no more fillin' yer lungs with that damn black coal dust. Jes' good clean country air 'n purely satisfyin' respect'ble work. 'N somethin' more, Pa, Laura Becker 'n me's goin' git married, 'n she'll be helpin' us run the horse ranch."

This last bit of news, on top of the rest of it, was more that Caleb could absorb. Tears filled his eyes. "Son," he began, "I jes' don' know what to say. Since yer ma died, ain't really much good's happen'd to me...'n you bein' run off...I jes' 'bout gave up on ev'rythin'. I know I ain't bin much of a pa to you..." He buried his face in his hands, shaking. Jonas held him by the shoulders.

"Pa, it's gonna be all right. It really is."

"I guess I wanna believe that. You've given me a lot to think about."

Benji's eyes grew larger and larger as Jonas revealed each segment of his story. He was bubbling with pride for his older brother. "Jonas, all that really happened? I can't believe it. 'N you got a horse ranch, a real honest to gawd horse ranch for us to live on?" He had a hundred other questions, lasting well into the night.

30

Next day, Jeb ordered a bottle of whiskey from the barkeep at the Claremont Hotel. It was mid-afternoon and the bar was practically deserted, but for a few men glued to the bar and one unkempt man seated at a table in a darkened corner, nursing a glass of whiskey. Jeb had left

Savage in the upstairs room he shared with Jonas, afraid the huge dog would draw unwanted attention.

The room was large for a Jericho establishment, strewn with round wooden tables with checker tablecloths, four spindle backed chairs to a table. Each table sported an oil lamp, more lamps hung from the low ceiling. Wooden stools fronted a long whiskey-stained oak-topped bar. An open archway separated the bar from the adjoining dining area, while a staircase led to the rooms on the second floor, where Jeb and Jonas had established quarters.

Jeb had no difficulty locating Jake Kellogg; Laura was quite sure he would be staying at the Claremont, hustling drinks in the barroom. Jake was the unkempt man in the dark corner.

Jeb pushed away from the bar and approached Jake's table, carrying the bottle and a glass. Jake didn't look up. His head hovered over his glass of whiskey, which he clutched tightly with both hands, guarding it as if someone might take it from him.

"Mind if I grab a chair, stranger? I shore hate ta drink alone. Hell, thet'd be like tellin' a joke with nobody ta laugh at it."

Finally, Jake looked up and regarded the shoddy, buckskin-clad old man. But his eyes went immediately to the full bottle of whiskey in Jeb's hand. Jake wasn't particular about who he drank with, as long as they were footing the bill.

"You meanin' to share that bottle, old timer?"

"Thet's my in-ten-shun. Like I say, I hates ta drink alone."

"Then sure, have a seat." Jake had been nursing his drink, not having the means to buy another. There wouldn't be any scrounging another one from the paltry gathering here at the bar. He'd long ago exhausted that option.

Jeb sat. "Here, lemme refresh yer glass. I'm Jeb, 'n what might yer name be, young feller?"

"You can call me Jake, 'n I don' care what yer name is s'long as ya keep the whiskeys comin'." Jeb leaned in closer. The low glow from the oil lamp gave the proceedings a sinister look.

"So tell me...Jake, is it? Tell me 'bout this har town of yers."

"Sure. It's a hellhole. All it's got is dirty miners 'n whores 'n backstabbers."

"Wahl, why do ya stick 'round then?" Jake gulped down his drink like a man possessed and proffered his glass for another. Jeb filled it.

"Ain't got nowhere else to go. 'N even if I did, I ain't got no way to git there, anyways. I'm plumb broke, mister." Jake leaned in closer. "Don' 'spose you could help a fella out a bit. I'm kinda down on my luck. It's only temp'rary like, 'till I kin git back on my feet."

"Mebbe I kin help ya. Depen's."

"Depends?...depends on what?" Jake thumped his empty glass on the table.

Jeb poured him another whiskey. "Wahl, I got in a peck of troubl' a ways back. Yep, got me a bartendin' job, 'n they caught me skimmin'. Hadn't bin for my nephew, I 'spect I'd a bin up fer a stretch at the county's expense. Now, my nephew, he ain't much ta speak of, but somehow he got himself well-heeled. Don' know whar he got it, 'n I weren't 'bout ta ask, but he shore hepped me out of thet sit-i-ation. Money shore talks. The point is I figger I owe one. So I'm thinkin' mebbe I might repay thet favor, dependin' on how I take to ya."

"Hell, man. You think I was always like this?" He threw down another whiskey. "I used to be a top man in the minin' comp'ny here. You ask anybody. Jes' ask 'em."

"Yeh, so what happened to ya?"

"Happen'd?" Jake shot back. "I'll tell you what happen'd." Jake grabbed the bottle. "You mind?"

"Hell no, thet's what it's here fer."

"Here's whaz happened," slurred Jake. "I got me a raw deal." Jake glanced around the room as if checking for prying ears. His words issued through clenched teeth, like a loud whisper. "This sons-a-bitch. I thought he was my pard...my friend. 'N I did 'im a real favor." The words tapered off as Jake became absorbed in thought.

"Look. I don' wanna 'pear nosey 'r nuthin', but what ya got agin' this har feller anyhow?"

"Huh?" Jake snapped out of his reverie. "Whaz I got agin' him? Hell, I'll tell you whaz I got agin' him. He ain't no good. He ain't no buddy a'tall.

'N I know things 'bout that rascal. I know plenty. 'N he better start treatin' me right, or I jes' might tell some things...serve 'im right.

"Jes' what kinda things, young feller? Might do ya good ta get it offa yer chest."

"Yeh, well...maybe." Jake forsook his glass and took a swig directly from the bottle.

"For one thing, Dirk...er, this fella that is..." Jake looked around nervously again, "he had me pick a fight with some kid that was foolin' 'round with his gal. We got him blamed for stickin' me with a knife. Likely kilt me, almost. Hurt like hell. It weren't his fault...was my knife, but ole Dirk, he wanted this kid run outta town. So whaz I git for gratitude? Hell, he ups 'n fires me, thas what I git. Said he din't have no room for no screws-up like me. 'N to keep my mouth shut 'bout all that, 'n 'bout other things he'z bin up to...wahl, he says he'd pay for my room here at the Claremont. 'N now he'z e'en quit payin' for that. So...whaz ya think mister...hep me out some?"

"Shore sounds like ya bin up against it, shore enuff." Jeb gave Jake a long close look. He drew his chair even closer. "I'm thinkin' ya bin giv'n a raw deal. Tell ya what. I like ya, Jake. I guess b'cause weren't so long ago I was in a similar fix. Wahl. I'm feelin' gen'rous today, 'n here's what I aims ta do fer ya. I'll pay fer thet room of yers, for a bit. But you gotta do somethin' fer me 'n for a friend of mine, thet bein' my nephew."

"Whaz kinda somethin' you talkin'about?"

"I'll shore git to thet. Meet me har tomarra night, 'n we'll share us anuther bottl', 'n sort this thing out. Till then, hang in thar pard." If Jake was at all suspicious of Jeb's request, Jeb was certain the promise of free whiskey and free board would bring him back the next night.

31

Early next morning, Jeb found Laura at the Becker Estate stables. She ran to him and threw her arms around him. "Oh, Jeb, you're here. It's bin so long. Is Jonas with you? Where's Savage? Oh, tell me ever'thing."

"Easy, lassie," said Jeb, somewhat embarrassed and overwhelmed. "We got har safe 'n I'm har ta tell ya, yer ta meet up with yer in-tended this very mornin' o'er at his farm." Jeb described exactly where. "Now I best git b'fore anyone sees me."

Laura ran to the house and changed into a dress, then quickly saddled Saca and rode to the McNabb property, passing through the meadow where she'd first seen Jonas. She found the designated meeting place, dismounted and waited there for Jonas. She found it difficult to contain her enthusiasm.

"What a wonderful time of the year," she thought. It was springtime, everything was reborn. Dogwoods were budding, pushing out lily-white blossoms and filling the air with their sweet fragrance. Daffodils, tulips, and crocuses were sneaking looks at their new world. Cherry trees were in bloom; a particular cherry tree hosted two cardinals resplendent in crimson glory, chirping an alarm at Laura's intrusion. Their warnings morphed into a more pleasant, long clear whistle as they became accustomed to her presence.

Laura sat with her dress splayed out around her. Ordinarily she would wear riding britches when out with Saca, but she hadn't seen Jonas since last fall and she wanted to look special. The cameo necklace Jonas had given her dangled prominently around her neck. She turned her head toward the sky and felt the warm sun on her face. A gentle breeze caressed her hair.

She noticed two grey squirrels gamboling about in a nearby dogwood tree. *How wonderful that they can jump from one tree top to another and run along narrow branches without falling. I wish I could do that, or soar in the air like that hawk, or even sing like a cardinal.* She seldom wished for things she couldn't have, or even thought about her personal needs. *But to sing like a bird would be like a prayer, a prayer of thanks...that I'm so happy.*

She pursed her lips and tried to imitate the cardinal's high whistle. *Whhheeeettttt, wheeeeeettt, wheeeeeeeeeeeeeeeettt...*

"Howdy, ma'am. Aire you some kind of a loony bird?"

Laura gasped as Jonas appeared, taken aback by his bedraggled appearance. Her lips spread into a wide grin.

"Well, tarnashun, I didn't 'spect no mountain man. I'm here waitin' for my lover boy, a good lookin', clean shaved fella I bin dreamin' 'bout all winter." She laughed. Then jumped up and threw her arms around him.

"Well, hey, Missy...reckon I'm the fella that fits that description, 'neath all this fur. 'N it's you I bin dreamin' 'bout for that same spell of time." They kissed.

She broke the kiss and leaned back. "That's quite a git-up. It's a wonder I even recognized you myself."

Jonas explained to Laura the plan he and Jeb had devised. In turn, Laura told that she hadn't been able to learn much that would help, except that Jake was staying at the Claremont Hotel. She really couldn't approach Jake at all, could only report what others said about him. And there was no way she could talk to Dirk about Jake.

"Laura, you did jes' fine. Jeb was able to find Jake 'n git things rollin'. 'N he found out some mighty int'ristin' things concernin' Dirk and Jake." Jonas described Jeb's meeting with Jake in the bar and the information Jeb had weaseled out of him.

"Seems Jake and Dirk were up to their necks in some things nobody ev'n knowed about. Tonight, me 'n Jeb'll be meetin' with Jake. I gotta feelin' that whatever we find out, it's gonna help me outta my fix."

"Jonas...oh, be careful. What if he recognizes you?"

"Ain't likely. Not 'till I want him to, leastwise. Jeb'll be feedin' him a few whiskeys ev'n before I git there. That'll loosen his tongue, 'n he won't be seein' so good neither. You, yourself, might not've recognized me, if you hadn't knowed I was comin'. We aim to pump Jake real good 'n find out what he knows about that fight we had, 'n about Dirk 'n whate'er else he's mixed up in. Then we'll cut 'im a deal. I figger Jake'll do jes' about anythin' for a few bucks right now, bein' he's so down 'n out. 'N Jeb says Jake is mighty resentful concernin' Dirk, 'n 'bout ripe for the pickin'."

"So," continued Jonas, "the plan is to give Jake 'nuff money to give 'im a chance to start over somewhere else, or to drink hisself to death if he's got a mind to. Don' much matter to me either way. But, for that money, Jake's got to set the record straight about that stabbin'. 'N he's gotta come forward about any other shady dealin' Dirk's involved in. By comin' forward, I mean Jake's got to own up to his part in all this to the sheriff, 'n to yer pa. I need yer pa to know I ain't no rascally character, so when I tell 'im I'm gonna be marryin' his daughter, he'll be less likely to punch my teeth out."

This made Laura laugh. "Oh, Jonas. D'you think it'll work? Oh, I hope so. But, in truth, yer gonna be marryin' his daughter no matter what her dad thinks."

They kissed again. "I'm happy to hear you say that, Laura. But I want us both leavin' here in good standin'. I don't want my name besmirched no how, 'n I sure don't want you talked bad about for hitchin' up with me. I think we got a good chance of workin' this thing out. If all goes as planned, I'll be askin' you to set Jeb 'n me up a meetin' with the sheriff and yer pa. 'N you got to get Dirk there too. Me 'n Jeb'll be there with Jake in tow."

They hugged again and talked of more pleasant things, future plans, green rolling hills, sunsets, bubbly creeks, and babies.

▲ ▲ ▲

Toward evening, Jebediah was back in the Claremont Hotel bar once again sitting across the table from Jake Kellogg. A bottle of whiskey sat between them and was emptying quickly, mostly of Jake's doing. Most of the diners had left by now. Anyone remaining was more interested in booze than food, or a grizzled old stranger. The tables were unoccupied but for Jeb and Jake—what few customers remained stood at the bar.

"Hey, Jeb, who's yer friend here?" inquired Jonas, just arriving on the scene. Jeb had selected a table that was in dim light and out of hearing range of the rest of the patrons. Jonas had his wide brimmed hat pulled down, partially shielding his face. With the ragged mountain man attire, full beard, mustache, and straggly long hair, there was really no chance of a whiskey-dulled Jake recognizing Jonas as the young man he had once tangled with. "Ker if I join you?"

"Slim, this hars Jake, my new pal," said Jebediah. "Jake, meet Slim, my nephew, the one I was a tellin' ya 'bout. Take a load off, Slim."

Jonas joined them but kept his imbibing at a minimum. Jake had attained just about the right degree of ripeness that Jonas felt he could start working on him without raising suspicion.

"Jake," Jonas began. "My pard tells me you've come on some rough times." Jake was unshaven and drawn looking. Judging from the stench, Jonas doubted he'd bathed anytime recently.

"Yeh, hell. You kin say that agin."

"Well, tell me 'bout it pard. I kin maybe help ya out."

Jake went on to repeat most of what he had told Jeb the preceding night, sensing it might improve his situation—couldn't get much worse. It had been a while since anyone had lent Jake a sympathetic ear. The second time around he seemed even more embittered, as the whiskey kept flowing and his tongue loosened.

"So, sounds t' me," said Jonas, "that this Dirk feller's done turned his back on you, 'n if he ain't helpin' you out no more, I guess you don' have to keep yer mouth shut no more neither. If I was in yer shoes, I'd sure fix that doubl' dealer good'n proper."

"Yeh, sure. 'N git myself kilt good'n proper. That's 'bout all would happen if I shot my mouth off now."

"What? You don' mean that rascal actu'ly threat'ned you?"

"Naw, he don' need to do that. I jes' know what he's cap'ble of, thas all."

Jeb was staying out of this conversation, satisfied to make sure Jake's glass remained full.

Jonas continued. "Well now, feller. You ain't alone no more in this. You've found yerself some allies. We ain't 'bout to let no harm come to you, I kin guarantee that. That is if we come up with us a deal. Now listen up. I think I know how you kin git back at that cheatin' varmin'. You mentioned you had some other stuff on this Dirk character, stuff he might not be too anxious for you to tell 'bout. Well, yer among friends here, 'n it don't seem you got a whole lot of them anymore, due to the terribl' deal you got. Why don't you jes' tell us 'bout it. I imagin' it's likely eatin' you up inside."

"What're you guys, the law 'r some-thin'?" Jake shuffled in his chair and looked around the room. "Why should I stick my neck out?"

"Jake, yer right to wonder about us. Let's jes' say we got as much int'rist in bringin' Dirk Fisher down as you do, maybe more. We ain't askin' fer no favors. You do for us 'n we'll do for you. Hell, we ain't the law. Dirk done me wrong, just like he done you."

Jake stared at Jonas. "'N jes' who in hell are you mister?"

"We'll git to that. Now, about our deal..."

"Yeh? Well refresh me, jes' what the hell do I get outta all this?"

"Like Jeb here tole you, we'll pay yer hotel bill while yer here. Plus we'll put a wad of change in yer pocket for yer trouble, enuff money to git you clear away from here, so's you kin git a new start somewhere else."

"A wad of change you say...like how much?"

"More'n you've ever seen b'fore."

Jake pondered a bit. He again looked around for prying ears. Then, figuring he really had nothing to lose, he sat forward in his chair and spoke in almost a whisper. "Yeh, I got lots I kin tell. But don' you be spreadin' it 'round. I ain't lookin' for no early grave."

Jake proceeded to reveal much more than Jonas had dared to suspect, now practically jumping at a chance to attain revenge on his former pal, and prodded by the prospect of "a wad of change".

He'd already told Jeb about Dirk setting up the fight that led to the knifing and about "that McNabb lad" being blamed for it. He then went on to tell even more. Frederick Becker, it seems, put a lot of trust in Dirk Fisher. He made him his right hand man, handing over to him many of the responsibilities for the operation of the Becker Mining Company. Becker had lapsed into a hands-off policy concerning the miners and their affairs, trusting Dirk to see to the dirty work. Thus, it was Dirk Fisher who handled the actual dealings with the miners, often with no accountability to Becker. And it was Dirk who handled the financial transactions between Becker's Company and the coal buyers. Jake revealed that Dirk had cut deals with some of the coal buyers, allowing him to record lower profits than were actually gained. Dirk and the buyers split the differences. Jake was often present at these transactions and got his cut, as did Larry Jansen, the third supervisor.

Jonas was appalled at the raw deal Dirk had been giving the miners, which included Jonas's father. Jake revealed that the miners never received the full amount of pay they were due. Part of their pay was held back for imaginary expenses, trumped up by the three mine company supervisors, Dirk, himself, and Larry. Deducted from the miners' pay were such intangibles as job protection fees, safety fees, equipment fees, and just about any other "fees" Dirk Fisher could dream up. The supervisors pocketed the fees with Dirk getting the lions' share. Dirk used the Corps, the Company's chosen enforcers, to ensure that the miners raised no objections to these unwarranted fees. According to Jake, Becker was unaware of these activities.

"My gawd, man," exclaimed Jonas. I don' guess you got any proof of any of that?"

"Proof? Well, hell, yeh. All ya gotta do is take a look at Dirk Fisher's bank account o'er there in Cedar City. I know for a fact he's got a pile of money in that bank, 'n there ain't no way he came by it all honestly."

Jonas wasn't quite sure just how he would use all this information. But for what he intended to do next he needed to get Jake upstairs to his room, which was just down the hall from where he and Jeb were staying.

"Pard, what say we git you up to yer room. I got a pro-per-si-shun for you, 'n this ain't the place to be offerin' it. Jeb, grab that bottl' 'n let's help our friend here up the stairs."

So long as the bottle was accompanying them, Jake raised no objections.

Once in Jake's room, Jonas removed his hat. Jake sat on his bed. Jonas pulled up a chair and sat facing him. "Jake, take a good look at me. D'you know who I am?"

"Huh...whaaa...who you are?"

"I'm Jonas McNabb. I come back to git things straightened out."

"McNabb? Whaaa...whaz in hell you doin' here?" Jake attempted to rise but Jeb held him down.

"Now, don' go doin' nuthin' foolish-like feller," warned Jeb. "Jes' listen ta what the lad's gotta say."

Jonas continued. "I ain't got nuthin' agin' you. That's o'er 'n done with as far as I'm concerned. But I need to have some things cleared up. You've got to tell folks that I weren't to blame for that knifin', that it weren't even my knife."

"Why should I do that?"

Jeb poked a finger in Jake's chest. "Now you jes' shet up 'n listen. When Jonas is done 'splainin' things, then ya kin talk."

"Like I said," continued Jonas, "we got a heap-a cash here for you. 'Nuff for you to get a new start, anywhere of yer chosin'. But you got to do somethin' for me. First, you clear my name, like I said. You tell folks about the knifin' 'n all, that it weren't my fault."

Jake looked to Jeb, seeing if was all right to talk. Jeb nodded. "How mush cash are we talkin' 'bout here?"

Jeb pulled a roll of bills from his pocket and thumbed through them in front of Jake's bulging eyes. Jake seemed to sober quickly.

"Well...okay, but how'm I 'sposed to tell folks, 'n what 'bout Dirk. How you gonna keep him offa me?"

"When we git done, you ain't gonna have to worry none about Dirk," said Jonas. "He's gonna be put away for a long spell, 'n you kin be long gone by then. Now here's the rest of the conditions for you to git that money. We'll have us a meetin' over at the sheriff's office. It'll involve the sheriff, Mr. Becker, yerself, Dirk Fisher, 'n me 'n Jeb here."

There was a knock on the door. Jeb opened it and admitted Sheriff Turner. "Sheriff, we bin expectin' you." Jeb had pre-arranged this.

"Well, let's find out if what the old fella, here, tole me is true," said the sheriff. "Haw, is that you, Jonas, underneath all that hair?"

"Yeh, it's me, Sheriff, 'n Jeb didn't tell you no lies. 'N there's even more. Jake here'll ver'fy ev'rthing."

Though somewhat hesitant, Jake finally admitted to Turner that it wasn't Jonas's knife and that the stabbing was accidental.

"'N Jake's got some more int'ristin' information for you, Sheriff," said Jonas. "'N if Jake comes through for us, I'm thinkin' you'll arrange to keep him outta jail."

Jake considered the money shown him, his resentment for Dirk Fisher, and the promise of leniency. He opened up completely and told Sheriff Turner everything—implicating Dirk, Larry, and even himself.

"Sheriff, the only proof we got of all this," said Jonas, "is Dirk's bank account o'er in the Cedar City Bank. I'm hopin' you got the authority to check out his deposits in that bank. I suspec' they clearly outdistance his salary. I'm also suspectin' that Jake's testimony will have Dirk sweatin' a bit, 'n Mr. Becker's bound to have some way of checkin' on the way Dirk's bin cheatin' him on the coal sellin'. 'N I'm also guessin' that my pa, 'n some of the other miners will back up what Jake's tellin' us about all them fees they've bin subject'd to."

"Wahl, I'll be horn-swaggl'd, "said Sheriff Turner. "All this goin' on 'n nobody knowin' nuthin'. Jonas, if this checks out, this here town's gonna owe you one hell of an apology. I'll head out for the Cedar City Bank come mornin'. If we kin git Dirk Fisher on this, 'n if Jake's willin' to testify, I'm sure we kin strike a deal for Jake. 'N I'll talk to the miners, see if I can't git some of them to come forward."

"Hang on a minute har," said Jeb. "I'll be right back." Jeb left the room and soon returned with Savage in tow. "Jes' ta make shore Jake don' git it in his head ta skee-dattl' sometime durin' the night," added Jeb, "we'll jes' leave ole Savage har ta keep 'im company. Savage ain't had nuthin' to eat fer some spell now, 'n I suspec' our pal Jake won't be giv'n 'im no trouble." Savage stood before Jake, issuing a slight growl.

So it was agreed. Tomorrow, early, Sheriff Turner would make the twenty-mile journey to the Cedar City Bank and check out Dirk Fisher's bank account, giving special attention to his deposits.

Jeb would be meeting with Laura and inform her of the latest developments. Then it would be up to Laura to get her dad and Dirk Fisher to the meeting at the jail the following morning. Jonas specifically expressed that Laura not be at the meeting, fearing what direction events might take.

"I jes' gotta feelin' it ain't goin' be no place for a woman," said Jonas.

32

The sheriff's office was a one room affair squeezed between the Claremont Hotel and the Bank of Jericho. An open archway in the back led to a windowless holding cell, secured with steel bars. The holding cell was just that—about adequate to hold a few prisoners for a short period of time. Any serious lockup time would be relegated to the state penitentiary at Moundsville, further upstate. The cell was presently unoccupied.

Supported by pegs on the wall behind the sheriff's desk was a twelve-shot Winchester .44 carbine and just beneath the rifle hung a two-barrel sawn off scattergun. Sheriff Turner's sidearm—a holstered Colt Army Revolver "six-shooter" and ammo belt—hung on a peg beneath the larger guns. Pete had never had occasion to use any of these weapons against anyone. He liked it that way.

On the appointed morning, Sheriff Turner leaned against a desk cluttered with paperwork, mostly concerning complaints from the locals, nothing serious since Jonas McNabb's altercation with Jake Kellogg last year. Counting the sheriff, seven men and one dog were crowded into the small jail room. Jebediah Hart and Jonas McNabb had escorted a nervous Jake Kellogg to the proceedings, with Savage assuring Jake didn't bolt. Frederick Becker, Dirk Fisher, and Larry Jansen believed they were responding to the sheriff's summons—something about trouble in town involving a few of Becker's men.

Jonas noticed a lone wanted poster on the wall—an old one deeming Jonas McNabb a wanted suspect in a stabbing incident.

"Well, Pete," said Becker, "What the hell's this all about? I'm a busy man." He hadn't recognized Jonas.

"Frederick, I think you'll find this worth yer time," replied Turner. "Go ahead, Jake, 'n repeat what you tole us the other evenin'." Jake had been reassured he'd get the money he was promised, as well as clemency for his involvement in the mining company scams.

Jake looked over at Dirk Fisher. Dirk glared back. But Jake had already chosen his path and wasn't about to be intimidated. *What do I have to lose anyway? For that kind of money, a man takes his chances.* Jake actually smiled—a smile of derision.

"All right," he started, still looking at Dirk. "I'll tell my story. Why the hell not?"

Jake began his disclosure, taking pleasure in getting back at Dirk for the way he'd been treated. First he admitted that he had instigated the fight with Jonas McNabb because Dirk was upset with McNabb for *messin'* with Laura Becker, *his property,* and that Dirk wanted to teach McNabb a lesson and appointed him to administer it. Jake explained that it was his knife, not McNabb's that was involved and that the stabbing was accidental. "So this here boy ain't to be held responsible," stated Jake, indicating Jonas.

"Wha..." exclaimed Becker. "This here's Jonas McNabb? Pete, what the hell's goin' on here?"

Dirk Fisher interrupted, rather, exploded. "You ain't goin' believe this lyin' lowlife drunk, are you? Hell, he'd say anythin' for a drink 'r two. McNabb musta promised him..."

"Now hold on Dirk," ordered the sheriff. "You'll git yer say. Jake, you go on with yer story and ever'one shet up till he's done. You too, Frederick." Dirk was puzzled and apprehensive over Jonas's presence. He thought he had Jonas out of the picture for good.

Jake told it all—about skimming the miners' pay, about pocketing part of the profits from coal sales, and the kickbacks to the coal buyers. Becker stared back and forth between Dirk and Jake, at first confused, then with growing rage.

Dirk became more and more agitated.

"You can't prove none of this," he snarled. "It's jes' lies, bald-faced lies 'cause he's upset I fired him. He's incompet'nt 'n a damn drunk. Ain't nobody gonna believe him."

"Well, you can believe this," said Sheriff Turner. He produced a document from his desk drawer. "This here's an official listin' of yer deposits in the Bank of Cedar City, verified and signed by the bank president himself. Frederick, take a look at these here figgers."

As Becker studied the document, Dirk slowly edged over to where Sheriff Turner's gun lay holstered on a hook on the back wall. He knew the bank account figures would incriminate him and that further investigation into his dealings with the miners and coal buyers would seal his fate. He edged the gun out of the holster while the others were intent upon the document.

All but Savage.

The dog growled at Dirk, drawing everyone's attention.

"Okay folks, jes' stay put, or I swear I'll use this thing," Dirk threatened. "'N hold that damn white devil back or he gits it first."

Jeb steadied Savage. "Larry," continued Dirk, "take them keys offa the wall there, 'n open up that cell in the back."

Larry hesitated. "Are you sure about this, Dirk? We could jes' be buying more trouble."

"Don't start thinkin' on me, Larry," said Dirk, waving his gun Larry's way. "It ain't yer style. Jes' do it."

Larry jumped to the task.

"Dirk, for God's sake," said Becker. "This is insane. I don't understand none of this." He stepped toward Fisher. "C'mon, Dirk, gimme the gun... we'll work this out."

"Stop right there, old man. I won't hesitate to shoot you or anyone else that keers to argue with this gun. Now...all of you...into the cell. 'N keep yer mouths shut. Larry, grab that scattergun, 'n make sure it's loaded. It jes' might come in handy."

"Dirk, I won't stand for this," said Becker. "Don't be a damned fool. Give me that gun," He moved toward Dirk.

Larry had the scattergun and had herded the others into the open jail cell. As Becker approached Dirk, Larry swung the shotgun around and accidently discharged it at Becker's foot, sending Becker sprawling to the floor. Larry stood dumbfounded, but Dirk was quick to reach the jail cell door, clanging it shut before anyone had a chance to react.

"You too, Boss," said Dirk. "You ain't hurt that bad. Larry, idiot that you are, you think you might manage to git this old man into the cell, b'fore you blast both his feet off?"

Larry got Becker to his feet and helped him hobble to the cell. Dirk inched the cell door open to admit Becker, keeping his six-gun pointed to the other occupants. He singled out Jake. "Jake, old buddy. No need for you to be locked up. Step out here, I got somethin' for you."

Jake hesitated. "Git out here now, Jake," said Dirk. Dirk stuck his pistol under Jake's chin, grabbed him by the shirt and hauled him from the cell, then slammed the butt of the gun against Jake's head. Jake slumped to the floor and Dirk administered a few hard kicks to his ribs. "Damn turncoat. Yer lucky I don't jes' shoot you. Larry, drag this stoolie back inside with the others. I'll hold the shotgun." Larry did so and clanged the cell door shut and locked it.

All this time, Jebediah kept a tight grip on Savage fearing his dog might get hurt trying to protect him and the others. Savage continued to snarl at Fisher. Dirk stuck the shotgun muzzle through the bars, nudging Savage's jaws.

"You want some of this, boy?" he teased the dog.

Jeb pulled Savage back. "Easy boy, you'll git yer day."

"Yeh, right," said Dirk, backing off. "'N hear this, McNabb, no one gets Laura but me, *no one*. Wahl folks, it's shore bin fun, but I got to be goin'. Enjoy yerselves now." He took the keys and he and Larry exited, locking the front and only door.

▲ ▲ ▲

Back at the Becker Estate, Laura was down in the stables tending to Saca after a morning ride. She was brushing the Appaloosa down with a stiff currycomb when Dirk Fisher entered the stables.

"Laura!" he yelled. "Come quick. It's your father. He's had a heart attack or somethin' o'er in town. Come quick."

Larry Jansen had the buckboard waiting, the same buckboard he, Dirk, and Becker had taken to town. Laura knew the three of them had gone into town for a meeting, so she didn't question Dirk's terrible news.

"Is he all right...oh, please...is he all right?"

"I think so, he's askin' for you."

They boarded the buckboard, Dirk taking the reins, with Laura between the two men. But they didn't head toward Jericho. They headed the opposite way.

"Why're we goin' this way?" asked Laura. He didn't answer. "Dirk, what's goin' on...Dirk?" He stared straight ahead, in silence. "Dirk, what about my father? Stop...stop this buggy. Tell me what's goin' on."

Dirk reined up the horses. He turned to Laura and grabbed her roughly by the shoulders. Laura struggled, and screamed, "You let me go...what is this?"

"Tie her hands, Larry. I'm takin' you, Laura. Ain't no Jonas McNabb goin' to have you. Yer 's'posed to be mine, 'n I'm takin' you." Laura struggled as Larry bound her hands in front of her. She continued to yell at Dirk.

"Stop this, Dirk Fisher. Stop it right now. I ain't goin' nowhere with you. What have you done with Jonas?"

"Stop yer screamin', Laura, or I'll have to gag you too. 'N I'll do it. I mean it." He shook her.

Laura settled down. Her confusion gave way to fright. Tears formed in her eyes. "I jis' don' understand," she said more quietly. "Why're you doin' this? You haven't hurt nobody have you?...Dad?...Jonas?"

"Ain't nobody hurt," Dirk lied. "'N there'll be no more men-shunin' of no Jonas. All you got to know for now is yer comin' with me. 'N I don't want no more talkin' till I say so."

33

Around noon, one of Sheriff Turner's deputies arrived at the jail to relieve the sheriff for lunch. Using his own set of keys, he released Turner and the others from the cell. Frederick Becker limped from the cell with Jonas's help. Jonas had given up his shirt to wrap around Frederick's foot to stem the bleeding. Jake had regained consciousness and was to able vacate the cell on his own.

By this time, Dirk and Larry had a three-hour start.

"I imagine them rascals'll be headin' for the Cedar City bank first, to git that money out," said Turner.

Jonas spoke up. "Sheriff, somethin's botherin' me about what Dirk said...'bout nobody gettin' Laura but him. I think we should ride out to Becker's place 'n check on Laura."

"My God," exclaimed Becker, "if anything's happened to her..."

"Frederick, I'm sure she's fine," said the sheriff. "Let's not git alarmed till we know diff'rent."

Once outside, Becker found his buckboard missing. "Damn, they've taken the buckboard. Somebody get me a horse. I'll kill that damn boy if he's done anythin' to Laura."

"Frederick," spoke the sheriff. "You're not going anywhere 'cept to see Doc Adams to git that foot cared for. The rest of us will see to Laura, then we'll go after Dirk 'n Larry."

"Well let's git goin' then," said Jonas. "I really think that bastard's gone after Laura."

"Hold on, young feller. Let's do this proper. I'll rustle up a few men to help us, jes' in case."

"You do that, Sheriff, but I'm headed out. I'll meet you at Becker's place, Jeb, you comin'?"

"You go ahead Jonas, yer gonna be doin' some hard ridin' 'n I'd only slow you up. B'sides, there's somethin' I'll be wantin' ta check on. Me 'n Savage'll be ready when ya need us." Jebediah peeled off his shirt and offered it to Jonas. "Here, take this, ya might want ta cover up a bit b'fore ya go stormin' off. I'll git myself anuth'r one...'n keep yer rifle handy."

From experience, Jebediah knew there was no reason to be rushing off. *What's done is done.* If Fisher had Laura, it was going to be a long, hard haul getting her back. "Jake, what say you 'n me have us a little pow-wow," said Jeb, dragging Jake aside. In the subsequent conversation, Jake confirmed something that Jeb had suspected.

"Jake," said Jeb afterwards, "orn'ry critter thet you aire, at least ya did what we asked ya to. I suspec' ya've earned yer money."

Jeb paid Jake off and offered him a last bit of advice. "Ya best be clearin' out of these har parts. The miners ain't gonna take too kindly 'bout how ya've bin cheatin' 'em."

▲ ▲ ▲

Jonas arrived at the Becker Estate well before the others. He reined up and leaped the front steps to the Estate house and rapped hard on the front door. Gini opened the door.

"Jonas, is that you, I'd have hardly recognized you if Laura hadn't said you were back." Gini saw the urgency in Jonas's eyes. "Jonas, what's wrong?"

"Where's Laura?"

"Laura? Well, Dirk Fisher came by a few hours ago in a buckboard with another man. Laura went with them. Oh, Jonas, what is it, what's happened?"

Jonas hurriedly filled Gini in on the details of what had happened in Jericho. Gini told Jonas that Laura had seemed distraught when she left with Fisher.

"Did she say anything?"

"I'm not sure, I was in the house. They left before I could get outside."

"Gini, I think Dirk's taken Laura under some kind of false pretense." Jonas was visibly shaken. "You got any idea which way they went?"

Gini pointed the way.

"Jes' like Sheriff Turner figgered," said Jonas. "They're headed for Cedar City."

Jonas waited for Sheriff Turner, who arrived shortly with several other men and provisions for a few days. Soon they were all on their way to Cedar City.

▲ ▲ ▲

Jonas rode in silence, leading the group, stretching the limits of his horse. His was a stern, determined visage—filled with anger and apprehension. The trip took over two hours. Sheriff Turner and Jonas went directly to the Cedar City Bank, while the rest of the men grabbed a bite to eat at the hotel.

Dirk had withdrawn his money, just as suspected. Turner asked around town and discovered that a man of Dirk's description had sold a buckboard at the livery and picked up three more horses. Then, after purchasing a few supplies at the mercantile, he had ridden north out of town. He was alone.

Jonas and the sheriff pondered the situation. "Okay," said Turner. "Looks to me like Dirk left Laura with his flunky Jansen somewhere outside of town, then rode in for the money 'n any supplies he might need for wherever they're headed."

Jonas pictured Laura alone with Larry, probably tied up, confused and frightened.

Safe?

He intended to do everything within his power to get Laura back, unharmed. A deep pain gnawed at his insides.

"Folks here say he's headed north," continued the sheriff. "Now, that don't mean he intends to stay on that course, could be he's jes' tryin' to throw us off. He could be headed anywhere. In that he swapped the buckboard for more horses, I suspec' he might be headed up into the mountains. Now, unless one of us is a bloodhound, it's goin' be mighty hard to track 'em."

"I don't care how hard it'll be," said Jonas. "I'm goin' after them, 'n I won't quit till I git Laura safe."

"Now hell, boy, nobody's talkin' about quittin'. We'll go after them all right. But first, we gotta git organized 'n think this thing out. We ain't got all that much daylight left, so's it makes sense we put up here for the night, 'n take off after 'em in the morning."

"In the morning?" said Jonas. "Why give 'em any more of a head start than they already got?"

"I know yer itchin' to git on their trail, lad, but let's be smart about this. I suggest we have us a talk with the sheriff here in Cedar City. Maybe he can git us some men that know the countryside, 'n maybe have some idea where Dirk might be headed. 'N we'll need to pick up some more supplies ourselves if we're goin' be out there for a spell."

Jonas could see Sheriff Turner's reasoning and though anxious to get started, he decided it made sense to wait until morning.

"And another thing we might consider," added Turner. "This jes' might end up with a ransom situation...jes' a thought. Anyways, Dale Clifford is Sheriff here, 'n I've know 'im for quite some time. He's a good man and he'll sure help us out if there's any help to be had."

Jonas and Turner stepped into Clifford's office. Clifford was a tall, lean man, without mustache or beard, but always looking as if he was trying to start them. A chaw of chewing tobacco bulged his cheek and now and then he would stroll to an open window and spit, as he was in the process of doing now. Jonas hoped no passers-by would intercept a load of the vile juice.

"Pete, what brings you to these parts?" asked Clifford, wiping dribble from the corner of his mouth with the back of his hand.

"Think we'll be needin' yer help, Dale."

Sheriff Clifford was fascinated by the story Pete Turner then related to him.

"Shoot," said Clifford. "We ain't had nuthin' like this goin' on in Cedar City, or anywhere here-a-bouts for quite some spell. To tell the truth, it's bin downright borin' 'round here. So could be a kidnappin', you figger?"

"Dale," said Turner. "There ain't no way that gal would've accompanied Fisher willin'ly. He's dragged her off for sure. I ain't got no idea of his intentions at this point. Now, where might a feller start lookin' for a coupla fugitives on the run?"

Sheriff Clifford thought a minute. "Hmmm, I'll tell you, Pete. If they got a place to hole up, maybe up into the mountains, yer gonna have a hard time diggin' 'em out. But gimme a description of these fellers, 'n if I see them hereabouts, I'll bring 'em on in, 'n they won't be escapin' me. Nuthin' personal, Pete. 'N the gal, leave me her description too. Best I kin do is keep an eye out for 'em, 'n I'll pass the word on to folks around here to be on the lookout for 'em in their travels."

"Obliged to you Dale, but a-nuther thing. You think you kin round us up a few of yer local boys to help us find these critters? I figger we got a better chance with some men that knows the countyside."

"I kin sure do that. I'll have a few boys for you by mornin'."

"Thanks, Dale, 'n tell 'em we might be out for a spell, so have 'em pack accordin'ly."

This had been a long day and Jonas hadn't realized how hungry he'd become. The last thing he had eaten was a few biscuits for breakfast. "What say we take us a meal 'n rooms for the night," Jonas suggested.

"I was about to propose the same thing," said Turner. I'll round up the rest of the boys 'n make arrangements at the hotel."

▲ ▲ ▲

Jonas couldn't sleep, too much weighed heavily on his mind. Just when it appeared that all was going well—with Jake's testimony vindicating him, and Jonas thinking he'd soon be back at his ranch with Laura as his bride, fate intervened with another twist. Once again, things didn't turn out as anticipated. "Dam-na-shun," he thought. "That's puttin' it mildly."

Whether or not Laura was to be ransomed didn't matter to Jonas. He was only concerned with her safety. Jonas knew he needed to find Laura and find her fast. He cringed at the thought of Laura in the hands of two desperate men—unpredictable men, and the longer they held her, the greater the chance of her being harmed—or worse.

But he would save Laura; that was his unrelenting course.

Jonas's restless night continued as he was unable to free his mind of lingering thoughts of Laura at the mercy of Jake and Larry. What must she be going through? His heart ached for her. He wanted to believe Dirk would treat her well if he had any feelings for her at all. And certainly Larry wouldn't dare approach Laura inappropriately with Dirk around. But in reality, just what might Dirk be capable of, now that he had shown his true colors. Such thoughts only added to Jonas's distress. He had to think positively, to cling to the notion that all would turn out well.

Jonas had killed already—in protecting Jebediah—but then he'd had no choice. How might he react if confronting Fisher and Jansen? He'd be carrying a rifle and a sidearm, and knew he would stop at nothing to protect Laura. He hadn't hesitated to kill that mountain man, Zeke, when Jeb's life was at stake. It bothered him, but he knew he'd do the same again if necessary. And if it came to that with Dirk and Larry, and if he discovered they'd harmed Laura in any way, he might even savor it.

But what were his chances of actually finding Laura and freeing her? Jonas wished Jeb and Savage were with him. He should have insisted that Jeb come along, but at the time, he was in such a hurry to be after Laura that he wasn't thinking clearly. Undoubtedly, Jebediah had hunted, trapped, and prospected much of the country around here. If anyone knew where Dirk might be headed, it would be Jeb. And Savage would be invaluable in tracking them. With the instincts of a wolf and a dog's loyalty, Savage could comb the wilds and uncover anything that remotely pertained to the whereabouts of Laura and her abductors. Jonas decided that one way or the other, he had to get Jeb and Savage here.

Jonas's mind continued to work over the events of this day, sleep being elusive. It figured that Dirk and Larry had ridden off with Laura, heading north. But Sheriff Turner was right—they could have headed north just to deceive any pursuers. Then they could have taken a different direction, or even doubled back south. When Jonas had fled a year and a half ago, he'd headed for the mountains to avoid discovery. If Dirk had that in mind, they'd be heading east. And if they meant to ransom Laura, they wouldn't go far, not until they got the money. So, as Jonas saw it, they'd have to hide out someplace, maybe somewhere short of the mountains. And not somewhere conspicuous, where people might become suspicious and divulge their whereabouts—the news of the abduction would soon be widespread. Jonas figured that would rule out small towns and villages. They could lose themselves in a city, but the closest city of any size was Charleston, more than seventy miles away, and should ransom be their intent, negotiations would be difficult from such a distance.

Jonas's best reasoning was that Dirk would find a place to stay while he conjured his next move, figuring that Dirk had acted spontaneously at the jail and hadn't had time to formulate a well-thought-out plan. Finally, mercifully, Jonas slept.

34

"Hey, boy, what-cha goin' do, sleep yer life away?"

Jonas awoke to see Jebediah standing over him with Savage at his side. "C'mon, roust outta there, sleepy-head, we got us some trackin' ta do," said Jeb.

"Jeb?" said Jonas, feeling somewhat incoherent after a sleepless night. "Wha...what'r you doin' here?"

"Same's you aire. Settin' out ta find yer gal friend. But *I* got a plan."

Jonas got up, threw on some clothes, and splashed water on his face to clear the cobwebs.

Jebediah revealed his plan.

"After ya left in sich an all-fired hurry, I spoke ta Jake 'n found out somethin' int'ristin'. Then I knew me 'n Savage would have ta git up har 'n help ya out. Now listen up. Jake tole me Dirk Fisher's got 'im a huntin' cabin somewhar up in the foothills nor'east of here. We gotta find thet cabin, 'n check it out. Thet's whar me 'n Savage come in. We got the best chance of trackin' the three of 'em. Hell, the sheriff 'n his townies couldn't track a herd'a cows in deep snow in the broad daylight. So we'll keep this in-for-ma-shun to ourselves. Jake didn't know exactly whar the cabin was, only thet it was somewhar up in them yonder foothills. Chances are good Dirk 'n Larry's taken the girl there, ta hole up fer a spell, maybe figger out what ta do next, thet is if we kin give either of 'im credit fer a brain."

"Speakin' of brains," said Jonas. "I think maybe mine's started wor-kin' agin. What you say makes sense, Jeb. Dirk got his money out of the bank here all right. No one at the bank seemed to know anythin' useful. So, I checked around town yesterday, figgerin' I'd recheck every action Dirk took here in Cedar City b'fore he headed off. Dirk sold the buckboard at the livery stable 'n purchased three horses to go along with the one he had. Again, that seems to confirm yer belief that Dirk's headed for rough country, the foothills, or possibly the mountains. For sure, no place for a buckboard. I was able to learn what supplies Dirk bought himself at the general store. It seems he was preparin' for an extensive stay somewhere." Jonas fished a list from a shirt pocket. "Here's a few things he bought: canned fruit 'n beans, flour, coffee, dried beef, soda biscuits, salt, bacon, grease. He didn't buy any kind of cooking utensils or any bedding. Could be Dirk's headed somewhere that's already stocked with them items. That would suggest a cabin he's already familiar with. Like a huntin' cabin."

Jonas continued down the list. "Clothing—both male and female, mind you—two fifty pound sacks of grain, playing cards, writing paper, envelopes and pencil—for a ransom note?—some reading material, toi-letries, hunting knife, rope, canteen, bullets for both rifle and six-gun, 'n shotgun shells. So, I guess you're right 'bout them holin' up somewhere. 'N the female items confirms that Laura is with 'em, 'n there ain't no way

222

it could be voluntary." Thinking about that sent a shiver up Jonas's spine.

"The large grain purchase seemed curious," continued Jonas. "Gen'rally horses can find enough grass 'n such to feed on in the wilds without the need for grain. Unless Dirk's destination had a lack of natural feed, like in a heavily wooded area. It would make sense that he'd choose to keep the horses hidden, rather than allowin' 'em to graze in the open grasslands where someone might spot 'em. The grain would keep 'em fed where there weren't no other feed available. So, it seems more'n reasonabl' he's got some well concealed spot all picked out, like you said, Jeb. Several people did see a man fitting Dirk's description, riding north out of town, by himself, leading three horses, 'n packin' a lot of gear. He must've left Laura and Jansen hid somewhere outside of town and picked them up when he rode out."

"Wahl, Jonas, 'scuse my biscuits fer short-changing' ya in the plan- ning' de-part-mint. Yuv bin scurryin' 'bout like ya knowed what ya were doin'. So I guess we're in agree-mint. They's headed fer thet cabin of his, shore as shootin'."

▲ ▲ ▲

When Jebediah, Jonas, and Savage arrived downstairs to the Cedar City Hotel dining area, they were greeted by Sheriff Pete Turner and the men he had brought with him from Jericho. Of those present, the loudest and most boisterous was Frederick Becker. His foot was heavily bandaged and he leaned on crutches. Becker had arrived early this morning by buckboard, along with Jeb and Savage, an unlikely alliance. Doc Adams had insisted Becker stay off horseback due to the severity of his foot wound. Jeb had commented, "That foot looks like a hornet's nest the way ole doc's got it all wrapped up."

"I don't aim to get left out of this search, Pete," Becker assured the sheriff. "I can still get around on a buckboard."

Becker noticed Jonas. "Well, howdy, McNabb. 'Bout time you got around. Grab yerself a coffee 'n a few biscuits. Well, boys, looks like we can get goin' now. I'm anxious to get my hands around that cheatin', connivin' Dirk Fisher's neck. 'N the sooner we get goin', the sooner we get Laura back. By the way, McNabb, I'm jes' wond'rin, what's yer involvement in all this?" The question came off more like an accusation than a query.

Jonas hesitated, searching for just the right way to put this. "Well sir, I guess you should know how it is between yer daughter 'n me." Jonas spoke with more confidence now than he had when he faced Frederick Becker for the first time back in his office, so long ago. "Mr. Becker, me 'n yer daughter have made plans. I got a horse ranch now, up in the Shenandoah Valley. Laura's bin there 'n she loves it. We plan on marryin' 'n livin' there..."

"Hey now," interrupted Becker, "jes' who d'you think you are? You can't really think you 'n my daughter could ever..."

"No, Mr. Becker, I don' think it, I know it. 'N I'll go to the ends of this earth to find her 'n bring her back. If them vermin have harmed Laura in any way, there'll be hell to pay. I don' mean to offend you, but you need to know how things stand."

"Well, I'll be damned...Jonas McNabb 'n my Laura. We'll talk more on that later. Right now, we jes' gotta get her back. Gawd-almighty, my Laura 'n Jonas McNabb." Frederick Becker pondered this, rubbing his chin. "Can't say I feel too good about that."

The few locals promised by Sheriff Clifford arrived and plans were made to get underway. A gathering of men on horseback, contingencies from both Jericho and Cedar City, waited in the street in front of the hotel. Each man had provisions for an extended pursuit.

Jeb pulled Sheriff Turner off to the side.

"Sheriff, I got my res-er-va-shuns about this Becker. He ain't gonna be able to do no trackin' from thet buckboard of his. Most likely he'd befoul any tracks thar was. 'N thar ain't no way no wagon could git up into the foothills anyways, let alone into the mountains. 'N considerin' he's all lamed up, it makes more sense thet Becker goes back to Jericho 'n waits fer news of Laura, jes' in case thar's a ransom attempt."

"Been thinkin' the same thing myself, Jeb. I'll have a talk with him."

Frederick Becker sat on his buckboard, anxious to get under way. Sheriff Turner approached him. He stood with one foot on the buckboard's running board, pulled off his hat and ran a handkerchief around the inside of the brim. Without looking at Becker, he spoke. "Frederick, we've known each other for quite a spell, 'n I suspect we have a mutual respect for each other. I kin well appr'ciate yer anxious to ketch them mavericks 'n git yer daughter back."

Turner replaced his hat and now looked directly at Becker. "Here's what I got to say. There's the possibility that all this might be about them wantin' ransom money for Laura. Now hear me out...if a ransom request was to be sent to you, it'd be sent to yer home, 'n you'd need to be there to receive it. And considerin' yer bad foot, 'n you needin' to be traveling by buckboard, it seems to me you'd be helping Laura a whole lot more if you were back in Jericho. Now, think about it before you git all ornery."

Becker's jaw tightened, an eyebrow raised. After a lengthy hesitation, he sighed. "I guess yer right, Pete. I know my daughter. She's pure headstrong. There ain't no way she'd take up with Fisher, not after what he's done. 'N Dirk may be many things, but he ain't stupid. When he figgers it out that there's no way he can have Laura for himself, he's gonna want to make sure he gits somethin' out of all this. So I guess it makes sense he'll try to ransom her. But damn it, I don't want any stone left unturned. You find her, Turner. I don't care what it takes. Now, where's that boy, McNabb?"

Becker sighted Jonas, lingering close. "McNabb," he called out, "we'll talk about yer fool idea concernin' my daughter when she's back 'n safe."

So it was determined that the search for Laura and her abductors would take a four-pronged approach. Becker would go back to Jericho to await any ransom attempt. Sheriff Turner and his men would join up with Sheriff Clifford's locals to scour the countryside for any evidence of Laura's whereabouts, and Clifford would remain in Cedar City in case anything or anyone turned up there. Jonas, Jebediah, and Savage would strike out on their own—Jeb saying, "I jes' wants ta play a hunch I got."

Jonas knelt down and scratched the back of Savage's head.

"Well, boy. Looks like we'll be countin' on you once more. If anyone can sniff them vermins out, it'll be you. Now find Laura, boy...find her." Tears filled Jonas's eyes. He hugged the dog. "You jes' gotta find her for me."

Jonas didn't realize that burned into the back of Savage's mind was the image and smell of a man poking the muzzle of a shotgun into his face.

▲ ▲ ▲

Laura rode in silence. She was confused and she was angry and her wrists hurt from the ropes that bound them. Dirk led her horse and Larry followed close behind, all riding at a steady pace. The forth horse carried the supplies. With her hands tied, Laura found it difficult to maintain the saddle. Her legs were sore from using them extensively to stay seated.

She'd always suspected there was something unsavory about Dirk Fisher. She never really trusted him. But she never would have dreamed he'd stoop to something like this. She wondered what could have driven him to do such a thing. Laura finally ventured to ask. "Dirk," she yelled ahead, "can we talk?"

Dirk allowed her to catch up to his mount. "S'long as you don't go into no hysterics agin."

"I jis' don' understand. Why're you doin' this? It'll jis' git you into a mess of trouble."

"I'll tell you, Laura dear, there's things you jes' don't know. I guess you deserve some sorta ex-plan-a-shun. Me 'n the boys've bin cheatin' yer old man, ever' which way," he said proudly. "Con-se-quently, I ac-cum-u-lated quite a pile of money. Unfortunately, though, we got caught. That back-stabbin' Jake gave us up. 'N that Jonas McNabb had a hand in it too. So, me 'n Larry had to leave rather a-brupt-ly."

"But nobody got hurt...right? You said nobody got hurt."

"That's what I said. Nobody got hurt." Dirk lied again, no use further riling Laura.

"What...are yer intenshuns...for me?"

"Well now, Laura, I guess that sort of depends on you. I intend to get far away from Jericho, 'n start up agin somewhere else. 'N I want you to be with me."

This last statement scared Laura more than anything else that had gone before. She didn't think Dirk would hurt her, or, God-forbid, force himself on her. But, how could he think she could ever care for him. He was a thief, and a liar, and had actually kidnapped her. Laura was scared because she now thought Dirk Fisher must be insane. He had to be to think he could get away with all this. There was no telling what he might be capable of now. She sure didn't think she could reason with him. She had no choice but to play along and hope to find an opportunity to escape.

PART V
The Search

▲ ▲ ▲

35

Two riders and a dog headed north out of Cedar City, then east and into the foothills of the Allegheny Mountains, approximately twenty-four hours after their quarry had entered the same foothills, some five miles further to the north. Jonas was armed with pistol and rifle, Jeb with just a rifle. Both riders carried whatever additional supplies they would need for an extended pursuit, should that become necessary. Meanwhile, Sheriff Pete Turner and his men set out to check on neighboring towns, homesteads, and the surrounding countryside to see what they could turn up.

Dirk, Larry, and the girl began a gradual assent into the foothills, entering a dense forest. It seemed to Laura that they had been riding for days, though it had been but hours. She was exhausted, her legs ached, her wrists were throbbing, and she was thirsty—but she rode on in silence. She would not give Dirk the satisfaction of knowing of her discomfort.

As the countryside became rougher and the trees more closely bunched, they rode a circuitous route—avoiding the ravines, steep inclines, and dangerous drop offs. Still, the footing was treacherous and Laura's mount slipped while climbing a moss covered, rocky incline. Even with her hands tied in front and holding the pommel, she could not maintain her seat and rolled off her horse. Her momentum carried her back down the incline, barely missing the hoofs of Larry's horse. She could not hold back the screams as pain ripped through her leg and her ankle folded beneath her. The two men were soon by her side. Laura pointed to her ankle. Dirk touched the ankle and Laura winced.

"Well, Laura," said Dirk, "looks like yer ankle's broke, or least sprained. See if you can put any weight on it." Laura tried to stand but fell back down when a screeching pain shot up her leg. "Hell, looks like we're gonna have to wrap that ankle. I guess you've got a rest comin' anyway."

Dirk softened up a bit toward Laura and not only attended her ankle, but untied her hands and gave her a biscuit and water and a much needed rest. His manner became gentler and almost apologetic. "Laura, I know this is a terr'ble mess for you, you hurtin' 'n all. I didn't want it to be this way. It all happened so quick like, I guess I didn't have time to think things out much, 'n I expec' you pretty much hate me right now, 'n I don't blame you much. Well, I'm hopin' that'll change. But, right now, I can't trust you not to run off. So I'm gonna hafta keep you tied up most the time."

"But why, Dirk? Why the stealin', 'n the deceivin', 'n now all this?"

"Why? You dare to ask me why? How could you know what it's like for someone like me?" Dirk's manner changed suddenly. "You've nev'r had to fight for anythin' in yer life. Yer paw gave you everything. Anythin' I ev'r wanted, I had to scrape 'n fight for. It's brains and hard work that got me to be yer dad's top man, 'n I ain't apologizing for doin' what I did to git there. Don' you be judgin' me, Laura. You ain't earned the right. So jes' shut up about all that."

Laura had not seen Dirk this angry before, not with her anyway. It alarmed her that he had turned from gentle and apologetic to full rage so quickly.

Laura stared at Dirk. The reality of her situation was slowly sinking in, with disturbing clarity. She was injured and at the mercy of two desperate fugitives, traveling into an unknown, wild region where conceivably she had no chance of being rescued. Laura could only guess as to what Dirk might have in mind for her, and no guess on her part seemed to lead to a favorable outcome. She didn't want to cry, she didn't want to give Dirk the satisfaction, but tears came anyway.

Dirk pulled her up rather abruptly, disregarding her anguish and lifted her onto her horse. This time he didn't tie Laura's wrists, but he did rope her mount to his. Again, they rode on, now in silence. They entered a valley with a creek running through. Dirk allowed the horses to drink, then proceded along the creek. Sometime later, he led the group up and out of the valley and into dense foliage. Laura did not see the cabin until they were practically upon it, as trees and thick undergrowth had kept it well concealed.

Dirk and Larry secured the horses behind the cabin and stripped off their saddles. The four horses quickly attacked several bales of hay that lay upon a small platform. No grazing was available. Dirk unlocked the cabin's front door and assisted Laura inside.

The cabin was sparsely furnished—two bunks with blankets and pillows, a wood burning stove with a cook-burner on top, a table with two chairs, two kerosene lamps, cooking utensils, and several shelves. The windows were secured with heavy locks. Generally, such cabins are kept unlocked, with the understanding that anyone who might use the cabin would treat it with respect and leave it as they found it. But Dirk always locked up, trusting no one but himself.

They left the door open and opened up the windows as well to air out the cabin.

"Damn, it's a bit cool in here," exclaimed Larry. "I'll git that stove goin' to warm 'er up, 'n heat up some grub too."

"No fire," said Dirk. "Somebody's liable to see the smoke. Someday, Larry, maybe you'll have a thought that ain't clear rubbish. How's the ankle, Laura? Feelin' better?"

"It hurts, but I'll survive."

"One good thing about that ankle, Laura, dear. I won't hafta tie you up so much. You ain't goin' anywhere on a busted ankle. 'N being yer a girl, you get one of the bunks for yer very own. So, Larry, I guess that leaves the floor for you."

Dirk deposited her on one of the bunks. Laura welcomed the relief, but she knew her situation was still grim. Less than a week ago, she'd been on top of the world. She remembered meeting Jonas in the secluded spot beneath the cherry trees, with birds singing and the sun warming her face. How soon fate could change even the most sound of dreams. How could Jonas possibly find her—so well hidden—somewhere at the ends of the earth. She knew Jonas would try and that he'd never rest until he did. But how? Tears dampened her cheeks.

"Aw, Laura, come on now," said Dirk. "Things ain't all that bad. Yer jes' tired right now, but I aim to take good care of you. You'll see, ev'erthing will turn out fine."

Dirk's assertion did little to comfort her.

He again tied her wrists. "Sorry, dear. Just a precaution while we all sleep."

36

Jeb and Jonas scoured the foothills in search of any signs that might put them on the trail of Laura's abductors. They allowed Savage to range far and wide over the countryside. With his keen sense of smell and hearing, and a proven uncanny sense for being in the right place at the right time, Savage would have the best chance of finding Laura.

Jonas felt a sense of urgency—the more time that elapsed, the more chance that harm might come to Laura, or that her virtue be compromised, and the less chance she might be found at all. So far, the search had proved disappointing, with no encouraging signs. They encountered only run-down and abandoned shacks with no indications of recent occupancy. The area to be searched was vast. Laura and her captors could be anywhere.

"Don't lose faith, lad," Jeb encouraged Jonas. "Trackin's a painstakin' 'n delib'rate sort of thing. Savage'll find 'em, you kin bet on thet."

But would it be in time?

As darkness set in, they picked a deserted cabin as shelter for the night, intending to continue their search at first light. The terrain was difficult to negotiate by day; at night, it would be practically impossible. More likely, they'd tumble to the bottom of a ravine, or a horse would trip and break a leg.

▲ ▲ ▲

Laura was so exhausted that she slept through the night despite the discomfort of the painful and swollen ankle. Next morning, Larry went outside to tend to the horses, giving Dirk a chance to talk to Laura alone. He gently shook her from her sleep and ushered her to a seat at the table, opposite him. He untied her hands.

"Laura. I bin thinkin' a lot on how to proceed. When I took you and brung you along, I guess I thought we could run off together. Now I ain't so sure. Maybe if we had enough time together, it would work out, but I need to be more sure of the way things stand. So I'm gonna give you a choice. Now, what I'd really like is for you to come with me willin'ly. Maybe we can find a place for ourselves where we won't be bother'd by nobody. I got lots of money, so that ain't no problem." He hesitated a bit, looking at Laura. She remained inscrutable. Dirk went on.

"The other choice is...we ransom you." Laura gasped. She hadn't anticipated that. "Yer dad will pay big bucks to get you back. I'm figgerin' $50,000. So, it's up to you to decide. 'N you got to decide quick-like. I need to know, so I can set things up, one way or the other. You can stay with me 'n we can try'n find a nice life together somewhere, or I swap you for money. Yer choice." Dirk left the cabin.

Laura weighed her alternatives. If she went with Dirk, maybe she could escape somehow. That was one choice. And the other? She knew her father would pay the ransom. But should she make such a demand on him? Even for him, $50,000 was a huge sum of money. But then too, it was probably partially her father's fault that all this happened. He'd let Dirk have free reign in the mining company. Her dad should have kept closer tabs on things. And her father's insistence that she marry Dirk was almost ironic. If she ran off with Dirk, her father would get his wish, though not as he expected. If she didn't, he'd have to pay the large ransom.

Laura figured the surest way of getting back to Jonas was to concede to the ransoming, but she had to present her decision to Dirk in such a way as to not offend him. She knew he could be volatile and unpredictable. Her decision would soon be tested as Dirk reentered the cabin.

"Well Laura, what'll it be...me...or the ransomin'?"

"Dirk, I jis' wanna be back home. It's the only life I know...with dad 'n my horses. I'm jis' not brave 'nuff to run off with you."

"Then yer chosin' the ransomin'?"

"I guess I am."

Dirk sat back, folding his arms in front of him. "Haw! Gal, you think yer foolin' me? I know yer wantin' to go back to McNabb. You 'n that no-account miner. I wish I could see the look on Becker's face with you tellin' 'im yer wantin' to hook up with one of his miners. Well, hell, what do I care? I'll take the money o'er some gal ain't got no more sense than that. It's settled then. Larry, get back in here," he yelled out the door.

37

Fifty thousand dollars would put a hurtin' on Becker, but Dirk knew the old man was good for it. As today was Tuesday, it was set that Larry would travel to Cedar City and post the ransom note. It would be in Becker's hands by Wednesday, as mail was delivered daily between Cedar City and Jericho.

The ransom money was to be in hundred-dollar bills and placed in a saddlebag, which Becker was to deliver to L. Smith at the Claremont Hotel in Cedar City on Friday morning at 10:00. Then, Becker was to leave and not look back. When Dirk was in possession of the money, Laura would be put on a horse and sent home.

The ransom note ended with Dirk's threat: *Boss, if you want Laura back in one piece, you'll follow my instructions exact.*

Dirk wasn't overly confident in Larry's part in this plan, but neither did he trust leaving Larry with Laura, not for that period of time. So Larry had to be the one to pick up the money.

He delivered his parting instructions, "Larry, yer part in this is critical. You screw it up 'n there'll be re-per-cushuns. You don't do nuthin' to make yerself con-spic-u-ous. You don't carry no side-arm, 'n you keep yer scattergun with your horse at the livery. Stay in that hotel room most all the time, 'cept to eat 'n you kin do that right at the hotel. You got no need to leave there. 'N no boozing', they'll be plenty of time for that when this thing's all settled. Soon's you git the money, you hightail it back here, 'n make sure you ain't followed. I know you ain't the brightest critter around, but jes' heed what I tole you. You got that?"

234

"Sure Dirk, they ain't nothing' to it."

"Jes' don't screw it up."

Within the hour, Larry left for Cedar City with the ransom note sealed in an envelope.

38

Tuesday. Cedar City. Larry Jansen arrived, posted his envelope, and took a room at the Cedar City Hotel under the name L. Smith. He left word at the desk that he'd be expecting an important visitor Friday morning at 10:00. That left him with nothing to do until then. *Sure, stay in my room...don't screw up...he thinks I'm some sort of a moron. Hell, this ain't much diff'rent than bein' in a jail cell.* By Thursday, Larry had had all he could take of the isolation. He decided a few drinks and a little company wouldn't hurt.

Dale Clifford, Sheriff of Cedar City, had noticed a stranger taking meals at the hotel. This wasn't all that unusual, except this particular stranger seemed to fit the description of one of the two men that the McNabb lad had been inquiring about several days ago. Sheriff Clifford assigned a deputy to watch the movements of the stranger, who had signed into the hotel as L. Smith. So when Larry Jansen settled in at the hotel bar, the deputy took a nearby table within easy hearing distance. The evening wore on and Larry's whiskies piled up. He became boastful and mentioned to several of the ladies at the bar that he was expecting a windfall due to a daring venture he and his pard were involved in. Encouraged by Larry's bravado, one of the women accompanied him to his room.

The deputy reported this to Sheriff Clifford. Clifford now had no doubt that L. Smith was one of the men Jonas McNabb was looking for. He instructed the deputy to continue the vigilance on the stranger.

On Friday morning, Frederick Becker rode into Cedar City by buckboard. He left the buckboard in front of the Claremont Hotel and entered the establishment, a crutch under one arm and a saddlebag over his shoulder. Sheriff Clifford's deputy observed Becker go upstairs to the suspect's room. The deputy alerted Clifford and the sheriff took over from there. He awaited Becker outside the hotel.

Soon Becker came downstairs without the saddlebag. He dropped a note at the bar and went outside through the batwing doors. Sheriff Clifford stopped him.

"Frederick...Frederick Becker, what gives?"

"Sheriff, what d'you mean?"

"Well, what're you doin' back here?"

"Dale," said Becker, rather loudly, feigning irritation. "I reckon that's my business, now ain't it? I'll let you know if anythin's goin' on I need you to be involved in."

Becker intended that this conversation be overheard, figuring that Larry would be watching and listening to make sure that Becker left town without incident. But due to an overhanging porch roof blocking the proceedings below, Larry couldn't know that Becker whispered instructions to the sheriff to check at the bar for a note he had left there.

"So, excuse me, Sheriff, I'm in a bit of a hurry."

Becker climbed gingerly up onto the buckboard and headed out of Cedar City toward Jericho.

Sheriff Clifford obtained the note from the bartender, which read:

Dale,

I gave $50,000 ransom money to Larry Jansen, registered as L. Smith, for the return of my daughter, Laura. Watch for him to leave the hotel, then follow him. I'll be down the road outside of town. Send someone to let me know when Jansen heads out. I'll come back to the hotel and stay until this whole mess is cleared up. If you do your job right, we'll have Laura back and them two villains in tow.

Becker

▲ ▲ ▲

The Claremont Hotel was near the end of the main street of Cedar City, with only the blacksmith shop remaining between the hotel and the town's limits. There were three ways to enter or leave the hotel—the bar entrance (the batwing doors), the restaurant entrance (so women wouldn't have to go through the bar to get a meal), and a side door to the restaurant for bringing in supplies and taking out refuse. Sheriff Clifford chose a concealed spot in the blacksmith shop from which he could observe all three exits. He considered whether he should seek additional help, but other than the deputy, most available men were already out looking for the abducted girl. He would dispatch his deputy to inform Becker when Jansen left the hotel. Then he would follow Jansen.

*If I do my job right...*Becker's message had said. *Well, shoot*, thought Clifford, *if you did yer job right, we wouldn't even have this situation.* Clifford saw this as perhaps his biggest challenge in all of his twenty-one years as sheriff of Cedar City. "I guess I've had it pretty soft up till now. No tellin' what this might involve. Wahl, Dale, ole boy, you said you'd welcome a bit more excitement." He bit off a chaw of tobacco and began his vigil.

Cedar City was a small town; not a whole lot happened here that demanded much of the sheriff. He'd never had to face anything that might involve gunplay. He'd never even unholstered his gun in the line of duty. Generally, his duties involved settling domestic quarrels or throwing an unruly drunk in jail overnight—things like that. So, how would he react if faced with a dangerous situation that well might develop if he were to locate the two kidnappers?

Dale was seriously considering retiring soon, maybe spend some time fishing and hunting—even visit his brother over in Kentucky. He'd never married and his brother's family was the only family he had left. His brother owned a nice farm and he'd been after Dale to come and help him run it. Maybe he'd just do that.

Jansen left the hotel by the side door, carrying the saddlebag. He ducked into the livery, obtained his horse, and soon was riding north out of town. Sheriff Clifford emerged from his concealed spot, mounted his already saddled horse, and took off after Jansen.

39

That Friday morning, early, back in the foothills, Dirk tied Laura to a chair, binding her hands and feet.

"I got to be off, Laura. I got a suspicion that pard of mine ain't gonna be able to resist the tempt-a-shun of all that money...think he jes' might try 'n run off with it. Well, I aim to be there when he makes that purely selfish 'n unpardon'ble decision, 'n, may I add, unhealthy one. So, sorry for the inconvenience, but I won't be long."

Dirk left with all three horses, and Laura finally got the chance she had been waiting for—an opportunity to escape.

The previous evening, as Laura was drawing a drink of water from the pump she had slipped a bar of soap up her sleeve, anticipating that at some point Dirk would leave her alone in the cabin, which meant she would have to be tied up again. Her thinking was that when Dirk tied her hands, the hidden soap bar would create a gap between her wrist and the rope, a slippery gap. Then she could force the soap from under the binding and loosen the rope sufficiently that she could wriggle her hands free. Now, with Dirk and Larry gone, Laura jumped at her opportunity.

As it worked out, freeing her hands was more difficult than she had anticipated. She lost precious time working the bar of soap out from under the tight rope binding. Fortunately, perspiration from the effort made the soap slick enough that it finally slid free. After that, the plan worked perfectly. The rope was now loose enough that she was able to slip her hands free and untie her feet. Her escape, of course, would be hampered by the sprained ankle. She would be on foot, since Dirk had taken the horses. Still thinking soundly, Laura threw a few necessary articles into a pillowcase—dried fruit, matches, and a canteen of water. She found a knife, albeit a small one from the cooking gear. "God forbid I'll ev'r have to use this agin anyone," she said aloud. She used the knife to create a slit in the pillow case, enabling her to slip the bag over her shoulder, thus freeing both hands for the trip ahead. She slid the knife into her belt. Finally, she threw a blanket around her shoulders and ventured outside into the early spring air.

Laura surveyed her surroundings. She wished she had paid better attention during her journey in, but at that time she wasn't thinking too clearly. She knew from which direction she had come and that she had traveled along a creek for an extended time. So it seemed plausible that she should head back, find the creek and head in that same direction, all the while looking for a viable path leading out of the valley, where hopefully she'd have a better chance of eluding Dirk on his return.

The pain in Laura's ankle increased with each step she took, rendering progress exceedingly slow. "Phew, no way I'll ever make it out of here at this rate," she thought. Looking around she found a fallen tree branch suitable to serve as a crutch. With a bit of practice and a whole lot of pain, she was able to establish a reasonable rate of travel. Reasonable, but still slow. Forturnately, she located the creek and began her escape along its bank. She was aware that she was leaving a trail in the soft ground, but there was no way to avoid that as the crutch and the disabled ankle precluded any possible way of covering her tracks. She could only hope to get out of this valley before Dirk caught up to her. Laura realized that there was really little chance of success, but this seemed her only hope.

40

Larry Jansen headed out of Cedar City. After riding a few miles north, he headed east, unaware that Sheriff Clifford followed a safe distance behind. Unbeknownst to either of them, Dirk Fisher had assumed a concealed position outside of town to observe Larry's departure. He saw that Larry was being followed.

"So, that idiot pard of mine managed to attract a crowd after all."

Dirk circled ahead of Larry, anticipating where Larry would enter the wooded area that led into the foothills and to the cabin. He stationed himself off the trail in a well-hidden thicket that looked down upon Larry's route. Dirk pulled his rifle from the scabbard on his mount and hunkered down into a thicket. Larry passed by, not twenty yards from Dirk's vantage point. Some minutes later, the sheriff rode into sight.

A shot rang out, reverberating through the trees. Larry looked back, startled.

"Aw geez," he thought out loud. "It's jes' some damn turkey hunter. Git a grip on yerself." He rode on, carrying a saddlebag filled with $50,000. Of course, he had never seen or expected to see anywhere near that kind of money. He could go anywhere. Do anything.

He feared Dirk, but he also knew that his share of the bounty would be nowhere near an even split. *$50,000!*

"Hell," he thought, "why not chance it. I'll never get anuth'r opportun'ty like this." Larry altered his course, intending to head back out of the foothills and travel north, as far as he could get from Dirk Fisher. As Larry urged his horse back around and started on his new course, there before him waited Dirk Fisher.

"Howdy pard," said Dirk. "Seems to me yer sorta headed in the wrong direction. The cabin's off that-a-way."

"Dirk, yeh...I...I got lost. I jes' ain't no good at direct-shuns."

"Yeh, Larry, pard, I see you ain't. You know, I got all kinds'a screw-ups in my employ. First Jake, 'n now you. Figgerin' on keepin' all that loot for yerself?"

"No...Dirk...nuthin' like that. I jes' got lost. That's all. I wouldn' dream of crossin' you."

"Yeh...yeh...yeh." Dirk drew his gun and trained it on Larry. "I see you still got that scattergun."

Dirk reached over and pulled the scattergun from a scabbard on Larry's horse. He raised it and casually pulled the trigger. The resounding blast knocked Larry off his horse and into eternity.

"Oops...tole you this here gun might come in handy. Damn...so hard to git good help these days. Guess you won't be needin' yer share no more."

240

He looked down on Larry. Dirk figured he had killed two men, inside an hour. A sheriff, and now a partner. He'd never killed a man before. Something stirred within him, an excitement of sorts. Had he actually enjoyed killing? He did feel a certain thrill, a sense of power perhaps. "Hell, I bin a thief, I bin a swindler, 'n I bin a kidnapper. 'N now I'm a twice-o'er killer. Is there no end to my talent?"

On the return trip to his cabin, Dirk pondered on what to do about Laura. "I guess I've sunk 'bout as low as I kin go. Ha. But I got the money, 'n I still got Laura. Ain't gonna make matters no worse no matter what I do with her. She wants that low-life McNabb o'er me—well, so be it. But he ain't gonna be gittin' no un-tarn-ished goods, 'n that's a promise!"

Dirk arrived back at the cabin, with his second horse carrying the saddlebag of money he had confiscated off Larry. The other horses, he left behind.

The cabin was empty.

"Well, that li'l bitch. One thing for sure, she can't git far, not on that foot."

Dirk had no difficulty in finding Laura's trail. Due to her bum ankle, he knew she would have to pick the easiest route, which would be along the creek. No way she would be able to climb out of the valley.

"Hmmm, lookee here," he observed, "We got us a footprint, 'n we got us a hole in the ground. She got more moxie than I give her credit for, done found herself a crutch."

He set out after her, still leading the second horse and the $50,000. "Ain't sure you'll need this cayuse, Laura. Jes' ain't sure what I might do," he said to himself. "But I know one thing for sure. When I catch you, 'n I will catch you, Laura, my dear, we're goin' have us a reckonin'."

▲ ▲ ▲

Jeb and Jonas's efforts to find Laura had thus far proved futile. This day marked the fourth day of their search. Even Savage had uncovered nothing. They had spent the previous night at the entrance to a valley, next to a creek, sleeping under the stars as no refuge was available. Jonas's sleep had been sporadic. He couldn't get Laura's travail out of his mind, fearing he'd be too late to do her much good. His heart ached and his mind reeled with various possible scenarios, all unfavorable.

Jeb and Jonas urged their horses along the creek. Savage had gone on ahead as usual. Up ahead they heard barking and they stepped up their pace. They found Savage standing guard at the entrance to a cabin, well hidden up the slope from the creek, and so well concealed they never would have spotted it on their own.

The cabin door was open.

The two men dismounted and approached the cabin cautiously, rifles at the ready.

"Hello, the cabin," shouted Jeb. "Anyone in there?" Receiving no response, Jonas led the way into the cabin.

"Somebody was here recently," said Jonas, noting the dirty dishes in the sink, the rumpled bedding, and toiletries (some feminine) scattered on a shelf. Lying on the floor beside an overturned chair were lengths of rope and a sliver of soap.

"They were here. Laura was here," said Jonas. He squatted and picked up a length of rope. "Looks like they had'er tied up. Ain't sure what this piece of soap is all about. You suppose she got away somehow, Jeb?"

"Let's have us a look out back," said Jeb. "Mebbe we'll find out 'bout thet." They found where the horses had been kept in back of the cabin. Before they could draw any conclusions, they heard Savage barking down by the creek.

"Let's git on down thar," said Jeb. "I think Savage's found somethin'."

Even the least qualified tracker could piece together what had occured. The earth was soft and wet along the creek bank, due to the early spring snow melt-off. Jeb discovered sets of small footprints, with indentations evenly spaced alongside.

"Looks like Laura's footprints," said Jeb, "'n judgin' from these har holes in the ground, I'd say she's got 'er some kind of a crutch."

"Oh no," exclaimed Jonas, fearing Laura must be hurt.

Jeb was an experienced tracker, having lived in the mountains for much of his life, reading tracks of all kinds, animal and human. He knew that there were two horses, one ridden and one without a rider, judging from the depth of the tracks. So, it seemed the abductors were now short one man.

"These tracks'r recent," said Jeb. "Not more'n an hour or so cold, 'cause the grass ain't even straighten'd up yet. To me, looks like yer Laura did escape somehow 'n hightailed it up along the creek har. I'd say her tracks are older than the other ones, so at least she's got her a head start."

Savage was barking furiously up ahead. "Easy boy, we're right behind you," said Jeb. Jonas wondered why Savage was so agitated.

"You got some personal stake in this, ole boy?"

With Savage leading the way, Jeb and Jonas were able to follow the tracks on horseback at a good rate. Jonas's mind teemed with possibilities. *Just one person on horseback, following Laura. 'N Laura was on foot, 'n most likely 'injured. How fast could she travel? Probably not fast enough, Jonas feared. 'N her pursuer—Dirk Fisher, most likely, would be in a vile mood when, 'n if, he caught up to her, considerin' that she had escaped him.* "I jes' gotta reach her in time," he thought.

▲ ▲ ▲

Laura struggled on ahead. The makeshift crutch did little to alleviate the pain that throbbed in her ankle. She didn't know how much of a head start she had, but suspected Dirk would be on her trail sometime soon. She only hoped she wouldn't encounter him on his return route.

How long had she been gone now...an hour...two hours? The effort was so intense and painful that it seemed like an eternity. She had to rest. She slumped down against a tree, drew the blanket around her, and closed her eyes. She clutched the cameo necklace Jonas had given her. Tears filled her eyes and ran rivulets down her cheeks. *Oh, Jonas...please find me.*

She didn't hear Dirk ride in on her.

41

"Well, howdy, Laura. Are those tears b'cause you missed me?"

Dirk dismounted and stood in front of Laura. She tried to rise, but the pain and the exhaustion were too great.

"Oh, don' get up on my account. Now, Laura darlin'. What did'you think you'd accomplish by runnin' off? 'N after all I did for you," he chuckled.

"Dirk, I...was afraid, that's all. I was afraid I'd be left all alone there in the woods..." Her voice trailed off. She was acutely aware of her plight— injured and alone, far away from any possible rescue and faced with a man she now considered a madman. She looked down at the knife she'd inserted into her belt—the small, ridiculously small knife.

"Now, Laura. Let's not be lyin' to each other. What kind of a way is that to start a re-la-shun-ship? Lemme help you up. I see yer havin' some difficulty there."

Dirk reached down and grabbed Laura by the front of her shirt, throwing off her blanket and brusquely lifted her to her feet. Laura gasped as Dirk pulled the knife from her belt, looked at it, smiled, and tossed it casually aside.

"You know, we never did git a chance to seal our re-la-shun-ship with no kiss 'r nothin'."

He pulled Laura to him, kissing her hard on the lips. Laura pushed him away and slapped him hard.

"Haw. Now ain't you li'l miss proper," said Dirk, rubbing his cheek. "Well, maybe it's time we took a littl' starch out of yer britches." He hit her hard across the face with the back of his hand.

Laura fell back against the tree. Stunned, she sank to the ground. Dirk pulled her back up by her shirt-front, this time ripping the shirt open.

"When I git through with you, Laura dear, you ain't goin' be fit for no one, let alone yer lover boy, McNabb. I bin waitin' a long time for this."

He roughly drew her to him, kissing her hard on her neck and ex- posed shoulder. Then he pushed her back to the ground. "Now, we have some fun."

Laura saw the vicious grin on his face. She cringed and rolled onto her side.

Suddenly, Dirk was flying backwards, but vaguely aware of the white blur that barreled into him.

The force of the dog's leap sent Dirk sprawling to the ground. Dirk rolled and came up with his gun in one motion. Savage leaped for him again. Dirk fired, he fired again.

Savage went down.

Then rifle shots rang out from behind Dirk, and Jeb came riding down on him. The first shot caught Dirk in the shoulder as he turned toward Jeb. Jeb kept pumping bullets into him, *fire...cock...fire...cock...* Jeb dismounted *...fire...cock...fire...cock.*

"You worthless bastard." *Fire...cock.* "You devil."

Fire...cock...fire. Jeb continued this ritual even after his rifle's hammer fell on an empty chamber. *Click, click, click.*

Jeb went to Savage and kneeled down to him. The dog wasn't breathing.

He was gone.

"Noooooooooo," Jeb wailed. He buried his face in Savage's thick neck hair and clutched the dog to him. He then gently laid the dog down and slowly rose. He went over to where Fisher lay in a bloody heap. He reached down, grabbed the dead man's feet and dragged him to the edge of a nearby ravine. The ravine was not deep but the sides were steep. Jeb put his foot on Dirk's limp body and pushed him over the edge. Dirk rolled to the bottom, like garbage into a pit.

"Yer whole body ain't' worth a hair from thet dog's back," snorted Jebediah.

Jonas had dismounted and was tending to Laura. He picked her up in his arms. She seemed to be in a daze. "Oh Laura, I'm so sorry I didn't git here sooner. You'll be all right now...it's all over."

"Jonas..." she whispered. "Jonas...you're here. It was so terrible... Dirk...he..."

"Never mind, Laura. It's over. Dirk will ne'er bother you agin." Jonas was somewhat alarmed by the ferocity of Jeb's handling of Fisher, yet he wasn't sorry about it. But he was extremely sorry over the loss of the great white dog, and felt the pain of Jeb's loss. He tried to express this to Jeb, but couldn't find the words. "Jes' take care of Laura, there," said Jeb. "Ain't nothin' more to be done for my dog, 'cept ta bury 'im."

Jonas turned back to Laura. "Kin you ride?"

"I...think so."

"I want to get you to a cabin we saw a ways back, so we kin fix you up, 'n you kin rest the night. We ain't got time to git anywhere else b'fore dark now."

"Jonas," said Jeb quietly, "ya go on ahead. I'll be takin' Savage up into the mountains whar he belongs. I don' want him spendin' no eternity anywhar near thet vermin down there. I'll find Savage a nice peaceful spot, somewhar I know he'd love, with rabbits, 'n foxes, 'n wolves, lik'n whar he came from."

Tears ran down Jeb's cheeks. "When I git him properly settled in, I'll be joinin' ya agin. Sometime tomorrow, I 'spect."

"Jeb." said Jonas, fearing the old man might do something rash in his despondency. "You know how bad I need you with me. Yer the best friend I got in the whole world. I ain't movin' out of this valley, till you git back."

"Don' worry none. I'll shore be back. Yer all I got left now."

Jonas helped Jeb get Savage up and slung over his horse and secured with a length of rope, and said his last goodbyes to the great white dog. Laura put a hand on Jeb's shoulder, she laid her other hand on Savage.

"Jeb," she said, "I jis' want you to know, I never loved any animal more'n I loved Savage, not even my horse, Sacagawea. I jis' want you to know that." Jonas helped Laura up on one of Dirk's horses and they rode out, following the creek, with the second horse carrying the $50,000 trailing behind.

Jeb began the arduous climb out of the valley and into the mountains.

He selected a spot for Savage's final resting place. It was a peaceful spot, although Savage's life was anything but peaceful. "You deserve a nice quiet restin' place, ole boy. You earned it a hundert times o'er." Tears filled Jebediah's eyes as he placed the dog in a shallow grave and covered him with dirt and pine branches. He placed a huge rock atop the grave and sat the night in solemn reflection.

▲ ▲ ▲

Early the next day, Jeb caught up to Jonas and Laura, who'd spent the night in the deserted cabin. Laura was rested, but still hurting. The three of them rode out of the valley, but without the great white dog.

Jonas felt deeply the loss of the great dog; he could only imagine how much worse it was for Jeb. He gazed over at his partner as they rode along, searching his face for some hint of what he was feeling.

"Young feller," said Jebediah. "I know yer concerned for me, but it's over. Savage is gone. He's at peace, 'n thet's thet. I ain't gonna linger o'er it. So let's jes' git on with the biz'niz at hand. For instance...what in blazes happened to thet other fella we was trailin'?"

Laura told about the ransom plan and that Larry had been the one to go into Cedar City to get the money from her father and that Dirk had followed later to check on him.

"Wahl, then," said Jonas. "Seein' as how Dirk had the money on him when we caught up to 'im, 'n Jansen is nowhere ta be found, I s'pect Dirk disposed of 'im somewhar back thar on the trail. We'll let the sheriff in Cedar City know 'bout it, 'n leave it up to him ta figger out what happened."

42

Frederick Becker was waiting for his daughter when she, Jeb, and Jonas arrived back in Cedar City. Sheriff Clifford was nowhere in sight, but his deputy lingered in the background. Becker was glad to have his money back, but was even more elated to see Laura returned safely. "You gave us quite a scare, young lady. Now, what the hell happened out there?"

"Oh, Dad, it was terrible. I don't know what got into Dirk. He..." Laura began sobbing. Jonas put his arms around her shoulder.

"You better let me tell it, Laura," said Jonas. "Yer still pretty upset o'er the whole thing.

"Sir, there ain't no more courageous gal nowhere than yer daughter." Jonas went on to relate the incidents leading up to Laura's rescue. Becker listened without interruption.

"Quite a story," said Becker, "quite a damn story. Laura, seems Jonas here's savin' you 'bout ev'ry other day now. Mighty obligin' to you once agin, young feller. Real sorry about yer dog, Jeb. But know, I'm mighty grateful to all of you. Hell, I can't imagin' what got into Dirk. I guess maybe I ain't such a good judge of character. Anyway, Jonas, I want you to know, you got yer old job back, 'n I see you as becomin' real important in my company."

"Well, I shore appreciate that, Mr. Becker. But I guess I got other plans. I told you about my horse ranch, 'n me 'n Laura's plans to marry..."

"Now hold on there, boy," interrupted Becker, "I'm willin' to reward you for all you did for Laura, but I got other plans for my daughter. You got to be reasonable."

"Dad, it ain't up to you no more." Laura spoke up, in anger. "I sure want yer blessin', but regardless, we're gettin' married anyway. You picked out Dirk Fisher for me, 'n look what come of that. Now, I think I'll do my own pickin'."

"Laura, honey," said her father. "Maybe if you give me some time..." In truth, Becker was not nearly as opposed to Laura matching up with Jonas as he projected. His objection was mainly the residue of a feeling that his daughter, his only child would marry someone of a high standing. The irony is that he himself didn't hold the well-to-do in particularly high regard, especially considering how things had turned out in his own marriage. He could find little not to admire about Jonas, and had yet to admit, even to himself, that he actually favored Laura's choice in a man.

"Sorry, Dad," said Laura, "there's a beautiful horse ranch up north that needs my...our...attention," she said, looking at Jonas. "We're *goin'* to git married, 'n that's settled."

Once again, Frederick Becker realized he had little influence over his daughter.

"We best be gittin' Laura back home," said Jonas. "But first, let's check in with Sheriff Clifford, 'n let 'im know all's bin happenin'."

"Clifford? He's over at the docs, gittin' patched up," said Becker, axious to change the subject. "Oh yeah, you had no way of knowin'. Let me catch you up. Clifford came draggin' in here yesterday, all shot up. Says he got bush-wacked trailin' that Jansen huckleberry. Wait, let me back up here some more. I dropped the ransom money off to Jansen, 'n had Clifford follow him when he left town, figgerin' he'd lead us to you, Laura. Well, Clifford got himself shot 'n he was confused as to what might've happened to Jansen. He did say he heard another shot a few minutes later, most likely a shotgun blast. Said he wasn't in no shape to follow up on it, but he did manage to climb up on his horse and make it back here. His deputy went searchin' for Jansen and found him jes' off the trail 'n brung 'im back to town. Can't say too much good about Jansen after what he done, but he sure didn't deserve that kind of an endin'."

"N Clifford," continued Becker, "he wasn't in too good shape, but he sure was talkative. Said somethin' about him givin' up the sheriff business. Y'know, it's almost funny. I understand he said somethin' about how he'd welcome a little more action around here. Now, he got a little action 'n he's ready to throw in his badge. Yep, almost funny. Well, anyway, that's about the size of it. Don't think I left too much out."

"Din't know about the sheriff," said Jonas, "but we had it pretty much figger'd about Jansen. Maybe it was a fittin' endin' for him, maybe it wasn't; bin a terr'ble bizniz for all of us." Again, Jonas thought of Savage. "So what say we look in on Clifford, 'n then be on our way."

"I s'pose someone should go see 'bout that Fisher fella," commented the deputy.

"The hell you say," said Jeb. "Let that devil lie jes' whar he's at. He's got a fittin' grave, right whar all the low creatures of the earth kin git at 'im. He kilt my Savage, 'n 'bout got at Laura, too. Let the vermins gnaw on his bones, 'n the devil take his soul. He's jes' whar he b'longs—in hell."

▲ ▲ ▲

Laura rode back to Jericho in the buckboard with her father.

"Guess we're quite a sight," she said. "Us all bandaged up 'n all. Dad, there's somethin' else I need to talk to you about, somethin' besides Jonas." She laid a hand on her father's shoulder—her look grew firm. "All that's happened has got me to thinkin'. It should be obvious to you by now, that you got to make some changes in the minin' company. It ain't fair to the miners. Now that you know how Dirk was cheatin' 'em, 'n who knows who else is, you got to set things straight. I want you to take the money you was goin' to pay for the ransom, 'n use it to help the miners, 'n their families. Some good should come out of all this."

"Aw, Laura, come on. Yer not only fixin' to run off on me, now yer wantin' to tell me how to run my business."

"Dad, I can't believe if you knew what was goin' on...about how the miners were being treated, that you wouldn't do somethin' about it. Jonas tells me about some of the things he saw was goin' on at the mines. 'N yer Corps, they've jis' turned into a bunch of ruffians. The miners' are too scared to speak up, 'cause they might git a beatin'. They got to work long hours in conditions that ain't safe, 'n they hardly make enough pay to live on. Dad, I know yer a decent man, 'n I got every faith you'll be settin' things straight now."

Frederick Becker was reluctant to admit that he wasn't in control of his own company—that things had been going on he wasn't aware of. He had always prided himself on his ability to oversee a tough business, involving rough and unpredictable men. He knew the miners had it hard—working in a coal mine was not a job for the faint of heart. Now, here's his own daughter telling him he needed to change the way he handled things.

No doubt, his reputation had been hurt by the devious actions of his supervisors, Dirk, Larry, even Jake. He had to bear part of the blame for that. Maybe he was getting too old for this business, or maybe just tired of it.

Finally he spoke. "Honey, I know I haven't been keeping a tight enough rein on the Company, 'n things have gotten outta hand. But, I think I can fix things up more to yer likin'. Maybe not right away, but I'll work on it."

"Oh, Daddy." Laura hugged her father. "'N give Jonas a chance too. I know you'll take to 'im too, jis' like I do."

43

Jeb and Jonas rode together back to Jericho, just ahead of Becker's buckboard. Jonas kept looking back at Laura and her father, wondering what drift their conversation might be taking. Jeb, of course, would have preferred to be on the buckboard, but felt no inclination to interfere with Laura's reunion with her father.

Though still several miles away from Jericho, Jonas heard bells clanging. His body stiffened. The bells could mean but one thing—disaster at the mines. Jeb was the first to spring into action, spurring his horse into an all-out sprint toward Jericho, a reaction that broke Jonas's stupor. Soon Jonas overtook Jeb as they raced toward the mines. The alarm bells could be heard for miles around.

Jonas arrived at the mine well ahead of Jebediah. Lucas, the miners' acknowledged leader, was frantically issuing orders and assignments to a group of workers at the mine's entrance. Dust spewed from the entrance covering the site like cannon smoke at a battle scene.

"Lucas," shouted Jonas, "what's happened?"

"Jonas. I heard you were back. And we can sure use you. We got a number of miners trapped inside. Damned cave-in."

"How many...who?"

"Ain't sure yet. Give us a hand clearing the entrance." A sense of dread gripped Jonas like a bear's grip. *Not Pa!*

Jeb reigned up, quickly grasping the gravity of the scene. "Jonas, where'er ya need me, I'm here."

Soon after, Becker and Laura arrived. Becker jumped from the buckboard seat, ignoring his crippled leg and fell face first to the ground. Laura rushed to him as best she could, considering her lame ankle, but it was one of the Corps that got to Becker first, giving him a hand up. "Don' look like yer in much condition to help out here, Boss."

"Never mind that," said Becker, "jes' help me over to the mine entrance. Least I can do is help see things run smoothly."

"Dad," said Laura. "Why don't we go over 'n see if we kaint help the families some?"

"The families? My responsibility is to the mines. You go help the families."

"Dad, we ain't in no shape to be totin' rocks 'r nothin'. We'd jis' be in the way. Come with me, please."

"Daughter, what could I possibly say to them?"

"Jis' try. They're scared. It could mean a lot to 'em."

Becker, as usual, gave in to his daughter. Though he was completely out of his element, he did issue reassurances to the miner's families that all would turn out well. He, perhaps, even derived a certain personal satisfaction in his efforts. Laura could not be more pleased.

▲ ▲ ▲

Benji was digging furiously at the rocks and debris blocking the tunnel leading to the trapped miners. A rap on his shoulder alerted him to the arrival of his brother.

"Jonas, Pa's in there." No other words were exchanged.

Jebediah joined the two brothers. They worked with scores of miners and other Jericho residents, clearing the rubble from the entrance in an all-out attempt to reach the endangered men. They were all aware that if they didn't reach the trapped miners soon, there was a real possibility that those inside would suffocate, or they could die from injuries sustained from the cave-in.

Families of the miners congregated in small groups with hopeful, yet apprehensive looks on their faces. The worst had happened, what all the mining community feared. A cave-in. Could it involve a husband, a father, a brother? Up to this point, the Becker Mining Company had been lucky. There had been no major incidents—plenty of minor scrapes, but no deaths.

Little by little, the rubble was cleared away, then dumped into hampers and unloaded outside the mine. The workers maintained a frenzied pace. They listened for any indication that the trapped miners were still alive—maybe a tapping sound, or cries for help—anything to give them hope. The digging went on throughout the day and into the night. Lanterns were hung to facilitate the effort as the rescuers were committed to working around the clock to liberate the unfortunate miners.

Jonas was a madman, working to the point of exhaustion. Yet, his thoughts drifted. *Why? Every time one situation gits fixed, another pops up. I feel like I'm being bounced around like a caged badger.*

Finally, Jonas detected a faint tapping. "I hear somethin' men...I hear it."

The digging stopped as the men listened.

"I hear it too," shouted Benji. "Someone's tappin', jes' up ahead."

They dug with greater frenzy. Rocks and debris were flying about in a whirlwind in a renewed effort triggered by the signal from within the mine. The tapping grew louder and the rescuers heard shouts up ahead, cries for help. They in turn shouted back encouragement—that help was on the way. Finally, Jonas, who was in the lead, broke through a final blockage and stumbled into an open area. He was welcomed by cries of relief from the huddled miners inside.

The rest of the rescuers poured through the opening. Triumphant shouts could be heard all the way back to the cave's entrance.

"They're alive! They're all alive!"

Some of the trapped miners had sustained injuries. Caleb suffered a broken leg and a severe bump on the head. He was carried out unconscious.

As the injured miners were administered to at the site by their families and by Doc Adams, the mining community reveled in the news that there were no deaths.

Caleb soon gained consciousness. Doc Adams set the leg and inspected the head wound.

"Doc, I'm seein' two of you," said Caleb, reminiscent of his war wound.

Jonas and Benji took their father home. Soon, Caleb was resting comfortably and Jonas and Benji collapsed on their bunks and slept for ten hours.

The consequences of the mining disaster were far-reaching. For the McNabbs, it punctuated the need for Caleb to quit working in the mines, and for Benji to abandon any thoughts he might have of pursuing such employment.

More significantly, the mining accident was a wake-up call for Frederick Becker. When Laura again emphasized to her dad the need to improve the conditions of the miners, Frederick finally listened.

▲ ▲ ▲

For the first time in a year-and-a-half, Jonas was now able to see his family freely and openly as he'd been completely exonerated of any fault in the stabbing incident. Nostalgia gripped him as he looked around the small farmhouse that had once been his home—where he had last seen his mother. A lump formed in his throat as he told his father it was time to sell the family farm.

"Pa, it ain't really much good for nothin' anyway. Maybe someone can use it for pasturin'. I want you 'n Benji to come 'n live with me 'n help me run the horse ranch. Yer gonna love it up there in the Shenandoah Valley.

You'll never have to work in the cursed mines again, 'n Benji'll sure never have to even think about workin' there. 'N Pa, you kin jes' take it easy, like Jeb aims to do, if you got a mind to. You 'n Jeb's gonna be great pals."

"Benji," said Jonas, addressing his brother, "there'll be plenty of work for you. 'N more schoolin' too. We'll be needin' somebody in the family with a biz'ness head. That is if we can keep you away from them school gals." Jonas ruffled his brother's hair.

Jonas thought his pa seemed less depressed, despite the broken leg. Maybe, finally, with a change of location and some hope for the future, his father could get past the loss of his Lonica.

"Son, I guess I wouldn't mind unloadin' this place. It sure ain't much to brag about. I guess what yer sayin' makes sense. But, one thing, you know yer ma's buried here on this property, 'n a lot of her kin. I won't have that li'l cemetery disturbed. Anyone comes to own this property has to leave them graves as is."

"Pa, ain't no question about that," said Jonas.

44

The mining disaster was, of course, the big news of the day, but there was another noteworthy occurrence in the offering—the wedding of Laura Becker and Jonas McNabb. The collapse of the mine delayed their wedding plans by two weeks. Frederick Becker had resigned himself to the probability that this wedding would actually take place and had subsequently promised Laura a weddin' affair she'd never forget. Little did Becker realize it would also mark a turn-around in his own life.

Folks would have to be dead and in their graves to be unaware of the upcoming wedding. Hand-printed posters were tacked up on every building, tree, and conceivable surface for miles around, proclaiming what was to be the most celebrated affair ever seen in these parts. Everyone was invited. The monthly Saturday dance would seem trivial by comparison.

Such was Laura's wish. To grasp an opportunity to bring together the entire community of Jericho in a joyous celebration in hopes that the beleaguered miners and farmers might share in the exhilaration she felt—anything to lift their spirits and relieve the hardships of their daily lives. Her father could well afford such an extravagant affair, and in Laura's mind, he needed to show more responsibility to the Jericho community—to those he employed and to those affected by his Mining Company.

Laura and Gini took charge of the wedding preparations. Laura's ankle was no longer an impediment, though she still slightly favored it. She had the final say concerning the wedding plans, but she relied heavily on Gini in all matters concerning etiquette and dress, pomp and circumstance, and anything else that Gini's sophistication might lend itself to.

▲ ▲ ▲

At the dining room table of the Becker Estate, Laura and Gini were pouring over the plans for the wedding. "But oh, *ma chére*," exclaimed an exasperated Gini. "Where shall we ever find the right wedding dress for you? We have such a short time and there's nothing available anywhere around here. We'd have to send to Charleston, or Richmond, maybe even Paris for a gown, or the material to fashion one. And only two weeks! Mon dieu, c'est impossible."

"Aha!" The exclamation came from Laura's father, who had entered the room and overheard Gini's concern. "I think I jes' might know where the perfect dress might be available." Frederick left the room and soon returned, carrying a garment, very white and very ornate. "Laura, this is the dress yer mother wore at our wedding, some ages ago. 'N this is the dress I'd like to see my daughter married in."

Laura gazed at the dress. Her father held it out at arms length so Laura might better see the entire dress in all its finery.

"It's beautiful, Dad, but will it be all right...I mean, you and Mother..."

"Laura, honey, it's okay if I say it's okay, 'n I insist."

Laura ran to her father and hugged him, dress and all. To Laura, her father's offering of the dress meant that he gave his approval that she marry Jonas.

Laura had written a long letter to Charly, telling about the kidnapping and all the events surrounding it, and that Savage had been killed in attempting to save her. She told of her upcoming wedding date and that she wanted Charly to be her maid of honor. Laura had come by this choice reluctantly, feeling perhaps her long-time companion, Gini, might want that honor. But, Gini had assured Laura that Charly was the right choice, that she and Laura were like two peas in a pod. "Besides, I've got all the honor I could wish for just seeing you happy."

Soon after, Laura received a telegram from Charly:

MY BAGS ARE PACKED – STOP – COMING BY TRAIN
– STOP – BE THERE ON THURS – STOP – RED TO
ARRIVE LATER – STOP
LOVE CHARLY.

Laura showed Jonas Charly's telegram as the two of them rocked gently in the porch swing of the Manor.

"Oh, Jonas, Charly'll be coming more than a week before the weddin'. She'll be here to help me with everything. It's all goin' so perfectly. Can you believe it? Hold me Jonas, don't let anythin' go wrong."

It had already been decided that Jebediah would be Jonas's best man, which Laura thoroughly endorsed. "If not for that wonderful old man," she gushed, "none of this would be possible. That beautiful ole mountain man, 'n his wond'rus dog. Jonas, I would make Jebediah, King of Jericho if I could."

Jonas pulled Laura close to him—this amazing woman—this girl who just a year-and-a-half ago had been but a fanciful dream. He didn't feel he deserved this kind of good fortune—to have both Laura and the horse ranch. He kissed her gently on the lips. He pulled back and looked into her eyes, then chuckled.

"Okay, mister. What's so durned funny?"

"Oh, it's somethin' Jeb said 'bout deservin'," said Jonas.

"Jeb? What about Jeb 'n deservin'?"

"Jes' mention it to him sometime about who deserves of what 'n you'll get an earful." Laura gave Jonas a puzzled look. "Huh?"

Jonas preferred to stay in the background during all the wedding planning. He was, after all, just the groom-to-be and happy enough to just absorb Laura's enthusiasm.

He now divided his time between Laura and his own family. Benji pestered him for every detail of his venture into the mountains. Even Jonas's dad showed an unusual verve over hearing about his son's exploits. Jonas explained as best he could about the horse farm in the Shenandoah, but to his dad the prospect seemed more fairytale than reality.

Jebediah took a room at the hotel in Jericho so as not to trouble anyone. "Besides," he said, "I got a special project I'm working on." Mysterious...

Gini, expert with needle and thread, was able to alter Priscilla's wedding dress to fit Laura perfectly. She further embellished the dress with a few French touches of her own to make the gown unique—garnishes of lace and a few other frills. Laura even allowed for a full bustle, despite her dislike for ostentation.

They were in Gini's room. Laura had put on her mother's wedding dress, replete with Gini's alterations.

"Oh, Gini, maybe it's too fancy for me. You know how I feel about such things."

"Well, *chére*," said Gini, "that's what being a bride is all about. You're supposed to be the center of attention."

"Oh, I guess, but...oh, never mind me. I know you know best. Jes' think, Gini, Charly will be here soon 'n I kaint wait to see her. 'N my mother will be comin'. I do so hope she won't spoil things. Ev'rythin's goin' so perfect."

"Honey, she won't. She can't. It will be your day and nobody's about to spoil it. You deserve every happiness there is on God's earth."

Frederick Becker heartily endorsed anything and everything his daughter wished for concerning the wedding plans. He had but one daughter, and he certainly had the means to make this a once-in-a-lifetime event. He still held some reservations about Jonas, but he put them aside for Laura's sake. And he wasn't altogether enthusiastic about the sweeping changes Laura wished for the miners. But he would take a closer look at his operation, at least to insure that no one would again take advantage of him.

The wedding ceremony would be performed by the Reverend Jacob Rife. He was the pastor of the Presbyterian Church and active in the community, particularly with matters concerning the welfare of the miners' and their families. This made him a local favorite.

Rife was a large man, very wide of girth, making his cassocks—his usual attire—seem more tent-like than a church garment. His complexion was perpetually red, as he huffed and puffed through his sermons, and afterwards applauded every favorable comment that might be offered on one of his homilies, as if he alone held the key to everyone's lasting happiness and success. But Laura had not chosen the Reverend for his views. He was the only cleric in town.

▲ ▲ ▲

When Charly arrived to Jericho by train, it was difficult to tell who was more excited—Laura to now have her close friend present to help with the wedding plans, or Charly to be seeing Laura for the first time since her ordeal with Dirk.

Charly and Laura flew into each other's arms and neither seemed to be able to talk fast enough or loud enough about the latest events, which resulted in them both enthusiastically talking over each other in a Babel-like confusion. Jonas, who sat by on a buckboard, couldn't help but laugh at the exuberance of the two girls. "Maybe you outta back off 'n try it again without all the yappin'," he joked.

Two days before the wedding, Red Phillips arrived in Jericho by train. Aside from his necessary luggage, he carried a rather small wooden box, with a series of holes drilled into its top. Charly received Red with great enthusiasm and led him to a waiting buckboard. She was to take him to the Becker Estate, where he would be staying.

"Before we go out there, darlin'," said Red, "I gotta look up Jeb and Jonas. Now jes' where might they be found?"

"Well, of course, honey. Jeb's in town here at the hotel, 'n Jonas most likely's out at the family farm. What's goin' on?"

"Let me show you somethin'." Red set the box on the ground and lifted the lid. Reaching into the box he pulled out a puppy—all white, and with red eyes.

"Oh Red, you've brought Savage's pup with you. 'N you never told me."

"Wahl, I never bin too sure 'bout wimmin keepin' secrets."

"Oh, you...well, anyway Jeb 'n Jonas are goin' to be thrilled, especially Jeb. I can't wait to see his face."

"Wahl then, let's head out and get Jonas first. Then the three of us can present this pup to Jeb."

So they did. Luckily, Jonas was at the farm and when shown the pup was overwhelmed by his likeness to Savage.

"What say we get this li'l critter right o'er to Jeb," said Jonas," that old man's in for one hell of a surprise."

And that he was. Jeb acknowledged a knock on the door of his hotel room and encountered Red, Charly, and Jonas standing there with woeful looks on their faces.

"Jeb, we got some terribl' news," said Jonas. "Come out here quick."

Jonas grabbed Jeb's arm and led him into the hallway. There, peeping out of a wooden box was a white pup with red eyes.

Jeb was dumbfounded, expecting bad news. "Wha...what is this?" He took a step forward and crouched down. The pup jumped out of the box and into Jeb's arms, licking his face. Tears rolled down Jeb's weathered cheeks. "This yer bad news, ya con-nivin' scoundr'ls?"

He looked back to the pup. "It's jes' the same as when Savage was a litt'l critter," said Jeb. "It is Savage, all o'er agin." He looked up at Jonas. "How...where?"

"You got Red to thank," said Jonas. "He brung the pup all the way from our ranch."

"It's Savage's pup, Jeb," said Red.

"Savage's pup? Ya mean him and that big ole white Malamute of yers...?"

"Yep. Guess they finally warmed up to each other," said Red.

"Wahl, I'll be callin' this here pup, Son of Savage. Mebbe Sonny, fer short," said Jeb, as he held the pup at arm's length and gazed into his eyes. "Don' know what I e'er done ta *deserve* this..." He looked over to Jonas. "Haw."

Jeb decided that Sonny would stay at the McNabb farm during all the wedding preparations. Of course, that's also where Jeb would spend a good deal of his time.

45

Priscilla Becker felt it necessary to attend her daughter's wedding, mostly because it was the proper thing to do, and if there was one thing Priscilla was, it was proper, at least from a societal perspective. Besides, it would provide interesting conversation once she returned to Richmond. Priscilla knew it would be awkward for all of them—the husband, the daughter, and herself. She had not been back to the Becker Estate since she had left her husband and daughter more than eight years previously. Of course, she was dead set against Laura marrying a miner's son, or farmer's son, or whatever he was.

On the day before the wedding, Priscilla arrived at Jericho by train, accompanied by her housekeeper, Caroline. Priscilla's intentions were to spend only two nights at the Becker Estate—the night before the wedding and the night after. Then she would return to Richmond.

Frederick Becker met his wife at the train station with a buckboard. He hadn't seen Priscilla in over two years, not since his last visit to Richmond. He greeted her with an awkward peck on the cheek.

"You're lookin' fine, Cilla. And Caroline, welcome to our humble country village. I'm sure you've heard nothing but good things about these parts," he added, giving his wife a glance. He'd meant to be more civil, but the slight just slipped out.

"Now, Fritz," commented Priscilla, "let's not start right off with the sarcasm. I intend to try to make this stay somewhat tolerable. And I haven't prejudiced Caroline against these parts or anyone in them. She's free to make up her own mind. You're looking quite fit yourself," she added, to Frederick's surprise.

"Well, thank you, dear. 'N it's bin a while since anyone called me Fritz."

"But your foot is looking a little odd, all wrapped up like that. Anything I should know about?"

"We'll get into the foot story later. Right now, let's get underway." Frederick, with lame foot and all, loaded the considerable luggage into the buckboard, then helped his wife and her housekeeper aboard and they headed for the Becker Estate.

"Cilla, may I talk freely...I mean in front of Caroline 'n all?"

"But of course, Caroline's almost like family." *Which was far from the truth.* Priscilla never really warmed up to Caroline, or any of the help. Caroline shrugged.

Frederick continued. "I know you don't approve of this marriage. I didn't either, at first. I know you wanted Laura to marry some well-off society boy from Richmond. But let me tell you about yer daughter...our daughter. She's an exceptional girl, 'n if you got to know her better, you'd know that. 'N she wouldn't of picked Jonas if he weren't exceptional too. She could've had anyone she wanted, no doubt about that."

Priscilla was becoming fidgety. "Now, hear me out," continued Frederick. "You owe Laura that much. Jonas has a partner who financed the purchase of a horse ranch up in the Virginia Shenandoah Valley. And from what I've been told, it's a damn good ranch, a promisin' one with a lot of ac'rage. You know how Laura loves horses, so it's a purty good deal for both of them. 'N my thinkin' is that Jonas will make a damn fine husband for Laura. 'N Cilla, he actually saved her life on several occasions."

Frederick told Priscilla about Laura's abduction and all matters surrounding it.

"Is it okay if I talk now?" asked Priscilla, slightly irritated.

"Of course. I'd be interested in what you got to say."

"First of all, why was I not informed of my daughter's misadventure? I'm glad she wasn't harmed...thank God, but I'm still her mother and as such should have been informed." Priscilla hesitated a moment, fighting back a tear, then collected herself.

"But you're absolutely correct, Fritz. I don't approve of this marriage. But I didn't notice anybody asking for my opinion. Our daughter, as pretty as she is, could do a whole lot better than a coal miners' son. Now, I'm grateful that Jonas has been watching out for our Laura, but he's sure not what I'd hoped for. Not for Laura."

"Just what did you hope for? A marriage like ours? Well, that's turned out just dandy, ain't it?"

"Fritz, please. Let's not discuss that just now. I don't want to fight."

"Just let me get this out. I know you didn't marry me out of love. I guess I was hopin' you'd come around to that eventually. Maybe you would've if we'd stayed in Charleston 'n you could've had yer society life you seem to crave so much. Cilla, I'm proud of what I've accomplished here. But I'm also sorry I couldn't make you happy. Now this is Laura's chance. 'N I'm right glad that she's hooked up with that boy." Frederick actually surprised himself by admitting this. "He's a fighter like me. 'N he really loves our daughter somethin' fierce. Those two belong together, 'n I won't have you interferin' with that."

"Fritz, are you trying to bully me? You should've learned long ago that I won't be bullied. And do you think I don't have feelings for Laura? Do you think I never had feelings for you? You must think me totally insensitive." Priscilla felt the anger building within her—an anger she had promised herself to avoid. She collected herself. "Oh, don't worry. I won't spoil your little party."

Becker looked at Caroline. "I'm sorry you had to hear all this."

The rest of the trip to the Becker Estate was made in silence.

▲ ▲ ▲

Laura was waiting for the buckboard as it pulled up in front of the Becker Manor. Charly stood by her side. Gini stood just behind Laura, ready to help if needed.

"Mother, how good to see you, I'm so glad you could make it." Laura greeted her mother, who was still seated on the buckboard.

"Laura, dear, you know I wouldn't miss my only child's wedding. Now help me down from here. I think this dress is about ruined from all the dirt and dust."

Laura helped her mother down. Priscilla hugged her daughter as if Laura were a guest for dinner. How different this was from Laura's enthusiastic reception upon her friend Charly's arrival. Frederick assisted Caroline from the buckboard and soon she and Laura were embracing, their greeting was warm and sincere.

"Welcome to the backwoods, Caroline," Laura said gleefully. "I really miss winnin' all yer money at...what did you call that game...oh yeh, con-qui'n."

"Now, don't you have that a bit backwards, dear?" responded Caroline. "Seems to me that most of the winnings ended up on my side."

Laura laughed. "I hope you ain't bin runnin' into no more buildin's with yer big-wheeled tricycle."

"Now I know you got things backwards." They both laughed.

The Becker Estate house looked about the same to Priscilla. Eight years...a twinge of emotion gripped her. Could she be feeling some nostalgia for the life she had rejected, that she professed to loathe?

"And, Mother," said Laura. "I'd like you to meet Gini. I can't say enough good things about her." Priscilla, of course, knew Frederick had engaged the daughter of his old friend, Henri Bucher, from Charleston, to be Laura's teacher and companion, in lieu of her absence.

Gini extended a hand to Priscilla. Although Priscilla took the hand, it was with ostensible haughtiness, indicating her disapproval of the manner in which this *au pair* had raised Laura.

"And this here is Charly, my best friend and soon-to-be my maid of honor," said Laura.

Priscilla greeted the girl with a limp handshake. "Ah yes, Charly, Laura's partner in crime," she quipped.

"Yep, that's me," said Charly, with a smile. "Glad to finally meet you, Mrs. Becker."

"Well, come on y'all," said Laura. "Let's git you inside so's you kin freshen up a bit. There's some folks comin' to supper that I'm anxious for you to meet."

Priscilla cringed. Ouch, the dreaded moment, she thought. Laura showed her mother and Caroline to separate bedrooms. Priscilla would not be occupying Frederick's room.

Laura rejoined Charly on the porch steps.

"Charly, I'm embarrassed about my mom, how she's treatin' ev'ryone. 'N she was rude to you. I don't know why she's like that."

"No problem, Laura. Let's jis give her a chance."

"I'm so glad you're here, Charly. I don't know what I'd have done without you this week. I expect, now that mother's here, I'll be needin' yer comfort even more."

Gini, of course, was still the one to see that everything ran smoothly, operationally at least. But she was thankful that Laura's friend, Charly, was around to help defray any contentions that existed between Laura and her snippy mother.

▲ ▲ ▲

Seven people gathered in the Becker living room—Laura, Charly, Gini, Frederick, Priscilla, Caroline, and Red Phillips. Caroline enjoyed her guest status. In Richmond, she was seldom invited to dine with Priscilla; Gini, in contrast, was in attendance because Laura always treated her as an equal in the Becker household. An ornate octagonal table was set with canapés and various spreads as before-dinner appetizers.

Jonas arrived with Caleb and Benji. Laura took Jonas' hand and proudly introduced him and his family to her mother. Jonas no longer retained the mountain man persona he'd assumed for his return to Jericho. The beard was gone, the mustache was gone, his hair was trimmed to a fashionable length, and his attire was more that of a banker than a farmer. Priscilla was quite surprised and even impressed by Jonas's gentlemanly appearance, not at all what she had expected.

"Well, I must say..." she started. "Laura has at least picked out a handsome young man." Priscilla lifted her hand to Jonas in greeting.

Jonas bowed his head and lightly kissed the back of her hand. "'N she sure was right 'bout what a fine lookin' lady you are, Mrs. Becker." Jonas extended a similar greeting to Caroline. Caleb and Benji were suitably dressed, but extended no hand kissing.

Jebediah arrived last, toting a large, curiously-wrapped package. There was no mistaking Jebediah for a banker. He was dressed in buckskins, but his clothing was clean and he was fresh from a bath at Jonas's insistence. Laura introduced him to her mother as "Jebediah Hart, a dear, dear friend."

"Glad ta meetcha, ma'am. Yers is shore a fine get-up," said Jeb, speaking of Priscilla's attire. The rest of the ladies, Laura included, were more simply dressed.

Priscilla ignored Jeb's comment. She had no intention of indulging this scruffy old man. Instead, she turned and whispered something in Caroline's ear. Caroline gave no response to her employer's rude behavior—which affected Jeb not in the slightest.

"I was hopin'," said Jeb, "ta take this op-per-tunity ta present Laura 'n Jonas har, with this weddin' gift I'm totin'. I know the wrappin's ain't too fancy, but I think you'll like what's inside it." Jeb looked around. "Where kin I set this thing?"

"Right here, Jeb," said Laura. "I'll clear you a spot on the table."

Jeb placed the large, loosely wrapped object on the octagonal table.

Laura looked at the ungainly package, then at Jonas. "Shall I?"

"You sure shall," replied Jonas, remembering that Jeb had mentioned he was working on a special project.

Laura began pulling aside the twine and loose wrapping.

She gasped. Before her was Savage, the great white dog that had been so integral to the lives of Laura, Jonas, and Jebediah. The woodcarving stood two feet high and captured Savage in a headlong leap, as if flying to the rescue one more time. The sculpture retained its natural oak coloring and was coated with a varnish to a soft finish. Laura was drawn to the red-tinted eyes, that, even though of wood, depicted the same penetrating gaze she'd seen in the living Savage. Jeb had given the carving the persona of a formidable protector, but more than that, he had imbued the dog with overtones of the mystical and spiritual. The woodcarving revealed Jeb's soul as well as that of his beloved companion.

Laura reached out to touch the woodcarving. Tears filled her eyes.

"Oh, Jeb. How could there ev'r be a better gift. You did this?"

Laura hugged the old man, tears flowing freely now.

Jeb grinned broadly. "I was hopin' ya'd like it."

"Like it? I love it. Oh Jonas, look at it. It is Savage, like he's come back to us."

"Jeb," said Jonas, "you've really outdone yerself this time." He was at a loss for further words, as he fought back his own tears, not sure if it was an emotional response to the woodcarving or to Laura's emotional reaction to it.

"Hmmph," uttered Priscilla. "So much fuss over a carving. Do you suppose there's any possibility we might eat now. I'm fairly famished." Though reluctant to admit it, Priscilla could not help but be impressed by the beauty of the sculpture, so life-like and with a vitality that seemed to take it beyond a mere artifact. She'd seen nothing to match it in Richmond. Perhaps she hadn't given enough credit to these back-woods people, especially the one called Jebediah.

Laura once more ran her fingers over the sculpture. She brought her hand to her eyes, dabbing away tears.

"Yes, mother," she said. "We can eat now."

Laura led the way to the dining room where a table was set with the finest of silverware and bone china, and various forks, glasses, and spoons, each designed to provide a separate function—a very proper table that might impress even Priscilla. Frederick Becker spared no expense for this occasion—a formal dinner in Laura's honor, prepared by his chef and served by the kitchen help, and quite possibly, a meal meant to show Priscilla that his was not a life-style without certain social amenities.

The soup came first, terrapin 'a l'Americaine, followed by a main meal of escalopes of salmon and baked Yorkshire ham a la Dixie. Vegetables included asparagus hollandaise, green peas, and sweet potatoes.

The meal was scrumptious, a worthwhile lead-in for the extensive festivities planned for the next day—the wedding, and the reception to follow.

Priscilla turned her attention to Jonas.

"So, you intend to marry my Laura...uh, Joseph is it?"

"Mother, it's Jonas. His name is Jonas and you know it," said Laura.

"Yes, ma'am," broke in Jonas. "I sure do intend to marry yer daughter. 'N you sure are lucky to have a daughter sich as her. She's the decent-ist person I ever met, 'n the purtiest. I guess she got that from you, ma'am."

"Well, at least you're polite...Jonas...in spite of your..."

"*Mother!*" Laura interrupted.

"Okay," said Priscilla, seeming to take pleasure in the tit-for-tat. "Then let me say, you're a polite boy and you're a nice-looking boy. At least Laura has some taste in one area..."

"*Mother!*"

"Yes, yes...I'm sorry, I apologize. I can't think where my manners have gone. So, Jonas, I understand we are to be beholden to you for the daring rescue of my daughter."

"Well, ma'am, it was more a combined effert, along with Jeb here... and most of the credit should go to Savage."

"And who, pray tell, is this Savage?"

"Savage," Jonas continued, "was Jeb's dog. He was jes' about the most mag-ni-fi-cent animal you could ever want to lay yer eyes on. He looked more wolf than dog, all white with red eyes 'n most as big as a horse. 'N ma'am, if not for that dog, ain't none of us would be here today...not me, not Jeb, not Laura."

"Really," said Priscilla, "and why haven't I seen this wonder dog of yours?" It was evident that Priscilla only believed about half of Jonas's heroic description of a mere dog. And from her haughty attitude, it was also clear that she meant to discredit the dog, as well as Jonas, and Jebediah. Her clothing, her manner of speech, the inflections in her voice—all meant to diminish Jonas in her daughter's eyes.

"Savage died saving Laura's honor, ma'am, 'n maybe even her life."

The blunt statement caught Priscilla off guard and her intended attack was cut short. Perhaps she was even ashamed of herself.

"Laura, Fritz...I'm feeling a bit tired, it's been a long day. I think I'll take an early retirement, if I may." Priscilla rose and unceremoniously left the table without waiting for a reply.

Laura turned to Jonas, "Oh Jonas, I'm so sorry. I was hopin' it wouldn't be like this."

"It's all right Laura. I'm sure she's jes' a bit overwhelmed."

Jebediah looked at Frederick Becker, forcing back a snicker. "Fritz?"

▲ ▲ ▲

Later that evening, Caroline singled out Laura.

"Laura, I hope you don't think I'm being discourteous or poking my nose in where it doesn't belong, but there's some things I feel I should tell you about your mother."

"Caroline, you know I think the world of you. If you know somethin' that kin help, please tell me."

"Thank you, Laura. It's just that your mother's been depressed lately. And I know she's lonely. She doesn't confide in me, of course, but I can tell. And also lately, she hasn't been going out nearly as often as she used to. Maybe she's been having problems with that man she's been seeing. I don't know. But she almost seemed glad to be leaving Richmond. Even for a few days. I guess I'm tellin' you this because I sense part of her sadness is that you're goin' on with your life without her being a part of it. I think she really misses you, Laura, and her husband, too. I just want you to be aware of that."

"Thank you for tellin' me this, 'n it does help. At least, a little."

46

The wedding was held at the one and only church in town, the Jericho Presbyterian Church, with Reverend Robert Rife presiding. By 11:00, Saturday morning, the church was packed. And twice as many folks were expected for the reception.

Priscilla and Caroline took seats on the bride's side. No lady present could begin to match the elegance of Priscilla's attire. She was not to be outdone by the locals on this occasion; even Caroline stood out. Their frilly, colorful bonnets alone elicited finger pointing and whispering from the wedding crowd.

The ceremony began with a fiddler and a piano player providing the entrance music, Wagner's familiar "Bridal Chorus", more commonly known as the "Wedding March".

Priscilla watched Laura move down the aisle, arm in arm with her father. Jonas and Jebediah awaited her at the altar. Priscilla noted that Jonas was dressed in a fashionable suit, a double-breasted frock coat over a simple white shirt with a high stiff collar and bow tie—maybe not up to Richmond standards, but admirable. Jebediah was similarly attired and obviously uncomfortable as he frequently tugged at his tie, as if in danger of strangling.

At least he had forsaken the buckskins! But Priscilla almost had to laugh at his shoes. Whereas Jonas stood in black shiny boots, congruous with his outfit, Jebediah wore thick leather boots, the same old boots he'd worn and repaired for years and "the only blamed footwear that don' kill my feet."

Priscilla was surprised that a lump formed in her throat and that her eyes watered as she looked at Laura—so beautiful, all in white, like a princess. The gown had been altered but Priscilla still recognized it as the gown she herself had been wed in so many years past. A tear moved down her cheek, which she quickly brushed away. She wished Laura would look her way—at least acknowledge her presence. But Laura had eyes only for Jonas.

Priscilla couldn't concentrate on the ceremony. She was only half-aware of Reverend Rife's comments as her mind was awash with conflicting thoughts. She wanted to be more a part of Laura's life, maybe even Fritz's, but how could she possibly live in a place like Jericho? It saddened her that her daughter would be moving on to a new life, an adventure in which she, her mother, would play no part. And grandchildren. There would be grandchildren and they would hardly know her. Was this the way she wanted it? Was her life in Richmond so desirable that she would continue to forsake her family ties? Her eyes again dampened, but with sadness, not with the joy the others were feeling. She was hardly aware that the ceremony had ended.

The recessional march began and folks stood and applauded as the beaming bride and the proud groom walked back up the aisle and out of the church.

The reception party followed immediately at the near-by Town Center.

A popular fiddle band in the region, the Blue Ridge Ramblers, had been hired by Frederick Becker to provide the music, but as was the custom, anyone who could conceivably lift a fiddle bow or stick thimbles on their fingers and bang on a washboard were invited to join in. Musicians filed in from all around—fiddlers, guitar players, wash boarders, juggers—they all came. The music was in full swing, even as the newly married couple entered the Jericho Town Center, which was filled to capacity.

Food came from everywhere—from the miners' families and from the Jericho eateries and even from as far away as Cedar City. The festiveness grew and the occasion became the largest, most singly celebrated event in Jericho's history. The fiddle band struck up jigs and reels and country waltzes as laughter and merriment filled the hall. Even Caleb, still sporting crutches, seemed to be enjoying himself.

Priscilla stuck with Caroline, trying to avoid the many folks that wished to congratulate her on her daughter's wedding, some that remembered her from her short stay in Jericho. She wished no association with these unsophisticated and simple country-folk. And she found the music crude and the dancing without grace. Yet, she couldn't help but acknowledge the warmth and joviality of the occasion.

She felt alone, even with Caroline at her side. Watching Laura and Jonas together saddened her. She knew she should be happy for them, but she felt left out of something important. They were beautiful together—even she had to admit that. They danced...they hugged...they laughed. Was she feeling rejected, that a stranger now was central in her daughters' life, and she was an outsider? She saw Fritz approaching her. He was still a handsome man. Priscilla felt nervous, almost like a schoolgirl.

"Cilla, I was hopin' you might try 'n enjoy yerself a bit. You might even try dancin'. What d'you say, should we give it a whirl?"

"What? Dance to this...this...whatever you call it."

"Yeh. I guess it don't hold up so well agin all that fancy music 'n dancin' yer used to in Richmond. Well, maybe you won't mind if I borrow Caroline for a dance or two. I bet she ain't quite so particular about the music."

"Well, that's up to her, though I can't think why she would want to."

"I'd be right happy to dance with you, Mr. Becker, and you're right, I ain't quite so particular. This music sets my feet to tapping."

"Please, the name is Frederick."

"All right...Frederick. I'd be delighted to accompany you."

Priscilla watched the two of them walk out on to the crowded dance floor. *Frederick indeed.* The fiddler and piano player were doing a credible job on a waltz, and Frederick and Caroline seemed to be enjoying the dance—and each other. If her husband's foot bothered him at all, it wasn't evident. Priscilla experienced an alien feeling; she had never even thought of Frederick with another woman.

Jealousy? Certainly not.

270

With Caroline gone, she now felt really alone, isolated and out-of-place. Once again, her eyes dampened. She felt overwhelmed...she had to get out of there...get some air.

She walked outside, seeking a place where she could be alone, away from the noise and the crowd and her mixed feelings. She found a deserted bench in a small park nearby. She had barely sat when she began to cry openly. She wasn't even aware of why she was crying, but she couldn't stop. The tears just seemed to pour out of her with a life of their own. She buried her head in her hands.

Something wet and warm pressed against the back of her hand. She looked up, startled. A huge white dog stood before her. At first, she felt fear, but as she gazed into the dog's eyes, his red eyes, she became calm, as if assured she had nothing to fear. Almost unwittingly, she reached her hands out to the dog, palms cupped up. The dog laid his head on her hands and continued to gaze into Priscilla's eyes.

The gaze was hypnotic. Priscilla became transfixed. Images of her life filled her mind as she stared into the dog's eyes. She saw a restless, dissatisfied girl become a restless and discontent woman; she saw that her life was a façade, a fakery, and that everything she'd centered her life upon for so many years was false—the opulent lifestyle, the fancy clothing, the partying, the parade of men. None of that had brought her love or a sense of belonging. She felt as if her very soul opened up. As she was held by the dog's eyes, she felt burdens being lifted from her, burdens that had encumbered her for years. Suddenly, she began to cry even harder, a cloudburst, but these were not tears of despair. They were tears of enlightenment. She wrapped her arms around the dog's neck and hugged him tightly. Her body shook in a flood of tears.

"Ma'am...ma'am...aire ya all right?" It was Jebediah. He'd strolled out for a walk himself and some fresh air and a bit of peace and quiet. He'd had about all the washboard clanging he could stand.

Priscilla looked up.

"I...I," she found it hard to speak between sobs. "Where is the dog?"

Jeb looked around. "Ma'am, I don' see no dog. He musta run off. Did he hurt ya, 'r somethin'?" Jebediah sat down on the bench beside Priscilla. He offered her a hanky. A clean one.

"Uh...thank you." She dabbed her eyes with the handkerchief. " No, he didn't hurt me. He...actually, he comforted me. But where has he gone?"

"Kaint hardly say, ma'am. What'd this har dog look like anyhow?"

"He was big. And white, all white, with red eyes. Yes, he had red eyes, wonderful red eyes."

"Red eyes, ya say, 'n all white?"

"Yes, that's right, and huge, bigger than any dog I've ever seen."

Jebediah gulped. "Ma'am, only dog I ev'r heard of like thet is my dog, Savage. *Was* my dog Savage."

Priscilla stopped crying and stared at Jebediah. She thought of the sculpture.

"Savage? The one that saved my Laura?"

"Yes'm. Ain't no other dogs like thet around."

"But you said he died saving her."

"Now that's the truth."

They both sat in stunned silence. A deep silence. A silence that grew out of sudden understanding and revelation. Priscilla's heart leaped and her mind lightened, as if a great pall had been lifted from her, much like before when she was hugging the dog...*hugging the dog?*

She turned to Jebediah. She took his hands into hers, but didn't dare tell him what else had transpired—the epiphany event that she had experienced.

Jebediah broke the silence. "Ya know. I ain't all that su'prised by what yer telling' me, considerin' the nature of thet dog, long as I knowed him. Yep, sure is somethin' ta set a man ta thinkin'."

"Jebediah...thank you...thank you so much." And she hugged him. "Would you escort a lady back to the party, sir?"

"Sir? Wahl, hell yes. Wahl, I'll be hornswoggl'd. If thet don' beat all."

▲ ▲ ▲

Laura was as happy as she could possibly be, in all respects save one. She had hoped her mother might enjoy herself more on this special occasion, *her daughter's wedding,* after all. How could she not see what a wonderful person Jonas was? Laura had even dared hope that her mother would somehow become a part of her family again, a family which now included Jonas. So far, none of these hopes had been even partially realized.

Laura saw her mother approaching as she and Jonas were breaking for refreshments.

"Laura, Laura dear," said her mother as she embraced her—a warm embrace. "I'm so sorry, so very sorry." Laura noticed that her mother's eyes were red and watery. "I've been so wrong. Can you forgive a foolish woman for being so selfish as to abandon her family?"

"Mother," said Laura, puzzled. "What's happened? What is it?"

"Laura, darling, if you'll give me a chance I'd like to be a better mother to you, a real mother. To you...and to you too, Jonas. Priscilla touched Jonas's shoulder. Laura, you couldn't have done better in picking a man. I can't explain everything to you right now, but if it's not too late, can you forgive me?"

"I don't know what to say. I don't understand...forgive you? All I want is for us to be a family again. That's all I ev'r wanted."

Mother and daughter again embraced. Priscilla kissed Laura lightly on the cheek. "I'll be back, honey. I've got something more to attend to."

The fiddler, the leader of The Blue Ridge Ramblers, had just finished a lively Virginia Reel that had all the dancers a-stomping and a-twirling up a storm. He noticed an elegantly dressed woman approaching.

"My good sir," said Priscilla, "may I ask if you are familiar with the 'Charleston Waltz'? I am the mother of the bride and would be grateful if you'd play this waltz that I might dance with my husband in honor of my daughter's marriage."

"The Charleston Waltz, you say?" mused the fiddler. "Wahl, I ain't bin up Charleston way much myself, but let me ask around." He turned to the musicians scattered around in back of him—maybe seven or eight of them at this time. "Any of you yahoos know the Charleston Waltz?"

"B'lieve I do," responded one of the fiddlers. "Spent a few yars up there 'bout a month ago."

"Purty funny, Marvin. Okay, folks," announced the bandleader, "we got us a request for somethin' called the Charleston Waltz. Now, Marvin here says he kin lead that music, 'n me 'n the boys'll jes' join on in. 'N ne'er let it be said thet the Blue Ridge Ramblers don't honor all requests. Boys, jes' follow ole Marv."

The fiddler began the introductory notes to the Charleston Waltz. The Ramblers picked up the cues easily and the waltz was underway.

The townsfolk had grown silent, wondering who would request such a highbrow number. They all watched as Priscilla, attired in all her finery, walked across the dance floor.

Frederick Becker had been in conversation with Caroline, who was relating stories about his daughter's stay in Richmond. He'd heard the band's announcement concerning the Charleston Waltz and now saw Priscilla walking toward him.

"Well, Fritz, do you think you'd remember how to dance to *this* music?" Without waiting for a response, Priscilla took her husband's hand and led him onto the dance floor. The townsfolk were unfamiliar with this type of music and stood aside as Priscilla and Frederick took the floor.

Priscilla curtsied, Frederick bowed. He hoped he could remember the steps. They began to circle each other, dipping to the flowing rhythm of the waltz. The large hall crowd grew silent. They had never seen this kind of courtly dancing before—formal and elegant. But they loved it and began to clap in unison with the music.

Priscilla felt delighted and relieved that the townsfolk were urging her on. She even laughed as a young lad, Jonas's brother, she believed—*my son-in-law's brother*—slowly began to ferret out the dance steps with his partner, a pert young lass who was every bit as adventuresome as he, while a group of young folks teased the awkward dancers, but nevertheless spurred them on.

As Priscilla and Frederick executed dips and twirls, steps and swings, adeptly performed to the engaging rhythm of the music, more and more townsfolk became active participants, giving a whole new country flavor to the Charleston Waltz.

The waltz ended and the band took up a slow dance piece, also at Priscilla's request. Priscilla wrapped her arms around her husband, drew him close and they began the slow number.

Frederick started to speak, but Priscilla placed a finger to his lips, shushing him. As they danced, Priscilla drew her husband closer and looked up into his face.

"Fritz, I've been such a fool. I'm so sorry. I've been selfish and inconsiderate, and, well...wrong. I know it's probably too late for me. I can only hope that..." her eyes moistened. "Can you give me another chance to see if we can't work something out?"

"Cilla, I hardly know what to say. You seem so diff'rent."

The woman he faced seemed no longer the distant, detached person that his wife had become. There was softness in her eyes and a gentle yielding of her body to his as they danced close together.

"Maybe I haven't bin all that fair either, 'spectin' you to settle for a simple country life. But judging from how folks here reacted to yer dance, maybe our world's ain't so far apart, 'n I bin thinkin' 'bout a few things. I think we got a bit of talkin' to do, if yer serious 'bout tryin' to work somethin' out."

"Talking about what, Fritz? What do you mean?"

"Let's save it for later, after things have settled down a bit."

The dance ended and Frederick escorted his wife to the refreshment table. Laura joined them and asked if she might borrow her father for a minute. Priscilla consented and Laura drew her father aside, away from the festivities.

"Dad, isn't it wonderful? It's all like a dream. Mother seems to have changed so. 'N Jonas is my husband 'n everythin' is so perfect now. And you...you've given the miners hope with the changes you made."

Indeed, many changes had taken place. The $50,000 Becker had put up as ransom would now be used to establish a medical clinic, providing sorely needed care for the miners and their families. Also, Becker had dissolved the "Corps" and intended to fill in the supervisory positions from amongst the miners, rather than use outsiders as he'd done in the past. And he would personally oversee all operations to assure that they ran smoothly. No more shady dealing would get by him.

"Yes," he said, "this is a great occasion. Jonas is a fine lad'n I couldn't be happier for you. Laura, I'm sorry that I let things get so outta control at the mining company. But then too, daughter, know that I ain't gonna turn into one of them soft hearted liberals, either. A man's gotta be tough to run this sort of operation. These miners are hard men 'n it takes a hard man to keep 'em in line. But I'll try to be more fair. And besides, I'm thinkin' 'bout some changes I ain't tole you about. We'll discuss it later...with yer mother, and Jonas."

The wedding and reception lived up to their promise and became the most memorable affair ever in Jericho. The event brought together miners and bosses, shopkeepers and farmers, young and old, in a way Jericho had never experienced before. This town would be losing the McNabbs (including Laura, the newest McNabb), but gaining a new spirit and a new hope.

The celebration continued throughout the afternoon, the evening, and well into the night, even though the honored couple had left.

47

Frederick Becker had asked the newly married couple to meet with him and Priscilla at the Becker Estate, as they had some important news. Jonas and Laura, fresh from their wedding reception, now awaited them on the porch steps of the Becker Manor. Although this was their wedding night, Jonas and Laura would not be spending the night together. Instead, Jonas would be heading back to the McNabb farm while Laura would remain at the Estate. They both agreed that their nuptial consummation should take place at their new home in the Shenandoah Valley—the JJ&L Ranch.

The evening was warm and a slight breeze kept the pesky bugs at bay. Laura's anticipation of good news from her father (how could it be otherwise) only added to exhilaration she felt over the events of this day, her wedding day.

Frederick and Priscilla arrived by carriage. They reined up and Frederick helped his wife down from her seat. Laura discerned a stern look on her father's face as he and Priscilla approached the porch. "Let's go inside," he said, "somethin' has come up. We need to talk."

Once inside, Frederick asked that everyone take a seat. Laura and Jonas sat together on a couch. Priscilla sank into a chair and gave her daughter a concerned look. Frederick remained standing. Laura winked at Jonas and patted his knee. "Okay, Dad," she said, with a smile. "Let's have the terribl' news."

"Girl, I never could put anythin' over on you." He laughed. "Okay, here's the terrible, wonderful news. Your mother and I want the two of you to be the first to hear what we've decided." He paused. "I'm seriously considerin' sellin' the mining company. I know there'll be intristed buyers, 'n I won't have any problem gittin' a decent price for it. If I kin make a favorable deal, I'm 'bout sure I'll sell."

Laura started to say something. Her father shushed her. "Now, no interruptions 'till I get this all out. If I get this sellin' deal done, 'n most likely I will, well, your mother 'n me have talked it over and we've decided to git back together."

"Dad, Mother, that's wonder..."

"Now hang on" said Frederick. "We still ain't done, yet. Cilla, you tell 'em the rest."

Priscilla rose from the chair and stood by her husband. "Laura, Jonas," she said, "when your father sells the company, he intends to retain a part share in it, enough so he can have some say in the way it's run. I guess you know he's already started to make some changes and he means to see them through. Now, here's what else we've decided."

Frederick placed an arm around Priscilla's waist. "We've decided that seeing as there won't be any need for your father to remain in Jericho...well, we're thinking of finding us a place in Waynesboro. That way we can keep the family close, just in case there'll be some little children around needing a grandpa and grandma. Is that everything, Fritz?"

"That about sums it up, dear. Okay, now you can talk."

"Oh, 'n I thought this day was already perfect," said Laura as she jumped up and hugged her mother and father. "'N now you tell us all this. It's the most wonderful day of my life, by far."

Jonas stood and congratulated them. "And I want to thank you both for allowing me to marry yer daughter, 'n for givin' us a great weddin'. I'll be takin' my leave now if you all don' mind."

"Wha...leaving?" said Frederick. "But you and Laura..."

"Dad, Jonas won't be spendin' the night here. We decided to have our weddin' night at our ranch."

"Well, I'll be. If that don't beat all," said the astonished father.

"Now, Fritz," said Priscilla. "It makes perfect sense to me." She kissed Jonas on the cheek. "My daughter has chosen well, Jonas."

Frederick and Priscilla decided to call it a night. Frederick led his wife to his bedroom. Laura could not hide a huge smile.

Laura said her good-byes to Jonas on the front porch. She settled into the porch swing and watched him until he rode out of sight. She was too wound up over the day's events to even think about giving up on the night for sleep.

A carriage arrived with Gini and the Becker house guests, fresh from the wedding festivities. Gini noticed Laura alone on the porch swing.

"Laura, what's wrong? Where's Jonas?"

"Wrong? What could possibly be wrong?"

Laura once again explained her and Jonas's reasoning about their wedding night.

"I'm jis' stayin' up for a while. I'm too excited to ev'r git to sleep."

Everyone congratulated Laura once more and went inside to their rooms.

A quiet settled over the Becker household. Outside, Laura felt a warm breeze against her face. She gazed up at a thin cloud drifting across the face of a half-moon. A sea of stars decorated the night sky and a chorus of tree frogs and katydids created a symphony to her happiness.

▲ ▲ ▲

The next morning promised a brilliant day. The sun appeared and chased away the low-lying morning mist that had descended upon Jericho.

Eight travelers awaited the train at the Jericho station.

The festivities of the previous day were still fresh in their minds and by now everyone was aware of Frederick Becker's far-reaching plans.

A clanging bell signaled the arrival of the steam engine. Smoke spewed from its wheels as it screeched to a halt.

Jebediah, Jonas, Laura, Caleb, Benji, Charly, Red, and Gini would be boarding the train to Waynesboro, Virginia. Frederick and Priscilla Becker would remain in Jericho to settle certain business affairs—specifically, the transference of the mining company to new ownership and the sale of the McNabb farm. Priscilla and Caroline would then head back to Richmond. Caroline would remain in Richmond, close to her family ties and friends, with regrets, but warm memories of her time with Laura. After wrapping up her affairs in Richmond, Priscilla would return to Jericho to assist her husband in whatever particulars remained unsettled.

Everything the eight travelers wished to take with them was loaded onto the train, including Laura's horse, Sacagawea. Soon, they all headed north to begin new lives in the Shenandoah Valley.

Epilogue

On the Train

Jericho to Waynesboro would be about an eight-hour trip by train, ample time for each of the eight passengers to reflect on past events and consider future expectations.

Laura sat next to Jonas. Her thoughts bounced from one joyous event to another as she clung to Jonas's arm. This handsome boy, who less than two years ago was unknown to her—then a romance that had developed so suddenly and unexpectedly—and now he was her husband forever. Her mother and father being re-united, and the promise of a real mother, one she could confide in and catch a gleam in her eye as she fussed over her grandchildren...*grandchildren? Oh, let there be a mess of them.* The JJ&L Ranch—a dream come true. All that's happened, a dream come true.

And thoughts of her harrowing kidnapping. *My God!...stolen away 'n nearly brutalized.* But then, the $50,000 that would be used to help the miners; the whole episode changing her father's attitude concerning his mining company, and certainly his attitude toward Jonas. And the wonderful dog that had come flying to her rescue—that saved Jonas all those times. A tear fell at this memory. Laura sighed a regret that she would probably lose Gini as a companion, despite her insistence that Gini stay on. But most of all her thoughts were of Jonas, who had captured her heart and completed her dreams. She squeezed his arm and laid her head on his shoulder.

Jonas felt the squeeze and marveled at this beautiful, wonderful creature—*his wife*—who now rested her handsome head on his shoulder. Sunlight streamed through the train window and transformed her hair to gold. All past travails were worth it to make this moment possible. He kissed her forehead and settled back, gazing out the window, with the scenery flying by faster than he could properly appreciate it. This was his first travel by train—what a contrast to the similar long, arduous trip he and Jeb had undertaken but a short while back—the unrelenting downpour dampening his spirit and implanting doubts about his future plans.

He glanced back a few seats at Jebediah. This old man, this wonderful old man, so instrumental in making all this possible. And while thinking of Jeb, it was impossible not to reflect on Savage, not a mournful memory but as one that instilled awe and admiration and gratitude. In his mind, the great white beast was immortalized, attaining an almost spiritual status. His thoughts strayed to his father, and to Benji—he felt grateful that he could provide them an escape from the daily drudgery of the coal mines. But, how would his father react to life at the JJ&L? Was there still a spark left in him, a spark that could be rekindled? And Benji, full of enthusiasm and ideas for what might lie ahead for him. *Sorry li'l brother. You got schoolin' ahead of you.* He thought of his ma and envisioned her as now being content—wherever she was—that the family would be together once more. Had he fulfilled his promise to her? Jonas threw an arm around Laura, closed his eyes and allowed his mind to drift to thoughts he and Laura now shared—thoughts about what was at last to be their wedding night.

Jeb, in an attempt to get his mind off this "damned noisy con-trap-shun thet gits a man too far 'n too fast fer his own good", bombarded his seat-mate, Caleb, with non-stop confabulations. Eventually, even Jeb settled into his own thoughts. He wasn't one to dwell on the past, or the future—"hell, what's bin done's bin done, can't change it, 'n what's gonna be's gonna be, ain't no sense ta be worryin' 'bout it". In spite of this bit of philosophy, he missed Savage. "Sure wish ya could be here, boy," he thought, "it jes' don' seem the same without ya." He stroked the head of the pup that quietly rested beside him. The pup gazed up at Jeb, there was something in his look...

Caleb respectfully endured Jeb's incessant chatter. He even enjoyed some of Jeb's tales of life in the mountains with his great white dog, Savage. But he was relieved when Jeb finally quieted down and he had time to collect his own thoughts. He'd been doing a lot of soul searching lately. His boys seemed so enthusiastic about their new home—about life in the Shenandoah. Caleb feared he might cast a shadow on their fervor.

He felt he had already failed in so many ways—as a father, husband, soldier, and farmer. Why should things be different now? His thoughts drifted to Lonica, to his first sight of her as he regained consciousness in the field hospital and gazed into her angel eyes. Somehow, *she* had seen some good in him.

Caleb looked at Benji in the seat ahead, then further ahead to Jonas, with Laura resting her head on his shoulder. These were good boys, boys to make a man proud. This was his family and in his boys his beloved Lonica lived on. Maybe in his sons he hadn't failed all that badly. *Lonica dear, maybe's there's some hope for me yet.*

No one on the train was more excited than Benji. He sat across the aisle from Charly and Red and pestered them for all they could divulge about the Shenandoah Valley and Waynesboro and the Cooper Ranch and particularly, the JJ&L. Eventually Benji wore down and assumed a more reflective mood. He gazed out the window and yielded to the hypnotic effect of the passing timberlands and distant mountains.

He idolized his brother. Jonas had made all this possible. He was the Ulysses Benji had read about in books—a courageous and adventuresome hero, venturing into the unknown and overcoming all obstacles. And now Jonas would be a part of his life once more. But the schooling—why would he need more schooling? All he wanted was to be a part of the horse ranch, which he imagined would be full of excitement and bold adventure. He imagined a life not unlike that of the cowboys he'd read about in dime novels about the Wild West. But then, maybe he could fit in some schooling. Jonas had assured him, "there's gals in them there schools, buddy boy, more'n you kin shake a stick at."

"Yep, a bit of schoolin' wouldn't be so bad," thought Benji.

Charly Cooper was thrilled that her best friend, Laura, would be living so close-by. The one thing lacking at the Cooper Ranch was a girl her own age to relate to and confide in. And soon she would confide a secret she'd been bursting to reveal, about herself and Red. Hers was a happy life and now could only get better. She gazed over at Red and winked.

Gini sat alone. She was faced with some difficult decisions. Laura wanted her to be a part of her new family at the JJ&L, in whatever capacity Gini might wish. But how could that possibly work out? Laura would no longer need her as a housemate or surrogate mother. She had Jonas now, and her own mother would soon be close by. So where would Gini fit in?

Frederick and Priscilla had also invited her to join them when they took up residence in Waynesboro, again in any capacity she wished—*everybody is so concerned with my wishes!* But she now felt the need to be on her own and to make a life for herself. She would still be close by as she was strongly considering setting up a dress shop in Waynesboro. Frederick Becker had provided her with a generous salary and she had more than enough money saved to get started. Her dress shop in Charleston had failed because of her handicapped leg and her lingering remorse over the loss of her parents. Now she walked with scarcely a limp. With new ideas and a great deal more experience, she felt sure she could succeed this time. And she would love to teach again—maybe just part-time at a school, or maybe as a tutor. *I'm still young, just thirty-five years old. Je suis une jeune! Plenty young enough to think about meeting someone special.* Charly, with a twinkle in her eye, had said there was a certain "Frenchie" at the Cooper Ranch she just might want to meet.

Jebediah Hart lifted the pup onto his lap—the new Savage. Tears filled his eyes as he gazed out the window at the distant mountains. He could almost see the old Savage, the great white dog, outlined against the pale blue sky—like a statue, high on a ridge, maintaining a protective stance over eight passengers bound for the Shenandoah.

Readers Guide

1. Three factors played an important part in the lives of the Jericho residents: the Civil War, the influx of the railroads, and the coal mining industry. Discuss how these factors altered or influenced the main characters and Jericho residents in general.

2. Both Frederick and Priscilla Becker experienced major changes in their attitudes. What events or revelations precipitated these changes?

3. A depressed Caleb could not work the farm, but was able to work in the mines. Why?

4. What attitudes toward the Civil War are reflected in this book?

5. A certain theme saturates this story—*deserving*—who deserves what and why? Jonas is torn between incidents of good fortunes and bad. What are his reactions to each? How does Jeb philosophize about who deserves what and why?

6. Jeb seem to be a steadying influence throughout the story. In what ways does he inter-react to ameliorate difficult situations?

7. Who did you admire the most in the story? Who did you despise, and why?

8. An ongoing theme in the story is man's need to live in harmony with nature. As the coal mining industry invaded the Jericho area, how did it affect the town, the countryside, the McNabb family? The coal mines are presented as being an affront to nature, whereas Jebediah maintained a close connection to his surroundings. Discuss the differences in the miner's lives and outlooks as opposed to Jeb's.

9. How did Jeb's sculptures influence Priscilla to reconsider her opinion of country folks?

10. Jeb could be called a down-to-earth philosopher. Review his views on the coal miners life, on mountain living, on women, on life in general, on God and Church (consider Jeb's statement, "...seems ta me them places (churches) jes' take what rightly b'longs in a man's heart 'n tries to make all sorts of laws about it." and "I got my feelin's 'bout God, 'n I'll tell ya true, they's all wrapped up in these har mountains, 'n this har critter (Savage)."

11. In what ways did Savage add spiritual overtones to the story? In what ways was he integral to the story's outcome?

12. The story involves four locales: Jericho, the mountains, Richmond, and the Shenandoah Valley. How do lifestyles within these areas differ? How does each contribute to the outcome of the story?

13. At what point does Jonas take charge of his own destiny, as opposed to being bounced back and forth by fate (good luck and bad luck)?

14. If the story were to continue into the 20th Century, which character would you wish to follow and why?

15. Discuss how romantic entanglements are so vital to the story—Caleb and Lonica's unlikely coupling—even more unlikely, the relationship that developed between Jonas and Laura—Frederick Becker's marriage to Priscilla, their separation, their reunion.

16. The author has attempted to portray the speech mannerisms of the four main locales represented in this story. In what way does this add to the authenticity and differences of the characters involved? Or did you find the dialogue difficult to follow? But, if so, consider Jebediah, the mountain man. Would you believe his character without his colorful way of talking? How did Laura's way of speaking underline her character?

CPSIA information can be obtained
at www.ICGtesting.com
Printed in the USA
FFOW02n2139210514
5471FF